A FAMILY'S TRUST

LOUISE GUY

Boldwood

First published in 2022. This edition first published in Great Britain in 2024 by Boldwood Books Ltd.

Copyright © Louise Guy, 2024

Cover Design by Becky Glibbery

Cover Illustration: Shutterstock and iStock

Every effort has been made to obtain the necessary permissions with reference to copyright material, both illustrative and quoted. We apologise for any omissions in this respect and will be pleased to make the appropriate acknowledgements in any future edition.

A CIP catalogue record for this book is available from the British Library.

Paperback ISBN 978-1-83533-140-8

Large Print ISBN 978-1-83533-141-5

Hardback ISBN 978-1-83533-139-2

Ebook ISBN 978-1-83533-142-2

Kindle ISBN 978-1-83533-143-9

Audio CD ISBN 978-1-83533-134-7

MP3 CD ISBN 978-1-83533-135-4

Digital audio download ISBN 978-1-83533-137-8

Boldwood Books Ltd
23 Bowerdean Street
London SW6 3TN
www.boldwoodbooks.com

For my much-loved Js.
Judy, JJ and Jamie.

1

Why had she agreed to this meeting? It was pointless. She could never forgive him.

Jess tapped her foot against the chair leg, her nerves mounting. The buzz of the coffee shop was usually comforting, but today, the murmur of voices accompanied by the aromatic wafts of espresso was anything but. People went about their morning routines, laughing and smiling as if nothing in the world mattered or had changed. But it had, or at least it was about to.

'Jessica?'

The hesitancy in the deep tone caused her heart to race.

'Jessica?' A tall, slim man with silver hair and a

tentative smile, his blue eyes friendly and warm, stood in front of her, repeating her name.

She nodded.

He motioned to the chair across from her. 'May I sit?'

She nodded again, the exchange so awkward the hairs on the back of her neck stood on end. Her *father* was standing in front of her. Her flesh-and-blood father. As much as she wanted to be angry and make sure he knew how much she hated him, part of her also wanted to cry. He looked like such a nice man.

Martin sat and cleared his throat. 'Sorry. This is harder than I imagined. I realise this is difficult, and I do appreciate you seeing me today.' He gave a small smile. 'I wasn't sure if you'd come. I expected your mother might try to stop you.' He cleared his throat again. 'How is Paula?'

Jess shook her head. If he'd bothered to stay in touch, he wouldn't need to ask that question. 'She died when I was five.'

Shock flashed in Martin's eyes. 'What? I'm so sorry. I had no idea.'

'She was hit by a truck while riding her bike home from one of the dead-end jobs she was forced to work.' The bitterness of Jess's words sliced the air.

Martin ran a hand across his chin. 'I'm sorry, Jessica. I wish someone had told me. Your Uncle Joe should have contacted me.'

'He probably assumed, as you'd abandoned us before I was born, that you wouldn't be interested.'

Silence fell between them, and Jess swayed between a sense of satisfaction for inflicting shock and pain on him and guilt that she could be so cruel. 'Why did you want to see me now? You've had forty years to get in touch.'

'Two reasons. I had a brush with cancer recently and my lawyer, who is also a friend, made me realise that as none of us live forever, if I wanted to meet you and apologise, then I needed to do it sooner rather than later. Secondly, Wednesday is the anniversary of my wife's death. It's been a difficult time, but the last twelve months have found me doing plenty of reflection. Of things that could have been. That should have been done differently. While it's obviously far too late, it made me realise how precious life is and how selfish I've been. Alice didn't know anything about you or my relationship with your mother. It's not something I'm proud of.'

'You made it abundantly clear when you took off that you were ashamed of us.'

The colour drained from Martin's cheeks. 'That's not what I meant. I meant I wasn't proud of my behaviour towards any of you. My wife had a right to know, and you had a right to be in my life if you and your mother had agreed to that. Part of the reason for wanting to meet you is to apologise. I know that words will never make up for the fact that I wasn't there, but I do want you to know that I'm sorry. Neither you nor your mother deserved what I gave, or more to the point, didn't give you.'

A waitress interrupted and took their coffee orders.

As she retreated to the service counter, Martin searched Jess's eyes. 'What did you mean when you said your mother worked a dead-end job?'

'She was working two jobs when she died. Early morning shelf packing at one supermarket, and afternoon and evening on the register at another. The combined income wasn't enough to cover the rent most months.'

Jess frowned as Martin closed his eyes and shook his head. Was this all an act? If this information distressed him, why hadn't he done something about it sooner?

Martin opened his eyes. 'Where's Joe these days?'

Jess shrugged. 'No idea. After Mum died, he visited me occasionally at the different foster homes I lived in. My eighteenth birthday was the last time I saw him.' It had also been her last opportunity to confide in him – to tell someone what had happened three years earlier – but she'd lost her nerve. 'He said he was going overseas and wished me luck with university. I hardly knew him, but he was proud that I'd managed to get myself into a good course.'

'What did you study?'

'A Bachelor of Social Work initially. Later, I did further study in psychology.'

'Did your uncle offer to help you with tuition?'

'Joey? No. He was always complaining about maxing out his credit cards and being short of cash. Although he would usually take me out for a meal, which in his situation was generous.' She smiled at the memory. 'He was my only family and my last link to Mum, but once he was gone for a few years, I put him out of my mind and got on with things. I learned from a young age that the only person who was going to look out for me was me.'

Martin continued to shake his head.

'What?'

'Jessica—'

Jess cut him off. 'It's Jess.'

'Okay. Jess, when I realised I couldn't continue my relationship with your mother or be a permanent part of your life, she told me to leave.' He frowned,

perhaps remembering that moment. 'That's an understatement. She threw things at me and told me in
very colourful language to never show my face
around her again. I tried numerous times to talk to
her, but each time she shot me down.'

'That's understandable.' Jess didn't blame her
mother but also remembered her fiery temper. When
Paula was upset, everyone knew about it.

Martin ignored the barb. 'I approached Joe as a
last resort. Your mother was close with him, or so I
thought, and I assumed he had her best interests at
heart.' He took a deep breath. 'I set up a bank account specifically for you and your mum and gave Joe
access to it. I sent your mum a letter with the information too. I guess she might have thrown it out
without reading it, or perhaps Joe intercepted it, and
she never saw it.'

'Why would he do that?'

'Possibly to keep the money for himself.'

Jess's mouth dropped open. 'No, he wouldn't do
that.'

'I put a sum of fifty thousand dollars in it to start
with.'

Fifty thousand! Was he kidding? It would have
taken her mother years to save that kind of money.

Martin continued. 'I wanted to ensure Paula

would have enough money to get everything she needed for when you were born and pay for doctors, specialists, and anything else she might need. I asked Joe to let me know when you were born, which he did.' His eyes clouded over. 'The twenty-third of April was the saddest day of my life. My first child was born, and I wasn't there to witness it.'

'That was your choice.'

'It was, and it was the wrong choice. Plenty of times, I wanted to come and see you. I even called Joe and asked him whether he thought Paula would allow me to visit. He laughed and told me she'd threatened to have me killed if I ever set foot near you or her again. I knew she wouldn't do that, but I also knew I had to respect her wishes. I couldn't turn up once or twice without making more of a commitment to both of you, and I knew I couldn't do that. I had other responsibilities.'

'You think Joey took your fifty thousand dollars and left Mum broke?'

'It wasn't only fifty thousand dollars. I'm quite wealthy, Jess. Following your birth, on the twenty-third of each month, I deposited ten thousand dollars into that same bank account. The payments continued until your eighteenth birthday. On that day, I deposited one and a half million dollars.'

'What?' Jess's head was spinning. There was no way this could be true. She couldn't begin to calculate how much money he was talking about, but it was a lot.

'It was a sum that I hoped would provide you with security for life. I knew you'd be working at some point and able to look after yourself, but I hoped the extra money would help with university and buying your first house. I also thought Paula might need some assistance. I sent a letter to Joe explaining that this was the last payment and to contact me if there was ever a need for more money. I never heard from him.'

Their coffee order was delivered as silence descended. Jess stared at the man sitting in front of her. If he was telling the truth, then not only was her uncle a cheat, but her mother's death had been completely avoidable. She did her best to blink back tears.

Martin shook his head. 'I can't believe this. I really can't. It was the one thing I thought I'd done right by you and Paula.' He exhaled. 'I'm sorry, Jess. If only I'd known, I would have changed the arrangement, and I certainly didn't mean to upset you now.'

'How do I know you're telling the truth?'

He considered her question. 'My lawyer will have

a copy of the letter I sent Paula and Joe explaining the arrangement, and then there are bank statements. I don't have them here, but I can send you the statements for the eighteen-year period. I have them all on file at home. I'm sure my accountant and my lawyer can also provide additional documentation to prove the transactions took place.'

Jess nodded. She wasn't sure she needed to see the documents. Everything about Martin Elliot suggested he was telling the truth.

Concern filled his eyes. 'I'm so sorry that you ended up in the foster care system. Did you find a nice family?'

Nausea churned in her stomach. *Nice.* A simple word that she would have given anything to have found the definition of when she was a teen. 'No. I was moved from one foster family to another. The longest I spent with any one family was three years. That was when I was twelve. On my fifteenth birthday, they told me they couldn't handle a teenager, which meant it was time for me to move on to a new family.' She did her best to keep her voice level. If only they'd allowed her to stay. *It* would never have happened. *He* wouldn't have happened. She took a deep breath. She wouldn't let her thoughts go back there. 'By the time I turned eighteen, I'd lived with seven different families.'

Martin brought his hands to his face. 'I'm sorry. So, so sorry. I don't know what your mother told you about me, but I wish I'd known, as I would have helped.'

'I was only five when she died. Up until then, she'd led me to believe you were dead. It was Joey who told me when I was twelve that you weren't, but you'd abandoned Mum and me before I was born, and Mum said she didn't want you in her life or mine. I decided to respect her wishes and never considered trying to find you.'

'But you still came today.'

'Curiosity got the better of me.' She sighed. 'I'd planned to tell you what I thought of you. How I hated you and thought you were a terrible person for what you did.'

'I don't think you're wrong about that.'

Jess stared at him. 'Maybe not, but the fact you thought you were supporting us does put a different spin on things.'

Martin scraped his hand through his hair, and Jess noticed a slight tremble in his fingers.

'If you were open to it,' Martin said, 'I'd love to get to know you. Help make up for the past.'

The lines in his forehead had deepened considerably in the short time they'd been talking. Jess was pleased to see his distress and realised he wasn't the monster she'd imagined him to be. He seemed genuinely upset at how events had unfolded. She, however, had no intention of letting him into her life. He'd done enough damage.

'Making up for forty years is not something you'll ever achieve.'

He nodded. 'I'm aware of that, but I'd like to get to know you and offer any financial support I can.'

'I don't need your money,' Jess said. 'It's been interesting to meet you, and I'm glad that you're not the complete deadbeat I'd always imagined. That you made an effort to look after us goes some way in helping me forgive you. But that's it.' She pushed her chair back and stood. 'I don't want a relationship with you, and I'd like you to respect that I never want to hear from you again.'

She experienced a mixture of satisfaction and sadness as shock crossed his features. She might as well have slapped him. 'Joey is my only remaining family, and if he did what you're suggesting, then it proves I'm better off without blood relatives in my life. I'm surrounded by wonderful friends who mean more to me than anyone I'm unfortunate enough to share DNA with.'

Martin looked torn. 'I'll respect your wishes, but I'll be honest—I'm disappointed. I'd hoped to get to know you and introduce you to Reeve.'

Jess turned to leave, doing her best to not be affected by Martin's tear-filled eyes. He'd stayed out of her life for forty years. Why should she feel anything for him now? She swallowed. That was the problem. A tiny part of her did feel something. A connection? A link? She stopped and turned back to him, unable to help herself. 'Who's Reeve?'

'Your younger sister. You're two months older.'

A wave of emotions swamped Jess. *A sister*? 'Two months? They were pregnant at the same time?'

Martin nodded. 'Paula didn't tell me until she was four months along, but I knew Alice was pregnant at six weeks.'

'And you chose Alice.'

The red splotches on his cheeks darkened. 'Yes, I chose my wife.'

'What if Alice hadn't been pregnant? What would you have done then?'

Martin gave a sad smile. 'I'm not sure. Part of me was relieved the decision was made for me. Very cowardly, I know.'

Emotions continued to sweep over Jess. She had a sister. A sister she'd desperately wanted at the age of three was materialising thirty-seven years later. When she was young, her mother had taken her to sit on Santa's knee for a photo. When he'd asked what she was hoping to get for Christmas, she'd answered, 'A sister.' She'd said the same the next year and the next. The Christmas she was six, the first without Paula, she'd worked out that Santa couldn't exist, and neither could God. For if he did, her mother would still be alive, and she'd have a sister.

But now it was real. She did have a sister.

'If you change your mind about me or about meeting Reeve, please get in touch. I'd love to hear from you.'

Jess nodded. There was too much to process right now: what Joey had done, that her father wasn't the ogre she'd imagined, and that she had a sister.

2

Reeve hummed as she ran her metal scraper under hot water, wiped it clean with a small towel, and set about the final smoothing of the chocolate buttercream.

Footsteps, followed by a low whistle, entered the kitchen as she ran the scraper over the top of the cake for the final pass. She smiled as Luke's strong arms encircled her from behind.

'Mm, think I've found something I'd like to devour.'

Reeve laughed and turned to face her husband.

He grinned and kissed her. 'The cake looks edible too. Although it's a bit over the top, isn't it?'

'Definitely,' Reeve said, slipping out of his arms

and turning on the tap to start the clean-up. 'But it's Bella's favourite, and I'm looking forward to seeing her. I always enjoy the first couple of days when she's with Nick, as it's nice to have some time to ourselves, but by the end of the week, I'm missing her and want to do nice things for her.' While the custody arrangement had been in place for four years, Reeve experienced the same emotions every week.

'And you're still feeling okay?'

Reeve frowned and turned back to face her husband. It was the second time he'd asked her this since they'd woken earlier. 'I told you I'm fine. Why are you asking again?'

Luke averted his gaze and sat down at the kitchen counter. 'I'm getting a little worried. You said some strange things last night when we were in bed.'

Reeve's gut clenched. *Not again.* This was not the first time he'd mentioned she'd said things she had no recollection of saying.

'You said...' Luke paused and took a deep breath. 'You said you want to have sex with other men.'

Reeve gasped. 'What? I would never say that.' She could see by Luke's face that he was repeating exactly what she'd said. But how was it she had no memory of it? 'I'm sorry. Even if I said it, I haven't been thinking it. For a start, why would I? You're amazing in bed, and we're so compatible.' And they were. It was some of the best sex Reeve had ever had. Luke had joked early on when she'd writhed in pleasure below his touch that she was benefiting from the fact that his hands were those of a surgeon. *Learning the magic touch was my ulterior motive for going to medical school.*

'Please forgive me.'

Luke smiled. 'It's okay. But I think you should see a specialist. I'd like to think it was a type of sleep talking, but I'm pretty sure you weren't asleep last night. I think it's worth checking that it's nothing else. With your mum and everything.'

The concern in Luke's eyes caused Reeve's bottom lip to quiver. She couldn't bear the thought that she might follow in her mother's footsteps. Luke stood and pulled her back into his arms. 'Hey, don't get upset. I believe you didn't mean it, and it's possible you were sleep talking. Getting checked out isn't going to hurt.'

A car door slammed in the driveway.

'Bella's home,' Luke said. 'Forget about this and get your happy face back on. You were dying to see her only moments ago. Sorry if I wrecked your mood.'

Reeve pulled out of his embrace. 'You didn't

wreck anything, and as much as I don't want to, yes, I'll go and see someone. Now, I'd better say hi to Nick.' She did her best to push the conversation from her mind as she made her way down the passageway to the front door.

Her excitement of earlier had been replaced with concern, but she still couldn't wait to wrap her fifteen-year-old in her arms. She plastered a smile on her lips and opened the front door as Bella, with Nick behind her, reached it.

Reeve's smile slipped as she took in her daughter's appearance. Bella's face was tear-stained, her lips pursed in anger. She pushed past Reeve and stomped up the stairs towards her bedroom. Reeve's mouth dropped open as she watched her go before turning back to face Nick. 'What happened?'

Her ex-husband pushed his floppy black hair from his forehead and sighed. 'I have no idea. She won't tell me. She's been great all week, and then this morning, she had a meltdown. We walked Freddie, stopped for breakfast at her favourite cafe – you know that place with the giant glass windows on Chapel Street – and all was fine. When we got home, she was glued to her phone for about an hour, and then crying. She wouldn't talk to me. All I got from her was it was something to do with school, and she was going to kill you.'

Reeve's stomach roiled. 'Me?'

Nick nodded. 'Sorry, I wish I had more information. I guess you'll find out soon enough. Did anything happen last week?'

Reeve stared at her ex. It was hard on Bella having her mother working at her school. She knew that. But she couldn't think of anything she'd done or said that would have impacted her. She'd been looking forward to Bella coming home and now this. She realised Nick was shifting from foot to foot, and she was still staring at him, not speaking. 'Sorry. I'm being rude. No, nothing happened out of the ordinary. Do you want to come in for coffee?'

Nick glanced at his watch. 'Better not, I've got invoices to get out to clients. But call me if you need me to do anything, okay?'

Reeve nodded, noticing Nick hesitate.

'I...' He dropped his gaze to his feet. 'I need to tell you something.'

Reeve took a step back. 'The last time you used those words it was to tell me you'd cheated on me. We're no longer together, so it's not cheating.'

Nick's cheeks flamed red. 'It's nothing like that. It's about the extra money you asked me for.'

'The money for Bella's computer and phone?'

'Yes. I don't have it now. I'm sorry, but things are tight. I invested in a commercial development, and it hasn't gone to plan.'

Reeve's stomach knotted. 'Oh no. Did you lose a lot?'

Nick hung his head. 'All of my savings. About forty grand.'

Reeve gasped.

'I know, it's not good. And I'm sorry, okay? I'll do my best to keep up with my child support, but the mortgage is an issue, so you might have to wait.'

'Have you told Bella?'

Nick shook his head, shame etched into every wrinkle.

'You know Luke will offer to cover your half of the cost of the phone and computer, don't you?'

Nick nodded. 'And I don't want him to, but if Bella needs them urgently, maybe we could ask your dad?'

Reeve folded her arms across her chest. 'Why would you accept money from Dad and not Luke? What's the difference?'

'Your dad's family, and maybe you should ask yourself that same question.'

'What do you mean?'

'You'll accept Luke's money but not your father's.'

'It's hardly the same. Luke and I are married.'

Nick shook his head. 'Look, I should go. I'll do my best to get some money to you soon.'

'Are you going to be okay financially? You know, in the bigger picture?'

Nick managed a wry smile. 'Probably not, but in the worst case I can always sell the house.'

Reeve stared at him. 'But you love that house. You always said that you'd have to be carried out in a box. That you'd never leave by choice.'

Nick sighed. 'It won't be a choice. But I have responsibilities and I don't expect or want you to be paying my share. I'll figure something out.'

Reeve nodded and watched as he headed back to his car. She'd always warned him that karma would bite him one day for what he'd done to her and their marriage, but this wasn't what she'd pictured or hoped for. This affected Bella too.

She walked down the hallway to the kitchen to find Luke rummaging through a pile of papers stacked on the sideboard. He looked up as she flicked on the kettle. 'You haven't seen that fishing magazine I showed you last night, have you? You know, the one you rolled your eyes at and suggested I actually go fishing rather than just read about it.'

Reeve stared at him. *Fishing magazine. What*

fishing magazine? Surely she'd remember talking about fishing as it was a new hobby Luke was exploring. 'No, sorry, I'm not sure where it is.'

'Strange. Another thing that's disappeared.'

Reeve flinched as a loud bang came from Bella's room.

'Slamming more doors,' Luke said, his eyes lifting towards the ceiling. 'What's going on?'

'Apparently, I've done something at school that's upset her.'

'Really? What?'

She sighed, taking a tray from the cupboard and setting it on the bench. 'No idea. But I guess it's time to find out.'

* * *

Reeve cut two slices of the white chocolate mud cake and added them to the tray with a pot of her daughter's favourite peppermint tea. She carried it up to Bella's room and knocked on the door.

'Hon, can I come in?'

'No.'

Reeve recoiled. The amount of venom Bella was able to inject into the only word she'd spoken since she'd arrived home was intimidating.

She swallowed and tried again. 'I need to speak to you, and I'm carrying a heavy tray. The slices of mud cake were bigger than I realised.' She held her breath. When Bella was little, the promise of cake or anything sweet would instantly have her on her best behaviour and going above and beyond to please Reeve. She wasn't sure at fifteen it would work the same magic.

But it did.

The lock turned, and the door opened. Bella retreated to her bed as Reeve brought the tray in.

'Leave it on my desk and go.'

Reeve placed the tray on the desk, took a deep breath, and turned to face her daughter. 'Dad said something happened this morning, and you need to kill me as a result.'

'Yes.'

'Are you planning to share with me what I've done? It would make it a lot easier on my deathbed to understand why I was being murdered.'

'It's not a joke. You've completely screwed me. I can't ever show my face at school again.'

Reeve frowned, trying to think of anything she'd done that could have affected Bella. There was the situation with Maddie Bryant and Grace Harper. She'd had no choice but to give them detention when she discovered them vaping on school grounds. 'Is this about Maddie and Grace? Are they angry with you because of the detention? I can't turn a blind eye even when it's your friends, hon. You know that. I wasn't unkind to them. It's a school rule, and they knew they broke it. If they get caught again, they'll be suspended.'

Bella stared at her mother, an incredulous look on her face. 'Vaping? You think I'm upset because you caught my friends vaping?'

'Well, not the vaping part, the detention maybe.'

Bella continued to stare.

'Look, unless you tell me what's going on, I can't do anything to help you.'

'Help? You emailed Dale Cross's mother and told her what a loser he is. Everyone knows. How are you going to *help* fix that?'

'What? I did not.'

'And now you're going to lie about it, too?'

Reeve folded her arms across her chest. 'I'm not lying. I didn't send an email.'

Bella stretched an arm across her bed and picked up her laptop bag. She took out the computer and opened it. 'You said what a pain he'd been last week, and then you go and do this.'

'He was a pain, but that's nothing unusual for

Dale.' Some days Dale was a delight to teach, and others, he was a challenge. Reeve tried her best to understand and support him, but for the past two weeks, he'd started randomly screeching like a chicken during class time, and it had become wearing. Reeve wasn't the only teacher to comment, and a support teacher had been brought in to remove him from the classroom environment and work with him independently when deemed necessary.

Bella found what she was looking for and shoved the computer at Reeve. 'That was posted to Insta and Facebook yesterday, and this morning Maddie tagged me in a group Snapchat message. That's when I saw it.'

Reeve glanced at the screen. It was a screenshot of an email. A chill ran down her spine. It showed her email address as the sender. The subject line read: *Your pain in the arse son.* She sank onto the end of the bed, her legs beginning to tremble. Her eyes scanned the body of the message.

You've ignored the teaching staff for years, but we can't stand it any longer. GET DALE TESTED or get him out of our school.

Do you think burying your head in the sand

is fair to anyone? Dale needs a diagnosis so he can be helped.

Do your son and everyone who has to interact with him a favour and look after him. Your lack of care is abuse.

Below is a link to a website where you'll find help. Please make an appointment.

Yours sincerely,

The staff of St Helena's

Reeve closed her eyes, nausea swirling in the pit of her stomach. This vile message had come from her email account. Or at least had been set up to look like it had. Her eyes flicked open. 'I didn't write or send this.'

'It's from your email address. The evidence is pretty damning.'

'I didn't send it, and I can prove it.' She put Bella's computer down and held out her hand. 'Come with me. I'll show you.'

Bella didn't take her hand but stood. 'This had better be good.'

Reeve grimaced. This was a set-up, and she could easily prove it. She led Bella out of the room, down the passageway to the fourth bedroom she'd set up as a home office. 'Check my emails,' she said. 'Look in the sent box. I did not send it.'

Bella sat down at her mother's desk. 'You probably deleted it after.'

'Then it will be in the deleted items or trash folder,' Luke said, entering the room. He looked from Bella to Reeve. 'What's going on?'

'Bella thinks I sent an awful email to someone. I'm trying to prove I didn't. What's the trash folder?'

Luke rolled his eyes and grinned at Bella. 'I think that answers your question as to whether she's deleted something.'

Bella gave a faint smile, and Reeve recognised a glimmer of hope in it.

'Bell, I haven't done anything wrong. I'm not sure how we'll prove it to everyone else, but I do need you to know.'

Bella nodded. 'If you didn't, I'll find out who did, don't worry about that.'

Reeve watched as her daughter clicked the mouse button numerous times, her eyes scanning the screen. Her mind raced. The first priority was to get Bella back on her side, and then it was to find out who'd done this. If this had gone to Dale's parents, the school needed to swing into damage control mode very quickly. It must have been a student – one who hated Dale and had it in for her.

She flinched as Bella slammed her fist on the desk and pushed the chair back with such force it careened into the overloaded bookshelf behind her. 'For a split second, I believed you, but look.' She pointed.

Reeve's heart raced as her eyes refocused on the screen. Her hand flew to her mouth. Sitting at the top of her sent items was the email to Dale Cross's parents. She turned to Luke, the horrified look on his face reflecting her own feelings.

Bella didn't wait for her to speak. She pushed past her and out of the room.

Reeve sank into the office chair. 'I swear, Luke. I didn't write this.'

The creases in Luke's forehead deepened. 'Ree, as much as I want to believe you, I'm worried. This email was sent at eleven thirty on Friday night. We'd had quite a few drinks. Remember?'

Reeve nodded. She'd woken with a pounding headache on Saturday morning.

'And it seems when you've had a few drinks lately, you're doing things that are totally out of character.'

'You can hardly compare skinny dipping in the spa with this,' Reeve said. 'I remember deciding to do

that. I remember doing it, and I remember you enjoying every second of it.' She pointed at the computer. 'But I don't remember this.'

'What about the text message to Charisse?'

Reeve's face flushed. Two weeks earlier, Luke's
friend Justin had called Luke wanting to know why
Charisse had received a text message from Reeve
saying he was having an affair. Again, Reeve had no
recollection of sending the message, but it had been
sent late at night when she'd had a few drinks while
waiting for Luke to get home from work.

'We need to get you some help, Reeve. Whatever's
going on is getting out of control. I'll ask around at
work. A behavioural neurologist is probably the
place to start. I'll find out who our best person is and
see if I can get you in. And in the interim, you'd
better call Aaron before he calls you.'

Reeve closed her eyes. He was right. She needed
to give the principal of St Helena's a heads-up before
someone else did. But how could she explain the situation when she had no idea herself what was going on?

* * *

Relief washed over Reeve as she ended the call to Aaron. The principal, while concerned, had sided with her.

'Reeve, you're one of my best teachers. If you say you didn't send it, I believe you. We've had some issues with the IT system being hacked lately. I'll call the Cross family and make them aware of this. I'll also draft a memo to all parents to explain the situation and to ask other families to get in touch if they receive any inappropriate messages.'

'Thanks, Aaron. I'm a little worried it's not about the school IT system, though. The message is in my sent items on my own computer.'

There was silence at the end of the line. 'What sort of email are you using?'

'Gmail.'

'Good.'

'Why's that good?'

'If someone knows your password, they can get into your account and send emails. If you've logged into your personal email at school, there is a possibility that our resident hacker has scraped your information and used it. It happened to Xavier Bartlett last month.'

'Really?'

'Yes, although his was used to praise a student rather than tear them down.'

'Praise a student? Wouldn't that suggest the student sent it?'

'It does, and through our investigations we were able to see that someone logged in to Xavier's Gmail account from an unknown ISP. They were clever enough to be hiding behind a VPN so, while we have our suspicions, we've not been able to confirm who it was. My guess is we'll find a similar scenario with your email. The main thing is not to worry. This is something the school needs to be concerned about, not you. Although you do need to change your password.'

Reeve wasn't sure about ISPs or VPNs but trusted Aaron knew what he was talking about. After she ended the call, she found herself smiling as she made her way downstairs to the kitchen where Luke was ending a phone call.

A quizzical expression crossed his face as he put his phone down on the counter. 'As pleased as I am to see you looking happy, I'm confused. I take it the call to Aaron went okay?'

'Better than okay. Hold on, and I'll get Bella down. She needs to hear this.'

Reeve called up the stairs to Bella before re-

turning to the kitchen. 'I do need to change my password as a priority. I'll do it as soon as I've explained.'
She frowned. 'Although the way I've been acting, I'll
probably forget it.'

Luke reached across the counter and squeezed
her hand. 'We'll get you checked out, Ree. There's
probably nothing to worry about.'

'Hopefully.' Reeve swallowed. Forgetting things
had become a regular occurrence, and she had to admit, it was beginning to scare her. Her thought was
interrupted when a reluctant Bella appeared in the
kitchen doorway.

'Sit,' Reeve said, pointing to the stool next to
Luke. Bella ignored her and, arms crossed, remained
standing in the doorway.

Reeve took a deep breath and went on to tell
them what Aaron had said.

'You were set up?' Bella asked.

'Definitely. I would never send an email like that,
Bell. You should know that.'

'How would I? You've done some out-there stuff
recently.'

Sweat tickled the back of Reeve's neck. 'And I'm
going to see someone about that.'

'I still don't want to go to school tomorrow.'

'An email will go out later today from Aaron explaining what's happened. He'll also have spoken to the Cross family. You not going to school will look like I've done something wrong.'

Bella sighed. 'Can I change schools?'

'Because of this?'

'No, because I hate going to the school you work at. You always said it was because of the fee discount you get by teaching there.'

'It's true. Your dad and I couldn't have afforded it otherwise.'

'Oh, come on,' Bella said. 'Granddad's offered to pay for me to go to a top private school for years. And' – she blushed – 'I'm pretty sure Luke could afford it too.'

Luke stood, kissed Reeve on the forehead, and turned to Bella. 'I'm going to leave you and your mum to chat about this. I'm happy to support whatever decision you both make, but as much as I like your dad, I'm very aware of his feelings about my "truck full of money".' He grinned as he did his best impersonation of Nick. 'I get where he's coming from. I'd probably feel the same if my daughter was being raised part-time by another guy. Anyway, let me know the outcome.'

Reeve couldn't help but smile as Luke left the

room. 'He's right, you know. Your dad won't want him paying for your schooling or anything else.'

'Anything else? Like the phone and computer you promised me?'

'Did Dad tell you he couldn't pay for that?'

'He didn't need to. I heard him on the phone the other night. He was practically crying to whoever he was talking to.' She folded her arms across her chest. 'He's lost all of his money.'

'Did you ask him about it?'

Bella shook her head. 'He would have been upset. I didn't want to add that to his problems. What about Granddad? He could afford the school fees. And the computer and phone. He always offers money and you say no.'

'I prefer to be independent,' Reeve said. 'Granddad's always wanted to pay your school fees, so he might agree to that. But your friends are at St Helena's. Wouldn't you miss them?'

'I won't have any left if you keep giving them detentions and emailing their parents.'

'I didn't email anyone.'

'Whatever.'

Reeve shook her head. 'No, not *whatever*. You can't get angry with me when I've done nothing wrong. I won't accept that. I will accept that having your mum at school isn't ideal and I'm happy to talk to your father about it. If he's open to letting Granddad contribute, then it might be an option.' And a relief for Nick based on his current financial situation.

'The local high school is also an option.'

'With its reputation for drugs and underage sex, it's definitely not.'

'Every school has both of those on offer.'

'You can buy drugs at St Helena's?'

A small smile played on Bella's lips. 'That's the one you're worried about. Sex is okay, then? Does that mean I can go on the pill?'

Reeve rolled her eyes. 'Okay, smarty pants. I'm not keen on you experimenting with either of those.' She hesitated. She'd spoken to Bella about sex on a few occasions. 'You know you can talk to me about sex if it's something that comes up. The main thing is that you're safe.' *And ideally, not fifteen.* She bit her tongue to stop from saying any more.

'Is this your way of changing the subject? I'm not interested in sex or drugs, but I am interested in changing schools, and I don't care where to. As long as it's not the one you work at.'

Reeve winced. 'Let's talk to Dad first, okay?'

'Okay.' She pushed off the stool. 'I'm going to do

my homework. Let me know when that email's sent so I can show my face on Insta again.'

Reeve watched as Bella's long, lanky frame exited the kitchen. She lowered herself onto the stool. As relieved as she was that she wasn't responsible for the email, she had to admit she was concerned. There were too many unsettling things happening. Too many things that took her back to a time when she'd lived through similar events. Except then, it wasn't her experiencing them. She'd been a witness – a witness to the unravelling of her mother.

3

Jess was deep in thought as she walked the four blocks to the second-floor apartment she and her boyfriend, Sam, shared in Elwood. Martin was nothing like she'd expected, and as much as she wanted to continue hating him, she wasn't sure she could. She reached the apartment block, hardly noticing the passing scenery or the slight chill in the air. It might only be three o'clock, but the one thing she knew was she needed a drink.

She keyed in the code for the gate to the complex, the aroma of freshly cut grass lingering in the air as she let herself through to the communal front garden.

'Hey, gorgeous, what's happening?'

Trent, Jess's neighbour and friend, was sprawled out on a picnic rug reading a book. He had a can of cider, a bag of corn chips, and a cooler bag next to him.

She smiled. 'By the looks of it, you're having the better day. You do know that it's winter, right? You look set for a summer picnic.'

Trent laughed. 'I picnic all year round. Come join me. I'd love the company. As much fun as this looks, I'd rather be sharing it with someone.' He reached inside his cooler bag and pulled out a second can of cider. 'Now there's no excuse.'

Jess hesitated. 'Can you give me five minutes? I want to see if Sam's home first. We had a bit of an argument earlier, and I want to check everything's okay.' *A bit of an argument.* That was an understatement.

'He's not here. I saw him leave about fifteen minutes ago. Said he was going for drinks with a mate at the Espy.'

'Really?' Jess slipped her phone from her bag and checked her messages. Nothing.

'Guess he's mad at you then,' Trent said, holding up the can again. 'Come on. You can tell me all your woes and then listen to me make excuses as to why I'm lazing about reading and drinking when I've got a deadline. Don't look in the cooler bag. I've drunk two of these already.'

Jess smiled. An afternoon relaxing without the pressure of another argument with Sam or interrogation about her meeting with Martin would be perfect. 'Are you going to tell me anything about your current story?'

Trent mimed zipping his lips. 'Nope, you know the rules. You get to read the published version.' He sighed. 'I'm regretting signing the deal on this one. I'm ready to branch out and write something different. A psychological thriller instead of another spy story would challenge me. But enough about my author struggles, tell me what's going on with you.'

An hour later, Trent's eyes were wide as he pulled more cans from his bag. 'Let me get this straight. You met your biological father for the first time today, and you have other family members you never knew about?'

Jess nodded. 'And he was a decent guy. Not that I intend to see him again, but at least I know my genes from that side aren't the complete disaster I assumed they were.'

'And you have a sister you don't intend to ever meet and an uncle who disappeared with millions of your dollars.'

Jess laughed, the alcohol having gone to her head. 'When you say it like that, it sounds like the plot of a movie.'

'Or my next book. But assuming movie, you, my friend,' Trent said, waggling a very drunk finger at her, 'are the star of the story. We'd organise for Charlize Theron to play you. You remind me of the short-haired version of her. Those big blue eyes and perfect cheekbones.'

'The eyes are from my father,' Jess said. 'Mum had brown eyes. Martin's are a deep blue. I wonder if my sister looks like that too?'

'Your sister?'

Jess jumped at the sound of Sam's voice.

She stared at her boyfriend. Was he still angry from their argument this morning? The same argument they seemed to have when anything important was happening in her life; that she 'didn't include him'; that she 'didn't share her feelings'. She hadn't admitted it out loud, but his neediness was getting tiring. 'Sorry about earlier. I was stressed about today and wanted to deal with it on my own.'

Sam nodded. She'd like to think that all was forgiven, but she knew him well enough to know it would be brought up again. And again.

'She's no longer stressed,' Trent slurred. He took

another can of cider from his cooler and held it up to Sam. 'Can we tempt you? We're working out who to cast as the evil uncle in the movie version of Jess's life.'

Sam sat down on the edge of the picnic rug beside Jess. He nodded to Trent and took the can. 'Evil uncle?'

'Get this,' Trent said before Jess had a chance to speak. 'Martin, the dad, who incidentally turns out to be a top bloke, sent millions of dollars to Reeve over the years, which her uncle, the bad guy, stole. She never got a cent. Her mother might even still be alive today if it wasn't for the uncle.'

Sam turned to Jess. 'Really?'

She nodded.

'Are you okay?'

'Okay?' Trent gushed. 'She's amazing. Imagine going through what Jess has gone through and turning out like this. She's a legend. That's what she is.' He threw his empty can onto the grass next to him and lay down on the picnic rug. 'I'm afraid *I'm* not much of a legend right at this moment.'

Jess laughed, but a frown remained on Sam's face, extinguishing her laughter. She sighed. 'What?'

'I'm worried about you, babe, that's all. Your dad really sent you money?'

Jess nodded. 'I still don't really think of him as my dad. I think of him as Martin Elliot, and yes, he did. I'll tell you more later if that's okay. Right now, I think I need to lie down too. That cider's potent.'

Sam watched as Jess balanced her can on a flat rock next to them and lay down beside Trent. She couldn't help but notice the concern in his eyes. She could only imagine the questions that would come once they were alone. She knew she should love her boyfriend for wanting to be there for her, but his constant need to talk about everything and delve deep into her emotions was wearing thin. Right now, she needed a friend like Trent. Someone who could laugh about the whole mess rather than stir up the anger she had every right to feel towards both her father and uncle.

* * *

The next morning Jess dragged herself out of bed, discovering she was still fully dressed, and made a beeline for the kitchen and coffee machine. She switched it on, popped two paracetamols in her mouth and drank a very large glass of water. Had Trent pulled more cans from his never-ending cooler supply? She wasn't sure, but her head suggested he might have.

A note lay on the kitchen counter. She picked it up, unable to prevent a groan from escaping her lips.

Gone to work early. I can't believe you'll share your deepest and most personal secrets with the neighbour and not me. I care about you and want to be the one there when you need someone. But you never let me be that person. You constantly hold back. Not sure I can do this any more. S.

Jess stared at the note. She wasn't sure she could do it any more either. As much as she thought she loved Sam, he was too needy, always wanting to know what she was thinking and if she was okay. It was nice that he cared, but he took it too far. The constant need to know her emotional state had become annoying. Even when she did share her feelings with him, he wore a wounded look that suggested he didn't believe she'd shared enough. She reread the note, her eyes stopping on *you constantly hold back.* What Sam didn't realise was she *had* to hold back. Since she was fifteen, she'd conditioned herself to keep things close to her chest. If she told Sam the truth about her life, and specifically what had happened when she was fifteen, he'd end the relationship and most likely report her to the authorities. While it was twenty-five years ago, there wasn't a day that passed when she didn't relive some part of that nightmare.

4

Reeve did her best to walk into St Helena's on Monday morning with her head held high. She had nothing to be ashamed of and nothing to explain. Aaron's email had gone out to all families the previous night, and she'd been overwhelmed to receive personal messages reassuring her that the parents knew she was innocent and always behaved professionally.

The biggest surprise was the message she'd received from Dale's parents, echoing the sentiments of others. They were keen to find the culprit behind the email, and as Aaron suggested, they assumed it was a disgruntled student. He'd suggested she bring her computer into school later in the week when the head of IT would be onsite and could check whether an unauthorised person had logged into her email account; she'd already changed her password to ensure whoever had hacked her account would no longer have access.

The morning passed uneventfully. The occasional snigger had erupted from the back of the classroom, and she could only imagine what was being said, but she didn't let it get to her. She just hoped Bella wasn't on the receiving end of anything nasty.

She stifled a yawn as she made her way towards the staffroom. Even with Aaron's reassurances the day before, she hadn't slept well. What if she *had* sent the message? What if she'd done the things she couldn't remember doing? What if her mother's illness was hereditary? The *what ifs* were doing her head in, and caffeine was going to be the only way she'd get through the rest of the day.

The staffroom was bustling with chatter and laughter when she pushed open the door. She smiled at her friends Sloane and Michelle, who motioned for her to come and sit with them. 'I'll make a coffee first,' she called, and made her way over to the kitchenette, took her cup from the cupboard, and added the instant granules.

'You look deep in thought,' Aaron said, reaching across her for his cup. 'Everything go okay this morning?'

'It did.' Reeve smiled. 'That email you sent shut the whole thing down very quickly. Thank you.'

Aaron rolled his eyes. 'For you maybe, not for me. The Cross family want answers. I don't blame them, but it puts the school in a difficult position.'

'Aaron?'

Reeve and Aaron turned their attention to the door of the staffroom. Jaya, Aaron's executive assistant, poked her head in. Her face was flushed, and she looked incredibly agitated.

'Everything okay, Jaya?'

She shook her head. 'Parent code red.'

Reeve would have laughed at her description if she hadn't seen Aaron's reaction first-hand.

'Oh god.' His voice was low but laced with concern. 'What the hell's happened now?' He glanced at Reeve, his teeth clenched. 'At least you can relax with this one. No doubt whoever's causing us trouble has moved on to the next phase.' He hurried to the door and disappeared into the corridor.

Reeve took her sandwich from the fridge and, with coffee in hand, manoeuvred her way back to the table where Sloane and Michelle sat. 'Hey,' she said as she sat with them. 'What's happening?'

'It appears you're the star of the show today,' Sloane said. 'Why didn't you call me yesterday? I would have brought over a bottle of wine and helped drown your sorrows.'

'Thanks. I had a few fires to put out with Bella and Luke, and a bottle of wine would have gone down well.' Although based on her drinking sessions of late, she was beginning to think she shouldn't drink at all.

'Got the year nine test after lunch?' Sloane asked. She nodded.

'How do you think Oscar Ryan's going to do?' Michelle asked. 'We need him to get at least sixty per cent to remain on the football team.'

Reeve smiled at the sports teacher. Oscar's scholarship was a combined academic and sports scholarship, but it had become evident to the academic staff that he'd been brought to the school for his football brilliance, not his academic achievements. 'He's worked hard the last few months. He'll be fine.'

'He's got you to thank,' Sloane said. 'All those extra hours tutoring. You've gone above and beyond for that kid.'

'He's a good kid,' Reeve said. 'Worth the effort.'

Michelle held up her hand and crossed her fingers. 'Let's hope he lives up to that praise.'

* * *

An hour into the ninety-minute English exam, Reeve found her eyes continually returning to the one empty seat in the classroom. Oscar's.

She'd gone through a range of emotions, from concern to anger, finally settling on frustration. The mid-year exam was compulsory, and she could only hope he would have a doctor's certificate to enable him to sit it another day. She averted her eyes from his seat and did her best to concentrate on the document in front of her. Other than the occasional shuffle of feet and paper, the classroom was quiet, each of the twenty-nine students focussing on their work.

Fifteen minutes before the exam was to conclude, the classroom door opened. Reeve and most of the students looked up. William Klein beckoned to her with an urgency that had Reeve hurry to the door.

'Keep working,' she advised her students, her frustration level rising; there was a sign on the outside of the door that clearly said *Please do not disturb – exam in process.*

The students' heads turned back to their work as Reeve slipped out, shutting the door quietly behind her.

'You need to collect your things and go and see Aaron.'

Reeve stared at the vice principal. 'What? Why? I'm in the middle of supervising an exam.' Dread settled over her. 'It's not the Dale Cross situation, is it?'

'No, but you need to go. I'll take over for you.' He cleared his throat. 'And Reeve, for what it's worth, I want you to know that I've got your back.' He forced a smile before stepping into her classroom, closing the door behind him.

* * *

I've got your back. The words replayed in Reeve's mind as she sat in her car in the school's car park, tears rolling down her cheeks. *Sexual harassment.* She'd been accused of sexual harassment. She couldn't get her head around it. Why would Oscar do something like this? It made no sense. The news had been delivered by Kerry Marsh, the school's student wellbeing officer, and Aaron.

Now Kerry's words played over in a loop in her mind. 'We take the issue very seriously. You'll be asked to leave the premises today, and you'll be advised when the school would like to interview you. We'll contact the Department of Education's Employee Conduct Branch to ensure the complaint is documented and to seek advice on how they would like us to handle the situation. We'll advise exact procedures, but usually, we would ask you to respond in writing to the accusations, and then a meeting will be organised to explore the circumstances further.'

Aaron had then escorted her to her car. 'If you've done nothing wrong, your name will be cleared,' he'd said, opening her car door. 'Trust the system, okay?'

Reeve had nodded, doing her best to keep herself together. Tears threatened, but she managed to contain them until Aaron walked away. She was too worked up to drive. She needed to hear a friendly voice. To have someone tell her that everything was going to be alright. She slipped her phone from her bag and called Luke.

'Hey, gorgeous. What a nice surprise.'

Reeve closed her eyes as Luke's warm, loving tone echoed through the car.

'I thought you couldn't call me during class time. Aren't you supposed to be supervising the English exam?'

Reeve remained silent, allowing his soothing voice to bring her the sense of calm it usually did.

'Reeve, you there?'

Her eyes jolted open. 'Sorry.'

'Are you alright?'

Reeve shook her head, doing her best to contain the tears. 'No. I've been suspended.'

A sharp intake of breath filtered down the line. 'What? Why? What's happened?'

She did her best to fill him in, tears overcoming her at times.

'Oh Ree, I'm so sorry. We both know you'd never consciously do something like that. Do you want me to come and get you?'

Reeve glanced at the clock on her dashboard. It was almost two-thirty. 'Don't you have a big operation scheduled for three? The Parkinson's patient?'

'Yes, we're prepping for it now, but I can bump it if you need me. You're more important.'

Reeve smiled through her tears. 'No, don't be silly. I needed to hear your voice. You can't let your patient down.'

'Okay, but what are you going to do now? Bella's got drama rehearsals until eight, which means you're going home to an empty house. I'll be here until at least seven. Can you drop in and see Sloane when school is out, or your dad, perhaps?'

'Sloane's got a staff meeting after school, but I could go and see Dad.' She sighed. 'Although that brings with it a whole other problem.'

'Your mum?'

'Yes, it's the anniversary of her passing on Wednesday, and I know he's quite down.'

'Go and see him, Ree. You'll probably find it'll do you both the world of good.'

Reeve could hear the murmurs of someone talking to Luke.

'I'm sorry, I have to go. And I'm sorry that you've been put in this horrible situation. We'll chat more tonight. Love you, and I'll see you later.'

While Reeve felt slightly better knowing she had Luke's support, his words stuck in her head. *We both know you'd never consciously do something like that.* He'd used the one word that concerned her most: consciously. Her gut contracted, and she pushed open her car door in time to empty the contents of her stomach onto the bitumen of the car park. *Consciously.* It was what she might have done *unconsciously* that filled her with dread.

5

Jess waited for the automatic doors to allow her entry to Victoria's largest private foster care organisation. She'd worked for Safe Houses for seven years as the manager of the Carer Information and Support Service team. Her role was varied, and she often found herself dealing with situations well outside of her job description.

'Hey, Jess,' Marlee, the not-for-profit's receptionist, called out as she passed the front desk and continued to the open plan area housing most of the staff. 'Good weekend?'

'Great, thanks,' she called over her shoulder. She waved to a couple of staff who were busy on the phones as she passed their office cubicles. The tap of fingers against keyboards and the smell of freshly brewed coffee was familiar and comforting.

Jess pushed open the door to her office, her nameplate making her smile. It was a little touch, but its permanency reminded her that she'd come a long way. The office was small but inviting with its vibrant artwork adorning the walls, and the splash of greenery her indoor plants provided. She sat down at her desk and powered up the computer. She had the board of directors at four and needed to go through her presentation again. Butterflies flitted in the pit of her stomach as she considered the opportunity before her. CEO. If she got the job, she'd have an even bigger chance to make a difference within the organisation. It was the one promise she'd made to herself when she'd finally left the foster system on her eighteenth birthday: she would make a difference, she would do her best to ensure no child was put in the position she had been. She cleared her mind and studied the PowerPoint presentation in front of her.

'Knock, knock.'

Jess looked up from her work and smiled as her colleague, Harry Speck, entered her office and sat down across from her. In his mid-forties, Harry had worked in foster care for twenty years and was as dedicated as Jess. 'Ready for this afternoon?'

'I think so. Still tweaking a few things.'

'You realise it's a formality, don't you? You've got it in the bag.'

Jess gave a wry smile. 'I wish I had your confidence.'

'Oh, come on, Jess. Look at all you've achieved in the last twelve months, let alone throughout your many years here. There's no one else that comes close.'

'No one internal, but who knows who else they're talking to.'

Harry tapped his nose. 'I know, and the job's yours. But that's not what I came to talk to you about.' His smile was replaced with the serious frown Jess had come to know and respect. She sat up straighter in her chair.

'We have a situation.'

The hairs on Jess's arms prickled. 'Who?'

'Felicity Chandler. Craig Novak called a few minutes ago. Apparently, they found her standing over their son with a large kitchen knife, threatening to kill him.'

'Jesus.' Jess jumped to her feet and grabbed her bag.

Harry rose from the chair. 'You're going to miss this hands-on stuff when you get the CEO role.'

Jess managed a wry smile. 'I can probably forgo dealing with attempted murder before my morning coffee.'

* * *

Jess pulled up outside the Novaks' large Mediterranean-style home and took a deep breath. She needed to remind herself that Felicity was only fifteen, was grieving the loss of her mother, and had no other family. It was understandable that she was lashing out. But this was the third foster home she'd been in in a period of six months, and it was unlikely she'd be welcome to stay after this incident.

Jeanie Novak opened the door before Jess had a chance to knock. Her eyes were red, her face strained. 'I'm sorry, Jess, we can't do it. She's too much. I feel like I'm letting her and the system down, but she crossed a line. She tried to kill Billy!'

'May I come in, Jeanie?'

'Yes, please. Sorry, I'm on edge, and I've forgotten my manners. Would you like tea or coffee?'

'No, that's fine. But let's sit down and chat. I need you to tell me what happened.'

Jeanie ushered her across a small foyer into a

cluttered living room. Jess sat on the edge of a squishy grey couch and waited for Jeanie to talk.

'I came home to find Felicity standing over Billy with a knife, saying she'd cut his balls off and hang them on the washing line before she killed him.'

A chill ran through Jess. 'What led to this?'

'That's irrelevant,' a deep voice behind her said.

Jess turned as Craig Novak appeared in the doorway.

'She's been a problem from day one, and now she threatens my son. We want her gone.'

'Lower your voice,' Jeanie said. 'Felicity's upstairs, and we don't want her to hear us.'

Craig's face reddened, and his voice grew louder. 'Why not? She's not a baby. She needs to know that her actions have consequences. Billy's going to need bloody therapy after this.'

'Okay,' Jess said, 'I understand that you're upset, but I do need a little bit more information. Was there an argument prior to what you witnessed? Something that led to this situation? It's not a normal way to behave if you're not provoked.'

Craig shook his head. 'You're saying that if Billy called her a name or something like that, it's acceptable to threaten his life?'

'No, I'm not. I'd like some context of what might

have happened.' Jess glanced from Craig to Jeanie, realising she wasn't going to get anything from either of them. 'How old is Billy?'

'Sixteen,' Jeanie said.

Bile rose in Jess's throat. They'd placed a fifteen-year-old girl in the house with a sixteen-year-old boy? She knew that all the checks would have been done, but her own history confirmed that that didn't mean she was safe. She did her best to calm her breathing. 'Hold on. You're saying Felicity had a sixteen-year-old boy on the floor and was threatening to kill him?'

'She knows taekwondo,' Jeanie said. 'Billy was screaming for help.'

Jess only wished she'd known a martial art and had been able to use it during her years in foster care. Maybe— She couldn't think about that. Not now. 'I'd like to talk to Felicity. Hear her side of the story.'

'She's upstairs,' Craig said. 'Second bedroom on the left. I've already told her to pack her things. You can collect her and her bag of clothes while you're up there. She's not staying another night.'

Jess followed the directions to the second floor and knocked on the door that was Felicity's room. There was no answer, so she pushed it open.

'Hey.'

Felicity was sitting cross-legged in the middle of the bed, her dark hair tied back in a ponytail. She kept her eyes fixed firmly on the window.

Jess sat down on the edge of the bed. 'I hear you're having a rough time.'

'Have you come to take me away? They told me I had to stay in my room until you came and got me. That was last night.'

'Last night? Have you had anything to eat?'

Felicity shook her head.

Anger bubbled within Jess. There was an emergency number to call when situations got out of hand, yet the Novaks hadn't. They'd left ringing until this morning. No doubt their way of punishing Felicity. 'Okay, let's go and get you some food and have a chat. Have you got your things packed?'

Felicity's eyes widened. 'I'm going?'

Jess nodded. 'We'll find you somewhere to stay temporarily and then hopefully find a family who'd like to have you for longer. But first, you and I are going out for brunch, and you're going to tell me what happened here. Okay?'

Felicity hung her head but gave a slight nod.

'Hey,' Jess said. 'I'm on your team, remember?

This system can work well, but it's not perfect and can also let people down. Now, let's get going.'

When they reached the bottom of the stairs where Craig and Jeanie waited, Jess said, 'I'll be in touch later in the day. I need to get Felicity settled somewhere else, and then we can talk.'

'She owes Billy an apology,' Craig said. 'I'd like to hear it before she goes.'

'After I talk with her, if I feel Billy is owed an apology, he will receive a written one,' Jess said. 'But right now, as you haven't elaborated on the situation, and I haven't had a chance to talk to Felicity properly, I think it's best that we leave.'

'Hold on,' Craig said. 'It's not—'

'No,' Jess said, cutting him off. 'I won't hold on. When a sixteen-year-old boy is involved in an altercation with a fifteen-year-old girl, I'd like to know every side of the story before I demand apologies from anyone. Especially as Felicity is underage.'

'What are you suggesting?'

'I'm *suggesting* I'll chat to Felicity and get back to you.'

'There's no way our Billy would have done something... well... something like you're implying,' Jeanie said, her face even redder than before.

Jess glanced at Felicity, whose eyes were fixed

firmly on the floor. 'Good, I'm glad to hear it. I'll be in touch.' She put a hand on Felicity's back and guided her out of the house.

* * *

Ten minutes later, Jess sat across from Felicity in a small cafe in St Kilda. She watched Felicity pick at her toasted ham and cheese sandwich, surprised she hadn't wolfed it down. Although, Jess wouldn't have had an appetite either if she'd been assaulted. She could only hope this wasn't the case. She took a sip of her coffee and replaced the cup in its saucer. 'I hope you know you can trust me. I'm here to look out for you and hopefully make the system work in your best interests.'

Felicity nodded.

'Let's start by you telling me what happened. You're not going to be in trouble, but I need to know what made you react the way you did.'

Felicity's eyes remained firmly focused on her food, causing a ripple of fear to surge through Jess. She needed the facts, but she was almost too scared to hear them.

'Did Billy do something he shouldn't have?'

Felicity nodded.

'Can you tell me what? I need to know to help you but also to make sure the Novak family don't foster any more girls if he's been inappropriate.'

Confusion spread across Felicity's features as her eyes met Jess's. 'Girls? They shouldn't be allowed to foster girls or boys. He's awful. So are they.'

Jess nodded. 'Okay. Tell me why he's so awful.'

'He...' Felicity's eyes filled with tears. Jess wanted to reach out to her, pull her into a hug and tell her it would be alright, that she'd go around to the Novaks herself and kill him. No girl, not at fifteen or twelve or any other age, should have to go through this.

'He said my mum killed herself because she hated me as much as he and his parents hate me.'

Jess sat back in her chair. 'What?'

'He said it's why I have no family. That no one would want to be with me, and even if any of them were alive, they'd do what my Aunt Meg did and disappear so no one could find her. I never even got to meet her.'

Jess nodded, trying to get her head around what Felicity was saying. 'Did he do anything else? Hurt you?'

'Only with his words. He didn't punch me or anything like that.'

Jess let out a breath. What she'd been thinking

had happened wasn't even on Felicity's radar. She might be fifteen, but she was a very young and naive fifteen in some respects.

'He said that to you, and then what? You pulled out the knife and threatened him?'

'I wasn't going to hurt him. He's bigger than me, and I wanted to show him that he shouldn't mess with me.' Her lips curled into a small smile. 'I haven't used my taekwondo since I stopped training. It was good to know it still works. I took him down with a simple leg sweep, and then the knife happened to be on the kitchen bench next to me. I don't think he thought I was going to kill him. It was Mrs Novak who freaked out. Billy hates me and played it up, hoping he'd get rid of me.'

Jess had to bite back a smile. She'd like to deck that kid for saying such nasty things. He had no idea what it was like to have no family. But at least it wasn't the scenario she'd imagined. 'You must miss your mum.'

Felicity nodded, her gaze returning to her sandwich.

'My mum died when I was five,' Jess said. 'I still miss her.'

Felicity looked up. 'Really? But you're...' She blushed.

'Old?' Jess laughed. 'Thank you for noticing. It never goes away, Felicity. It does get easier. As time goes on and you get older, you'll still miss her, but you'll have other people in your life who help to make it better.'

'Flick,' Felicity said. 'My friends call me Flick.'

Jess nodded. 'And that Billy, well we both know he's an entitled little shit.'

Flick's mouth dropped open. 'Are you allowed to swear?'

'Asks the girl who pulled a knife on a teenager and threatened to kill him.'

Flick smiled and picked up her sandwich. 'Fair enough. What happens now? Do I go to some other horrible family who doesn't want me?'

* * *

Jess returned to the office mid-afternoon. She'd organised emergency care for Felicity with Heather Frawley, a foster carer she'd known for fifteen years and always knew, no matter the situation, that she would make the child feel welcome, safe, and loved, even if it was only for a few nights.

'You okay?' Harry asked as she passed him in the corridor.

'Sorry, yes. I was thinking about Felicity Chandler.'

'Did you get it sorted?'

'For now. I had to remove her from the family.' She frowned. 'She flattened their sixteen-year-old and threatened to kill him after he kept saying that her mother killed herself because she hated her as much as he and his parents hate her.'

Harry shook his head. 'Poor kid.'

Jess nodded. 'Who needs that on top of every-thing else? Her father died in an accident, and her mother was unable to cope and took her own life. It's not a nice feeling being completely on your own. She said something which surprised me. Something about an aunt who'd disappeared. I thought she was orphaned when her mother died.'

Harry shook his head. 'No, there is an aunt some-where. We tried to contact her when Felicity was first brought into the system. From memory, she'd moved to the States or Canada twenty years ago and disap-peared. We weren't able to make contact.'

'I might have a look into it. See if she can be tracked down. If she has family out there, it would be nice to see if we can reunite them.'

'Possibly,' Harry said. 'If she's disappeared, it's quite likely she doesn't even know her sister died or that she has a niece.' He checked his watch. 'I'd better get going. I've got a meeting in a few minutes. Good luck with the presentation, not that you need it.'

Jess smiled and continued to her office to discover a courier package had been left on her desk. She sat down, slid the package in front of her, and read the label. It had been sent from DS Legal. She opened it and took out a large, stapled document and a covering letter. Her heart thumped as her eyes flicked to the sender's name. Martin Elliot.

Dear Jess,

It was an honour and pleasure to have finally met you. Your independence and the manner with which you conduct yourself is a credit to you. I'm devastated to learn about Paula and that you did not receive any of the financial assistance I provided.

I have had my lawyer, Devon Saunders, provide you with copies of the bank statements for the eighteen-year period, as well as a copy of the signed agreement between myself and Joseph Williams. I am happy to share original documents with you if you feel you'd like further proof.

I would like Devon to do some searching on my behalf into Joseph's current where-abouts but would like to discuss this with you first – ideally in person, but a phone conversation would work too.

I realise you may not want my money, but Safe Houses might. I would be happy to become a major sponsor and donate the money to your workplace or another cause you are passionate about.

Martin

Jess stared at the letter for a few moments before leafing through the documents he'd sent. She'd known in her gut that he was telling the truth when they'd met. A flicker of hope ignited in Jess. Maybe Martin Elliot would be worth getting to know. After forty years, she might have someone in her life that she could call family. She pushed the thought from her mind as quickly as she'd had it. Why would she bring someone into her life who would most likely let her down or disappoint her? She glanced at the clock. It was ten to four. She slipped the documents back into the box and put them out of sight under her desk. She'd deal with that later. Right now, she had a presentation to give.

6

After half an hour spent pulling herself together, Reeve stopped outside the gates of her father's Toorak mansion. She opened her car window and pressed the button for the intercom. The massive iron gates swung open as the camera that sat above the gate recognised her midnight-blue Land Rover, a present from Luke for her fortieth birthday three months earlier. She drove through the gates, the crunch of gravel on the driveway a familiar and comforting sound, and parked at the front entrance of the historic 1913 Edwardian villa. Martin's work as a leading hedge fund manager had earned him millions in bonuses, allowing him to purchase what Reeve's mother constantly referred to as her 'dream home'. The green panelled door opened, and her father stepped out. He walked towards her, meeting her part way along the hedge-lined path.

'And to what do I owe this pleasure?' His smile crinkled the corners of his deep blue eyes.

'I need comforting,' Reeve said. 'An awful day at work.'

Her father put an arm around her shoulders and led her into the house. 'Come on in and tell me everything. It might only be half three here, but it's five o'clock somewhere and time for a drink.'

Reeve allowed Martin to guide her down the long hallway, past the formal lounge and into his study. The fire was crackling in the hearth, and the sweet smell of cinnamon filled the room. Reeve drew in a deep breath. It was a scent that drew her back to her happy and privileged childhood. Her father had insisted on burning cinnamon sticks to purify negative energy from the home. He'd joked about it, and it wasn't until she was in her early twenties and more aware of the impact her mother's mood swings had had on her father that she realised what negative energy he was trying to erase.

She accepted the glass of single malt whisky he passed her, sat down in one of the grey wingback chairs positioned in front of the fire, and started to talk.

* * *

Martin was pacing in front of the window by the time Reeve finished telling him what had happened. He refilled his drink, knocked it back in one gulp, and then came and sat back in the chair next to her. 'We fight it,' he said in his calm, *we'll fix this* manner. 'I'll speak to Devon later and get his advice on the best approach. He's an excellent lawyer.'

A feeling of unease settled over Reeve.

'I know what you're thinking,' her father continued. 'That you don't want to use my money to get you out of trouble, but sometimes you need to accept my help. You kicked up enough fuss about those investments of Mum's I transferred into your name.' He reached across and took her hand. 'Let me help you, sweetheart. You know Mum would march right into the school and flatten that kid, don't you? She'd want me to do the same, but we'll do it the legal way.'

Reeve smiled at the memory of her feisty mother. He was right. She would have insisted on helping sort out the situation. 'I miss her, Dad, I really do.'

Martin's smile fell as he let go of Reeve's hand and leant back in his chair. 'Me too.'

'I can't believe it'll be a year on Wednesday. Are you sure you don't want to spend the day together? I was taking the day off, not that it's relevant now.'

Martin gave a sympathetic smile. 'How about this. Let's have a late breakfast, say at nine, and then go to the cemetery together. After that, I'd like to spend the day on my own if you don't mind.'

Reeve nodded.

'Do you think Bella will want to come?'

At the mention of Bella's name, Reeve dropped her head to her hands. 'Oh no. Bella. She's going to kill me.'

'You've done nothing wrong. Let me call Devon. I'm sure he can get something put in place where the kid's not allowed to talk about it to anyone until the situation's resolved.' He stood, pulled his phone from his pocket, and paced in front of the fire.

'Get me Devon Saunders,' he barked into the phone when his call was answered. 'It's Martin Elliot, and it's urgent.'

Within thirty seconds, he had Devon on the line.

Reeve half-listened to her father's side of the conversation but found her mind wandering to a place she'd done her best to avoid all day. The *what if I did it* place. She'd been acting so out of character, saying terrible things and forgetting what she'd done, that realistically anything was possible. As much as she dreaded the thought, she was going to have to see someone and have tests done. Patricia Fields might be a place to start. She'd been her mother's psychiatrist, and Reeve had had several sessions with her following Alice's death. She would understand why Reeve was concerned as she knew Alice's case well.

Her thoughts were interrupted as her father finished his call. He slipped the phone into his pocket and sat down across from Reeve.

'Devon will call you tomorrow. He's going to speak to the school and find out the next steps. He thinks there's usually an interview process where they'll want to question you, and he'll be there with you if this happens. He said to tell you not to speak to any staff or students about the situation in the interim and to tell Bella not to discuss anything. He's going to do his best to have a gag order put in place so the kid can't discuss the complaint either.'

Reeve nodded and forced a smile for her father's benefit. 'Thanks, Dad. I don't know what I'd do without you.'

Martin's jaw clenched. 'Hopefully, that's not something you'll have to deal with for some time.

Now, do you want me to come home with you and talk to Bella? She might need to hear from someone else how she should handle this situation.'

Reeve appreciated his offer but knew she was the one who needed to deal with her daughter. 'No, I'll be fine, but I should tell you, as you'll probably get a call from her, she's hoping you might help her change schools. It's nothing to do with the Oscar situation. She brought it up on Sunday. She hates being at the same school as me. I understand that, but Nick and I can't afford fees at one of the more expensive schools, and there's no way he'll let Luke pay for her.'

Martin laughed, quickly turning it into a cough. 'Sorry. Yes, I'd be more than happy to help.'

Reeve folded her arms across her chest. 'What was the laugh for? Nick's always done his best to provide for Bella, you know that. But electricians don't exactly make the same salary as surgeons.'

Martin sighed. 'Reeve, I've been paying Bella's school fees since the day she started. The only change was when you split up with Nick and started paying half yourself. Of course he can't afford it, and he was too proud to tell you. He married into a wealthy family and there's no way he could keep up.'

Reeve's mouth dropped open. 'You're kidding. Why didn't you say anything?'

'Because I understood. Nick's a hard worker and he has his pride. Although, from what I gather, he was happy to accept money from me, he just knew how against handouts you are and didn't want you to know.'

'Why tell me now? Has Nick asked you for more money?' Reeve's stomach churned as she thought back to Nick's admission that he'd lost all of his savings. Surely he wouldn't ask his ex-father-in-law to bail him out?

Martin sighed. 'I promised him I wouldn't share any of our discussions with you.'

'So he has?' Reeve couldn't believe it. She and Nick were divorced and he was going to her father for money?

'Let's not get into it. The bottom line is, Nick's willing to accept help, which is good as his situation affects my granddaughter, and you should too. Whether it be for school fees or legal help or anything else. We're in a privileged position to be able to engage the best resources available, and we should. The words "I can't afford it" should never pass your lips.'

Reeve was about to object. It was fine for him to talk like this – her father had amassed a small fortune – but she hadn't. Not everyone wanted to be dependent on someone else.

Martin held up his hands, seeming to sense her defensiveness. 'Nope, no more discussion. Don't mention to Nick what I've told you, and act delighted when he agrees to let me pay for the school fees. Now, the head of St Margot's is someone who owes me a favour. I'll have a chat with her and see if there's any chance of Bella starting next term. And I will say I'm elated that a daughter of mine is finally willing to accept some money.'

'A daughter of yours? That sounds like you've got a bunch of us hidden away.'

Martin's cheeks coloured. 'I...' He hesitated. 'I sometimes wish it was the case, Reeve, that I'd given you the chance to grow up with siblings. That I hadn't taken that from you.'

Reeve stood and crossed the room to where her father stood. 'Don't be silly.' She leant forward to hug him. 'It was hardly your fault Mum couldn't get pregnant again. It was one of those things. We were destined to be a family of three.'

Martin opened his mouth, seemed to think better of it, and shut it again. 'Perhaps.'

Reeve frowned. 'Perhaps? Dad, it's not your fault, and anyway, I enjoyed being an only child. You spoilt me rotten.' She gave a small laugh. 'I might have objected to sharing your affections with someone else.'

'You're a good daughter, Reeve. Always remember that, won't you.' His eyes glistened. 'There are things in my past that I'm not proud of, but the one thing I've always known is how much joy you've brought me and how much I love you. Let's meet at nine on Wednesday, okay?'

Reeve nodded. Wednesday was going to be a difficult day for her father, and the words he'd spoken suggested his emotions were already getting the better of him. He wasn't usually one for displays of affection. 'Flaxton's?'

Martin smiled. Flaxton's had been her mother's favourite breakfast haunt. 'Perfect. And Reeve, don't worry too much about this school business. Devon will fix it. There's never been a situation he hasn't been able to sort out for me. Sometimes it requires fighting to ensure the truth is told. As a last resort, I'm sure the school would appreciate a big donation, as would the family of this kid.'

'No.' The word escaped Reeve's lips before she even had time to process it. 'I could never show my face again at the school if I had to buy my right to be there. I'm innocent, Dad. If that can't be proven, then I walk away.'

'You make me proud, love. Okay, I'll tell Devon we're fighting this your way. No payoffs, no bribes.' He grinned. 'He'll find it hard to believe we're related.'

After farewelling her father and manoeuvring the Land Rover down the long driveway and back out to the road, Reeve did her best to shake the feeling of unease. Her mind whirled with concerns about the situation she was in. Devon was a fantastic lawyer, she knew that, but the biggest problem she faced was not proving her innocence; it was whether or not she actually was innocent. She needed to make an appointment with Patricia as soon as possible and organise tests. She considered calling from the car but hesitated. Once she attended the appointment, there was no going back. She would find out for sure if she was, in fact, sick.

* * *

Reeve was slumped at the kitchen counter, her head resting on her hands, when Luke arrived home from work that evening. She did her best to hide her misery as she explained what her father had organised with Devon.

Luke took her in his strong arms and rubbed her

back. 'We'll fight this, Ree. You've got nothing to worry about.'

Reeve pulled back, her eyes meeting Luke's. 'But what if I do? With all the crazy things I've been doing and saying, it's possible I did this.'

Luke fell silent.

'I think you're right about me needing to get tests done,' Reeve continued, 'and as soon as possible. If there isn't anything wrong with me, then at least I'll know that I didn't do anything wrong at school.' *But how will I explain the other things?* Reeve pushed the thought from her mind, refusing to give it airtime. The possibility that she had what her mother had was too frightening to cope with.

'I meant to ask at work who would be best for you to see. I'll ask tomorrow and get a recommendation.'

Reeve shook her head. 'I think I'll go and see Patricia. You know, the psychiatrist who treated Mum and who I saw after she died.'

Luke nodded slowly. 'She's not a behavioural neurologist, who is the person you really need to see.'

'She's not, but she's a psychiatrist who specialises in early onset dementia. So she's a good starting point. She also has the contacts to refer me to the right neurologist or another specialist. And she knows Mum's history, so it won't be as daunting.'

Luke leant forward and kissed her forehead. 'That sounds like a good starting point. Have you rung for an appointment?'

Reeve nodded. 'She's booked out for the next two weeks, but she put me on the cancellation list when I explained it was urgent.'

'Good. Now try your best not to stress about it. We're luckier than most in that we can afford the very best when it comes to specialists and lawyers.'

'Speaking of that, Dad's insisting on paying for the lawyer. Says it's something Mum would want him to do.' She wrung her hands together. 'Hopefully this will be resolved quickly, and I can get back to work. I'm being paid during the investigation at least.'

A smile danced in his eyes. 'I know I've said this before, but I'm going to say it again. You don't need to work. You could become a lady of leisure. Do all those things you've said one day you'll do. Join the tennis club, learn to play golf, or do some charitable work. I know you like to be independent, but I do earn enough for both of us. And there's your dad's money too. Those investments he *forced* on you are worth a fortune.' He laughed. 'I can't imagine anyone except you who'd consider that kind of gift to be an inconvenience.'

Reeve sighed. 'I don't want to be reliant on Dad's

money. I've always been independent, and the fact that he insisted those investments of Mum's be put in my name makes me feel sick. It'll go to charity down the track. But it's not only about the money. I love what I do. I'd be letting my students down for a start, but imagine if you were suddenly told you couldn't go to work any more and your skills weren't needed. What would you do?'

'Enjoy myself.'

Reeve raised an eyebrow. 'Then quit your job. You keep saying you have enough to live a comfortable life. Why keep working?'

Luke laughed. 'Okay, point taken. Yes, it'd be like someone cut off my arm. I didn't study for all those years to stop now.' He raised his arms and stretched. 'Although, after a day like today, it's tempting.'

'Bad day?'

'Long. The last operation was fiddly. The concentration required always takes it out of me. One of those every few days would be enough, but today I had two quite similar, and tomorrow I'm supervising the interns.' He took her in his arms. 'I'm not starting until eleven on Wednesday, which means I can spend the morning with my lovely wife. How about I take you to Zander's for breakfast, and then we can take a walk along the esplanade if the weather's good?'

'I can't,' Reeve said. 'I promised to meet Dad for breakfast and then go to the cemetery with him. It's Mum's anniversary.'

Luke tapped his forehead. 'Sorry, you mentioned it on the phone earlier. Do you want me to come?'

Reeve thought about it for a moment. 'No, I think this should be something that just Dad and I do. Hope that's okay?'

'Of course,' Luke said. 'It's an important day for you both. A sad one, but one to celebrate too. From everything you've shared with me about your mum, it's obvious that she wasn't the sort of woman who'd want you to sit around moping. She'd want her life celebrated.'

Reeve nodded. It was true. Prior to her illness and diagnosis, Alice had always been the life of the party.

'So.' Luke pulled her close, kissing her forehead. 'How about I make a reservation for dinner on Thursday night at Dominic's. I'll be home too late on Wednesday night, so we can postpone our celebrations for your mum until Thursday. And Bella loves it there, and I'm sure she'd want to celebrate her grandmother's life with us.'

Reeve frowned. 'I'm not sure how Bella's going to react to what's happened today. Based on her meltdown on Sunday, I can't imagine it's going to be good.'

'I'll make the reservation for three anyway. They can always remove a chair if she decides not to come.'

'Thank you. Thank you for everything.'

Luke raised an eyebrow. 'Everything?'

'For being you. For being there for me and for being flexible about Bella and for not telling me what to do.'

Luke laughed. 'I'm still learning the ropes on how to navigate the world of a teenager, but as for you, I'll always be there, Reeve. I love you.' He kissed her gently on the lips before pulling away. 'Now, I'm going to go and have a shower and wash the hospital off me and then we'll open a bottle of that expensive Penfolds we bought for special occasions.' He winked. 'Don't worry. I won't let you have more than two glasses.'

'I hardly think the day I got suspended is a special occasion.'

'It doesn't happen often,' Luke said, his eyes teasing her playfully, 'so we'll consider it a special occasion.'

Reeve's phone pinged with a text as Luke disappeared upstairs, and she took two crystal wine glasses from the cabinet that housed them. She slipped the phone from her pocket. It was Sloane.

> Hey hon, are you okay? Call me when you get a chance. I can't believe that little prick would do this. Love you. x

Tears filled Reeve's eyes. So much for Devon suggesting they enforce a gag order. If Sloane knew, then all the teachers did and no doubt the students too. The rumour mill had already started, and her name was being blackened. She knew how it worked. Guilty until proven innocent, and even then, people would always question her actions. She sent a quick text back to Sloane.

> I'm okay. I can't believe it either. Guess it's a case of no good deed goes unpunished. No free tutoring from me moving forward, assuming I still have a job. Call you tomorrow. Waiting for Bella to get home. Not looking forward to that!

A message came back almost immediately.

> Better still, how about drinks at Rocco's on Wednesday? I can meet you at six. I know it will be a difficult day.

Reeve smiled through her tears. She'd known Sloane for over twenty years. They'd met at Monash University doing their Bachelor of Education degrees and had become best friends. Three years earlier, Sloane had told Reeve of the available position at St Helena's, and for the first time in their teaching careers, they worked at the same school. She hesitated. Devon had said she wasn't to talk to anyone at St Helena's. But it was Sloane. A genuine long-time friend had to be an exception.

> Rocco's sounds good.

> Great. See you Wednesday, and don't stress. The truth will come out. x

Reeve placed her phone on the kitchen counter, opened the wine fridge, and took out the bottle of the Penfolds Luke had suggested. *The truth will come out.* She only hoped it was a truth she wanted to hear.

* * *

A permanent ache seemed to have settled in the back of Reeve's throat. She was on edge, and her ears pricked for any outside noises that might be Bella coming home. She was an hour late and not answering the text messages Reeve had sent her. She'd had one glass of wine with Luke but wasn't willing to risk a second. She needed her wits about her when she spoke to her daughter.

A text message pinged on her phone as she sat in the lounge room waiting. She grabbed at it, expecting to finally have communication from her daughter, but it was Patricia Fields.

> Reeve, I have a cancellation at 10:30 a.m. tomorrow. Would that suit your schedule? Best, Patricia.

Reeve's insides twisted as she stared at the message. Tomorrow was too soon, wasn't it? She wasn't ready. She took a deep breath. But she had to be. She had to know what was going on and hopefully rule out dementia. She sent a quick confirmation text before she could change her mind.

A little after nine, a car door slammed in the driveway. The front door opened, and Reeve listened to the familiar sound of Bella tossing her bag into the nook that led off the hallway. She took a deep breath, doing her best to control her nerves. She was dreading the conversation she knew she was about to be forced to have.

Reeve stepped out of the living area and into the hallway, a smile fixed on her face. Bella was already halfway up the stairs.

'Hey, hon, how was drama?'

Bella stopped momentarily before continuing up the stairs as if Reeve hadn't spoken. She slammed her door when she reached her room.

Luke came up from behind Reeve and slipped his arms around her. 'That went well.'

Reeve's eyes stung with tears. 'This is incredibly unfair. It's bad enough trying to deal with a teenager on a good day. Having to convince her of something I didn't do, again, isn't on.'

'Do you want me to talk to her?'

Reeve turned to face Luke. 'No. I need to. But thank you.'

He pulled her to him and kissed her forehead. 'It'll be okay. You've done nothing wrong.'

Reeve nodded. For the moment, that was what she needed to believe. If tests proved otherwise, she'd deal with that then. For now, she needed to hold her head high. She pulled out of Luke's embrace and marched up the stairs to Bella's room. She didn't knock. She wasn't going to ask her daughter permission to speak to her.

'Get out.'

Bella was sitting at her desk, her back to the door, Snapchat open on her phone.

Reeve took another deep breath. 'No. We need to talk about Oscar and what's happening at school.'

Bella turned to face her mother. 'Do you know what you've done? The names I'm being called, and the horrible things people are saying?'

'I can imagine, and I'm sorry you're having to go through that. But I've done nothing wrong. Oscar's accusations are lies. There's no truth to them. I would never abuse my position as a teacher. To make sexual suggestions to a fifteen-year-old? I'm old enough to be his mother.' She shuddered at the thought.

'Why would he make up a lie like that? You said it: you're old enough to be his mum. Who wants to be with their mother? If he was going to lie, he'd say he'd had sex with Miss Lewis. At least she's half your age.'

'The accusations are sexual harassment, Bella, not abuse. He's accused me of saying inappropriate things, not doing them. And why would he do that? I wish I knew the answer. I've bent over backwards to help him the last few months, and this is the thanks I get.'

Bella snorted. 'Yeah, bent over backwards. That's pretty much what the kids are saying too.'

Heat rushed to Reeve's cheeks. She wasn't going to continue this line of conversation. 'If it's any consolation, I won't be allowed back at school to teach until the situation is resolved.'

'It doesn't make any difference to me. I'm not going back to that school, so don't even try to give me your stupid reasons as to why it will be okay. You're not the one copping horrible comments and being shoved in the corridors because your mum's a child molester. Even if you're fired, I'm not showing my face there ever again.'

The venom in Bella's voice hurt more than Oscar's accusations. Her daughter didn't believe her and wasn't going to support her. 'If you feel that way, why did you go to drama this afternoon? You can't continue if you're planning to leave St Helena's.'

Bella laughed, a high-pitched strangled noise erupting from her lips. 'I didn't go to drama.'

'Where did you go then, and who dropped you home?'

'I went around to Mason's house. He was the only

person who showed me any decency today. We hung out.'

It was getting worse. Mason Walker was the one kid at St Helena's you didn't want your daughter going near. Rumour had it that his father was a drug dealer, and his mother was currently in prison for possession. Mason was rough, had his arm around a different girl every week, and last year had got a sixteen-year-old student pregnant. He didn't cause trouble at school, which meant there were no grounds to get rid of him, but he was a constant topic of conversation and source of concern in the staffroom. 'Mason's not a good influence,' she said. 'I don't want you going to his house again.'

Bella's jaw tightened in defiance. 'Yeah, and I don't want you telling my classmates you want to have sex with them. When you stop, I'll consider listening to you. For now, get out of my room.'

Reeve stared at her daughter, unsure how to proceed.

'I said get out,' Bella repeated. 'Dad's back tomorrow, and I'm going to his place. I won't be coming back.'

'Hold on, what? That's not our arrangement.'

'I'm fifteen. Your *arrangement* isn't my arrangement. I'm telling you what I'm doing. I'm not staying under the roof of someone accused of what you've been accused of. I'm pretty sure Dad will agree with me when I tell him what you've done.'

'I'm pretty sure Dad will support me and know there's no way what Oscar's said is true.'

'How would he know what to believe? Look at all the terrible things you've said and done in the last few months. You don't even remember any of them. How would you know if you'd done anything with Oscar or not? You called me a spoilt little bitch the other night. Let me guess, you have no memory of that, do you?'

'What? I never...' Reeve's words petered out as Bella's eyes hardened. 'Why didn't you say something?'

'Really? You want us to fill you in with all the bizarre stuff you're saying and doing? Luke told me we should protect you until you've seen a doctor. Something you should do sooner rather than later before you completely ruin my life.'

Reeve had no response. She turned before Bella could see the tears rolling down her cheeks and slowly retreated from the room. How many other things had she done that she'd be crushed to know about? And as for ruining Bella's life, she wasn't sure which scenario was the best. That she wasn't sick and therefore had no explanation for her actions, or that she was and, assuming she followed in her mother's footsteps, Bella would be subjected to watching her mother deteriorate and eventually die. The one thing she knew for sure was that she couldn't put her through that.

7

It was close to seven by the time Jess pushed open the front gates of the apartment complex and walked through the garden area to the stairwell.

'Hey,' Trent called down from his third-floor balcony. 'How's your head today?'

Jess looked up at him and smiled. 'It wasn't great this morning, but the day's ensured I've got a raging headache and want to go to bed.'

'Does that mean bad news from the Board?'

Jess frowned. She didn't remember discussing this with Trent, but then again, they had had a lot of drinks.

'Sam mentioned it last night,' Trent said, his

cheeks colouring. 'He also said to tell you to call him when you were ready to share more of your life with him.'

'He said that last night?'

'No, he said it about an hour ago when he left.'

'He left?'

Trent nodded. 'With half of your apartment by the looks of what he and his mate, that red-headed one, took with them.'

Jess's stomach churned. 'He moved out without even talking to me?'

'Sorry, chick. Let me know if you need anything, okay?'

She reached the second floor, pushed the key in the lock, and opened the front door. The change in the energy of the apartment immediately hit her. The picture hanging above the vintage oak hallway console was gone, as were the ornaments and photo frames that had adorned it. Her eyes scanned each room as she made her way to the kitchen. All signs of Sam had vanished. The rug beside their bed, the throws over the couches, and the pictures from most walls. As they'd purchased most of them together, that was a bit rude, although at this point, Jess wasn't sure she cared.

She reached the kitchen, dumped her bag on the counter, and opened the fridge. As she poured a glass of wine, she noticed a letter propped up against the fruit bowl.

She took it and her glass into the living area and sank onto her favourite cream couch. The bright blue cushion was noticeably missing. She took a large sip of wine before unfolding the page. Her heart rate quickened as she read it.

Jess, I can't do this any more. I need to be with someone who wants to share more than their physical presence with me. I need someone who's willing to share their thoughts, their feelings, and their emotions. I'm sorry if life has made this too difficult for you to do. I hope you find happiness. S.

She threw the note onto the coffee table. Why was being private and reserved such a big deal? She needed someone who loved her for who she was and didn't constantly feel the need to try to psycho-analyse her. It wasn't as if she'd changed since she met Sam and suddenly clammed up. She let out a deep sigh. Just that morning, she'd thought it might be best if they broke up, but the way he'd done it was a shock.

Jess sipped her wine, her thoughts shifting from Sam back to Martin and his letter. That he wanted to find Joey suggested her uncle *had* taken Martin's money. Anger surged in her. If he'd taken the money meant for her and her mother, he was responsible for both her mother's death and Leo's. *Leo.* She shook herself. She couldn't allow her mind to take her there right now. She had to deal with one thing at a time. The first being Joey. She needed to find him and confront him.

* * *

Jess reached a dead end quickly in her search to find her uncle. She wasn't sure where to start. She found herself knocking on Trent's door a little before ten.

'Sorry, I know it's late,' she said.

'No worries, I was about to make hot chocolate. Want to join me?'

She nodded.

'What's going on?' Trent asked as, a few minutes later, they sat across from each other, nursing steaming mugs of hot chocolate at the small kitchen table.

'I found out today that my uncle most likely did take the money that Martin sent each month, and I want to speak to him.'

'To the uncle?'

Jess nodded. 'I need an explanation. I can't imagine it'll be anything that will excuse what he did, but I guess part of me is hoping there is an explanation other than that he stole it.'

'What if that is the explanation?' Trent asked.

'I'm not sure. I guess I decide whether I want to pursue any legal avenues.'

'Okay. Did you want me to come with you to speak to the uncle?' Trent made a fist. 'I'd be very happy to speak to him with this.'

Jess smiled. 'No, it's not that. I have no idea where to start trying to find him. I did the obvious Google searches but didn't find anything useful. I thought you might know with your journalist background how to find people.'

Trent nodded. 'I know someone who tracks people down for me. I can't access the info myself. Hold on a sec.' He stood and left the kitchen, returning moments later with his laptop. 'I'll email Hamish. He's going to need his full name, date of birth, last known address. Ideally, birthplace if you happen to know it.'

'I've only got his name and date of birth,' Jess said. 'Joseph Cairo Williams.'

Trent raised an eyebrow. 'Cairo?'

Jess blushed. 'Family tradition. Mum's middle name was Paris, mine's Adelaide.'

'Okay, but I still don't get it. Why name you after places?'

'Places we were conceived. My grandparents enjoyed a lot of overseas travel.'

Trent laughed. 'Mm, okay. Too much information. But the good thing is, Cairo is an unusual name.' He typed an email and sent it off to his friend. 'Hamish is quick at turning around favours for me. I imagine we'll hear from him sometime tomorrow.'

'Thank you.'

'What's the plan of attack once we have his contact details?'

Jess sighed. 'Honestly, I have no idea. It's an awful situation to be in. The fallout from what he's done is almost too much to deal with.' Her eyes filled with tears. 'If we'd had that money, Mum might still be alive. She wouldn't have had any reason to be working a dead-end job or riding a bike to it.' *And I would never have been put in a position to lose Leo.*

Trent reached across the table and placed his hand on her arm. 'I'm sorry, Jess.'

'Me too,' Jess said. 'What Joey did set off a chain of events that had devastating consequences. It wasn't only Mum.' She hesitated. She'd never told anyone about Leo. For a split second, she considered telling Trent but then changed her mind. It wasn't a case of not being able to trust him with her darkest secret; it was a case of losing his friendship the moment he learned the truth about her. She wasn't willing to risk that.

* * *

The next afternoon, Jess waved to Trent as she walked through the front garden entrance of the apartments. Despite the crisp winter air, he was sprawled out on his picnic rug, a laptop in front of him. 'I'm supposed to be writing, but you could twist my arm and take me out for a drink.' He glanced at his watch. 'Although it's a bit early. Shouldn't you still be at work?'

'I didn't sleep very well after our chat last night. I decided to work from home this afternoon. Did you hear back from Hamish?'

Trent nodded. 'Have you checked your email? He rang me at lunchtime and said he had information on Joey for you and would send it directly to your email. He was in a rush, so I didn't find out anything else.'

Jess's heart began to race. 'He found him?'

Trent smiled. 'Check your email.'

Jess slipped her phone from her bag. She was about to find out where Joey was. She looked up at Trent. 'Imagine if he lives around the corner. I could confront him tonight.'

Trent raised an eyebrow. 'You could, but I'd sleep on it. Work out what you're going to say.'

Jess took a deep breath. She scrolled through the emails and found one from Hamish Woods. She opened it.

Dear Jess,

Trent has asked me to locate a Joseph Cairo Williams on your behalf.

Records indicate that Mr Williams left Australia in 1998 and has not returned. His last known address was George Town, Grand Cayman Islands. While I have been able to trace his initial movements in George Town, there has been no further record of him. It's possible that he changed his identity at this point.

I have a colleague who can assist you fur-

ther, but I'm afraid there will be fees involved.
If you'd like his information, please let me
know, and I will put you in touch.
    Best regards,
    Hamish

'He disappeared.' Jess looked up at Trent, unsure
what to think. 'Moved to the Caymans over twenty
years ago and hasn't been heard of since. Hamish has
a colleague who might be able to find out more information.'

'If you're happy to pay?'

Jess nodded. 'I am. I'd say I probably already have
my answer regarding the money, but I'd still like to
track him down. When I was eighteen, he told me he
was going travelling and would be back in a year or
two. He was going to tour castles in Scotland and
hoped to get some work in Europe to extend his trip.
Moving to the Caymans was never part of that conversation, and from everything I know about that
area, it's the perfect place to hide money if you
need to.'

'Are you okay?' Trent asked.

Jess swallowed, the compassion in Trent's eyes
almost undoing her. She slipped her phone back into

her bag. 'I will be. It's sad to think that my only living blood relative did that to me. He ruined my life in many ways. If it wasn't for him, Mum would be alive, and the whole foster situation wouldn't have happened.'

'He might not be your only living blood relative. Don't forget, Martin and his daughter might be related to you. And any other relatives on their side. Joey might not be the last blood relative.'

Jess nodded slowly. 'That's true.' She forced a smile. 'I think I'll head upstairs. Lots to think about.'

Trent stood and gave her a quick hug. 'I'll be down here for another couple of hours. If you need me, call out over the balcony. Okay?'

'Thanks. And thanks for getting Hamish to do that. I'll send him a message later to thank him and ask him to refer his colleague.'

She let herself into her apartment, walked through to the lounge, and flopped down on the couch. She closed her eyes, memories of Joey playing through her mind. It surprised her that, if he had stolen the money, he'd continued to visit her after her mother died. Wouldn't the guilt have been too much for him? Jess sighed, wondering if Martin had been notified after her mother's death whether he would have stepped up and done anything. Would he have been honest with his wife and taken her to live with them? Would she have had the opportunity to grow up in a loving family with a sister? All questions that would never be answered.

Only because you're too gutless to ask.

Her eyes flew open as Sam's voice entered her head. He would tell her to contact Martin. To ask all the questions she needed answers to. *Why sit there and let it fester into something bigger when you could ask the question, Jess? What have you got to lose?*

He was right. Jess picked up her phone, an ironic smile playing on her lips. She'd never listened to her boyfriend before, so why, the day after he'd left, did she suddenly start? She swallowed. Because she needed to hear the answers. That was why. She needed to hear that yes, Martin would have stepped up and been there for her. She needed to see him again.

She keyed a message into her phone and waited. A few minutes later, a response came back.

> I'd be thrilled to meet. How about Saturday morning? I'm so happy to hear from you again. Martin.

Jess smiled as she sent back a message confirming the time and place. Joey and his actions had cost her a lot, but maybe a father was something she would gain.

8

_____

The idea of how many other things she may have
done that she'd be mortified to know about played
over in Reeve's mind during the fifteen-minute drive
from South Yarra to Patricia Fields's office in East
Brighton. After her run-in with Bella the previous
night, she'd spent over an hour googling symptoms
of early onset dementia and wished that she hadn't.
Her emotions were a jumbled mess by the time she
reached Patricia's luxurious address.

Now, as she lowered herself into the ivory club
chair – the picture window opposite providing
sweeping views of Port Phillip Bay – she took a deep
breath. Her last appointment with Patricia had been
six months ago. She'd walked away feeling strong,

knowing she could cope moving forward without her mother and feeling extreme gratitude to the psychiatrist for her insights. She hadn't imagined she'd ever have the need to be back here, let alone so soon.

'Here you go.' Patricia's lips curled into a smile as she placed a teapot and cup on a side table next to Reeve, but Reeve couldn't help but notice the smile didn't reach her eyes. She had been surprised at how much the psychiatrist appeared to have aged since she last saw her. Reeve was aware that Patricia had been widowed a few years earlier. Perhaps she was lonely, and it was taking its toll. She now looked her age, which Reeve guessed was early to mid-sixties.

Patricia settled into a chair across from Reeve, blocking some of the view. 'From our brief conversation when you rang to book an appointment, I understand you're going through a difficult time.'

Patricia's words caused Reeve to reach for a tissue. She dabbed at her eyes, doing her best to control her breathing and contain the tears.

'When you're ready,' Patricia continued, her soothing voice helping to calm Reeve, 'tell me what's been happening.'

Reeve took a deep breath. She started off factual, about the events that had transpired, from the more minor events of forgetting the somewhat nasty, and at times unusual, things she'd said, to the issues at school, first with Dale Cross and now with Oscar.

Patricia's facial expression didn't change as she listened to Reeve and made notes. Reeve wondered, as she had during other appointments, what Patricia was thinking. Had she heard these kinds of stories before? Did she find anything new or shocking?

'Luke's worried about me,' Reeve said. 'And to be truthful, I am too. I can't comprehend that I'm saying and doing things that are not only out of character but that I also have no recollection of.'

'And I assume you're worried that the school situations might not be a setup. That you're responsible on both accounts?'

Heat flooded Reeve's cheeks, and she nodded. 'I've only ever acted professionally before, so it is hard to comprehend, but yes, in all honesty, I'm worried.'

Patricia nodded, consulting her notes. 'From what I understand, the incidents at home that you don't remember were linked to alcohol consumption. Is that correct?'

Reeve nodded.

'But the situations at school wouldn't have involved alcohol?'

'Definitely not. And with the Oscar situation, I

remember our sessions quite clearly, and I even went back and made notes about some of them. Detailing when and where we met, what was covered in the session, and what I did when we finished.' She pulled a small notebook from her handbag and passed it to Patricia.

Patricia began flicking through the notebook. 'From what I can see here, you've been able to account for all of your time with Oscar.'

'I believe so. But that's my biggest problem. What if I'm wrong? What if I don't remember saying something inappropriate? I could have conveniently blocked it from my mind.'

'Are you attracted to this student?'

'No.' Reeve's response was instant. 'He's the same age as Bella. I could be his mother.' An unpleasant metallic taste filled her mouth. She picked up her teacup and sipped her drink, hoping it would rid the taste and settle her stomach.

'Why, then, do you assume you might have crossed a line with what you said to him?'

'I'm not assuming I did, but I can't rule it out.' Reeve replaced her cup on its saucer. 'I said something to Luke a few days ago that I have no recollection of that worries me the most.' She took a deep breath. 'I said that I wanted to sleep with other men.'

'*Men.*' Patricia emphasised the word. 'Would you consider a fifteen-year-old schoolboy a man?'

Again, Reeve shook her head.

'The positive thing,' Patricia said, 'is that in the unlikely instance that you did cross a line with Oscar, it certainly doesn't seem to be premeditated. And regarding the email you sent to the other student's family, you say the school believes your email may have been hacked?'

'They do, but I'd been drinking the night it was sent, and that seems to be the common denominator with my behaviour. Was I drunk enough to not care? I'd been speaking about Dale and how frustrating I was finding him with Luke earlier that night.'

Patricia frowned. 'With your permission I'd like to speak to Luke and hear from him what's been going on.'

Reeve nodded.

'And I'd like to do a couple of tests to get a feel for where things are at. Are you up for it?'

Reeve nodded again. The ache in the back of her throat immediately reappeared. She was up for the tests. She just wasn't sure she was up for the results.

* * *

CLIENT MEETING SUMMARY

DATE: August 20
Client: Reeve Elliot
Duration: 90 Min
MMSE: 14

Reeve Elliot, 40-year-old female, presenting with depression and similar behaviour traits as her mother, Alice Elliot, who suffered from early onset dementia.

I treated Alice from May 2017 until her death in August 2018. Over that timeframe, her behaviour became more erratic and destructive. As is common with many dementia patients, she had no recollection of her outbursts or behaviour. As time progressed, Alice had very few moments of lucidity and became introverted, anxious, and at times aggressive.

Reeve is struggling with the recent suspension from her position of employment due to accusations of sexual harassment of a fifteen-year-old male student. Unfortunately, there were no witnesses, other than the boy himself, to corroborate his accusations.

Following the session I spoke to Reeve's

husband, Dr Luke Sheffield, who informed me that he has noticed strange behaviour over the last six months, but nothing until now that caused him to think she was anything but quirky. If Reeve's behaviour escalates, it may be beneficial for him to join our sessions.

MMSE and Mini-Cog test undertaken. Reeve struggled with her answers in both tests, scoring a concerning 14 on the MMSE. I will redo both tests next session as she was agitated today and possibly not performing at her best. A score of 14 does, however, suggest early onset dementia and possibly rapid decline.

I have referred Reeve for blood tests to rule out other dementia-like symptoms. Will organise CT and MRI scans following the next appointment.

I have created a plan for Reeve to follow to help minimise the triggers for her behaviour, i.e., alcohol consumption. She asked about medication for her nerves. At this stage, I feel it is best she removes alcohol from her system and see what drug-free feels like. Benefits of medication to be reviewed next session.

Next appointment scheduled for one
week's time.

* * *

Reeve drove away from Patricia's studio with a
mixture of feelings racing through her. Patricia hadn't
shared with her what her test results were, suggesting they weren't good. She'd simply said she'd
like to redo them next week when Reeve was more
relaxed. 'A first session is very confronting, Reeve. I
do the test to give me a starting point, but it is always
worth redoing them. We'll discuss the results once
we have all the testing completed. For now, get the
blood tests I've given you the referral for and elimi-
nate excessive drinking. We'll see how you go over
the next week and then explore further what might
be the root cause of the issues you're experiencing.'

She turned into her driveway and pulled into the
empty double garage. Luke would have left for work
an hour ago. She'd fill him in later.

She took a deep breath, opened the car door,
stepped into the garage, and stopped. The moment
she walked through the internal access into the
house, she'd have to deal with Bella. Part of her
hoped her daughter would be more forgiving this

morning, but the part that understood her teenage daughter knew it was unlikely.

She walked through the internal access, arriving in the hallway next to the front door. She sucked in a breath. Two suitcases sat at the bottom of the stairs. Her hope for forgiveness was not going to eventuate. By the looks of it, Bella intended to carry through with her threat and move in with Nick.

'Bella?' Reeve looked up the stairs as she called her daughter's name.

'What?' she snapped back.

Reeve took a deep breath and counted to five, mustering every bit of strength to answer in a reasonable tone of voice. 'Could you come down, please? I want to talk to you.'

Silence.

Reeve waited before calling Bella's name again.

A rap on the front door made her jump. She opened it to find Nick standing on the doorstep, his brows furrowed.

'Hey. What's going on?'

Reeve sighed and motioned for him to come in. 'I'm in desperate need of coffee. Do you want one?'

Nick nodded towards the suitcases and raised an eyebrow. 'The hysterical phone call wasn't a joke last night? She wants to move in with me.'

'Apparently.' Reeve led him towards the kitchen.

Nick followed and sat down on one of the stools at the counter while she busied herself with the coffee machine. 'Bella accused you of some terrible things last night. I couldn't make out everything as she was crying, but she did say she couldn't live here any more.'

Reeve looked up from the coffee machine. 'You've come to pick her up?'

Nick shook his head slowly. 'Not necessarily. I need to hear what's going on. Are you okay? From the things she said, it sounded like you might be in trouble.'

Reeve blinked back tears. Before he ruined their marriage, Nick had always been caring and compassionate. After everything they'd been through, it was nice to know he was still there for her. When she'd left her father's the previous day, she'd been tempted to contact him and question whether he'd really asked her father for money, but she'd hesitated. Her father had asked her not to and maybe this was her way of being there for Nick – by staying out of it.

'I am in trouble,' she admitted. 'One of the students at school has accused me of sexual harassment. Dad's organised his lawyer for me. I'll be speaking to him after you leave.'

Nick's mouth dropped open. 'You're kidding... But the school know you'd never harass a student.' He raised a clenched fist. 'Who's the kid? I'll go sort it out.'

Reeve smiled through her tears. 'Thank you. It means a lot that you'd do that.' She managed a small laugh. 'You and Dad make a good team. I'll be speaking to Devon later this afternoon. See what he advises. Bella seems to believe this kid over me, and she's horrified to show her face at school.'

'Not wanting to go to school's understandable.'

'Yes, it is!' Bella entered the kitchen and flung herself down on the stool next to Nick. 'Thanks for coming to get me. Can we go?'

Reeve placed a coffee mug in front of Nick, causing Bella to frown.

'Can't we stop for coffee on the way?'

'Really,' Reeve said, unable to stop the sarcasm shaping her words. 'You can't even spend ten minutes here with me while I explain to your dad what's happened?'

Bella crossed her arms. 'How can you explain what's happened when you have no idea yourself? For all you know, you did sexually abuse Oscar. He certainly seems to think you did. Snapchat's going mad about it. Apparently, some of his friends witnessed what you did.'

Bile burned the back of Reeve's throat. 'I've been accused of harassment, Bella. Verbal harassment, not sexual abuse.'

'That's not what Snapchat's saying.'

'I wouldn't believe anything you read on Snapchat,' Nick said. 'If those kids had witnessed anything, they'd be under clear instructions not to discuss the matter.'

Bella snorted. 'I doubt that would stop them.'

'Why don't you go upstairs and check you've got everything,' Nick suggested. 'Give us ten minutes to drink our coffee.'

Bella rolled her eyes, turned dramatically, and stomped out of the kitchen.

Reeve stared after her daughter. It was like dealing with a stranger. How could she get through to her that she had done nothing wrong? She turned to Nick, deciding to concentrate on him and ignore Bella. 'Thanks for your support.'

'We both know you wouldn't do something like that, Reeve. Did you do something else to upset the kid, and he's getting his revenge by getting you fired?'

Reeve shook her head. 'No. I'd been tutoring him

outside of class. He was making an effort, and we had a bit of a laugh as we were studying.'

'Did he ever make a move?'

'No. Why would you think that?'

He shrugged. 'I wondered if his behaviour was revenge. If you'd rejected him or something like that.'

'Definitely not. My dealings with him were always appropriate.' She paused.

'What?' Nick picked up on her hesitation.

'I've been having a few issues with my memory.' Her cheeks heated as she spoke. 'When we were together, did I ever do or say anything strange?'

Nick laughed. 'Where do I start?'

She punched him lightly on the arm. 'I'm serious. Did I ever say anything out of character?'

Nick frowned. 'Not that I can recall. Why?'

She went on to tell him about the unusual things she'd said and done, which she had no recollection of.

'You always were a lightweight when it came to drinking,' Nick said. 'It could be as simple as cutting down on that.'

'Even if it is alcohol-fuelled, it seems strange,' Reeve said. 'For a start the situation with Oscar was at school and not drinking-related. But I'm also saying things I've never thought.' She blushed as she told him she'd said she wanted to have sex with other men.

Nick snorted. 'Bet that went down well with surgeon boy. Must have made him question his manhood. You certainly *never* said anything like that while we were married. But then' – he winked – 'you had no need to.'

Reeve couldn't help but smile. He was enjoying this admission far too much. 'Okay, we agree that the Bella situation isn't ideal. She wants to change schools, and she wants to live with you.'

'Change schools?'

Reeve nodded. 'She hates being where I teach, and considering the current circumstances, I don't blame her. Dad's lawyer wants her to stay for appearances, to show her support for me and to reinforce that I've done nothing wrong, but she's not willing to go along with that.' She blinked back tears as she considered her daughter's current hatred towards her.

'She'll come around. Once this is all cleared up, she'll be back.'

'You don't mind having her full-time?'

'I don't mind, but she'll get sick of me very quickly, that much I guarantee. She is fifteen, though, and should be able to choose where she lives. I'll encourage her to come home to see you, but I can't promise anything. What should we do about the schooling?'

'Dad's offered to talk to a few of his contacts to see if we can get her into another private school. I said I'd talk to you first and see how you felt about that. He would like to pay her tuition, and I would really like it this time if you agreed. With the cancer, we have no idea how long Dad will be around for. It would give him great pleasure to know he was doing something to help Bella.'

Nick smiled. 'I don't think I've ever heard you agreeing to accept money from your dad.'

She shook her head. 'I've always wanted to be independent of it. He did amazingly well with his business, but I know some of his wealth was gained at the expense of others.'

'I'm usually the first to say no to help too,' Nick said.

Reeve couldn't help but notice his cheeks redden. He'd been accepting help from Martin for years, but she wasn't going to let on that she knew. Martin was right. Nick was a very proud man.

'But,' Nick continued, 'even with the discount you get by working at St Helena's, the school fees bite each term. And with my current financial situation looking rather grim, I'd be happy for your dad to pay. If the money has come from less scrupulous activities, then we look at it as putting the money to positive use. But' – his face clouded over – 'I'm not happy for Luke to contribute. I know he'll probably offer, and please tell him I appreciate it, but I can't accept his money. Martin's Bella's blood relation, which is different. If he'd like to pay the fees then I'll gratefully accept his contribution, but if he changes his mind, then I'll come up with the money, okay?'

Reeve nodded. 'We'll work something out about the finances too. If Bella's with you full-time then I'll contribute child support like you normally do.'

Nick didn't make eye contact as he finished his coffee and pushed his stool back. Reeve felt for him. If she lost all of her savings, she didn't know what she'd do. She had Luke and her father as backup, of course, but she wouldn't want to have to rely on them.

'Thanks, I appreciate the offer. I'd better get Bella. And don't worry. This will all blow over, and things will be back to normal before you know it.'

* * *

Back to normal. Reeve tossed and turned most of the night, wondering if Nick's words were true. She could only hope so, but watching Bella storm out of the house to Nick's car, a suitcase in each hand, had left her with a feeling of dread. Was this the start of the end of her happy existence?

After finally nodding off around four, Reeve woke with a heaviness weighing on her. She knew she needed to do her best to push all thoughts of the work situation from her mind and concentrate on what was important. Today, it was family, although without Bella, it wouldn't feel right. Tears filled her eyes as she remembered her beloved mother. She did her best to blink them away as Luke snuggled behind her, an arm pulling her to him.

'You okay?' His voice was sleepy. He struggled in the mornings, and after an exhausting day like yesterday, he would probably want to sleep in.

She nodded, not wanting her voice to give away her emotions.

He tightened his arms around her. 'Your mum will be looking down on you, like she does every day, thinking how proud she is.'

Tears rolled down Reeve's cheeks. 'I hope so.'

'I know so,' Luke said, turning her over to make eye contact. 'You've got a heart of gold, Reeve Elliot, and every person who comes by you knows that. Make sure you never forget.'

Reeve managed a small smile.

'Now, what time are you meeting your dad?'

'Nine. I'd better shower and get ready.' She leant forward and kissed him. 'And let you get some more sleep.'

He shook his head and leapt out of bed. 'I'll make coffee while you shower.'

'Thanks, I think I'll call Bella and double-check if she wants to come. After yesterday I'm sure she won't even take my call, but I should at least give her the option.'

Luke pulled her to him and hugged her tight before pushing her gently in the direction of the ensuite. 'Why don't I speak to Bella? That way, if she's going to be incredibly rude, you don't have to deal with that on top of everything else.'

'Thank you. Tell her I'll pick her up from Nick's in forty-five minutes if she's coming.'

'Will do. Now go and immerse yourself in your memories.'

An hour later, she sat across from her father without Bella.

'She said "No thank you",' Luke had said.

Reeve had raised an eyebrow. 'She was that polite?'

'It's my translation of her actual words. She was a little more descriptive. Ignore her. You don't need her drama today. You'll have enough of it tomorrow and the next day and the next.' She'd agreed, pushing Bella and everything else from her mind so she could focus on her parents.

Now she reached across the table and squeezed her father's hand. She'd been shocked to see him this morning, his face pale, his eyes red. She knew he'd struggled since her mother died, but he'd done a good job of hiding his pain. This morning, however, it was raw and on show for all to see. 'Are you doing alright?'

He gave her a sad smile. 'I spent last night looking through photo albums. Probably wasn't the smartest thing to do as it brought back floods of memories.'

Tears blurred Reeve's focus as the pain in her father's face became more prominent.

'Good memories,' he continued, 'but I guess that made it harder. Remembering the good times and what I've lost. *We've* lost, I should say.'

'Oh Dad, you should have told me you were planning to do that. I could have come over last night and kept you company.'

He shook his head. 'No, it was something that me and my bottle of brandy needed to do. I'll be fine, Reeve. I think of your mother every day, but anniversaries do something strange to us. I wanted to look at the photos to keep the happy times in my mind rather than dwell on her last couple of years. That was hard on both of us.'

Reeve nodded. It had been. Watching someone you love suffer from dementia had been awful. Her mother had exhibited strange behaviours throughout Reeve's childhood, but it was once Reeve turned twenty that Martin alluded to there being a problem. If anything, her mother had outlived many of the life expectancy predictions that were given to her. Ten years maximum, one specialist had said. She'd continued for nineteen past diagnosis. But the last two years had been poor quality of life for both Alice and those around her.

'There's guilt mixed up with everything too,' her father said. He paused as their coffee order arrived.

'Guilt?'

Tears filled his eyes. 'Her passing was a relief and...' He hesitated, his eyes not reaching Reeve's. 'There are things I should never have done during our marriage.'

Reeve stared at her father. It was the second time

in the last few days he'd alluded to doing things he wasn't proud of. Their food arrived, and while her appetite was non-existent, Reeve forced a mouthful of the omelette she'd ordered, carefully considering her next words. She didn't want to know about the things he wasn't proud of, but she did want to be honest with him. She put down her fork. 'It wasn't only you who felt relief. I did too.'

His eyes widened. 'Really?'

She nodded. 'I think it's normal, Dad. We both loved Mum, she knew that, and we both knew it. But seeing her deteriorate was heartbreaking. She was a completely different person, one who wasn't very nice to be around. Feeling relief at not having to be confronted with that every day and being able to grieve the woman we both loved is completely natural.'

Martin smiled as he cut into his blueberry pancakes. 'Is that you or that shrink of yours talking?'

Heat flooded Reeve's cheeks. 'Both probably.' The sessions she'd had with Patricia following her mother's death had helped her understand that her reactions to her mother's passing were normal. That it was completely acceptable to feel relief that she no longer had to deal with her mother's unpredictable nature. Hearing her mother refer to her with names that included phrases such as *fucking whore* and *smug motherfucking bitch* was disturbing. Patricia had been able to help her understand her mother a little better and also get some closure on her death.

'Well, you're probably both right,' Martin said. 'Now, I promised myself we'd celebrate Mum's life, not be maudlin. Tell me one of your favourite memories, and I'll share one of mine.'

The morose mood lifted, and the rest of the breakfast passed with laughter as they reminisced.

They finished their second cups of coffee, paid the bill, and left the restaurant.

* * *

With the morning traffic along High Street being heavy, it was close to twenty minutes later when Reeve pulled into the parking area at the Kew Cemetery alongside her father's Jaguar. He was standing by the cemetery's gate with his hands pushed into his jacket pockets. He looked exceedingly uncomfortable.

'You okay?'

He nodded. 'I'm not a fan of cemeteries. It's why I don't come as often as I should.' His cheeks reddened. 'I've only been twice since the funeral.'

Reeve linked her arm through his. 'There's no right or wrong way to deal with death. We both know that Mum's in your heart. The rose memorial is what she wanted, but visiting isn't for everyone and doesn't mean that you love her more or less by coming. I come occasionally, but I feel closer to her when I'm doing things that remind me of her rather than staring at a small plaque next to a rose bush that has her name on it. Sitting with a glass of champagne and listening to one of Wagner's operas is the thing I do when I want to feel Mum's presence.' *It was one of her favourite pastimes.*

Martin chuckled as they passed by manicured lawns, gravestones, and a beautiful decorative flower garden. 'Not sure why we're here in that case. I could have come to you, listened to music, and drunk champagne.'

Reeve smiled. 'Maybe next year. I guess being the first anniversary, it feels like something formal needs to be done.'

They fell into a companionable silence as they weaved their way through the older sections of the cemetery, finally reaching the memorial garden. Reeve stopped at the row of rose bushes leading to the one her mother's ashes were interred at the base of. A woman stood in front of it, her long blonde curls hanging down her back.

'Who's that?'

Martin frowned. 'No idea. A friend of your mother's, perhaps?'

They continued, reaching her mother's rose bush as the woman turned.

'Carol?'

The woman in her late fifties smiled. 'Hello, Reeve, Martin. It's lovely to see you both. I wanted to pay my respects today. I hope you don't mind.'

'Mind?' Reeve said. 'After everything you did for Mum, of course we don't mind. Do we, Dad?' She turned to her father, whose cheeks had flushed. 'Dad?'

'Sorry, no, of course we don't mind.' He stared at Carol longer as if he was about to say something else, shook his head instead, then bent down to clear some leaves from the plaque at the base of the rose bush.

Reeve stared at her father. She couldn't imagine why he was acting strangely. Carol James had been a godsend. For the last twelve months of her mother's life, she'd been her full-time caregiver and she'd been the one to introduce Luke to the family. 'He's a wonderful man,' Carol had said, nudging Reeve when she was speaking of Luke. 'He's a favourite with all of the nurses, but I think he'd be perfect for you.' Reeve had almost choked on the coffee she was drinking. 'Don't even think about setting me up with someone. There's no way a surgeon is going to be interested in me.'

'Incorrect.' A tall, dark-haired doctor with perfect cheekbones and a chiselled chin had entered Alice's room. 'You must be Reeve,' he said, his blue eyes twinkling. 'And from everything Carol's told me, I'm already interested.'

He'd made a point after that first meeting of visiting her every day in the hospital, bringing her small, usually edible gifts and showering her in compliments. He was a bright light in what was otherwise an awful time in Reeve's life. He'd provided a distraction as her mother's condition deteriorated and she eventually passed, and somehow it had been natural that their catch-ups moved away from the hospital and became proper dates.

She turned to Carol and lowered her voice as her father continued to tidy the area around her mother's plaque. 'Sorry about Dad. He's struggling today.'

'Completely understandable. I should have thought to ask him the other week at the hospital if he'd mind me coming by.'

'At the hospital?'

Carol nodded. 'Yes, I've moved into the oncology area.' She frowned. 'I hope I haven't spoken out of turn. You did know he's been scheduled for further treatment?'

Reeve swallowed. Her father hadn't told her anything about further treatment, had he? She wasn't willing to admit this to Carol in case he had and she'd forgotten. 'Yes, of course.'

Carol's face relaxed. 'Thank goodness. Now, try to focus on the happy memories today, won't you? Your mother was a strong and amazing woman.' She gave Reeve a small smile, glanced briefly at Martin, then walked away.

Reeve turned back to face her father. He stood in silence, staring at the plaque. Reeve's heart contracted. Eight months earlier, he'd been given the good news that the radiation had slowed the cancer considerably. He wasn't cancer-free, but with developments in treatment, he might one day be. She couldn't bear it if the cancer was back. She wanted to ask her father, but this was not the time or place. He was grieving, and she needed to let him do that. She would question him about Carol's words later.

* * *

Relaxed and overflowing with both patrons and decadent wines, Rocco's wine bar was the perfect venue for discreet midweek drinks. Soft jazz mixed with muffled conversations and laughter reverberated from the oak-panelled walls. Reeve leant back in her chair, relieved that the day was nearly over. She'd loved spending time with her father, she just wished it had been under different circumstances.

'I can't believe it's this busy on a Wednesday,' Sloane said as a waiter placed two flutes of champagne in front of them.

Sloane lifted her glass, ready for a toast.

Reeve hesitated briefly before lifting hers.

Sloane raised an eyebrow. 'Problem?'

'Drinking seems to be a common factor in the memory problems I've been having. I'm becoming a bit wary.' She was wary but, after a day like today, she was also desperate to embrace the numbing effects of the alcohol.

'We'll stop at one then,' Sloane said. 'To Alice.' She raised her glass higher. 'May she be dancing on the stars tonight.'

Reeve clinked glasses with her friend before taking a small sip. She replaced it on the table, determined to pace herself.

'I know you saw your dad this morning,' Sloane

said, 'but have you had some time with your own memories today? I imagine it's what you need.'

Reeve sighed. 'The last twenty-four hours have been rotten. Absolutely rotten. It's been one thing after another.'

'The Oscar situation?'

'That's only part of it. There's the Dale Cross email and Oscar, which has had me suspended and caused Bella to move in permanently with Nick. Then there's Dad and the anniversary.' She went on to tell Sloane about seeing Carol at the cemetery.

'Are you going to ask your dad about it?'

Reeve nodded. 'I can't stop thinking about it – that and a couple of comments he's made this week about doing things he regrets. Dad's already outlived his prognosis. At his last check-up, they said the radiation had been so successful he could have several years left. But it's cancer. If it's attacking another part of him, then he could be in trouble.'

'Go and see him tomorrow, hon. Find out what's going on and hopefully put your mind at rest. He'd have ongoing check-ups, so it might have been something routine like that.' She lifted her champagne flute and nodded at Reeve's. 'For now, let's listen to the jazz, enjoy the bubbles, and try to block out all of the stresses you're dealing with.'

Reeve smiled. 'Tell me something about you. What's happening with that guy you started seeing?'

Sloane launched into a monologue about the thirty-something model she'd started dating. Reeve did her best to listen but found her mind wandering from her father, to Bella, to the situation at school, to her mother, and even to Luke. She gave herself a little shake. Her mind was all over the place. She needed to calm it down, concentrate on Sloane's conversation, and enjoy their time together.

As she smiled and did her best to tune back into Sloane's words, the sharp trill of her ringtone interrupted them. 'Sorry.' She ignored the phone as it clicked to voicemail.

'I was saying,' Sloane continued, but she was interrupted as the ringtone blared again.

Reeve slipped it from her bag. 'I'd better check in case it's Bella or Luke.' She glanced at the screen. The caller display showed Larry Reynolds, her father's neighbour. She frowned as she pressed the green button to accept the call. 'Larry, everything okay?'

Reeve's breath came in short bursts as the gravity of his agitated words registered with her. 'Is Dad okay?'

Alarm flashed in Sloane's eyes as the words left Reeve's lips.

'I'll be right there.' She ended the call and, legs trembling, stood. 'Dad's house is on fire and the emergency services are there trying to get it under control.'

Sloane grabbed her bag. 'Come on, I'll drive you. What did he say about your dad? Is he okay?'

'He doesn't know. Said they're not sure if he was home and to get there as quick as I can.'

Sloane threw some money on the table. 'It'll be okay, hon. He's probably not even there.'

Reeve nodded, praying to herself that she was right as they hurried out of the wine bar.

9

Jess tried her best to push all thoughts of Joey and Martin out of her head and concentrate on her job. She didn't want the distractions of her personal life impacting her work. Now, as she made her way home after a meeting in Hawthorn, she found the thoughts slipping back into her consciousness.

She turned up the radio, hoping it would drown out the 'what ifs' that had begun to gnaw at her, and tapped her foot on the floor of the car impatiently. She'd been stuck behind a truck for five minutes, the traffic stopped in both directions. Tackling Toorak Road at this time of night had been a mistake. She'd planned to pick up some Thai from her favourite takeaway in Prahran but now wished she'd forgone the detour and gone to the one in Elwood instead.

The truck in front of her pulled onto the wrong side of the road, revealing police cars and police officers directing traffic. Jess waited for the police officer's instructions before carefully following the truck through the area that had been set up as a detour. Smoke billowed up in large clouds ahead. She shuddered, hoping that whoever's house was burning was safe. A Toorak house too; a fortune was going up in smoke.

Her phone rang as she turned into High Street and continued along to Prahran. She hesitated, her in-car caller display showing it was a private number. She usually let them go through to voicemail, but something nagged at her to answer it. As soon as she heard the young girl's voice, she was glad that she had.

'I want to stay, Jess.'

Jess took a deep breath. She was going to have to speak to Heather about making the emergency stays less enjoyable. 'You know that's not possible, Flick. Heather only does short-term accommodation.'

'What if I spoke to her? I know she likes me. I think she'd let me stay.'

Jess hesitated. It was probably best that Felicity

heard directly from Heather that she wouldn't be able to offer her a long-term placement than for her to think it was Jess saying no.

'I'll be good. I won't do anything wrong if I can stay with Heather. I'll be my best self, I promise.'

Jess's heart contracted at the desperation in the young girl's voice. She knew that feeling. Of wishing with all your being that you could be accepted into a loving situation. Of seeing it from a distance but knowing it was unlikely to ever be for you.

'Jess?'

'I'm here, Flick. Look, you can certainly talk to Heather, but she has made it very clear to us that five to seven days is the maximum she's willing to foster for. I hate to think you'll have your hopes up and then be disappointed.'

'I can ask her?' The desperation had been re-placed with excitement. Flick either hadn't heard what she was saying or wasn't listening.

Jess sighed. 'You can ask. But don't get upset if she says no. I'm interviewing a lovely family tomorrow who I think you'll be a good match with.'

'I'll ring you back once I've spoken to Heather, and you can cancel your meeting tomorrow,' Flick said.

The call ended, and Jess shook her head as she

pulled up outside the Thai restaurant. She was confident she knew how the conversation with Heather would go. And while she'd be kind and lovely to Felicity, it was going to be another nail in her *no one wants me* coffin. She could only hope the Smith family, who she was meeting with the next day, would offer Felicity a long-term placement, or better still, that she was able to track down Felicity's aunt and give her a proper family connection.

* * *

On a whim, Jess ordered enough Thai for two and added a serve of fishcakes, knowing they were Trent's favourite. She considered calling him to see if he was home but decided to take the chance. Worse case, she'd have leftover pad thai for lunch the next day. Her thoughts were consumed with Felicity as she parked under the apartments and made her way up the stairs to the apartment entrance. She looked up to the third floor, smiling as she spotted a pair of Nikes propped up on Trent's balcony.

'Hey, famous author,' she called, getting his attention. He stood and grinned.

'At least you've finally got the hang of how to address me. The bestseller lists haven't quite caught up to the fact that I should be on all of them, but that's okay, can't rush things.'

Jess laughed and held up the white takeaway bag. 'Feel like Thai?'

Trent's eyes lit up. 'Yes, please! Give me a couple of minutes, and I'll meet you at yours. I'll bring wine.'

'Perfect.'

Jess walked up the two flights of stairs to her apartment and unlocked the front door. She took the food straight into the kitchen, got out some plates, and put them on the kitchen counter. As much as she'd like to eat outside, it was still too cold. The fact that Trent was always out in the winter air surprised her.

'Knock, knock.' The front door opened and Trent appeared, holding up a bottle of Sauvignon Blanc. 'I assume you've ordered pad thai and a Penang curry,' he said. 'This will go perfectly.'

Jess laughed. 'And fishcakes.'

'Really? But you don't like them.'

'But you do. Grab some wine glasses and come and sit down. I'd love to chat with you about something.'

A few minutes later, they were seated across from each other, Thai food in the middle of the table to share, and a glass of wine each.

'How are you after finding out about your uncle?'

'Fine. I'm meeting with Martin Elliot on Saturday morning, and I'll find out more about what he knows then. I don't want to talk about it tonight. I've done my best to put all thoughts of Joey and Martin out of my mind today.'

'Okay. What did you want to talk about? Sam?'

'Sam? He's the last person I want to talk about. He's in my past. I could never talk to him about anything important. He always turned everything into such a big deal.'

'But you can talk to me?'

Jess stared at him. She could talk to Trent. She liked the idea of asking for his advice and respected his opinion. She shrugged. 'Maybe the pressure of romantic relationships makes me clam up? Who knows? But I would like your advice.'

She went on to tell him about the situation with Felicity. 'She's probably in tears about now as Heather will have told her no to a permanent foster arrangement. It's an awful situation to be in when you have no one who cares about you.'

'You care about her.'

'I do, but I'm employed to deal with her. It's hardly the same as family. There's an aunt who disappeared before her mother died who I've been trying to track down.' She blushed. 'I thanked Hamish and asked if he could help me, but his powers don't extend beyond Australia. I believe the aunt went to the US.'

'I've got a mate in LA who might be able to help.'

Jess laughed. 'Really? Another mate who can track down people?'

Trent spooned some rice onto his plate. 'I have a third mate in Johannesburg who could do the same if you need anyone tracked down there. Logan, in the States, works for the Central Intelligence Agency.'

'The CIA?'

Trent nodded. 'I'm not suggesting he'll be able to track down the aunt himself, but I'd say he'd be able to pass her details on to someone who could.' He glanced at his watch. 'Eight o'clock here means it's about two in the morning for him. Let's give him another couple of hours to sleep and then call him.'

'Really?'

'He's used to my middle-of-the-night calls. He goes for an early morning surf before work most days, which means anything after about four o'clock his time is acceptable. Who do you think I use for book research?'

Jess was aware that her mouth had dropped open. 'How come I've never heard of this spy friend?'

Trent shrugged. 'I keep my work private. Most people get to read the final product if it's published, nothing else. I assume they'd find the rest boring.'

'Boring? You've got to be kidding. It's fascinating. Tell me more while we eat and wait for your friend to wake up.'

10

Reeve gripped her phone, her heart thudding the entire drive from Rocco's to Toorak. She couldn't lose her father. Not on the anniversary of her mother's death. It would be too cruel. She tried to calm her breathing as Sloane overtook another car on her quest to get from St Kilda to Toorak in record time.

As they turned from Toorak Road into Lansell Road, still several streets away from her father's, they could see black smoke billowing high into the sky.

'Jesus,' Sloane said. 'I wonder how it started?'

Reeve couldn't respond. All she could think about right now was her dad. She lifted her phone to her ear and called his number. Once again, it clicked through to voicemail. That wasn't unusual – her father often left his phone at home when he went out – but it was frustrating.

Sloane turned into Fourth Street, and Reeve gasped. The street was crowded with emergency services vehicles. Sloane edged the car as close to number six as she could, and Reeve jumped out and hurried towards the front gates. Neighbours were crowded on the footpath, looking on in horror. She recognised Larry Reynolds, who stepped out of the crowd when he saw her, his eyes wide, his face strained. She ignored his gestures, hurrying straight to the front entrance, which was blocked by two police officers.

'This is my father's house.' She hardly recognised the high-pitched squeal of her voice.

The female police officer took her arm and, with Sloane now following, guided them through the gates. She stopped once they were inside the property. 'We're best to stay here. There's nothing you can do to help. It's far too dangerous. Do you know if anyone was home?'

Reeve shook her head. 'My father could be. I had breakfast with him this morning, and he said he was coming home. He would have been home by about eleven.'

'How old is he, and what vehicle does he drive?'

'Sixty-six and a silver Jaguar,' Reeve said.

The police officer nodded. 'Hold on.' She stepped away from Reeve and Sloane and spoke into her shoulder mic. Reeve couldn't make out all her words but did catch *sixty-six* and *silver Jag*.

The officer listened for a moment before nodding and returning to Reeve and Sloane.

'While there is no confirmation at this stage of anyone being inside, it appears there is a silver Jaguar parked in front of the house.'

Reeve's legs went weak, and as if in slow motion, she was falling. Then everything went black.

* * *

'Ree. Come on, Ree, wake up.'

Luke's gentle voice broke into Reeve's consciousness, and the sense of dread she'd been feeling was replaced with relief. She was drowsy but relaxed. She was lying down, Luke was with her, and the bad thing was nothing more than a dream. But what was the smell?

She forced her eyes open to find Luke staring at her. His eyes filled with something she didn't recognise. Fear? The room was bright and sterile. She was in the hospital.

Luke took her hand. 'Thank goodness you're okay.' His voice cracked as he spoke. 'Sloane's outside. She's worried sick about you.'

'What happened?' Reeve croaked.

Luke let go of her hand and poured a plastic cup of water from the jug that sat on the table straddling the bed. 'You passed out, and when you came to, you were distressed, and the paramedics sedated you and brought you in. They believe you went into an extreme state of shock.'

Reeve's mind was jumbled and foggy. She did her best to search her memory. 'I was at Dad's.' Her head swirled as soon as she remembered. She grabbed Luke's hand. 'I think I'm going to be sick.'

Luke helped her sit up and deftly handed her a sick bag. She dry retched, her stomach cramping. She lay back against the pillows as Luke stroked her cheek. She searched his eyes, but he was unusually evasive, not making eye contact.

'Did they find him?' Her voice was barely a whisper.

He nodded.

'Alive?'

Luke took a deep breath. His voice shook when he spoke. 'No, Ree. I'm sorry. They found him in his chair in his study. They're assuming he might have fallen asleep earlier and then suffered from smoke inhalation. It appears to be the cause of death.'

Reeve's heartbeat quickened as an ice-cold blanket descended upon her. Her father was dead? No, he couldn't be. It was unfathomable. Luke took her hand, but she snatched it from him as her legs began to shake.

'I'm going to ring for the nurse,' Luke said, his face full of concern. 'This is a huge shock.' He reached across and pressed the call button.

Moments later, a nurse hurried into the room. 'Everything okay?'

'My wife needs something to relax her,' Luke said.

The nurse picked up Reeve's chart. 'Let me check a few things, and we'll see what we can do.'

What could they do? A single tear rolled down Reeve's cheek. Her father was gone. Gone on the anniversary of her mother's death. There was nothing anyone could do.

11

Jess couldn't believe how quickly things had proceeded since her conversation with Trent's friend Logan the previous night. She'd woken to an email with current contact details for Margaret Chandler, Felicity's aunt. Now, having arrived at work, she read through the details once more.

> Margaret Chandler, forty-five years old, goes by the name of Meg. She is currently living in North Utica, outside of Chicago. Divorced, no children, running a small cafe in the main downtown area. Her phone number, address, and email are supplied.

Jess shook her head as she checked the time difference. It was concerning to think how quickly personal information could be found. However, most people didn't have access to a spy agency. She smiled, thinking about Trent and his connections. No wonder his spy series of books was such a success with real-life spies at hand for answering his research questions. He was full of surprises, that was for sure. Still, on this occasion, it played in her favour. It would be 4 p.m. in North Utica, hopefully a good time to call. She took a deep breath and dialled the international number.

* * *

Jess's heart contracted that afternoon as Felicity wiped her eyes with the back of her hand, desperate not to show how upset she was. As Jess had expected, Heather had confirmed she couldn't offer her permanent accommodation. It was hard enough dealing with the emotions of the younger children, but a fifteen-year-old who was doing her best to be tough was even harder.

'Look,' Jess said, 'I met with the Smith family today, and they're lovely. They've invited you to come and do a trial stay with them to see if you like them.'

Jess was dying to tell Felicity the news about her aunt, who she'd spoken with earlier that morning, but didn't want to get the teenager's hopes up if nothing came of it.

'To see if I like them? The other way around you mean.'

'Both, I guess,' Jess said, 'but they're nice. They have two younger girls with them, and they're hoping you'd be a good role model for them.'

Felicity snorted. 'Did you tell them I tried to kill my last foster sibling?'

Jess smiled. 'Wasn't it self-defence, and the knife happened to be handy?'

Felicity shrugged. 'What does it matter. This will be another failure.'

'You know,' Jess said, 'I used to feel like you do too. I get it, but I can tell you right now, this family are nicer than anyone I ever got sent to. Give them a chance, okay?'

'Fine, whatever. When does the torture begin?'

'Now, if you're ready. I said I could bring you over before lunch. The other girls are at school, which will give you a chance to get familiar with Shay and Chris and the house before they get home. They've got a dog too. A big fluffy thing. I think you'll like him.'

'I hate dogs,' Flick said, although Jess couldn't help but notice the spark of interest in her eyes. She was protecting herself. Not getting her hopes up, knowing the most likely scenario is they would be crushed later. Jess sighed. She knew that feeling. Expect the worst and never be disappointed.

An hour later, Jess's mind drifted back to Flick's aunt. It had been a difficult conversation as Meg had left Australia twenty years earlier. She didn't know of Flick's existence or her sister's death. She'd gone silent when Jess told her about her sister but recovered quickly. 'I guess I shouldn't be surprised after all this time that something awful happened. I severed all ties when I left Melbourne.'

'Did you have a falling out?'

'No, nothing like that. It was more like I was being held back, that I wanted more than what my family and Australia could offer. Funnily enough, I've been thinking about coming home recently. But I'm not sure what I'd be coming back to if Gillian's not there any more. We didn't have any other family.'

'You have Felicity.'

Meg laughed. 'I guess I do. Does she know about me?'

'She knows you exist but doesn't know I've been trying to find you. I didn't want to get her hopes up.

She's had a difficult time since her mum died and has been passed from one foster home to another. She's looking for stability right now, and I need to be careful with what I tell her. If you were interested in considering fostering her, then that's something we could discuss. If, on the other hand, you aren't interested, then you might still like to make contact with her, but we can make that clear upfront, so there are no misunderstandings.'

'Foster her? As in, have her live with me? I can hardly afford to look after myself.'

Jess heard the note of wonder in Meg's voice. She was being put on the spot and would need time to let everything sink in. 'Why don't we speak again in a couple of days,' Jess suggested. 'In the meantime, I can email you information about the foster system here and what's entailed. It will give you a chance to digest everything and prepare any questions you have for me. Also, have a think about whether you'd like to meet your niece, regardless of the foster situation.'

Upon finishing the call with Meg and agreeing she would contact her early the following week, Jess rang Trent.

'I wanted to thank you,' she said when he picked up.

'Mm, a thank you,' Trent said, a teasing note in his voice. 'I don't think words will do the trick with that one.'

'No? A present, perhaps?'

'No, I'm thinking dinner. I'd like to be treated to something fancy where we can dress up, drink too much, and have a good laugh.'

'It's a date,' Jess said. 'Now, I'd better go and think up something amazing in the way of saying thanks.' She ended the call, her smile slipping as she thought back to their conversation. *A date?* No, it wasn't a date. It was a thank you... wasn't it?

* * *

Early on Saturday morning, Jess found her hand had a slight tremble to it as she did her best to coat each lash with mascara. She was more nervous about meeting Martin today than she had been last weekend. This time there was more to lose. Last weekend she'd had no intention of getting to know him, but now she was contemplating the possibility of him becoming part of her life. *Martin.* She wondered if she'd ever get to a point where she saw him as *Dad.*

She shook her head and placed the mascara back in her make-up bag. She was getting way too far ahead of herself and creating a fantasy that, based on her life to date, was most likely going to come crashing down. She needed to take things slowly, decide whether there was a place for him in her life and vice versa. She certainly didn't want to form a relationship with him to find herself abandoned again. She took a deep breath, did a final appearance check in the mirror, and glanced at her watch. She still had forty minutes before she was due to meet him. She went back into the bedroom and grabbed her bag. She would walk there. It would only take half an hour. Hopefully it would rid her of some of her nerves.

Jess left the apartment and walked along Dickens Street, noticing that many of the trees on the nature strips were now bare of leaves. She crossed Marine Parade at the lights and joined a busy throng of walkers and cyclers on the Bay Trail next to the St Kilda Marina. The sky was a brilliant blue, but the chill in the air was an instant reminder it was still winter. She slipped her hands into the pocket of her fleece coat, her mind wandering back into her past as she wound her way around the Marina Reserve on her way to Fitzroy Street. By the time she arrived at Blush, her head was full of thoughts of her mother. It was hard not to wonder how different life would be if Paula was still alive.

Jess decided to avoid the busy outside tables, opting instead for a quiet table at the back of the cafe. She was ten minutes early, but it didn't stop her heart from racing. She returned the smile of one of the wait staff who passed her with a tray spilling over with dirty dishes. 'Grab a seat,' he said. 'I'll be back in a minute to take your order.'

Jess slid into the comfortable cushioned chair, her eyes automatically travelling to the front door. He might be early too. She took a deep breath. It was a calm space, yet her nervous energy was likely to ruin the breakfast experience of others if she didn't relax.

The waiter returned with a pad and pen and pointed towards the specials board. The artistic writing on the chalkboard made the specials on offer sound incredibly inviting, but she wasn't sure she'd be able to eat anything. 'Latte, please. I'm waiting for someone.'

She wondered if Martin was as nervous as she was. She wanted to talk to him about the Joey situation, but she also wanted to ask him about other family. Having been on her own for such a long time, she was intrigued to know if there was a much bigger family out there. The waiter returned with her coffee, and she sipped it slowly as time ticked past.

Ten o'clock came and went, and Jess's nerves escalated. What if he didn't come? That wasn't a scenario she'd contemplated. She'd be extremely disappointed not to see him. She slipped her phone from her bag and checked the text messages. They'd said ten, and still did. But it was only ten minutes past, and parking was never easy in St Kilda.

As she replaced her phone in her bag, it pinged with a message. She grabbed it, her heart lifting. He must be running late. But the message wasn't from him. It was from Felicity.

> Hate it here. Can I go back to Heather's?

Jess sighed. She'd hoped Felicity would try with the Smith family. She'd respond to the message later. Right at this moment, she had family issues of her own to contend with.

At eleven, fifty minutes and another coffee later, Jess conceded that he wasn't coming. She'd been stood up. She picked up her phone, tempted to send him a scathing message, but she changed her mind.

What if there'd been an accident or something un-avoidable had happened?

> Checking you're okay? Sorry not to have seen you today. Please ring or text to reschedule. Jess.

She sat staring at her phone for twenty minutes, willing a response to appear, but it didn't. She got up from her table, paid her bill and left the cafe, sur-prised by the enormity of her disappointment.

12
_____

Reeve wasn't sure how she got through the next few days. She was released from the hospital the morning after the fire with strict instructions to rest. Luckily, she had Luke to ensure she did. She'd been prescribed sleeping tablets, and now, four days after her release from the hospital, she realised she needed to stop taking them. Yes, they helped her sleep, but they also left her feeling woozy and out of sorts. She needed to make arrangements for her father's funeral and advise people of his death, yet she couldn't bring herself to do anything. It was like she was operating inside a fog.

Now, Sunday morning, she turned to look at the clock on top of her bedside table. It was almost eleven, and she was in the same place she'd been since Bella had left on Thursday – in bed. She threw off the covers and, doing her best to ignore her unsteady legs, went into the ensuite and turned on the shower.

Half an hour later, she appeared downstairs, freshly showered, her hair dried, and wearing clean clothes. Luke looked up from the kitchen counter, where he sat typing something on his phone, his eyes widening in surprise.

'Hey, I didn't expect to see you down here today.'

'I need to get myself together,' Reeve said, switching on the kettle. 'Enough of the moping around. There are a ton of people to get in touch with and arrangements to be made.'

Luke put his phone down on the counter. 'I spoke with Devon on Friday. He's going to call back tomorrow morning as he's hoping to drop in and see you. He asked me to send you his love.'

Reeve's eyes instantly welled up at what she knew was genuine kindness from Devon.

Luke stood and came over and put his arms around her. 'And the police dropped around too.'

Reeve pulled back. 'The police?'

Luke nodded. 'They dropped in some of your dad's personal belongings. An envelope that has his phone and keys and a few other things from what they said. I put them away until you're ready for them.'

'Did the police say anything about the fire?'

'No, just that it was an ongoing investigation, and they'd be back in touch directly or via Devon.'

Reeve nodded, and Luke squeezed her hand. 'Are you feeling okay this morning?'

Reeve stared at her husband. It was an odd question considering what had happened. But the look in his eyes told her he wasn't asking her this in reference to her father.

Unpleasant tingles ran down her spine. 'I didn't do something else terrible, did I?'

'No,' Luke said. 'You said some things last night, that's all. You mentioned Oscar a few times, and your words were a little unsettling. Those sleeping tablets you've been taking can leave you feeling out of it and cause ramblings.'

The look in Luke's eyes confirmed it was anything but ramblings. Reeve's gut clenched. She had no recollection of saying anything about Oscar. 'Do I want to know?'

Luke shook his head. 'Probably not. Devon did mention that the school had been in contact with him to set up an appointment. He's explained the situation, and they've been accommodating in as far as agreeing to postpone.'

Reeve pulled out of his arms and took a green tea bag from the tin on the kitchen bench. She put it in a cup and poured boiling water on it. She couldn't deal with the Oscar situation right now. 'Has Bella been in touch?'

Bella had arrived at the house with Nick the day after the fire. Reeve had left calling her ex until she'd been discharged from the hospital. She'd told him what had happened over the phone and asked him to bring Bella over to break the sad news. When Nick and Bella arrived, Bella's tear-stained face confirmed she already knew.

'I had to tell her,' Nick said apologetically, his eyes damp. 'I'm not sure I could have got her here otherwise.' He'd hugged Reeve for a long moment.

Reeve and Bella had spent the day sitting together. Hugging, crying at times, and laughing with memories of some of the silly things Martin had done.

'He did offer to help you change schools,' Reeve told Bella. 'We spoke about it on Monday, after I'd found out about Oscar's accusations. He had some contacts he was going to talk to. Unfortunately, he probably didn't get a chance to do that, but he did offer to pay for your schooling, and your dad agreed that it was a good idea.'

Bella nodded, showing no real emotion regarding the school situation. 'I'm going to miss him so much, Mum.' She'd buried her face in Reeve's shoulder, allowing her mother to hug her tight. It had therefore been quite a shock when mid-afternoon Bella announced she was going to ring Nick to pick her up. Reeve had assumed Bella would want to stay close to her.

'I can drop you back,' Luke had said, overhearing the exchange. 'I need to go into the hospital this afternoon, and Nick's place is on the way.'

It was the last she'd seen or heard of her daughter since Thursday.

Luke shook his head in answer to her question of whether Bella had been in touch. 'No, although I would hardly expect her to be, considering the circumstances. You should probably call her.'

Waves of guilt overcame her. What kind of mother was she? She should have been checking on her daughter, making sure she was okay. She'd left Nick with that job, which was hardly fair. 'I'll ring her now.'

Luke took her phone from the charging station

on the kitchen counter and passed it towards her. 'I wouldn't count on her taking your call, Ree.'

'I think after what's happened with Dad, she'll put the other stuff behind us. For now, anyway.' She hesitated as Luke frowned. 'You don't think she will?'

'Thursday was pretty tough on her, that's all.'

'It was tough on all of us.' She glanced at the screen, seeing there were several text messages. She saw Nick's name and opened his message.

> Bella's upset about Martin and how things went down with you on Thursday. Probably best you stay away for now. Let me know if there's anything I can do to help and what the plans are for the funeral. I'll make sure Bella's there.

Reeve frowned. *How things went down with you on Thursday.* What did that mean?

'Everything alright?'

Reeve looked up from the phone and met Luke's eyes. 'What did you mean when you said Thursday was tough on Bella?'

Luke hesitated, his eyes evading Reeve's. 'It was a difficult day, that's all.'

'Nick's suggested something went down with

Bella and me on Thursday that upset her. I don't understand. She was upset about Dad but not upset with me. Our grief brought us closer. We shared a lot, and then she decided she wanted to go home. You drove her, remember?'

Luke nodded. 'I do remember. I also remember her decision to go home being sudden. You said you were surprised as you assumed she'd stay here for a few days or even go back to the normal arrangement.'

Reeve nodded. 'That's exactly what happened.' She sat down at the kitchen counter. 'Nick doesn't usually play games, but this seems a bit strange.'

Luke stepped closer and put one hand on each of Reeve's shoulders. 'Ree, you said some pretty horrible things to Bella, which is why she made the sudden decision to go home.'

'What? No, I didn't. And even if I did, how would you know?'

'She told me when I drove her back to Nick's.' He bit his bottom lip, the way he did when he was uncomfortable.

'Tell me.'

'I'd prefer not to.'

Reeve's stomach churned. 'I need to know what I'm dealing with.'

Luke closed his eyes briefly before speaking. 'You told her Martin said she was a little slut.'

Reeve drew in a breath. 'What? He never said that.'

'That's what I told Bella. I explained that there was something wrong with you, possibly a side effect of the sleeping tablets or whatever else is going on.'

Reeve dropped her head into her hands. 'That's awful. I swear I didn't say anything like that to her.' But even as the words came out of her mouth, she knew that she couldn't know for sure. 'Oh God, this is such a nightmare.' She pulled herself up straight. 'I can't think about this right now. I need to keep busy. Can you give me Dad's things, please? If his phone was there, I might be able to access the contacts, which will make letting people know what's happened easier.'

Luke moved over to a sideboard and pulled open a drawer. He took out a large white envelope and passed it to Reeve.

She took a deep breath, slipped her finger under the flap of the envelope, and tore it open. Inside was a mobile phone, Martin's wedding ring, his wallet, and a set of house keys.

'Is that it?' Luke asked.

She took the ring from the envelope and ran a

finger around its rim. 'He wore this every day for forty-six years.'

Luke sat next to her. 'You should keep it somewhere special. You could even consider turning it into jewellery you can wear. Keep your dad close.'

Tears filled Reeve's eyes. It was a lovely suggestion.

She reached into the envelope and took out the phone, then passed it from one hand to the other. 'At least I've got this now. It's full of his contacts, which will make organising the funeral easier.' It didn't respond when she tried to turn it on. 'Needs to be charged. I'll do that now as I should go through and check who needs to be contacted. From the messages we've already received, a lot of people learned what happened from the news reports, but I'm sure there will be some who are still unaware.' She closed her eyes. If emotional overload was a thing, then she was suffering from it. Tears rolled down her cheeks.

Luke took her hand and kissed it. 'What can I do to help?'

She opened her eyes and did her best to smile. 'Nothing. Just being here is helping. I'm sorry I'm such a wreck. It's too many things at once.'

'I know it is, and you've done an amazing job in handling everything. What with the school, then

Bella, and now your dad, it's a miracle you're not curled up in the foetal position.'

'Until this morning, that's pretty much where I've been. I need to pull myself out of that funk and get organised. Dad deserves an amazing send-off, and it will give me a distraction.'

Luke slid an arm around her shoulder. 'As awful as this situation is, I'm proud of you.' He hugged her to him and held her tight, unleashing another stream of tears from Reeve.

Eventually, she pulled away and stood. 'I'm going to charge his phone and start making a list of who I need to call.' She smiled at her husband. 'Thank you.'

'Me? What for?'

'For being here for me. I've been a nightmare for weeks now with everything that's going on, and it hasn't fazed you. You're amazing.'

Luke blushed. 'No, I'm lucky. While I hate that you're going through this, it's the way we handle things that affects us the most. I'm a big believer that life's challenges are there to bring us together, to strengthen our bond and highlight what we love about each other. External forces should never be allowed to tear us down.'

Reeve leant down and kissed him softly on the

lips before picking her father's phone up off the coffee table and moving through to the kitchen and the charging station. His words were beautiful and true, but from experience, she'd learned quickly that problems caused rifts in relationships. The issues that broke down her marriage to Nick were caused by external forces. If they'd been of Luke's nature and viewed them as opportunities to strengthen their relationship, would they still be together? She shook her head. No, she couldn't imagine any circumstances where she would have been able to rise above what Nick had done and forgive him.

* * *

Intent on keeping busy, Reeve went back upstairs to make the phone calls. First, she called Devon and arranged for him to come to the house at ten the following morning. She could hear in his voice how cut up he was. He'd been Martin's lawyer for over thirty years, and the two men were friends as well as business acquaintances.

She took a deep breath after ending the call. The next one wouldn't be as easy. She debated on ringing Nick's number or trying Bella's mobile. She doubted her daughter would answer, but she decided to try it first. It clicked straight to voicemail, forcing her to ring Nick's.

'Hey, how are you coping?'

'I'm okay. How's Bella?'

He gave a small laugh. 'Combination of sad and angry. A lot of loud music being played.'

'I saw your text message,' Reeve said. 'I'm sure I would never have said anything like that to her.'

'That's what I told her,' Nick said. 'But she's adamant that you did.' He cleared his throat. 'There's not something else going on, is there?'

Reeve frowned. 'Like what?'

'I don't know. I'm concerned that a lot of your problems, aside from Martin's death, are in areas of your life that Bella's involved in. The issues at school could see you fired, and as she doesn't want you there, that would suit her.'

Reeve drew in a sharp breath. 'You're not suggesting she's somehow responsible? She'd never do something like that.'

'I'd hope not. But she's spending a lot of time talking to that Mason kid. You know, that one you've always said is bad news.'

'Very bad news.'

'Don't worry, I haven't let her out to see him, but other than ban her from all technology, I can't stop her from being in contact. It got me thinking, that's all. Some of the things she's mentioned that you've supposedly done don't sound like you.' He gave a little laugh. 'If anyone was going to say you had issues, it'd be me. Having been with you for seventeen years, I think I know you better than anyone. And as much as I'd like to blame you for everything that went wrong in our marriage, we both know it was me, not you, that messed up. Other than yelling at me when I deserved it, you were never nasty to me or about anyone else. These things Bella says you've done aren't you, Reeve. I guess it worries me. It also worries me that the outcome of the school issues, if not in your favour, benefits Bella. Who knows what this Mason kid is suggesting she do? I don't want to think she's capable of manipulating the situation, but I can't rule it out either.'

A tear slid down Reeve's cheek. Nick had always been there for her, but this extra support was what she needed right now. 'I can't believe she'd do something like that. Sure, she hates me being at the same school, but this is too extreme. She's a good actress but not that good. Also, we've said she can consider moving schools. She doesn't need me to be fired to have that happen.'

'I hope she's got nothing to do with it,' Nick said.

'I'm looking for an explanation. I honestly don't believe you've done any of these things.'

'I'm seeing a psychiatrist on Tuesday,' she admitted. 'She's putting me through some tests and trying to get to the bottom of it. Because of Mum,' she added, knowing it would be enough information for Nick to understand what she meant.

'Oh, Reeve.'

She had to close her eyes at the sadness and sudden understanding the two words conveyed. Nick had seen her mother's deterioration firsthand. He'd loved Alice, and she'd loved him. He'd been as devastated as both Reeve and her father watching the changes in her behaviour and her gradual decline.

'Tell me anything I can do to help, okay?'

'Thank you. By the sounds of it, I'm going to need your help trying to communicate with Bella. Is she there?'

'Yes, hold on. I'll see if I can get her on the phone.'

She waited for a minute or two before Nick spoke again. 'I'll apologise in advance, but here she is.'

'Bella?'

'What? Dad said I *had* to speak to you.'

'Oh hon, I'm so sorry. I have no recollection of saying those awful things to you. If I did, I'm truly sorry. Granddad never said anything like that about you. He thought you were amazing.'

Silence greeted her.

'Bella?'

She heard Nick's voice, a low angry whisper in the background, telling Bella she needed to respond.

'Fine,' Bella said. 'Whether you believe you said it or not, you did. First, you called me a spoilt little bitch, and then you told me Granddad thought I was a slut. Whether Granddad said it or not, you did. I don't want to be around you. You always go on about how important trust is, and right now, I don't trust you at all. I don't trust what you tell me, and I don't trust that you won't do something awful to embarrass me more than you already have.'

Reeve recoiled. Bella's words dripped with anger and resentment.

'For now, I want you to leave me alone,' Bella continued. 'I'll be at Granddad's funeral, and I'd like to speak. Can you let Dad know the details?'

'Of course.'

'Okay. Here's Dad.'

Reeve listened to a brief exchange between Nick and Bella.

'That was awful,' she heard Nick say.

'I don't care. She deserves it after what she said to me. She's ruining my life.'

Nick sighed into the phone. 'Sorry. I'm not sure how to deal with her.'

'I appreciate everything you're doing,' Reeve said, and she did. 'I'll be in touch tomorrow about the funeral.'

'Okay, and Reeve, I meant it when I said to let me know what you need from me.'

She ended the call, grateful for Nick's support but heartbroken at Bella's rejection of her. She closed her eyes. She'd been in Bella's shoes, watching as her mother drew away from her and became someone else. It had been gradual and unsettling at first. Her mother behaving out of character one day, doing and saying terrible things, and then being her normal self the next. When Alice flipped more frequently between her regular, loving self to the angry, nasty version dementia created, it was hard at times to forgive her.

Reeve shook her head. It was what was happening to her. Having watched her mother go through it, she'd always sworn that if she was in the same position, she'd end her life. Of course, she'd never expected to be in the same position when she'd made that promise to herself. But there was no way she'd allow her family to go through what she and Martin had. She opened her eyes, her gaze fixing on a photo of her and Luke. Could she do that to him? After all his love and support, could she be the one to check out early? And Bella, too; could she put her through the trauma?

'Phone's got some charge.' Luke's voice travelled up the stairs to the window seat in the office alcove where she'd sat to make the calls. She stood. She needed to stop these thoughts. She didn't even have an official diagnosis. *Yet.*

Reeve hurried down the stairs, determined to switch her mood into something positive. Advising her father's friends that he'd passed was hardly going to achieve this, but making a plan would give her mind something more constructive to think about.

'The phone's charged enough to use it,' Luke repeated, nodding at her father's phone, which sat on the charger next to the fruit bowl, 'and he got a text message.'

'Really?'

Luke nodded, picked up his coffee cup and took a sip.

Reeve took the phone from the charger. She swallowed as she looked at the screen. Going through her father's phone seemed like an invasion of privacy.

'It's password-protected,' Luke said.

She looked up at him. 'Did you try to access it?'

He shook his head. 'No, I noticed when it was charging.'

'Hopefully, it's the same as the code he used for the front gates at the house. It's what he used for everything.' She punched in the six-digit code she'd used many times when arriving at the Toorak address and smiled as she was given access to the phone. 'Dad was predictable. I'll give him that.'

She sat down at the counter next to Luke. 'There are a few new text messages and seven unanswered calls.' She touched the button, and the screen brought up the recent messages. She glanced down the list. 'His lawyer sent one of the text messages. He knows about Dad, so that's a bit weird.'

Luke peered over at the phone. 'No, they were sent the night your dad died.'

'Okay, that makes sense.' She opened the conversation and scrolled up to read earlier exchanges between Martin and Devon. It appeared to be about an investment opportunity and Devon needing Martin to sign some papers. Nothing out of the ordinary.

Reeve went back to the main screen and saw a name she didn't recognise: Jessica Williams. She opened the recent text message.

> Checking you're okay? Sorry not to have seen you today. Please ring or text to reschedule. Jess

'That was sent on Saturday morning,' Reeve said to Luke. 'Dad stood her up, whoever she is. Not that he could help that.' She returned to the phone and scrolled up through the messages between her father and Jessica Williams. They'd started a month earlier.

> It was quite a shock to get your message last week. Sorry for my delay in contacting you. I had a lot to consider. Yes, I am happy to meet with you. Jerrico's in Elwood make good coffee. How about this Sunday at two?

> Sunday would be wonderful. See you then.

'The next message is after they've met. Dad reached out to her.'

> I'm overwhelmed but delighted to have met you today. I'm devastated to have learned what you've been through and that the money never reached you. I understand your wishes, but I hope you'll change your mind regarding future meetings.

'There was no response from Jessica, but then she sends a message a couple of days later,' Reeve said to Luke, who was listening with interest.

> I received your parcel, thank you. I have many questions. Would you be free to catch up again?

> I'd be thrilled to meet you. How about Saturday morning? I'm so happy to hear from you again.

'They then went on to make plans to meet at Blush in Fitzroy Street at ten on Saturday. Dad was already gone by then and so obviously didn't respond to the last message, the one where she's been stood up. I wonder who she is?'

'Whoever she is, she doesn't know what's happened. Maybe you should call and let her know.'

Luke glanced at his watch. 'I'm sorry, Ree, but I'm going to have to pop out for a few hours. I postponed one of my operations on Friday as I took the day off, but I need to speak to the patient and get her ready for tomorrow. I'm afraid I'll have to go back to work as normal this week.'

'Sorry, I hadn't even thought to ask.'

Luke kissed her forehead. 'Nothing to be sorry about. You've got enough going on. As soon as you have the funeral details, let me know, and I can book the day off. I've told the hospital to hold off on scheduling anything for me on Thursday or Friday as I'm assuming it will be one of those days. But as a result, they've overloaded me for the first three days of the week. I'll pick up some Vietnamese on my way home later. Save us cooking tonight. There's a bottle of that Pinot Gris your dad loved in the wine fridge. We'll have a glass in his honour.'

'Not me,' Reeve said, shaking her head. 'I'm going cold turkey on the wine. You can enjoy a glass.'

Luke smiled. 'Good for you, and no, I'm happy to support you. Now, I'd better run. Good luck if you call this Jessica Williams. You can tell me tonight who she is.'

Reeve looked at her father's phone again as Luke grabbed his keys and wallet and went through the internal access to the garage. Nerves flitted in her stomach as she read through the messages between Martin and Jessica Williams again. She wasn't sure why she was so nervous. Jessica was obviously someone her father had enjoyed meeting and hoped to see more of. There was some history between them, and her father had been thrilled to receive the last message suggesting they meet. She frowned. While he lived his own life, Martin had loved filling Reeve in with the detail of his meetings, his trades, and his general day-to-day life. For him to be *thrilled* to see someone, it meant they were special. But not special enough to tell her about? She was intrigued.

She picked up his phone, deciding there was only one way to find out who this woman was, and that was to call her.

13

Jessica wound her way around the beachfront path, the icy chill from the ocean blasting at her cheeks. She smiled at a woman hurrying past in the opposite direction, pushing a pram and doing her best to keep up with her toddler, who was zipping ahead on a small pink plastic motorbike.

It was her first weekend without Sam, and she had to admit, she was enjoying the solitude. What she wasn't enjoying was the constant nagging at the back of her mind as to why Martin hadn't shown up or contacted her the day before. There could be numerous reasons, she knew that, but the one that kept surfacing was he'd changed his mind about getting to know her. She'd done her best to convince herself that this wouldn't be the case – after all, he was the one who'd initiated contact – but the past, and his history of abandoning people, was hard to ignore. Her phone rang, breaking into her thoughts.

Jessica slipped her phone from her pocket and glanced at the screen. She froze. It was him.

She cleared her throat and pressed the call button. 'Hello.'

'Is this Jessica Williams?'

She hesitated. It was Martin's phone, but the female voice wasn't Martin. 'Yes, it is.'

'Jessica, my name's Reeve Elliot...'

Her stomach lurched. Martin's daughter was calling her. Did she know?

'...I'm Martin Elliot's daughter,' she continued. 'I wanted to get in touch as I know you've been trying to reach my father.'

'That's right, I have.'

Reeve cleared her throat. 'The thing is, there's been an accident. A house fire.'

Jess's hand flew to her mouth. The Toorak house. Was it his? She'd wished him dead on many occasions in the past, but figuratively, not literally. 'Is Martin okay?'

Reeve's voice caught. 'No, I'm afraid he's not. He

was at home at the time the fire started and...' Her voice caught. 'He didn't survive.'

'No!' Jess's mouth dropped open.

'I'm sorry to tell you over the phone,' Reeve said. 'But I wasn't sure how you knew Dad. I have his phone and saw the text messages between the two of you. Do you mind me asking how you knew him?'

She has no idea. Jess remained silent. What should she tell her? The truth?

'Were you in a relationship with him?'

'I'm sorry, Reeve, I think I need to sit down. This is quite a shock. Thank you for getting in touch. Will you be making the funeral details public?'

'Yes. I'll put something in the paper on Tuesday. I'd be happy to send you the information when it's all confirmed. I'd be interested in meeting you and hearing about how you knew Dad. His messages suggested he was excited to see you.'

'Thanks, Reeve. I'm very sorry for your loss, but it's been nice to speak to you.' She ended the call, realising that had sounded a little strange. She doubted Reeve considered it *nice* to break this news about her father.

She shook her head. *Dead.* Martin Elliot – *her father* – was dead.

14

Reeve stared at her father's phone. So much for going direct to the source for information. She knew nothing more about Jessica Williams now than she had before the call. While shocked by the news, if Jessica was a business acquaintance, surely she would have said that. She put down the phone and sighed. She'd ask Devon tomorrow if he'd heard of her. For now, she should go through the rest of the messages on the phone and check her father's contacts. She had phone calls to make and was dreading doing them. Luke had offered to make them, but it was her responsibility.

It was after six by the time she heard the garage door open and Luke's car drive in. She was still sitting at the kitchen counter, a numbness having settled over her. She was finding it hard enough to deal with her own shock of Martin's death, and reliving it time and time again, as she broke the news to yet another person, was horrible.

She stood and stretched as Luke appeared in the doorway. He smiled and held up a plastic takeaway bag. 'Dinner is served.'

'How did you go at the hospital?' Reeve asked, getting some plates from the sideboard. Her stomach rumbled as the aromas of lemongrass and ginger filled the kitchen.

'Standard procedure,' Luke said, putting the bag on the counter. He slipped his arms around her waist and pulled her to him. 'How about you? Did you make any phone calls?'

'About forty,' Reeve said. 'It was horrible.'

Luke pushed a stray piece of hair from her eyes. 'You poor thing. You should have let me do it.'

She shook her head. 'No, I needed to.'

'And did you get on to that Jessica woman?'

She nodded. 'I did, and she sounded shocked about Dad. She didn't tell me who she was or how she knew him.'

'Did you ask?'

'Yes, but she was too shocked to talk. She implied

she'd come to the funeral. I guess I can speak to her then, and I'll ask Devon about her tomorrow.'

Luke kissed her forehead and pulled away. He opened the wine fridge, then closed it. 'I forgot for a moment that wine is off the menu. Shall I make some green tea? That goes nicely with Vietnamese food.'

Reeve hesitated. She would kill for a glass of wine. Even just a small one to take the edge off the day. 'Don't be silly.' She opened the wine fridge and took out a bottle of the Pinot Gris Luke had mentioned earlier. 'Just because I need to cut back doesn't mean you should miss out. It's been a big few days and you should be allowed to relax.'

'I want to support you.'

Reeve shook her head, took the bottle opener from the drawer and opened the bottle. She poured Luke a glass and handed it to him, before taking a second glass from the cabinet and pouring a small amount. 'Patricia said I should cut back. She didn't say I had to stop.'

Luke frowned. 'Do you think that's a good idea? Drinking's a contributing factor to the incidents we want to avoid.'

Reeve moved closer to Luke and slipped an arm around his waist. 'One small glass isn't going to hurt. Don't let me anywhere near my phone or computer and that way, if I do end up saying or doing anything silly, it'll only be you who knows. I know you're dying for a glass, and you hate drinking alone, but let's make sure it is only half a glass for me, not a drop more. Okay?'

Luke hesitated before nodding. 'Okay, but that's it. If you do anything unusual it's time to cut out drinking altogether. Now come on, let's take this outside. I'll light the patio heater, and we can enjoy dinner under the stars.'

* * *

Reeve had no recollection of going to bed, but at midnight woke with a pounding headache and the taste of stale alcohol in her mouth. She groaned and rolled over to check if Luke was beside her. The bed was empty. She dragged herself up to sitting, rubbing her forehead. What had happened? She remembered Luke coming home and the discussion about the wine and the Vietnamese food. They'd planned to take it outside and enjoy it under the stars. She'd poured the wine, and that was all she remembered. Had she blacked out? Her mouth and stomach suggested that was not the case.

She was bloated and uncomfortable, and she had

a pain in her side. The same symptoms she endured when she ate chilli. As much as she loved it, it didn't love her. Her physical symptoms confirmed at least that she had eaten dinner. But then what? Had she drunk the wine? Was the small glass enough to have her forgetting her actions again? And where was Luke?

She lay back on the pillows, her racing heartbeat causing acute pain in her chest. She took a deep breath. She knew this symptom well enough to know it was panic rather than a heart attack. What was happening to her?

A noise from downstairs alerted her. It sounded like broken glass being swept up. She slowly climbed out of bed, straining to listen. More chinking of glass. She pushed her feet into a pair of slippers and crept down the stairs. She assumed it was Luke in the kitchen, but what if it wasn't? What if there'd been a break-in?

'Jesus!' Luke's exclamation stopped her on the stairs, a mixture of shock and relief.

'Luke?' She hurried down the last of the stairs and into the kitchen, stopping in the doorway. Luke was holding his hand under the tap. Her eyes surveyed the scene in front of her. Broken glass was strewn over the countertops and on the floor. From the looks of the red liquid everywhere and the dark glass, it appeared red wine bottles had been smashed.

'What on earth? Have we been burgled?'

Luke looked at her and shook his head before turning his attention back to his finger and the tap.

'Is your finger okay?'

He nodded. 'Just a nick, thank goodness. I'm hoping it won't affect my work.' Luke often joked that his hands were so valuable they needed to be insured.

Reeve stepped her way carefully through the glass and stopped beside him. 'What happened?'

'You don't remember this one either?'

The anger in his voice caused a cold shiver to course through her. Luke never got angry.

He sighed and turned to her. 'Sorry. You probably don't.'

'Probably? I remember serving up the Vietnamese, and that's all I remember. I just woke up. I've got a shocking headache and feel like I ate and drank way too much. I have no recollection of doing either.'

Luke turned off the tap, grabbed some paper towels from near the stovetop, and wrapped them around his finger. 'You did both to excess.'

'I drank to excess?'

He nodded.

Anger surged through her. 'How could you let me do that?'

Luke gave a strangled laugh. 'Let you? Like you gave me a choice. Reeve, you excused yourself after dinner, saying you were going to make a list of the contacts you'd called today so you could cross-check it against the list Devon mentioned he had. The next thing, I find you sitting on the floor of the pantry, having drunk a full bottle of wine. It appears one glass wasn't enough after all.'

'What?' She shook her head. 'Why would I do that?'

Luke sighed. 'How would I know. You wanted another drink. I said no after the first small glass, but you decided to take matters into your own hands.' He stared at her, his features completely void of the concern and compassion he'd been showing the last few weeks. 'It can't go on. You've got a problem, and I have no idea how to deal with it. Now, go back to bed. I'll clean this up and come up soon.'

'But what happened here?' Reeve gestured to the broken bottles.

'You didn't like my reaction to finding you in the pantry. Your words were something like, "For fuck's sake, Luke, my father died, I'm on trial for abusing a student, and my daughter hates me. Why don't you go and fuck yourself and leave me to self-medicate?" You then threw a full bottle of wine at me, which smashed over the bench. That was followed by two more with you screaming that you should never have married me. That I am the arsehole and that you want me out of your *fucking* kitchen and preferably out of your life.'

Reeve hung her head in shame. 'I'm sorry. I would never knowingly say something like that. I love you so much. I'm humiliated.' And she was. She was living a nightmare. One she didn't know how to wake up from, or indeed whether she *would* ever wake up from.

'Go to bed, Reeve.'

She met his gaze. 'You do believe I didn't mean this, don't you?'

He nodded. 'It's still hard to deal with. Seeing you go crazy and speak in a way I don't even recognise. Let's talk in the morning, okay? Right now, I need to get the broken glass cleaned up and get to bed. I've got a big day tomorrow, and I need some sleep.'

Reeve turned and left the kitchen, her stomach churning. How could she be adamant in her denial of having done anything wrong with regards to Dale Cross or Oscar Ryan when her behaviour was out of control in her own home? She hurried up the stairs, only just making it to the bathroom in time, where she violently retched into the toilet.

* * *

The next morning, Reeve made herself coffee, partly disappointed that Luke had already left for work and partly relieved. She wasn't sure she could face him again this morning. She was grateful for the note he'd left on the kitchen bench.

Don't worry. We'll get through this. Sorry about last night; I'm just so worried. Love you. x

She knew that feeling of worry well. Poor Luke. She was putting him through a nightmare. She bet he wished he'd never met her. She'd showered and dressed, feeling incredibly seedy. No wonder, if she'd drunk as much wine as Luke said. A bottle was more than she'd ever normally drink, and to do it alone and in a short space of time was madness.

The clock on the wall above the kitchen table showed it was nine-fifty. Devon would be arriving any minute. She got up and pushed open the kitchen windows and French doors that opened out onto the backyard. The smell of red wine permeated the air, and she was hoping the icy chill of the winter morning would help remove it. The wooden counter-tops were stained with red blotches, a permanent reminder of a night, ironically, she couldn't remember.

She popped two paracetamol and drank a large glass of water before hearing Devon's Jag pull up out the front. He and her father had similar tastes in cars, and many of their discussions revolved around analysing different models of their favourite brand.

She opened the front door and watched as Devon stepped out of his car, briefcase in hand. He smiled as he saw her watching him and strode towards the front door.

He held his arms open and embraced her the way he'd done many times before. He was her father's lawyer but also a family friend and more like an uncle to Reeve than anyone else had been.

'Come in,' she said once he released her. 'I'll make some coffee.' She led him into the kitchen.

'What's the smell?' he asked, placing his briefcase on the counter. 'Did you guys have a party last night? It smells like a lot of wine was consumed.'

'A large breakage, unfortunately,' she replied. 'Now, coffee? White with one?'

He nodded and sank down on the stool and opened his briefcase. 'There are a few things we need to discuss regarding Martin's wishes.'

Reeve made the coffee and took two cups over to where Devon sat. She sat down next to him. 'Did Dad specify any requests for a funeral?'

Devon gave a wry smile. 'More than that. The whole thing is pre-paid and organised. Down to the time of day and catering. His preference is for a Friday afternoon so people can' – he picked up a piece of paper – 'I'm quoting here. "People can continue into the night and get smashed."'

Reeve laughed. 'That sounds like Dad. Hopefully, the venue he's chosen has availability this Friday. I guess it can wait until the following one otherwise.'

'They do,' Devon said. 'I checked and made a tentative booking last week. They said to call them later today if you'd like to go ahead. You may prefer to do your own thing and ignore Martin's instructions.'

Reeve shook her head. 'No, we'll do as Dad wanted. It wouldn't make sense not to.'

'There are a few things you'll need to arrange. The funeral home will put the details in the paper, but you'll need to contact Martin's list.'

'His list?'

Devon raised an eyebrow, took a three-page document from his file, and passed it to Reeve. 'Yes, his list.'

She scanned the document, which was titled, *People to contact upon my death.* She recognised some of the names but not all of them. She slowed as she reached the end of the third page. Jessica Williams was not listed.

'Okay, I can do this. Do you think it's acceptable to email or text message?'

'Definitely,' Devon said. 'I assume you've contacted his main friendship group and acquaintances already?'

She nodded.

'Yes, then an email or message will be fine. It's too many people to call directly. The other thing I wanted to talk to you about is the police investigation into the fire. I called Sergeant Butler on my way here. It's an unusual situation. All signs point to the fact that the fire started in the kitchen. He left a pot on the stove and must have forgotten about it. It's how a lot of house fires start. However, the police are still treating it as suspicious.'

'Really? Why?'

'Because the security cameras around the property were disabled at some time during the day. The last footage that was recorded was of Martin driving out in the Jag earlier that morning.'

'To meet me for breakfast and to go to the cemetery,' Reeve said.

Devon nodded. 'There's nothing after that which suggests someone got in there and removed the cameras directly after. That footage went straight up to the cloud, which is why we have it.'

'Wouldn't they have been caught on camera?'

'Not if they knew where the cameras were and how to approach them to avoid being seen. They were clever enough to disable the system at the control centre too. It was only accessing the house that was required.'

Reeve stared at Devon. 'It was someone who knew Dad?'

'That's the impression I got, although the police were vague.'

Reeve's mouth dropped open. 'No.'

'Unfortunately, I'm not joking. Martin had a few enemies, but no one I could imagine wanting him dead.'

Reeve nodded, trying to get her head around the implications of Devon's words.

'There's something else,' Devon said, unable to meet Reeve's eyes. He cleared his throat.

'You're scaring me.'

'Martin didn't want you to know, but he found out a few weeks before he died that the cancer was back.'

Reeve closed her eyes. She'd known it was likely, after speaking to Carol at the cemetery.

'It wasn't good,' Devon continued. 'He'd been talking to the doctors about more treatment, but he hadn't decided what he was going to do.'

Reeve's eyes flew open. 'What do you mean he hadn't decided?'

'I mean, he knew it might buy him a few months, but at a huge cost. He'd feel awful, probably need nursing, and he didn't want to put you through the pain of watching another parent die. After your mother, he didn't think that was fair.'

Reeve stared at the lawyer. 'What are you suggesting? That he killed himself so I didn't have to watch him die?'

Devon sighed. 'I hope not, Reeve, I really do. But he did say some things to me that suggested he might finish things himself before they got too bad.'

Reeve digested this information before slowly shaking her head. 'There's no way he'd do that to me. Not on Mum's anniversary and not without saying a proper goodbye. If the cancer was that bad, I'd believe he might end things early, but not like this. Also, he'd never burn down the house. God, he used to refer to it as his mecca. He might kill himself, but there's no way he'd do that to the house. He'd consider it sacrilegious.'

Devon released a long breath. 'You know, you're right. I'm sorry for even bringing it up, but it's been playing on my mind since the day of the fire. I kept playing over our last conversations looking for any hint of a goodbye, but there was nothing.'

'It was either an accident or foul play,' Reeve said. 'And hopefully it was a horrible accident and nothing more.'

'Hopefully. Now, there's more to go through with regards to your dad,' Devon said. 'His will, for starters. You are the main beneficiary. I was going to suggest we meet next week, once the funeral and formalities are over with, to go through the details.'

Reeve nodded again. She wasn't in any rush to do any of this.

'Now, to the next issue,' Devon said. He took a sip from his coffee before replacing it on the kitchen counter. 'The school. They would like to confirm a date to meet with us. I've explained the situation with your father's passing, and they've been very accommodating. They've asked for you to nominate a date when you think you'll be up to meeting with them.'

'Is never an option?'

Devon smiled. 'Only if you don't want to go back to work.'

'That's tempting right now.'

Devon cleared his throat. 'I must ask you one thing, Reeve, before I represent you. It's something I asked your father for every case he involved me in. Is there any truth to the allegations?' He held up his hand to stop her from talking before continuing. 'As I said, I always asked Martin this. It didn't change anything about my representing him. It meant I knew where he was coming from and helped me form the best plan of attack.'

'Whether you'd need to pay people off rather than legitimately win the case?'

Devon's cheeks coloured. 'I wouldn't go as far as admitting that, but yes, sometimes less conventional approaches were required.'

'I'm not looking for less conventional. I'm looking to clear my name. I have no recollection of saying any of the things Oscar's accusing me of.'

Devon's eyes narrowed. 'Hold on. That's not the answer I was hoping for, or the one Martin led me to believe. *No recollection*?'

Reeve nodded.

'Are you saying you didn't say anything, or you might have, but you don't remember?'

Reeve sighed. 'I'd better fill you in on what's been happening.' She went on to tell Devon about the strange behaviour she'd been exhibiting and the concerns that it might be linked to an illness such as her mother's.

'Oh Reeve. Did Martin know?'

Reeve's eyes filled with tears at the compassion in his voice. She shook her head. 'I wasn't going to say anything until I knew for sure, and even then, I'm not sure if I would have told him. Going through this twice would be too much for anyone.'

He nodded. 'Alice's condition was very hard on both of you. It does mean, however, that there is a possibility you could be guilty of these charges?'

'Yes, although it would be completely out of character.'

Devon sighed. 'This isn't ideal. We'll need a psych assessment before we try to defend the allegations. The problem is if your assessment comes back showing erratic behaviour due to mental illness, I can't see you keeping your job. The best-case scenario is that you did nothing wrong, and the kid's making it all up.' He frowned. 'The question is, why would he do that?'

Reeve remained silent. There was no reason he'd make something like that up.

'Would you like me to investigate a suitable doctor for an assessment?'

Reeve shook her head. 'No, I'm seeing a psychiatrist on Thursday who specialises in early onset dementia. I'll speak to her further and see what we can do to organise more testing. I can't imagine it will happen quickly.'

'I'm not sure the school will allow for a lengthy time frame. They want it resolved as soon as possible. Would you be happy for me to talk to your psychiatrist? I can explain that there is urgency in organising testing.'

Reeve nodded and picked up her phone and scrolled through her contacts. She wrote down Patricia's number and handed it to Devon.

'If you are guilty, and mental illness is involved, then how you are dealt with is very different from a premeditated scenario.'

Reeve lapsed into silence. Only a few days ago, she would have adamantly fought to prove her innocence, but doubt was now settling over her.

'We'll get you through this. There are plenty of people who will want to support you. People loved Martin, and they love you.'

Reeve nodded. 'Thank you.' The strange conversation with Jessica Williams came back to her. 'Did Dad ever mention a woman by the name of Jessica Williams?'

Something flashed in Devon's eyes briefly before his face took on what Reeve had always considered his *lawyer* look. Totally expressionless.

'He might have mentioned her. Why?'

'I found an exchange of text messages between them, and I called her and told her what had happened to Dad.'

'Oh?'

'She was shocked, but she didn't tell me who she was or how she knew him. She was extremely vague.'

'I guess that's understandable after the news you'd delivered.'

'I must say I'm intrigued. It's unlike Dad to have had secrets.'

Devon shifted uncomfortably in his seat.

Reeve eyed him up and down. 'You know who she is, don't you?'

Devon sighed. 'Yes, but I think it should be her decision whether she shares their history with you. It's certainly not my position to say anything. Although...'

'Although what?'

'Martin has left provisions for Ms Williams to be included in the distribution of the estate. We'll go through that next week when you come and see me over those matters. Hopefully, in the interim, she'll meet with you and tell you how she knew your father.'

Reeve sipped her coffee, the conversation with Devon unnerving her. 'Were they having a relationship?'

'Not in the context of what you might be thinking. She's someone from his past who he met up with more recently. What I can say is I know he was excited at the prospect of getting to know her better.' Devon drained his coffee and stood. 'I'll contact your psychiatrist and see if the tests can be prioritised and then contact the school and ask for the discussion to be postponed until you've had your medical diagnosis completed.'

He leant forward and kissed Reeve lightly on the cheek. 'I'm sorry you're going through this. I know Martin would be devastated knowing you were facing this on your own now.'

'I have Luke's support,' Reeve said. 'And Nick's too. I won't be on my own.'

'And I'm here,' Devon said. 'Anything at all you need. Now, will you call the funeral director today?'

'As soon as you leave,' Reeve said. 'I'll ask them to forward you the details, and I guess I'll see you on Friday, assuming it can be done this week.'

'The autopsy will be completed by tomorrow,' Devon said. 'Martin's body should be released after that. Let me know if you need any help, won't you.'

Reeve managed a wry smile. 'Sounds like Dad's done everything already. Although...' She hesitated briefly. 'I'm sure he'd be thrilled if you'd speak at the funeral.'

Devon blushed. 'Have a look through the file I've left you. He's nominated everyone he wants to speak and the order in which they are to go. He's included me, so I'd be delighted.'

'We'll half expect him to walk in and give us directions on the day,' Reeve said. She shook her head. 'Everything always worked out how Dad wanted, didn't it?'

'Generally, although now that we've agreed that he wasn't behind his own death, I doubt the way he exited the world was part of his plan.'

Reeve stared at the lawyer, a shiver running down her spine. Devon was right, and Reeve could only hope his death was proven to be an accident. She didn't think she could cope with the alternative.

15

Jess found a bench overlooking the windswept waters of Port Phillip Bay and sat down. Reeve's phone call the day before had stunned her. She'd hardly slept and had done something that morning she never did: rung in sick. She'd spent the morning in bed and had now dragged herself up for a walk to try to shake off the melancholy that had settled over her.

A wave of grief hit her as she sat down on the bench. He hadn't stood her up. He'd died.

She wiped her cheeks roughly with the back of her hand, her tears mixing with the salty spray from the ocean. What was wrong with her? She didn't even know Martin Elliot, so why was she feeling upset at his death? She took a deep breath and closed her eyes, willing the tears to stop.

'Jess?'

Her eyes jolted open at the familiar male voice.

'Are you okay?' Trent's brows drew together as their eyes met.

She shook her head, unable to speak.

He lowered himself onto the bench next to her and put an arm around her shoulder. 'Let's sit and enjoy this cold, blustery day, shall we.'

Jess sank into him, grateful for his comfort and that he wasn't demanding to know what the issue was.

A few minutes passed, and a sense of calm settled over her. 'Thanks,' she said. 'Probably not what you were expecting to encounter today.'

'I had no expectations,' Trent said, squeezing her shoulder. 'If you want to talk about it, I'm a good listener. And if you don't, I'm a good drinker, as you know, and would be happy to buy you a drink.'

Jess managed a smile. 'How about we combine the two, except I buy you the drink. There's that bar that's part of Mulligan's. Windbreaker or something.'

Trent drew her to her feet, and they walked in companionable silence along the walking trail until they reached Windbreaker.

With most people at work, the outdoor tables weren't very busy. They chose a table next to a patio heater.

'My shout,' Jess insisted when they were seated. 'What do you feel like? We could share a bottle of red if you're keen. Even with the warmth of the heater, it's too cold for anything else.'

'Perfect.'

Jess ordered a bottle of Cab Sav, and the waiter returned with the bottle and two glasses.

'To a better day tomorrow,' Trent said, raising his glass.

Jess sipped her wine, appreciating the immediate relaxing effect it had.

'So,' Trent said. 'What causes my favourite neighbour to be crying on a park bench on a Monday afternoon? The boyfriend perhaps?'

'Who? Sam?'

Trent laughed. '*Who?* How many boyfriends did you have?'

'Sorry, no, it's not about Sam.' She took a deep breath. 'It's my dad, Martin.'

'The one you were supposed to have coffee with on Saturday?'

This time Jess smiled. 'Yes, that one, not one of the others I've got hidden away.'

Trent gave a wry smile. 'Sorry. What's he done?'

'Nothing. He's dead.'

Trent put down his glass. 'What?'

Jess found herself wiping her eyes again. 'He died in a house fire on Friday.'

Trent stared at Jess, his face reflecting her own disbelief at the situation. 'I don't even know what to say. How did you find out?'

'His daughter, Reeve. She rang me.'

'He told her about you before he died?'

'No, she saw my text message after I thought I'd been stood up yesterday and wanted to let me know what had happened. She had no idea who I was.'

'Did you tell her?'

She shook her head. 'No, it wasn't the right time for anything like that. I'm not sure if there will be a right time now.' She took a large sip of her wine.

'Oh, Jess, I'm sorry. That's awful.'

'It is.'

'You said it wouldn't be the right timing to tell his daughter. Possibly not right now while she has a funeral to arrange and other formalities, but it will be at some stage. You said your dad suggested he wanted you to get to know her.'

She nodded. 'He did. But I'm not sure. She probably needs to hear his side of the story from him, not my version.'

'But you have his version from when you met him last weekend. You can tell her what he told you. There might be other friends or relatives that she knows who know the story too.'

'That's true. She's going to let me know when the funeral is. I guess I'll meet her if I go, but that wouldn't be the right time to tell her.'

'Did you want me to come with you to the funeral?'

'I wasn't sure whether I should go. I can't introduce myself to anyone.'

'You can say you were a friend if you're asked. Or we can blend into the background and make sure you're not asked anything.'

'Thank you,' Jess said. 'I think I do want to go. I wasn't part of his life, but I can at least be part of this. Hear what the people who did know him have to say about him. Paint me a picture of how he was perceived. And yes, I'd love you to come with me.'

'You'll still owe me that dinner,' Trent said, a smile playing on his lips. 'Don't think this gets you out of your date obligations.'

'About that,' Jess said. 'Can we call it dinner,

rather than a date? I've proved many times that I'm awful at dating but quite good at dinner.'

'Deal,' Trent said, holding out his hand as if they were shaking on a business deal.

Jess took his hand in hers, surprised at the butterflies that flitted in her stomach as she did. Dinner and friendship only, she reminded herself. Trent was her closest friend, and the last thing she wanted to do was mess that up.

* * *

By Tuesday, Jess was grateful to be buried in work after the revelations of the weekend. Anything to take her mind off the Martin situation was appreciated. She'd had a text message from Reeve early that morning with the details for Friday's funeral and had confirmed with Trent that he was still happy to go with her. It was a strange feeling to be grieving a father she hadn't known and, up until a week or so ago, had hated the thought of. She'd made many assumptions about him and blamed him for so much. Yes, she still had every right to be angry that he hadn't wanted her in his life until now, but his actions proved he wasn't the awful person she'd always imagined.

'Hey,' Harry said, poking his head around the corner of Jess's office door on Tuesday morning. 'I heard there's a big announcement happening later today.' He grinned. 'Should I put the champagne on ice?'

'Definitely not,' Jess said, returning his grin. 'Don't want to jinx anything at this stage.'

'Fair enough. Have you heard any more from Felicity?'

Jess had filled Harry in on the situation with Felicity after speaking to her aunt. 'She's not happy where she is, unfortunately. I can't tell her yet, but I had an email from her aunt overnight, and she's booked a flight to Melbourne. She's arriving in a few days. She's going to meet with me first to discuss the possibility of fostering, and then we'll arrange for her to spend some time with Felicity. For now, I've told Felicity to give it a couple of weeks, and if she hates the Smiths, we'll talk about it then. I need to buy some time to check out the aunt.'

Harry gave a low whistle. 'That's a pretty big step after only recently learning about her niece.'

'It sounded like she'd been thinking about coming back to Australia. This might be the push she needed.'

'Great,' Harry said. 'Let me know how it goes.

And for today, make sure you're back by four. A little bird told me that's when the celebrations are going to start.'

Jess couldn't help but smile as she left her office. It was very nice of him to be excited about her potential promotion, but it was also premature. The board said it would be the end of the week at the earliest that any announcements would be made. And the process would be that the person would be offered the job and need to accept it before anything was made public. The unsuccessful candidates would be notified at the same time.

A message popped up on her screen from Marlee at reception.

> Bruce wants to know if you are available for a quick meeting in ten minutes?

She typed a quick response.

> Yes, his office or mine?

Even as she typed the words, disappointment flooded through her. Seconds ago, Harry had her excited about the job opportunity, but a summons to see Bruce was confirmation she didn't get it. He would be delivering the bad news to the unsuccessful candidates. She already knew that. And as there was no other reason she'd be meeting with the human resources manager, she was sure that was what it was for.

His office, thanks.

Jess watched the clock tick around the full ten minutes before standing and making her way down the long corridor to Bruce's office. He was on the phone but smiled and waved her towards the empty chair across from him.

She admired the dramatic landscape he had hanging behind his desk. The rugged coastline and bright red cliffs had to be Cape Leveque north of Broome. She wondered if she'd ever get to explore such remote parts of Australia.

'Sorry,' he said as he hung up. He shuffled some papers on his desk before leaning back in his chair, his focus back on Jess. 'Now, there's something I need to talk to you about regarding the CEO role.'

'I gathered that's what it would be about.' She stood. 'It's no problem, Bruce. I know there were some great candidates. I'll look forward to working with whoever you've chosen.'

'It's not me personally who chose the person for the role,' Bruce said. 'As you know, the board have the final say.'

Jess smiled. 'Okay, I won't blame you then.'

He pretended to wipe his brow. 'Good, because I'd say the overtime is going to be something to complain about, and you can whinge to the board about that.' He grinned. 'Congrats, Captain.'

Jess sat down again. 'What? I got it?'

He nodded. 'I'm offering it to you, or at least trying to.' He took a sheet of paper from his desk. 'I think you're already aware of all of this, but here is the term sheet. Nothing's changed since you interviewed for the position – other than if you're happy with the terms, we'll need a signature. The unofficial announcement will be made to our staff at four o'clock by Duncan, the chairman of the board, but they want to make sure you're accepting it first, and it gives us time to call those who weren't successful. The official announcement to the media and broader community will be made next Tuesday.'

Jess's smile widened. She signed the document and practically floated back to her office. The last couple of weeks had been crazy – a breakup, a meeting with her biological father, the discovery of Joey's diabolical behaviour, the death of her father, a conversation with her sister, and now a new job. She was about to pick up the phone and see if Harry had the champagne chilling when a message from Marlee appeared on her screen.

Please call Devon Saunders, Martin Elliot's lawyer.

* * *

Jess only hesitated a second before picking up the phone. She'd hoped to have time to savour the elation of the promotion, but it wasn't to be. She was put straight through to the lawyer.

'Jess, thanks for getting back to me. There are a couple of things I wanted to discuss with you. Firstly, I'm sorry for your loss.'

'Thank you.'

Devon cleared his throat. 'It's been a very sad week, to say the least. Martin was my friend as well as a client, and I want to make sure that his wishes are all met. And then there is his will, which I will discuss with you, preferably in person.'

'I'm not expecting anything. I didn't even know him.'

'He has provided for you in his will, but again,

that's something we can discuss later. I'll be contacting all beneficiaries over the next week about that. It was the Joseph Williams situation I wanted to talk to you about. Martin was very distressed when he discovered you never received the monies that were meant for you and your mother. I believe you would have received the statements Martin had me prepare to show the payments?'

'Yes, I did, thank you. I've since found out that Joey fled to the Cayman Islands in 1998, and there appears to be no trace of him since then.'

'Martin's investigations discovered the same,' Devon said. 'I'm not sure if you are aware that he had investigators looking into the situation? He wanted to put together as much information as possible before talking to you about it and what you'd like to do.'

'He didn't find him either?'

'No. We assume he changed identities. Martin was happy to finance further investigations if you'd like me to continue with it?'

Jess hesitated. She already had Trent's friend looking into the situation. Was there any point doubling up? 'No, let's leave it for the moment. There's enough to deal with surrounding Martin's death. My desire to find Joey is to hear directly from him why he did what he did. It's not to retrieve the money. I'd hate for Reeve to think I was after her father's money.'

Devon cleared his throat. 'You're aware that Reeve doesn't know who you are, aren't you? I was wondering how you wanted to deal with that. I know Martin was hoping to introduce you but had mentioned to me that you'd said you didn't want anything to do with him or Reeve.'

'I didn't when I met him the first time. But after giving it more thought, I was open to getting to know him. I'm not sure telling Reeve now would be in her best interest. She doesn't need the memory of her father tarnished.'

'That's very good of you,' Devon said. 'But I think she'll question the way the will is left. Martin has left you a sizeable percentage of his fortune, and as Reeve is a beneficiary, she will be entitled to receive a copy of the will. She'll no doubt be curious.'

'Oh.' Jess wasn't sure what to say.

'I'm happy to explain the situation to Reeve. She's a lovely woman, and while I think initially she'll be shocked, I expect she'll also be interested as to who you are. You need to remember you've done nothing wrong. If she's angry with anyone, it will be Martin.'

'Maybe we should leave it until after the funeral. Allow her to grieve and deal with what's happening right now,' Jess said. 'I am planning to attend but won't speak to Reeve. I'll pay my respects and then leave. Then if you tell her sometime in the coming weeks, please let her know I'd be happy to meet with her and answer any questions she has. Not that I'll necessarily have the answers. We really needed Martin for that.'

'I've known Martin for many years,' Devon said. 'Hopefully I'll be able to provide some of those answers.'

Jess thought back to her meeting with Martin and him saying his lawyer had encouraged him to make contact with her. 'You two were good friends?'

Sadness laced Devon's words. 'Yes, very good.'

'From what Martin told me, I have you to thank for pushing him to meet me.'

'I wouldn't say I pushed him,' Devon said. 'I'm not sure how much he told you, but Martin was battling cancer and he'd had some bad news a few weeks before he died. He was discussing his estate with me, and he shared his regrets in never having met you. I simply told him that while he was alive there was no reason to have any regrets. That he could do something about it. He was the one who then initiated the search for you.'

'Cancer?' Jess's hand flew to her mouth, remembering her discussion with Martin. He'd mentioned it so casually she'd assumed it wasn't a concern, that he'd been successfully treated. 'He told me he'd had a brush with cancer. I assumed by that he meant he'd had treatment and was now cancer free. I feel terrible. I didn't even question it. You're saying he still had cancer?'

'He did. His time was running out, but he still had months, possibly longer.'

Jess wasn't sure how to react to this information. Guilt stabbed at her that she hadn't asked him about it. But worse was the realisation that even if Martin had lived, she wouldn't have had much time to spend with him. She ended the call a few minutes later after agreeing to meet with Devon the week after the funeral to discuss the will. It was hard to believe she was being included in the will of a man she knew was a multi-millionaire. She didn't want his money, but she thought back to the note he'd sent her with the bank statements that even if she didn't want it, maybe Safe Houses would. An injection of funds into the system would make a huge difference. While she wasn't interested in it for herself, she wouldn't discount accepting the money altogether.

16

Grief swept over Reeve in waves in the days leading to the funeral. The funeral home had been amazing from the first phone call. They'd confirmed the Friday service and had undertaken the bulk of the arrangements. While it was a huge relief, it didn't stop Reeve's stomach churning each time she thought of her father and what she'd lost.

Martin's body had been released by the coroner the previous day, and Reeve was still waiting to hear from Devon on the findings. Smoke inhalation was the most obvious cause of death, but the fact that an autopsy had been performed suggested the police weren't ruling out other potential causes.

Reeve had considered postponing her appointment with Patricia and would have if it wasn't for the urgency that was now required to have testing done. She dreaded the appointment and had been incredibly grateful when Luke offered to take the morning off work and come with her.

Now, as they made their way up the paved path to the door of Patricia's studio office, Luke took her hand. 'I'm proud of you.'

Reeve stopped and turned to face her husband. 'Why? There's nothing to be proud about with the way I've been acting.'

'I'm proud that you're here and that you're looking for answers. I see a lot of patients, and many would have given up already. Gone to bed for weeks at a time until hopefully, this all disappeared. You're facing things head-on at a difficult time, and I'm proud of you. Not many people would be making this a priority the day before their father's funeral.'

The door to Patricia's studio opened, not giving Reeve a chance to respond, and Patricia welcomed them inside.

'Before we start,' Patricia said once they were all seated, 'I did want you to know how very sorry I am about your father. While my dealings with him were in the capacity of discussing your mother's treatment, from the things I learned from your mother about him and from yourself, he sounded like a very loving and caring man.'

Reeve reached for a tissue from the box sitting on the side table next to her. She'd probably go through the entire box this session. 'Thank you. He was.'

'I imagine it has been a very difficult time for you. I had a call from your lawyer, Devon Saunders. He's explained the school situation in more detail and the need to speed up testing.'

'That's one of the reasons I didn't cancel,' Reeve admitted. 'That and an incident the other night scared me enough to suggest I might need help.'

Patricia nodded. 'Why don't you tell me what happened, and we'll go from there.'

Heat crept up the back of Reeve's neck. 'The problem is, I don't remember.' She went on to tell Patricia the details she could recall and what Luke had filled her in on.

Patricia made notes on her notepad before turning to Luke. 'I imagine this has been very distressing for you.'

He nodded, and Reeve was horrified to see his eyes fill with tears. 'Sorry,' he mumbled, wiping them with the back of his sleeve. 'It's been a real shock seeing the changes in Reeve. It's happening quickly, and it's frightening me.'

'You're a doctor, aren't you?' Patricia asked.

Confusion crossed Luke's features. 'Are you suggesting that because I'm a doctor, I should take all this in my stride? I'm a trauma recovery surgeon, not a head doctor, and I've had very little experience with dementia. If that's what we're dealing with.'

'I wasn't in any way suggesting you should be taking this in your stride. I wanted to check the information I have about you is correct.'

Luke's cheeks flushed red. 'Sorry. I'm on edge. I've been reading up about early onset dementia and, well, nothing has painted a very pretty picture of it.'

'Reeve hasn't officially been diagnosed with anything.'

'I know. But it doesn't stop me from being concerned.'

'It's completely normal that you'd be worried after the unsettling events of the last few months.' She smiled. 'From everything Reeve's told me about you, you're what's keeping her together.'

'It's true,' Reeve said, turning to Luke. 'You've been amazing.'

Luke took her hand. 'I love you so much, and I hope you'll always think I'm amazing, but this is hard. I'm worried you're going to do something to hurt yourself.'

Reeve dropped his hand. 'What? Why would you think that?'

Luke looked at Patricia, who nodded for him to continue. 'Last night, you woke me at one, telling me I was the only good thing in your life. That with your dad gone and Bella hating you, there was no point continuing. You said you were worried you had acted inappropriately towards Oscar and would never be able to show your face again at the school. You asked me whether I had access to strong drugs that would make it easy.'

Reeve closed her eyes momentarily before looking at him. 'Why didn't you tell me this morning?'

'I didn't want to upset you before this session. I figured it was best to discuss it here.' He looked at Patricia. 'The thing is, I'm not sure what I should do to control Reeve or stop her from doing anything dangerous. After the wine bottles the other night, I'm worried she might harm herself.'

'I would never do that,' Reeve said. 'I don't care what I said. You and Bella are my world. Sure, we're going through a hard time, but we'll fix that at some stage. I could never do what you're suggesting.' She swallowed. Yet she'd had the thought herself only a week ago.

Luke pushed his hand through his hair in frustration. 'You say you wouldn't do a lot of things, Ree. But look at what you've been doing. It's awful.'

Reeve was silent.

'I'm sorry,' he added. 'I'm not trying to make you feel bad, but I have no idea what to do.'

'As a starting point,' Patricia said, 'the best thing is to try to identify what's causing Reeve's aggression. Try to be understanding and calm when she's going through one of her outbursts. It's difficult but it may help diffuse the situation. I'll give you some reading material to take away with you, but there are some simple things you can try, which can be quite effective. Even playing calming music in the house can provide a soothing environment.'

Luke nodded, but Reeve could guess what he was thinking. From the way he'd described her outbursts, she doubted any calming techniques were going to stop her when she was in full flight.

'Okay,' Patricia said, 'Luke and I have done a lot of talking about you. Now it's time to give you a chance to speak.'

Reeve sat up a little straighter in her chair. 'About what?'

'About how you're feeling. Luke's made his feelings quite clear today, and I imagine it was hard to hear how worried he is.'

Reeve shut her eyes, willing the tears to remain at bay, but one betrayed her and rolled down her cheek.

'Oh Ree, I'm sorry.'

Reeve shook her head. 'You don't need to be sorry. You need to be able to say how this is making you feel.'

Patricia nodded. 'You both do. And this is a safe place where you can talk without judgement. I want to remind you both that we don't know what's going on with Reeve, so concluding that it's early onset dementia is premature. Regardless, you're dealing with a difficult situation and are in very different roles from each other, having to cope with it. The more open you can both be, the more likely you'll be able to approach it as a team and hopefully have it strengthen your bond rather than destroy it.'

'If that's even possible,' Reeve said. 'On the day he died, Dad said to me that it had been a relief when Mum passed.'

'I'd never feel like that about you,' Luke said.

Reeve shrugged. 'It's how I felt about Mum too. You can't predict how you'll feel until it happens.'

'*If* it happens,' Patricia added. 'Now, Reeve, why don't you try to explain how this is all making you feel and what you need from Luke to help you get through each day. I'm not only talking about your health. I'm talking about dealing with your father's death and the legal proceedings with your work.'

Reeve took a deep breath and started to talk.

* * *

CLIENT MEETING SUMMARY

DATE: August 29
Client: Reeve Elliot & Dr Luke Sheffield
Duration: 90 Min
MMSE: 13

Reeve's husband, Dr Luke Sheffield, is concerned with the nature of Reeve's aggressive outbursts. Provided suggestions for helping to defuse the situation when it occurs.

MMSE and Mini-Cog test repeated. Reeve struggled once again, with the tests scoring alarmingly low. CT and MRI referrals provided.

Blood test results showed no sign of infection, vitamin deficiency, or nutrient deficiency. Kidney, liver, and thyroid all functioning perfectly. The possibility for dementia to be caused by any of these can be disregarded.

At this stage, I believe Reeve to be in the middle stages of early onset dementia with possible rapid decline.

Discussions around enduring power of attorney, medical treatment decision maker, and long-term care options to be raised at next appointment.

A course of action to be determined following CT and MRI results.

* * *

Reeve smoothed down the front of her black Vivienne Westwood Timans dress, a tremble running through her hand. The session with Patricia the previous day already seemed like a distant memory. The whole week had passed in a blur, constantly shrouded in grief. She selected her favourite pair of Manolo Blahnik pumps from her shoe shelf, a small smile playing on her lips as she slipped them on. She could picture her father shaking his head, telling her there was no way she was wearing them to his funeral. Martin had commented on the green shoes every time she'd worn them in his presence, and the comments had not been particularly complimentary.

What, are you dressing like a frog these days?

She'd nearly spat out her coffee. These were fifteen-hundred-dollar shoes. Granted, she'd got them at half price, but they were the only expensive pair she owned. Did he have no taste at all?

They would add a splash of colour to her black ensemble and make him roll his eyes if he had any idea of what was happening.

'Reeve?' Luke's deep voice floated up the stairs. 'Are you ready?'

'Coming.' She collected her black blazer and handbag and walked out onto the landing. Luke was standing at the bottom of the stairs wearing a black suit with a deep turquoise tie.

'I'm not sure if it's appropriate to say this, but you look beautiful.'

'Thank you.' She gave a wry smile. 'Although Dad wouldn't agree if he saw my shoes.'

Luke returned her smile. 'And Nick called. He'll meet us there. Bella's been having a meltdown about what to wear.'

'Why didn't she call me?' Reeve said, ignoring Luke's raised eyebrow. Surely Bella could put their differences aside for a few days and get through the funeral as a family.

Luke held out a hand as she reached the bottom stair and guided her through the internal access to his car.

They arrived at Chalmers's Funeral Home in Toorak twenty minutes before the service was scheduled to begin. They were greeted by Greg Chalmers. Reeve had met with him during the week to finalise all arrangements. She'd sent through a slide show of photos, but other than that, her father had specified every detail, down to the wreath he wanted to be laid on the casket.

'We have a section up the front of the chapel for you and the family,' Greg said as he led them inside.

The first thing to hit Reeve was the sweet smell of carnations. Tears filled her eyes as she saw the overwhelming number of arrangements placed throughout the chapel. They'd been her mother's favourite flower. Even in death, Martin was making a tribute to his late wife. A beautifully carved casket sat at the front of the room, another arrangement of carnations on top of it.

'When we met with Martin a few months ago,' Greg said, 'he insisted he would need the biggest of our rooms and that even that might not be big enough. Hopefully, we'll be able to squeeze every-body in. The room seats three hundred.'

'Wow, three hundred!' Luke said. 'That's a lot of people.'

'He had a lot of business acquaintances,' Reeve said. 'From the list, about twenty per cent were friends and eighty per cent related to his working life. You know what Dad was like. He liked events and parties to be impressive. I guess this is his final chance to remind us of his "the more the merrier" motto.'

And *more* he got. With only a few minutes before the service was to begin, the room was at capacity. The only space was up the front in the section re-served for family. Reeve craned her head, hoping to see Bella walk in any minute. She'd kill Nick if they were late.

'Do we wait for them?' she whispered to Luke.

He glanced at his watch. 'I'll go and tell Greg that we'd like to hold off a few minutes, but with this many people here, I don't think you can leave it too long.'

Reeve nodded. Surely Bella wouldn't miss her grandfather's funeral out of spite for her? She'd find it hard to forgive her if she did.

'He'll wait until five past,' Luke said, returning

and sitting next to Reeve. 'Hopefully she'll be here by then.'

Three minutes past two, Bella walked into the chapel with a red-faced Nick following her. The congregation quietened as they walked to the front of the room and sat down next to Reeve. Reeve reached for Bella's hand, but her daughter shook her away. Reeve closed her eyes, grateful when Luke's arm slipped around her shoulders and gave her a gentle squeeze.

Greg Chalmers moved to the front of the room and welcomed the guests to the celebration of Martin Elliot's life. He smiled as he explained that Martin had planned the service down to the finest of details and that hopefully, the celebration would run seamlessly as Martin had insisted it would if they followed his lead. A ripple of quiet laughter ran through the room. Reeve smiled. Those who knew her father would know what a perfectionist he was.

Following the slide show, a eulogy from Devon, and speeches from Reeve, Bella, and John Steele, a friend Martin had known since he was ten, a final hymn was sung, and the congregation was invited to approach the coffin and say their goodbyes. With many in attendance, it took three songs for this process to be complete.

Greg thanked everyone for coming and reminded

them that drinks and canapés would be served for the next two hours on the lawns that sprawled out behind the funeral home. 'Martin has also booked a room at Flannigan's Hotel for those of you who would like to continue afterwards. He's insisted I advise you that the bar tab has already been paid, and he expects you to drink the venue dry.'

Reeve was pleased that Bella at least had the decency to walk from the chapel with her, Luke, and Nick before the rest of the congregation. As soon as they exited the room, Bella broke away from her and went straight out to the lawned area where drinks and canapés were to be served and sank onto a bench near a feature fountain. Nick placed a hand on Reeve's shoulder as she debated whether to follow her daughter.

'Leave her. She's angry, and she's grieving. Today's about your dad, and you don't want to remember it as the day you had a massive fight with Bella. There are a lot of people who will want to talk to you.'

A lump lodged in Reeve's throat. She forced a smile. He was right, but for her, the only person she wanted to speak to, and wanted approval from, was Bella.

'Reeve!' She turned as John Steele approached her, his arms wide, ready to embrace her.

Nick winked and walked away to find a drink as her father's oldest friend told her how sad he was that Martin was gone. They chatted for a few minutes before they were interrupted by a former work colleague of Martin's.

The two hours sped by as Reeve received condolences and well wishes from person after person. She noticed Bella was still sitting by the fountain but had been joined by a woman about Reeve's age. She didn't recognise her, although from a distance there was something familiar about her.

'Reeve?'

Reeve turned and smiled. 'Carol, thank you for coming.'

Carol James's smile was full of compassion. She placed a hand on Reeve's arm. 'How are you?'

Tears filled Reeve's eyes. Until being asked that question, she thought she was doing quite well.

'It was such a shock to hear of Martin's passing,' Carol said. 'Especially as I saw you both earlier that day. I still feel bad about that. I've been a nurse long enough to know to keep my mouth shut. At the time you said you were aware of your dad's situation, but I got the feeling that perhaps you weren't. I hope your father wasn't upset with me mentioning his appointment.'

'I never got to ask him about it,' Reeve said. 'I'd planned to the next day as I knew he didn't want to talk about it on Mum's anniversary.'

'I should never have said anything.'

Reeve sighed. 'It's not all that relevant now, is it? The cancer wasn't what killed him.'

Carol rubbed Reeve's arm as Devon, beer in hand, approached them. 'It looks like you've got lots of people wanting to pay their respects, so I won't take up any more of your time. But if there's anything I can do for you, let me know.'

Reeve nodded and managed a small smile as Carol left her and Devon to talk.

'Can I get you a drink?'

Reeve shook her head as a photographer moved past them and took a photo. Reeve raised an eyebrow at Devon. 'Photos?'

'Part of Martin's instructions were to capture the moment,' Devon said. 'I guess you'll be given copies down the track.' He gave a wry smile. 'Not sure he thought that one through. Funeral photos aren't something you'll find on most people's walls. Although knowing Martin, he's probably already organised for them to appear in tomorrow's paper. Now, a drink?'

'No, I'm fine.' Her eyes travelled to where Bella

was still in conversation with the woman by the fountain. 'Who's that with Bella?'

Devon's eyes travelled to where Reeve was looking, and he froze.

'Devon?'

'Um, I'm not sure.'

'Really? Because you've gone very pale and are acting quite strangely.'

'Excuse me for a moment, please, Reeve.' He didn't wait for her to respond but walked in the direction of Bella and the woman.

'You okay?' Luke arrived by her side with a wine glass in one hand and sparkling water in the other. He passed the water to Reeve.

'I'm okay, but I'm intrigued as to who that woman with Bella is. Devon practically hyperventilated when I pointed her out.'

Luke's eyes travelled to where Devon was now talking to the woman. 'Someone your dad worked with probably. She's a bit young to be anything else.'

Reeve stared at him. '*Anything else*? Like someone he dated?'

Luke nodded.

'Devon's reaction was strange. The moment he saw her, he began acting weirdly. It's someone he isn't comfortable with, that's for sure.'

'Interesting,' Luke said. 'One way to find out. Go over and introduce yourself.'

Reeve nodded, her attention turning back to the woman. She was familiar, but Reeve couldn't place where she might have seen her before.

* * *

The concern on Devon's face was clear as Reeve approached the small group. A tall, good-looking, blonde-haired man joined them with two glasses of wine, one which he handed to the woman. She said something to him, causing his face to light up with a smile.

She looked up and met Reeve's eyes. Reeve froze, holding her breath as she looked from the woman to Bella and back again. That's where she'd seen her before. Her features were similar to Bella's. Reeve's legs trembled. It had to be a coincidence, surely?

'Reeve,' Devon said, turning to face her. 'This is a friend of your father's.'

A friend. She continued to stare at the woman whose face had paled. Neither of them spoke.

'And I'm Trent,' the man said with a small wave. 'A friend of Jess's.'

'Jessica?' Reeve asked. 'Jessica Williams?'

Jessica nodded.

Reeve continued to stare at the woman sitting next to Bella. The likeness between the woman and her daughter was uncanny. She sucked in a breath, realisation dawning on her. How could he?

'Reeve!' Devon managed to get her attention.

She turned to Devon. 'Did you know? Did you know my father did this?'

Devon's cheeks flamed red as he nodded. He threw back his drink, looked from one woman to the other before shifting his focus to Bella. 'Bell, could you come with me and help an old man find another drink? I wanted to speak to you about a few things in private. Your grandfather had started the process of looking into alternative schools for you, and I feel he'd want me to fill you in with where he got to.'

Bella's eyes lit up, and she leapt to her feet. She turned to Jessica before she followed him. 'Lovely to meet you. Although I'm pretty sure we've met before, but I can't remember where. You're so familiar.'

'It's been lovely meeting you too, Bella.' Jessica smiled and the two women watched as Bella and Devon walked back towards the funeral home. Trent placed a hand on Jessica's shoulder. 'Would you like me to leave the two of you to chat?'

She nodded, and he disappeared towards the food tables.

'You have a lovely daughter,' Jessica said.

Reeve sank down onto the bench next to Jessica. 'Sorry,' she said. 'This is a bit of a shock.' *That's an understatement.*

'No, I'm sorry. I shouldn't have come. It wasn't my intention to meet you today. I'd hoped maybe at some point, but not today. Devon was planning to discuss the situation with you at a more appropriate time.'

The two women sat in silence for a moment.

'You look so much like Bella,' Reeve finally said. 'I'm surprised she didn't notice.'

'She appeared next to me before I had a chance to move away,' Jessica said. 'Again, I wasn't trying to cause a scene today. I wanted to pay my respects. Trent and I should have left after the service. But there was a part of me that wanted to observe Martin's family.' She gave a nervous laugh. 'Sorry, that probably sounds creepy.'

Reeve didn't respond, her eyes fixed firmly on her shoes.

'Are you okay?' Jessica's voice was gentle.

'Sorry, this is probably not the welcome to the family you were hoping for. I think I'm in shock. How could Dad have another child and keep it secret? Is it only you or are there others? Did he have a second family?'

'Only me from what I know. We met for the first time the Sunday before he died.'

Reeve's head jerked up. 'Hold on. You only met him recently? Why?'

'My mother wasn't honest about who my father was. For many years I was led to believe he was dead. I was contacted by a private investigator a few weeks back, saying Martin was trying to reach out. That he wanted to meet me.'

'So, he'd only just found out about you too. That makes it slightly better, I guess.'

'I'm not...' Jess started but then stopped. 'It's probably not the time or place to discuss the details of what happened. Perhaps we could catch up for coffee one day soon, and I can fill you in?'

Reeve hesitated.

'It's fine if you don't want to,' Jessica added. 'Honestly, I know this is a huge shock. It was for me too.'

Reeve stared at the woman next to her. Her sister. *She had a sister.* What type of upbringing had she had? Had she enjoyed the same privileges as Reeve? Had her mother given her a happy childhood? Was there a stepfather on the scene? She gave herself a mental shake and turned her focus back to Jessica. 'Sorry, I have a million questions to ask you. Yes, I'd love to catch up for coffee or lunch or something. I've already got your number on Dad's phone. I'll message you to organise a time.'

There was a surreal feel to the entire afternoon. She'd buried her father and now was meeting a sister she hadn't known existed.

The two women said an awkward goodbye as Jessica stood, suggesting it was time she left. Reeve remained seated, watching as Jessica walked over to the man she'd come with, linked an arm through his, and walked towards the exit.

'You okay, chick?' Sloane sank onto the bench and draped an arm over her shoulder. 'You're very pale.'

'I'm good,' Reeve said, moving her focus from Jessica to Sloane. She wasn't ready to talk to Sloane about Jessica. She needed to process it first. She managed a smile for her friend. 'Thanks for coming today. I appreciate it.'

Sloane hugged her. 'Wouldn't have missed it. But I do need to go. Dad's struggling to try to move furniture and has rung about twelve times since I got here. Hope you don't mind?'

'Of course not,' Reeve said. 'Give him my love and a big hug while you can.'

'Will do. I'll call you over the weekend, okay?'

Reeve nodded and watched as her friend strode across the lawns to the exit. She'd give anything to be in Sloane's shoes now; off to visit her dad.

* * *

The weekend following her father's funeral found Reeve going through the motions of sitting at the kitchen counter, drinking coffee, with her thoughts drifting to her father and Jessica. Coming to terms with the death of her father was hard enough but to find out he'd hidden that he had another daughter was devastating. They'd always been close, and now she was driving herself crazy, wondering what else he'd hidden from her. Were more children going to appear out of the woodwork?

It crossed her mind that Jessica Williams could be a fraud. Her father had never mentioned her, and then she turned up at the funeral of a well-known millionaire. Was she a hustler, hoping to get her hands on his fortune? She dismissed the idea almost as quickly as she had it. She looked so much like Bella, and Devon knew who she was.

Luke was as shocked as she was when she explained who Jessica was. He'd had the same thought and voiced it in the car on the way home from the funeral.

'As awful as this sounds, if she's here to claim from Martin's estate, you'll probably need to ask her for a paternity test.'

'It crossed my mind, but then she looks so much like Bella I'm not sure it would be necessary. Also, we don't know if that's her intention. She only met Dad a week before he died. From what I understand, her mother led her to believe her father was dead. It was Dad who went in search of her, not the other way around.'

'Perhaps,' Luke had replied. 'But you need to remember there's likely to be a lot of money at stake. Looking like Bella isn't enough to confirm paternity. If Martin has included her in his will, then that's different, but if she's not and she contests it, you'll need to be careful.'

'I'm sure Devon would have everything like that covered if it was required.'

Now, as she sat in her favourite spot at the kitchen counter, she could hear Luke speaking to someone at the front door. She'd been grateful when he'd said he'd go and check who'd knocked, as she

was dreading answering the door and finding the police with bad news in relation to her father's death.

'Ree, can you come here? Now.'

The tension in Luke's voice caused a ripple of
fear to pass through Reeve. She slipped off the stool
and reluctantly made her way to the front door. Confusion replaced her fear as she saw Michelle, the
sports teacher from school, standing with Luke, her
arms crossed and her eyes flashing with anger.
'Michelle?'

'What the hell, Reeve?'

'Whoa,' Luke said, 'there's no need for that. I just
explained to you that Reeve is struggling and is unlikely to have any recollection of sending you a
message.'

'She didn't send it to me,' Michelle said, 'she sent
it to Libby. My insecure and anxious partner. The
woman I love who packed a bag and moved back to
her parents' house after reading Reeve's message.'

'I'm so sorry.' Reeve forced the words from her
lips. 'I don't know what I sent her, but I promise, it
wasn't me. Well, if it was me, it was the sick version
of me.'

'I'll say you're sick. If you don't remember what
the message said, here's a reminder.' Michelle thrust
her phone at Reeve.

Reeve's hand flew to her mouth as she digested the vicious words.

Karma's a bitch. So is your girlfriend. Ask her who she was cheating with last night. You know her. In fact, you consider her one of your best friends. That's right, Michelle and Janey Rutch have a thing going.

It had come from her email address.

Reeve squeezed her eyes shut. When was this going to stop, and why would she try to cause problems for Michelle and Libby? For a start, she hardly knew Libby. She opened her eyes as this thought took over. 'Hold on, how would I have Libby's email address? I've only met her once or twice and certainly don't have any of her contact details.'

'You're saying you didn't send this?' Michelle waved the phone towards Reeve.

'I hope I didn't send it,' Reeve said. 'I can't imagine any motivation I'd have to send it either. I have nothing against you or Libby.'

'I have no idea what your motivation was, Reeve, but you and Sloane are the only people I confided in about my crush on Janey. A crush I never intended acting on and would not have jeopardised my relationship for. But you've done that for me. And her email is easy enough to find on her photography website, as are the rest of her contact details.'

'Can we speak to Janey?' Luke asked. 'Explain the situation? Reeve's going through a difficult time and we're waiting for tests to be conducted to give us some answers. I can assure you, this wasn't done maliciously or even consciously.'

Reeve wrung her hands together. 'I'm so sorry, Michelle. I don't know what to say. If I could take this back, I would.'

Michelle looked from Reeve to Luke and back to Reeve again. 'You're really sick?'

Reeve nodded. 'I think so. My mum had early onset dementia and all the signs are pointing to it being hereditary.' Tears welled in her eyes as she made this admission.

Michelle sighed. 'I'm sorry, Reeve. Really, I am. I wouldn't wish that on anyone.'

'Look,' Luke said, 'why don't I come with you and talk to Libby. Explain the situation and hopefully make things right between the two of you.'

Michelle nodded. 'Thanks, I think I'll need you to do that.'

'Did you want me to come?' Reeve's gut churned

at the thought of apologising to Libby. The situation was mortifying.

'No, you've done enough. I think she'll believe Luke.'

It was close to two hours before Luke returned, his exhaustion worn clearly on his face.

Reeve leapt to her feet the moment she heard the key in the door. 'How did you go?'

'It's all sorted out,' Luke said, guiding her into the lounge room and sitting down on the couch. 'Libby took a little convincing, but it appears she believed me. I have a feeling she had good reason to be jealous though. There was a bit of an argument where Libby alluded to Michelle cheating in the past.'

Reeve dropped her head into her hands. 'This is a nightmare. I think I need all access to technology removed. I can't keep sending random messages to people, destroying their lives.'

Luke moved closer to her, putting an arm around her shoulders. 'Ree, you heard what Patricia said on Thursday. We need to get those tests done. It might be as simple as getting you some medications. I know you're humiliated.' He took a deep breath. 'It's an illness, and we need to get on top of it. Patricia did say that stressful situations could cause someone with dementia to act out in ways they never dreamed possible. I honestly can't imagine anything more stressful than what you've been through this week with your dad and everything else. Something as simple as a mild sedative might make a difference.'

It was true. She remembered her mother's condition deteriorating in times of stress. Before she'd been taken into full-time care, her beloved Chinese crested poodle died. She'd become so aggressive that neither Martin nor Reeve could restrain her when she lashed out.

'Let's try and keep your stress levels as low as possible between now and the tests, okay? Hopefully, there won't be any surprises tomorrow morning when we meet with Devon.'

'Surprises? Like what?'

'Like other sisters suddenly appearing out of the woodwork,' Luke said. 'Of course you'd be stressed when there's an inheritance on the line.'

Reeve shook her head. 'If she's Martin's daughter, she's entitled to as much as I am. That's not the part of the situation that's stressing me. It's knowing he had another daughter to start with.'

* * *

The next morning Reeve found herself squeezing her eyes shut as Devon explained the details of the will. It wasn't the inclusion of Jessica Williams. It was the exclusion of Luke. It was unthinkable. How could he do this? And why? Luke had never been anything but respectful and friendly to her father, and in general, they'd enjoyed each other's company. A gentle squeeze of her hand forced her to open her eyes and turn to her husband.

'I'm sorry,' she said, speaking over Devon. 'I had no idea he'd do something like this.'

Luke gave a wry smile. 'It's not a problem, Ree. I'd probably have done the same myself if it was my daughter marrying someone she hadn't known for very long. I don't think it was personal. It just makes good business sense.' He stood. 'Now, in addition to ensuring I can't get my hands on Martin's estate, his instructions state that these meetings need to be held in private. I'll wait for you in the car, okay?'

Reeve's eyes swam with tears. She could only nod as Luke made his exit.

Devon handed her a tissue, and she dabbed her eyes.

'Sorry.'

'No need to apologise. I did warn Martin that this could create some issues when he died, but he was adamant that he didn't want Luke having immediate access to his fortune. As you know, a large percentage of Martin's estate is protected by the Elliot Family Trust. I have been the Trustee for the trust for twenty-five years, and Martin's wishes are that his role of Appointer of the trust is now moved to you. He has clear instructions on how he wants the trust to run.'

Reeve nodded. Her father had made it clear many years ago that he wanted the family trust to remain intact after his death and hoped Reeve, as the new Appointer, would follow his wishes.

'As Appointer, you do have the power to remove me as Trustee if you wish to,' Devon said. 'That would give you the freedom to do what you want with the assets depending on who you allocate the role to.'

Reeve shook her head. 'No. You've managed it successfully for twenty-five years. Dad trusted you for a reason.'

Devon nodded. 'Okay. Now, in addition to the assets of the trust, there is money to be distributed. Martin sold off a few assets when he was first diagnosed with cancer. He wanted to make sure that the cash could be distributed without needing to sell anything else. You are one of the beneficiaries listed to inherit. As it stands, prior to being able to inherit the percentage of the estate Martin has left you, you will need to rewrite your will to ensure this money is safeguarded from Luke if you should divorce within the next ten years or if something should happen to you. Martin has specific details of how he'd like the money distributed following your death if that was to happen. You will also need to name a new Appointer for the Elliot Family Trust. This cannot be Luke. If you divorce, the term becomes irrelevant, and you can allocate the monies in your will as you like. Except for gifting money to Luke.'

'But we can access the money now and do anything we want with it?'

'You can.'

Reeve shook her head. 'It doesn't make much sense. Luke can use and spend it how he likes in that case.'

'As long as you remain together, he can. But Reeve, I think the whole point of the will is Martin making it clear that he wants to see your marriage is solid before he includes Luke. Again, I'll reiterate that it wasn't personal, he just wants to ensure that the money is to help you and Bella moving forward, and it isn't for Luke to benefit from. Sure, he'll benefit if you buy a nicer house or indulge in holidays or luxuries, but he can't walk away with half of Martin's fortune if the marriage fails. That was Martin's main concern. He's worked hard his entire life to build up the assets he has, and he wants his family to benefit from that, not an outsider.' He held his hands up before Reeve objected. 'His words, not mine.'

Reeve sighed. 'Well, I hate to disappoint him, but the marriage isn't going to fail.' She swallowed. Unless she pushed Luke away with her medical issues, which she was beginning to think was highly probable.

Devon smiled. 'Again, it's not what he was suggesting, Reeve. He was just being overly cautious.' He paused, tapping his fingers on the desk. 'I probably shouldn't share this information, as it was Martin's confidential instructions, but I feel under the circumstances it would be beneficial.'

Reeve frowned. 'There's more?'

'Not more, it's just that I think you should know that Martin had the same stipulation in his will when you married Nick.'

'What?'

Devon nodded. 'The will was changed when Bella turned five. You and Nick had been married for seven years and Martin decided ten years wasn't necessary. He thought your marriage would last.'

'But it didn't.'

'No, but as Martin was still alive, your relationship with Nick wasn't relevant to his estate.'

They sat in silence for a few moments as Reeve digested this information. 'Thank you,' she said at last. 'It makes a big difference to know that Dad was looking out for me and it isn't personal towards Luke.'

Devon smiled. 'Now, there was something else I wanted to discuss with you, and that's the remainder of the estate. As you may have noticed, I said the *percentage* of the estate you've been left. Your father has left money to a selection of other people. He's asked me to explain who and why, so you're not left wondering.'

Reeve sat forward on her chair. She considered her father's words of only a few weeks earlier that he was leaving money to a few people who wouldn't expect it. That it was 'without explanation, so hopefully, they'll accept the money as a goodwill gesture'.

'I'm not sure if you'll recognise any of these names,' he said. 'There's a sum left to a Charles Manning, a sum to the family of Wesley Parsons, and an additional sum left to an Eleanor Budd.'

Reeve shook her head. 'Never heard of them. But why has he left the money to the family of the second one? Why not to him?'

'I believe he took his life a few years ago. Your father withdrew funds from a large investment, and the company went under. From memory, they were a construction company, and Martin was provided with information that their dealings weren't always legal. He didn't want his name associated with them from that point forward. Unfortunately, the ramifications for the Parsons family were too much for Wesley Parsons to endure. Martin felt incredibly guilty about that.'

'But he didn't do anything wrong if they were operating illegally.'

'No, he didn't, but he was upset that his actions had such an impact on Wesley's family. He wanted to gift them money when it happened, but I had to advise him not to. The investigation into his death uncovered the illegal dealings they'd been part of, and any connection to Martin could have been devastating for his business.'

'At least they'll get something now. Although won't it be an admission of guilt, which will have them come after more?'

'No. He's put a note for each of the three.' Devon flipped open his file. 'For the Parsons family, he's put: *To the family of a man I admired.* Not true, but he hoped it would prevent any questions.'

'I'm glad he's done something for them,' Reeve said.

'He's also left money to Nick,' Devon said.

Reeve nodded. 'We knew he was going to do that. Remember the dinner when he sat us all down and explained why we were not to contest his will?'

Devon smiled at the memory. 'Yes, it was certainly a little unorthodox.'

'You know, I only found out this week that Dad was helping Nick out with the school fees. I wish they'd told me.'

'Your dad was just trying to make things a bit easier on you both,' Devon said. 'It would have been a struggle for the two of you to cover your expenses with the school fees on top. I remember Martin saying how many of his friends had divorced in their forties over money issues. He wanted to make sure money wasn't something that caused stress for you and Nick when it didn't need to.' He smiled. 'He referred to it as his "small victory". That he was able to help you without you knowing. And Nick's a proud man, Reeve, like most men are. He wouldn't have wanted you to know he couldn't afford the fees, and he certainly wouldn't want Luke or Bella knowing.'

'Then why did he say that he was happy for Dad

to pay the fees when Bella wanted to change schools if Dad was paying them anyway?'

'From what Martin told me, Nick thought it was time that you saw some of the good that your dad was doing for you. He felt guilty that he was getting the credit for the fees when Martin was paying them.'

'Nick said that?'

'A version of that, I believe.'

Reeve's heart swelled with affection for her ex-husband. In that moment she realised she could never admit to Nick that she knew about the school fees.

'Now,' Devon continued, 'Martin's also distributed ten per cent of his estate amongst a range of charities, and then there's Jessica Williams.'

Reeve's insides contracted at Jessica's name. She'd promised to ring her to organise a coffee catch-up but hadn't yet. Part of her was full of questions, wanting to piece together her father's life, but another part wanted to bury her head in the sand and know nothing about it.

'He's left her a substantial sum. Not as much as you, but still a lot, and all cash. She's not listed as a beneficiary of the family trust and his instructions are very clear to me as the trustee that she is not to be made a beneficiary. The family trust is to protect the assets for you and Bella.' He passed the document across the desk to Reeve.

Her eyes scanned it, and she let out a low whistle when she saw how many millions her father had left Jessica. 'That's a lot.'

'It is, and you could certainly contest it if you wanted to. I should warn you that as a biological daughter who has been specified in the will, you might not be successful.'

'Did he provide financially for her when she was a child?'

Devon nodded. 'He did. He was very generous.' He cleared his throat. 'Which brings us to another issue. Before his death, Martin met with Jessica, as I believe you know, for the first time. He learned at that meeting that the monies he'd provided for her over the course of eighteen years had never reached her. It appears her uncle intercepted the money.'

'What, stole it?'

Devon nodded. 'Martin spoke to me about possible legal proceedings to reclaim the funds but wanted Jessica's input on this first. I believe he'd planned to speak to her about it but didn't get a chance. The uncle disappeared years ago. I will speak to Jessica about it when I meet with her later today,'

Devon said. 'Explain Martin's wishes and see what she wants to do.'

'You're meeting with her today?'

Devon nodded. 'And I'll be speaking with the other beneficiaries later this week. None of the funds will be available for some time, but as they are mentioned in the will, they are required to be notified.'

Reeve thought back to her conversation about paternity. 'Should we ask her to get a test? What if she's not Jessica Williams or she's not his biological child?'

'She has to provide identification as to who she is,' Devon said. 'Assuming her identification checks out, we could still request a paternity test, but due to the fact that she's named in the will it isn't a requirement.'

'And she looks like Bella,' Reeve said. 'That would be too big a coincidence if they weren't actually related.'

'We can still ask her if it would make you feel more comfortable.'

'I'll think about it,' Reeve said, exhaustion suddenly enveloping her. 'What do I have to do now with regards to Dad's estate or anything else?'

'Nothing for the moment. I'll handle the paperwork and start getting everything ready for probate.

The police case will need to be finalised before anything can be released. None of this will happen quickly. I wanted you to be aware of Martin's wishes and how he'd left everything.'

Reeve stood. 'Thanks, I appreciate it.'

'Reeve,' Devon added. 'The school will be in touch with me to organise a meeting for later in the week. Do you have a preferred day?'

'Any day's good.' As the words came out of her mouth, even Reeve could hear how hollow they sounded. Her gut feeling was that it would be the last time she set foot inside that, or any other, school.

* * *

Reeve glanced sideways at her husband. Luke hadn't said a word since they'd left Devon's office. His eyes were fixed on the road, and his foot was planted heavily on the accelerator.

'That was horrible. Are you okay?'

Luke forced a smile and glanced across at Reeve. 'I've been better. Your dad's decision has left me feeling a bit flat, that's all. As I said, it made good business sense, but I'd hate to think he didn't trust me.'

'Devon made it clear to me that it wasn't personal.

That whoever I was with would have faced the same restrictions. Dad just wanted to make sure the money was there for Bell and me. He's happy with us spending whatever we want while we're together, and if we make it ten years, then what's mine is yours.'

'*If?*' Luke said, his lips curling into a smile. 'I don't think it's a case of *if*, it's a case of when. As for the will, it's not a big deal. It's probably better it was me you're married to than Nick. Martin excluding him in the will would have been unforgivable. I'm sure Nick would have taken it that he wasn't good enough.'

'He did exclude Nick,' Reeve said. 'Devon explained that Dad's will excluded Nick for the first seven years of our marriage. He waited until Bella was five before removing the clauses that excluded him.'

'That makes me feel a lot better. It was a business decision, not a personal one.'

Reeve fell silent.

'You okay?' Luke asked.

Reeve took a deep breath. Luke would find out at some stage, so she might as well tell him now. 'He was excluded initially, but even after we split up, Dad kept him in the will. He's been left money.'

'What? How much?'

'Three million. He wanted to make sure Nick had

enough money to live comfortably moving forward, as how Nick lives also impacts Bella.'

Luke gave out a low whistle. 'Does Nick know?'

'I don't think Devon's spoken to him officially since Dad died, but Nick's known since Dad's diagnosis that he was a beneficiary. Dad catered a dinner for a small group when he thought he only had a few months to live to explain how he'd left his will. He didn't go into exact specifics, but he wanted those who were beneficiaries to be very clear that he'd left his will exactly how he wanted it and he'd be very upset if anyone contested it. He spoke privately with me and Nick and explained that he considered Nick family and therefore had left him a reasonable amount.'

'Your ex cheats on you and that's your dad's reaction? That's messed up if you ask me.'

Reeve sighed. 'I know, but I also understood. Dad wanted to make sure that Bella had a comfortable existence. He knew how reluctant I was to spend his money so hoped that Nick would at least give Bella the things he would have liked to. A car for her eighteenth, university paid for. That kind of thing.'

'Doesn't it concern you that Nick knew he was going to inherit and then your father dies in a suspicious house fire? You don't think the two things are connected?'

Reeve stared at Luke and then started to laugh. 'No, I don't. Nick knows he could have gone to Dad for money at any time. He didn't need to kill him to get to it.'

'Ree, your dad's been paying Bella's school fees for years because he knows Nick's too proud to admit to you that he can't afford it. You really think he'd be able to swallow his pride and ask Martin for money for other things? You said he'd lost forty grand recently in a development. He can't afford to contribute to Bella's new computer or phone or anything else from the sound of it. This seems a bit too good to be true.'

'Nick wouldn't hurt Dad. Not for money and not for anything. He lost his savings, but he's still earning money and electricians make good money. He would have got back on his feet.' And from the conversation with her father about Nick, it sounded like her ex had gone to Martin for help. He'd hardly do that and then turn around and kill him. It would be funny if it wasn't so ridiculous.

Luke shook his head. 'As long as the police are covering all their bases, that's all I'm saying.'

Reeve ignored his comment. Nick may have cheated during their marriage, but he would never hurt her father, or anyone else for that matter. 'You know, one thing Dad's death has made me realise is why he still respected Nick, even after Nick cheated. It never made sense to me until now. He could hardly condemn something he'd done himself. Now I think back, I can see why he was okay with what Nick did. I doubt Mum knew about his affair, and from what I've worked out, he had nothing to do with Jessica or her mother.' Anger boiled up in her. 'If he wasn't already dead, I'd kill him.'

Luke frowned. 'You don't mean that. He made some mistakes, as most people do. But he also did a lot of good, and you had a great relationship with him. That's what's important now, Ree. Your memories of what you and your dad shared. Not wills or money or anything else.'

Reeve took a deep breath. Luke was generous with his words, and he was right. Her love for her father was what she needed to focus on. 'I won't expect you to stay if it does turn out to be dementia.' The words slipped out before she could stop them. She'd wanted to say it to Luke for some time now but hadn't had the courage. Could she survive without him? More to the point, would she want to?

'I have no intention of leaving, Ree. You're my life. In sickness and in health. Remember?'

Reeve wiped at her eyes, annoyed at how easily she welled up these days. She couldn't imagine how she'd be handling all of this if she didn't have Luke by her side. She could only hope she could get a diagnosis and some help before she destroyed their relationship too.

17

Soft jazz tones muffled the sounds of murmured conversation and laughter in the busy Italian restaurant. Jess's stomach grumbled as wafts of garlic drifted from the kitchen. Toni's was her favourite restaurant in St Kilda and her choice for her dinner with Trent.

'You know tonight was supposed to be a thank-you dinner for me,' Trent said, his eyes twinkling. 'Not a celebration of your brilliance.'

Jess laughed and held up her champagne flute in a toast. 'It can be both. It's not my fault they made the official announcement to the media about me becoming the new CEO on the same day I was taking you to dinner.'

Trent clinked glasses with Jess. 'Congrats, you deserve the job. I'm proud of you.'

Heat flooded Jess's cheeks. 'And I'm proud of your success too. Harry, one of the guys I work with, forwarded me a review last night of *Codename Jackal*. Are you aware it's sitting on the *New York Times* bestseller list?'

Trent shrugged. 'Nah, I don't follow reviews or lists. My agent sends me emails with all that information, and I file them away. Maybe one day when I can't think up any more stories, I'll read them and bask in my former glory.'

Jess laughed. 'I have a feeling you'll be coming up with stories for many more years.'

'Speaking of thinking up stories, I have a real-life one unfolding in front of me. What with you and the new sister, the murdered father, the inheritance, and everything else. It would make a great movie.'

Jess frowned. 'I'm not sure anyone's saying he was murdered.'

'Sorry. I read something in the paper this morning that suggested possible foul play. I assume the police investigation hasn't been completed yet.'

'No, not yet. I met with Martin's lawyer today. You'd better take another sip of your drink before I tell you what he left me in his will.'

Jess had to do her best not to laugh at Trent's reaction to her news.

'He left you how much?' Trent's eyes were so wide Jess half expected they might burst from his head.

'Sixteen million.'

Trent burst out laughing. 'Sorry,' he said, holding his side, 'but you said that so calmly. Like he'd left you sixteen dollars, not sixteen million!'

Jess nodded. It was surreal. Her father, who she had known for less than one hour, had left her sixteen million dollars.

'If he left you sixteen million, what was his estate worth?'

'I didn't ask. Devon, the lawyer, told me that it wasn't the same percentage share as Reeve was getting, and I had every right to contest the will if I chose to. He also mentioned that a lot of Martin's assets are tied up in a family trust. I'm not a beneficiary but in theory could contest it. He was surprisingly upfront about that.'

'More fees for him, I guess.'

'No, I don't think so. He wanted me to know my rights. I'm not sure I'll accept the money Martin left me, and I certainly won't be contesting the rest of the estate. It's none of my business how he left it or what the family trust is worth.'

'What do you mean you won't be accepting the money?'

'I don't know. It feels wrong. Who knows if he's even my father? I wondered about that on the way there today. I asked Devon if he thought Reeve would agree to a DNA test. I think it would be good for both of us to know that we are related. He said he'd check with her. I'd kind of hoped she might have contacted me since the funeral to meet up. I've got her number, Devon gave it to me today, but I think I should wait to hear from her. It was a big shock, and maybe she changed her mind.' Jess wouldn't blame her if she had. If the situation was reversed, she wasn't sure how she'd feel about her father having a child that had been kept a secret. It was a lot to process.

Trent was shaking his head.

'What?'

'I'm guessing you are the only person in the world who, after they've been told they are inheriting millions of dollars, demands a DNA test to make sure they're eligible to receive the money.'

'It would make me more comfortable, that's all.' Her phone rang as she put her cutlery down and was about to reach for her wine glass. 'Sorry.' She took it from her bag, ready to silence it when she saw the caller display.

'It's her,' she whispered, pointing at the name *Martin Elliot* on the screen. She was calling from her father's phone.

'She can't hear you until you answer it.' He sipped his champagne, a smirk on his lips.

Jess's heart raced as she answered the call. 'Reeve?'

'Hi, Jessica.' Reeve sounded as nervous as she felt.

'It's Jess, actually. Jessica's a bit formal. I've been thinking of you, and once again, I'm sorry for turning up at the funeral and alarming you as I did. I hope you're okay?'

There was a brief silence at the end of the phone before Reeve cleared her throat. 'I am, thank you. And you don't need to apologise. I had a phone call from Devon. He mentioned you wanted to do a DNA test.'

Jess's face heated. She was glad Reeve couldn't see how embarrassed she was. 'I'm sorry. It probably sounds awful, me suggesting that Martin might have his facts wrong. He probably doesn't, but I did want to make sure. I hope you're not offended?'

Reeve let out a delighted laugh. 'I'm not offended. If anything, it most likely confirms that you are Martin's daughter. It's the type of thing he'd do. He certainly wouldn't accept something like an inheritance without knowing for sure he was entitled to it.'

'I'm not sure I'm entitled to anything,' Jess said. 'I didn't know him, and it seems very strange that he'd include me in the will. Regardless of the DNA results, I'm not sure if I can accept it.'

'Jess, could we meet up? There are a lot of things I'd like to learn about you, and I'm sure you have questions about Dad, and maybe me too.'

'I'd love to. I finish early on Friday afternoon. We could meet for a drink and dinner, perhaps?'

'That would be great.'

They finished the call, agreeing to meet at XO in South Yarra on Friday night.

Trent raised an eyebrow as Jess slipped the phone into her bag. 'How's the sister?'

'She sounded pretty pleased to speak to me,' Jess said, gulping her wine. Hearing Reeve laugh had been lovely. She couldn't help but smile. 'This is such a strange situation. I don't know what to think.'

'Don't think at all,' Trent said. 'Approach it with an open mind and see what happens. From what I can see, you have nothing at all to lose but plenty to gain.'

'Like sixteen million dollars.'

'Well, yes.' He grinned. 'That's certainly a bonus.

But I was referring to the one thing you haven't had for a lot of years, and that's family. Assuming the DNA test confirms it to be the case.'

A nervous flutter in her stomach surprised Jess. When she'd left Devon's office earlier that afternoon, part of her had hoped that a DNA test would prove that she wasn't related to Martin Elliot. But now, she realised she'd be disappointed if that was the case and she didn't have a sister after all.

18

On Wednesday morning, Luke insisted that Reeve remain in bed as he packed a bag for a conference in Sydney. 'I'll get an Uber to the airport, and you can pick me up on Saturday. Yesterday really took it out of you, Ree. I'd rather you rest up and be good for the weekend when I'm back.'

She'd been tempted to argue and insist she was fine to drive him but was hit with overwhelming tiredness just thinking about tackling the Tullamarine Freeway. 'Okay, thank you. I'll definitely pick you up on Saturday.' While the MRI hadn't been physically taxing, the stress of what it might reveal had prevented her from being able to sleep. Luke had tossed and turned a good part of the night too, so she knew it wasn't only her. They would get the results when they saw Patricia the following week.

After Luke left, she decided to get up, shower, and think about how she was going to fill in the day. Her thoughts reverted to her father as she opened the shower door and turned on the taps. She wished he was here to explain the Jess situation to her. She wanted to know what happened and whether her mother had had any idea of Jess's existence. She had a lot of questions and doubted Jess would be able to answer them.

Half an hour later, Reeve inhaled the smell of freshly ground coffee and sank onto a stool at the kitchen counter. She sipped her coffee slowly, her thoughts still with her father.

She was jolted from her thoughts as a key turned in the front door, and the door banged open. Had Luke forgotten something? She hurried from the kitchen into the hallway and stopped. Bella glared at her.

'I need to get some clothes.'

'Shouldn't you be at school?'

'I told you I wasn't going back there. I'm a joke thanks to you.'

'You can't drop out. Legally you can't leave school

in Victoria until you're seventeen. That's still two years away.'

'Devon's speaking with St Margot's for me this week, and if I can't start there, then I'll start at the high school next week. Dad said he'd go with me and fill out all the enrolment stuff.'

'And this is the first I hear about it?'

Bella started walking up the stairs. 'Dad said you don't need this too.'

Reeve sighed as her daughter disappeared out of sight. She was right. She didn't need this. Did it matter what school Bella went to if she was happy and learning? She sat down on the bottom stair, listening as the wardrobe and drawers in Bella's room were opened and shut. She wondered if she would leave anything behind.

Ten minutes later, she reappeared, dragging a large suitcase behind her. Reeve stood. 'Do you need a hand?'

'No, I'm good.' Bella managed to get the bag down the stairs on her own.

'Look, you're right. I do have a lot on my plate, but I love you and want to be there for you. I'm sorry, Bell, really, I am. If I did any of the things I've been accused of, I'd be absolutely devastated. You know that.'

'If? There's no question of *if.* I don't know what you've said to others, but I know what you've called me.'

'And I'm so sorry. I've been acting out of character with no memory of anything, and I'm worried.'

Bella stared at her, a flash of fear crossing her features. 'Do you think you've got what Nana had?'

Reeve blinked back tears. The anger had left her daughter and had been replaced with genuine fear and concern. 'I hope not, hon. I'm seeing a psychiatrist and will get the results for some brain scans and imaging next week. That will give us a bit of an idea if it's likely. Unfortunately, it would explain a lot of what's been happening. I hope it isn't the case, but if it is, then we have an explanation at least for what's been going on.' As she watched her daughter, Nick's words came back to her: *a lot of your problems, aside from Martin's death, are in areas of your life that Bella's involved in.* 'I need to ask you something.'

Bella nodded.

'I know you hate me working at the school and always have. I also know that you've been spending time with Mason Walker.'

Bella's forehead creased. 'So?'

'I'm wondering if perhaps Mason suggested he help you set me up.'

'Set you up?'

'Yes. Have Oscar agree to help you get rid of me. Send the email to Dale Cross's family. I would hate to think you would do something like that, but I would also understand. It's been hard on you having me at the school. I know that.'

Reeve found herself holding her breath as Bella stared at her. She'd be devastated on one hand if Bella was responsible for all of this but relieved on another. At least she'd know she wasn't going nuts.

Bella spoke through gritted teeth. 'You believe I hate you to the point that I'd try to get you fired?'

'I didn't say you hated me. I know you hate having me at the school.'

'And my only option would be to accuse you of horrendous things which make me look like a loser? Do you honestly believe I'd do something like that?'

Reeve shook her head, realising that of course Bella wouldn't. 'No, and I'm sorry I asked.' She could kick herself that she hadn't ignored Nick's words. She knew their daughter and she should have known better than to even suggest it.

'Even if I did set you up, which I didn't, how do you explain all the other things you've done? Calling me terrible names and saying you didn't? The things you've said to Luke and his friends? Smashing the wine bottles all over the kitchen?'

Reeve frowned. 'How did you know about that?'

'I overheard Luke telling Dad. He dropped in to see him. He asked Dad whether you'd done anything extreme when they were married. He's worried about you.'

Reeve swallowed. Luke had no right to speak to Nick about what she'd done. Although she could understand why if he was trying to find out how far her problems went back. 'I'm sorry. I guess part of me was hoping you might have done something, and I wasn't losing the plot.' She forced a smile. 'I really am sorry.'

Bella's face was now red with anger. 'Is this going to be another thing you forget you did? That you accused me of doing something I'd never do? Do you think I'm like that?'

Reeve opened her mouth to say no and closed it again. No. Maybe. Who knew? 'Sorry, Bell. That's about all I can say. I understand you don't want anything to do with me, but I hope that'll change over time. I'll support whatever decision you make regarding school. I'll give Devon a call and ask him if he's been able to have success with St Margot's, okay?'

Bella closed her eyes. Reeve hoped she was calming down and would forgive her, but when she opened them, they were raging with anger. 'Stay out of my life. I'll call Devon. I'm fifteen, and I can look after myself. If I need help, I've got Dad. You figure out what's going on with you. If it is what Nana had, then get some treatment or something.' She opened the front door, dragging the suitcase behind her.

Reeve walked to the door, realising a car was waiting in the driveway. Mason Walker sat in the driver's seat. His menacing stare sent a shiver down her spine. Regardless of anything that was happening, the one thing she was certain of was that boy was bad news.

* * *

The next morning, Reeve dragged herself to standing, surprised she'd slept deeply. She'd expected to toss and turn after the confrontation with Bella and the looming meeting with the school. She'd ended up cleaning most of the afternoon to distract herself, forced some dinner down and then—

She stopped halfway to the ensuite. And then what? She vaguely remembered turning on the television after dinner and making her usual night-time pot of chamomile tea, but that was where her memory ended. She must have fallen asleep on the couch and dragged herself up to bed when she woke. That wasn't unusual, although she usually did recall doing it.

A feeling of unease settled over her. If she didn't remember going to bed, had she done anything else she was going to regret? She returned to the bed and picked up her phone from the nightstand. She hesitated before opening her text messages, praying she hadn't sent anything inappropriate to anyone. The last message was to Luke, replying to his message from earlier when he'd landed in Sydney. It said she loved him and to have a good trip. Nothing else. She opened the email client on her phone and took a deep breath as she opened the sent items box. *Nothing!* She threw the phone down on the bed, a mild feeling of elation settling over her.

She returned to the ensuite, aware that while she was relieved, she was also exhausted, headachy, and nauseous. She hoped it was nerves and she wasn't coming down with something.

Twenty minutes later, showered and dressed, she made her way downstairs to the kitchen. She still had two hours before she was meeting Devon at a cafe near the school to discuss the meeting. Plenty of time for coffee and some toast to calm her stomach. She stepped into the kitchen and froze.

A bottle of red wine was open on the kitchen counter, three-quarters drunk. A glass lay on its side next to the bottle, wine spilling out onto the counter. A box of Reeve's favourite chocolates was next to the bottle, with half of the contents missing. Her hand flew to her mouth. No. She couldn't be responsible for this, could she?

She sank onto a stool at the counter, her head dropping into her hands. The way she felt this morning, headachy and nauseous, could be a result of this indulgence. But she had no recollection of even thinking about drinking or eating chocolate. She clearly remembered making a spinach and mushroom omelette and eating that with a small salad and a glass of the special guava juice she'd bought to enjoy instead of her usual glass of wine in the evening. She ate that and then sat on the couch and watched television. Then it was all blank.

Tears filled her eyes. It was frightening not to have control over what she was doing. No one else was home, and she was hungover and sick in her stomach. The tears turned to sobs. She'd been through this as a bystander, and now she was going to inflict it on others. She pulled herself together after a few minutes and took a deep breath. The hardest thing was this wasn't a disease like cancer. It wasn't something she could fight and have a chance to beat. It was already beating her and would defeat her completely in time, leaving a trail of carnage behind.

She thought of her conversation with Bella the previous day. The hurt and hatred were already there. Could she inflict years of this on her daughter? She'd hated her mother at times. The rational part of her had known it was a disease and that Alice didn't have control over what she was doing, but having the person you loved more than anyone in the world calling you horrible names and screaming abuse at you was hard to remain emotionless to. Resentment had grown within Reeve. Resentment that made her feel even more guilty when her mother was lucid and knew what she was saying.

She stood and crossed over to the kettle. She flicked it on and took a coffee mug from the shelf. No, she was not going to put Bella or Luke through this. She couldn't. She also wasn't going to waste away in a home where they'd feel obligated to visit her. She would get her official diagnosis, put her affairs in order, and take care of the situation herself.

* * *

Having made such a momentous decision, Reeve realised the moment she sat across from Devon to discuss their strategy for the meeting with the school that it was a waste of time. They needed to cancel the meeting.

'What?' Devon's mouth dropped open when Reeve said it might be best to resign. 'You've told me you didn't do anything wrong. Resigning would implicate you immediately.'

'I can no longer trust my own judgement as to what I did or didn't do,' Reeve said. 'I'll get the MRI and CT scan results next week, and I'm pretty sure I can already tell you what they're going to say.'

'Oh Reeve, I'm sorry. And I'm sorry Martin's not here to help you.'

'It's probably the only benefit of him already being gone – that he doesn't have to live through it again.'

'He'd want to be there for you. You know that, don't you?'

Reeve nodded.

'And there's no way I'm going to let you resign. If you are suffering from medical issues, then they need to be addressed before any of this is. I'll meet with the school and explain the situation. You are within your rights to ask for sick leave while your health issues are investigated.'

'No, I want to leave regardless of the outcome of any of this. If there's any truth to the allegations, then I'm not fit to be teaching.' She wasn't fit to be around anyone if they were true. 'And right now, I can't think of any reason Oscar would be making this up, which is more horrifying than you can imagine.'

'You know as well as I do that an illness such as dementia can see people doing all sorts of out-of-character things. As much as we don't want the diagnosis to be that, if it is, you'll at least know that you're not consciously doing these things. You have no control.'

'No, but I'm still expected to take responsibility for those actions. You should have seen Bella yesterday. She hates me. I don't blame her. Imagine being in her shoes right now. Her mother accused of sexually harassing one of her classmates.' She cringed.

'Which we both know you'd never consciously do. One good thing is that, like your mother, you do have the funds for the best available care if you require it.'

Reeve nodded, silently praying that she wouldn't need it. Money didn't help in this situation. Yes, it might buy you nicer accommodations and more expensive specialists, but it didn't stop the progress of the illness.

Devon checked his watch. 'Okay, I'll go and meet with the school. There isn't any need for you to come. I'll call you this afternoon and let you know how it goes.' He stood. 'By the way, when I met with Jessica earlier in the week, she mentioned she was hoping you would get in touch with her.'

'I have already,' Reeve said. 'We're having dinner tomorrow night.'

Devon sighed. 'What a mess Martin left you with. I'm sorry, Reeve. If you need anything at all, let me know.'

* * *

Reeve's phone pinged with a text message as she returned home from her meeting with Devon. She smiled as Sloane's message appeared on the in-car display.

Are you home? I'd like to drop in and see you after work today. Am finishing early, can be there by four.

Reeve instructed the system to reply.

> Would love to see you, and four sounds great. Would you like to stay for dinner?

> No. I'll see you at four.

Reeve forced herself to concentrate on the road and not the screen. Sloane was never abrupt, although, based on the time, she was probably hurrying back into class. She hoped nothing was wrong. She'd already checked her phone and emails and knew she hadn't done anything that could possibly offend her. She sighed. She was going to drive herself insane, if she wasn't already, with this type of thinking. There was probably a very reasonable explanation as to why Sloane's text was blunt.

When she opened the door to Sloane a little after four, one look at her friend's face told her something had happened. Her cheeks were drawn, her lips pursed. 'We need to speak.'

Reeve led her through to the living area. 'Please tell me I haven't done something to offend you.'

'You don't remember?'

'Oh no.' Reeve wanted to crawl under the cushions on the couch. She shook her head. She didn't want to know.

'You called me at midnight last night, Reeve. You ranted and raged for about twenty minutes about what a bitch I am. How I wasn't a real friend. That you'd lost your dad and the fact that I left the wake early to go and see mine was rubbing it in. That I hadn't been there for you, and you hated me as a result.'

'I have no recollection of any of that,' Reeve said, 'and I promise, hand on heart, I've never thought any of those things.' She fought back tears. It was as if someone had taken over her life and was ruining it. But that someone was her. 'Really, Sloane, it wasn't me.'

Sloane frowned. 'You did sound weird. I assumed you were drunk. But who else would know I left Martin's funeral to go and see Dad?'

Reeve shook her head. 'I don't mean I didn't make the call to you. I meant it isn't this me. The one you know. The one who loves you. It was the other me. The one that dementia, or whatever it is, is doing its best to ruin. Although' – this time, Reeve frowned – 'I checked my phone this morning as I was worried I might have done something terrible last night, and there were no calls, texts, or emails.' For a split second, she was filled with hope. Maybe it hadn't been her. Maybe it was a set-up.

'You rang from your landline,' Sloane said. 'It came up on my phone display.' She sighed. 'Oh hon, I don't know what to say. Why did you think you might have done something last night?'

'One of the things that seems to make me worse is drinking, which is why I'm not supposed to be drinking at all. I woke up this morning feeling rotten and discovered a bottle of red on the bench, three-quarters drunk. I can't recall opening it, and Luke's away in Sydney, so it was me.'

Sloane nodded. 'And then you rang me. No wonder you sounded weird if you'd drunk that much.'

'I don't remember drinking it. I'll get the test results next week from the MRI and CT scan. I guess they'll confirm that there's a problem. I'm sorry. I would never deliberately say something like that, and I certainly didn't mean it. I don't know what to do.'

'Perhaps lock up all the alcohol if that's part of the issue,' Sloane said.

'Better still, why don't you take it with you? The wine fridge is about half full, and there are some boxes in the garage of red we haven't had a chance to unpack. Consider it an apology.'

Sloane laughed. 'I don't think Luke would be impressed if I take all your wine.' She moved next to Reeve on the couch and took her in her arms. 'I'm so sorry, hon. We've been here before with Alice, and I can't believe it's happening again. Genetics are a bitch. Let's hope Bella...' She cut off her sentence, the words hanging in the air between them.

19

Jess was surprised at the onslaught of nervous energy that coursed through her system on Friday morning as she waited for Meg Chandler to arrive. Felicity's aunt had flown into Melbourne the previous day and had arranged to meet Jess at Safe Houses at ten o'clock. Jess's nerves were for her fifteen-year-old self. She could only imagine what a difference it would have made to her life if a relative had appeared wanting to foster her at that age. Not only would it have given her the love and stability of a family, but it would also have prevented the nightmare she'd endured.

'Jess.' Marlee poked her head into the office. 'Meg

Chandler's arrived. Would you like me to show her to the boardroom?'

'Yes, please. I'll be there in a minute. The plate of pastries in the kitchen is for our meeting. Would you mind bringing them in with any tea or coffee she asks for?'

'Will do.'

Jess thanked her before pulling out the small mirror she kept in her desk drawer and checking her make-up. She was being ridiculous. This was about Felicity, not her, but she didn't want to do anything to mess it up. She took a deep breath, stood, picked up Felicity's file, and made her way down the corridor to the boardroom.

She smiled as she opened the door and saw a dark-haired woman admiring the indigenous art-work on the boardroom wall. 'One of our foster success stories,' Jess said. 'Her paintings are getting well known worldwide.' Jess held out her hand. 'I'm Jess Williams. Thank you for coming today.'

Meg shook her hand and smiled. 'Thank you for tracking me down. I'm still not quite sure how you did that, but it's certainly had me thinking. What can you tell me about Felicity?'

Jess sat down and indicated for Meg to do the

same. She opened the file and took a photo of Felicity from it and passed it across the table.

'Wow,' Meg said. 'She looks like her mother at that age. Gillian had that pouty smile too.'

'She's a great kid,' Jess said. 'She's had a hard time since her mother died. Hasn't quite found her feet with a foster family yet.'

'That's possibly a good thing for me.'

Jess nodded. 'Possibly. Now, let me tell you how it all works.'

For the next twenty minutes, Jess walked Meg through the standard steps for fostering a child in Australia. 'Ultimately, we're looking for a good fit for Felicity,' Jess said, 'but when it's a family member, a lot of the usual criteria isn't relevant. You have that blood connection, which is considered incredibly important.'

'But I could be a criminal.'

Jess laughed. 'Yes, which is why we do a lot of checking, regardless of your blood tie.'

Meg nodded. 'You mentioned in our initial discussion that Felicity inherited Gillian's estate.'

Jess nodded. 'That's correct. The money is kept in trust until she turns eighteen, and then she can access it.'

'What about her living costs now?' Meg asked. 'Can that money be used towards them?'

'Not usually. Foster carers can apply for government assistance, which should cover most out-of-pocket expenses for Felicity until she's nineteen. It allows for a transition into adulthood from ages eighteen to nineteen.'

Meg nodded. 'Good. If I'm to move back to Australia to do this, I'm not sure how quickly I'll get employment. So, there will be assistance up until she turns eighteen or nineteen, and then she can rely on her inheritance?'

'That's correct. I would assume she'd be working in a part-time capacity by that stage as well,' Jess said. She smiled. 'Hopefully at university and working to help pay her way.'

'Her inheritance should mean she won't need to do that and can study and party,' Meg said. 'After all, that's what being eighteen is all about.'

Jess stared at the woman in front of her. The constant references to the inheritance were beginning to make her feel uneasy. Was this the reason she was here? For money? Jess pulled a document from her file and pushed it across the table to Meg. 'Here's a summary of what Felicity will inherit when she's eighteen. I think it's important you're aware of the amount.'

Meg's eyes widened with surprise. 'I assumed that would be confidential.'

It should be, but Jess's gut was telling her that this wasn't going to be the happy ending she'd hoped for. 'You're family, so we can make an exception.'

Meg nodded and glanced down at the sheet in front of her. She frowned and picked up the page and turned it over.

'It's just the one side,' Jess said.

Meg looked up at her. 'You're trying to tell me Gillian was only worth twenty-six grand when she died?'

'Unfortunately, yes. I believe she was struggling to make ends meet. This nest egg will mean a lot to Felicity when she receives it. I imagine she might use it for a car or towards her living expenses if she chooses to go to university. Perhaps both. The money is Felicity's, Meg. It isn't money that she is expected to share.'

Meg tossed the piece of paper towards Jess and stood. 'That paltry amount's not worth sharing. It cost me over a thousand dollars to come to this meeting, and I still need to afford the airfare back to the States. I wish you'd shared this information earlier.'

'Hold on,' Jess said. 'Are you telling me you're only interested in your niece if she comes with a decent bankroll?'

'I'm not putting my life on hold for three years to raise my sister's brat for no reward. I don't expect a lot, but I do expect to be compensated.'

Jess's heart sank. 'Your *sister's brat* is a lovely girl, and I'm relieved I never told her about you. I'm not sure she could take another disappointment right now.'

'Well, she's going to have to, isn't she? I don't want to foster her, but I want to meet her. Set it up, would you? Tell her I'm here for a few days and will be returning to the States so she doesn't get any ideas about me looking after her.'

Jess swallowed. She couldn't believe this was happening. She'd stuck her neck out trying to do something good for Felicity, and this was the result. A money-grubbing relative who couldn't care less about her, and now Jess was going to have to explain the situation to the teen. She shook her head. Life was incredibly unfair. Poor Flick, she could already imagine the disappointment she'd experience discovering there was someone out there related to her but who didn't want her.

'I'm going to book my ticket back to the States early next week, so arrange it for Sunday please, and send me the address details.'

Jess found herself nodding, wishing at the same time she didn't have a neighbour with secret service contacts.

* * *

Jess did her best to shake off the feeling of despair that had settled on her shoulders since the encounter with Meg earlier and lifted her wine glass in a toast as she sat across from Reeve at XO, South Yarra's busy Asian fusion restaurant. Reeve lifted her water glass, insisting she didn't drink, and clinked it with Jess's.

'To new beginnings,' Jess said. 'Hopefully, at least. This whole situation feels surreal. I'm sad that I never got to know Martin. I'm hoping you can tell me more about him.'

'I'd love to,' Reeve said. 'And I've got a million questions regarding your upbringing and everything you experienced as a kid.'

Jess wasn't sure if it was the wine or genuine emotion that had her welling up as she saw Reeve's reaction to the stories of her childhood and the foster homes she was placed in. She didn't go into any detail about what happened when she was fifteen, but she still painted a fairly accurate picture of a disrupted and unenjoyable upbringing.

'I'm sorry,' Reeve said for the fifth time, as ninety minutes later, after sharing a delicious dinner of steamed barramundi and Hainanese chicken, their dessert was delivered to the table. 'I honestly think if Dad knew, he would have done something. I'm still confused that he kept you secret. It's not like him. Well, not like the man I knew him to be.'

'He spoke a little about his decision when we met,' Jess said. 'He said he was put in a position of having to choose, and he chose his wife over my mother. I get that. It's a shame that he had the affair to start with.'

'You wouldn't be here if he hadn't,' Reeve said. 'And from everything you've told me, your experience has benefited so many kids that have ended up in foster care. You wouldn't have the perspective you have if you hadn't been through it.'

'True,' Jess said, although she would have been quite happy to have not been here and to have not gone through it. 'Now, I've monopolised the conversation. Tell me about you. I'm assuming you had a slightly different upbringing.'

As she tasted her ginger crème brûlée, Jess could tell that Reeve was doing her best to downplay the privileged upbringing she'd had. But when she started speaking about her mother and her dementia, Jess saw another side to her otherwise perfect life.

'The thing is,' Reeve said, 'I've had a few incidents happen that suggest I might be following her down that path.'

'Oh no,' Jess said. 'What sort of things?' She listened, horrified as Reeve, her face growing redder with each admission, talked about a situation at her school that had caused her to leave her job, possibly permanently, and then the numerous incidents that she couldn't remember, including the most recent of abusing her friend.

'Part of the reason I want you to know,' Reeve said, 'is so if you get any abusive phone calls, messages, or anything else from me, please know it's not really me. I have no control over what's happening. Once we get a proper diagnosis, hopefully there will be some treatment or a plan to minimise my outbursts, but I can't guarantee that.'

'Do you want to know if you do something?' Jess asked. 'Or would you prefer I keep it to myself?'

Reeve's face coloured. 'Please don't tell me I've already insulted you?'

Jess couldn't help but laugh. 'Sorry, no, you haven't. I wanted to check. That's all. The funny thing is, if you called me up and abused me over the will, I'd think you were totally within your rights. I wouldn't even question it. I don't feel I have a right to any of Martin's estate. It should go to you and your family.'

'That's crazy,' Reeve said. 'If anything, you could argue that you should have a much bigger share than me as you've missed out your entire life. I'm more than happy for that, by the way, or at least splitting our combined inheritance fifty-fifty rather than how Dad left it. I don't like that he's left it how he has.'

'He doesn't know me,' Jess said. 'Devon explained that there were investments he wanted maintained, and he was concerned that I might do things that wouldn't be in line with his wishes, whereas you'd probably do what he'd want.'

'I guess that makes sense. Now, would you like coffee or more wine?' Reeve stood. 'I need to use the bathroom, so I can order them on the way back.'

'A skinny cappuccino would be lovely.' Jess watched Reeve as she made her way to the ladies' room. She'd shared so much with her about her life, Martin, and her medical issues. Jess had a lot to process. The main thing she was processing was how easy this felt. The two women had clicked immediately. As cliché as it sounded, Jess felt she knew Reeve. She'd read articles about blood relatives having connections that couldn't be explained, and she was sure that was what this was. She could only hope Reeve was experiencing the same feeling.

20

Reeve stopped at the bar on her way back from the bathroom. She'd enjoyed the evening with Jess immensely. Hopefully, she wouldn't discover she'd ruined it in some way by doing something she didn't recall. She looked across to the table they'd been sitting at. Jess was still there. That was a good sign. She was glad that she'd found the courage to tell Jess what was going on with her. Having it out in the open, while horrible, was a relief.

'Can we get two skinny cappuccinos, please?' Reeve asked as the bartender approached her. She pointed to the table where Jess was. 'We're sitting over there.'

'Sure. I'll bring them to you.'

'Unless you'll allow me to buy you lovely ladies a bottle of the restaurant's finest champagne.' A deep male voice spoke from behind her.

She turned, facing a tall sandy-haired man. His dimples deepened as he smiled at her, his green eyes dancing. She held up her left hand, her wedding band clearly visible. 'Thank you, but we're not looking for company.'

He held up his hand, which sported a thick gold band. 'I shouldn't be either, but that dress you're wearing is corrupting me. You look gorgeous.'

Reeve gave an embarrassed smile.

'How about I give you this,' the guy said, taking a business card from his pocket. 'My name's George. If you ever change your mind about some company, please call. I think we could have a lovely time together.' He tucked it in the top of her bag before she had a chance to object, then walked in the direction of the bathrooms. She couldn't help but smile. As much as she wasn't looking for male attention, it was the first time in a long time that she'd been hit on. It was flattering. The fact that he'd run a mile if he had any idea of what she was really like was irrelevant. For that moment, she'd been desirable to someone who wasn't her husband.

* * *

An hour later, Reeve offered to drop Jess home rather than get an Uber. It was only a short drive from the restaurant and it gave them the opportunity to spend more time together.

'I've enjoyed tonight,' Jess said. 'I'd love to do it again soon.'

'Me too, and I'd like you to meet Bella properly, and Luke too,' Reeve said. It might be a way to break the ice with Bella, or at least give her a reason to want to come home for a few hours. 'How about we organise something for the weekend after next?'

'I'd love that,' Jess said. 'It's the next left.' She pointed to an apartment complex that sported a large fence and entrance gate. Reeve pulled over and leant forward to hug Jess.

'Thank you for not freaking out when I told you about the dementia possibility. I was worried it might scare you off.'

'Not at all.' Jess hugged her back. 'If you need company next week when you get those test results, let me know. I've got plenty of annual leave owing. I'd be happy to come with you.'

Reeve smiled and waved as Jess climbed out of

the car and pushed open the security gate that led into the gardens of her apartment building. She pulled back out into the road smiling to herself. She had a sister! A woman she was beginning to get to know and a woman she liked. To top it off, she'd had a guy hit on her tonight, which was flattering, and not a thing of the past which she'd assumed it would be around her fortieth birthday. Now all she had to do was go home and go straight up to bed.

It was as she walked into the kitchen that she realised she hadn't spoken to Luke at all today. That was unusual. Even when he was at a conference, she would normally speak and text with him. She took her phone from her bag, her heart sinking as she saw there was a text message from Luke. She crossed her fingers, praying she hadn't sent something nasty to him.

Hey hon, thank you for your lovely message. I love you too. The guys are all jealous, I think. My laptop was on the meeting room table and John Druitt read it out to everyone. I will be late tonight at dinner and won't get to speak to you. Let's chat tomorrow. Love you, L x

She opened her email to see what message he was referring to.

> Hi darling. I hope things are going well for you. I miss you and want you to know how much I appreciate and love you. You really are amazing. Having you by my side is the one thing that makes me think I can beat this. Love you so much. R xxx

She closed her eyes, relief swimming through her. She had no recollection of sending the message, but thankfully it was a message to remember, not one to be ashamed of. She reopened the message to see what time she sent it and frowned. The time of the message suggested she'd sent it while she was at dinner with Jess.

She picked up her phone and typed in a text message to Jess.

> I had a great time tonight, thank you! Strange question, but did I use my phone to send any messages while we had dinner?

The reply was almost instant.

> Loved tonight too. And no. You didn't take your phone out of your bag while you were at the table. Although you did go to the bathroom, so I'm not sure if you sent a message from there? Is everything okay?

Reeve looked at the message. It was possible she'd sent that when she'd gone to the bathroom, although she had a clear memory, she thought, of the bathroom visit. Would she have blacked out momentarily, or however it worked, to send a message?

She sent a quick text back to Jess, assuring her everything was fine and that she'd be in touch to organise their next catch-up, before switching on the kettle. She filled the tea infuser with her favourite chamomile leaves, added them to a cup, and poured boiling water over it. She took a deep breath as she carried her drink upstairs.

Sadness settled over her as she sat down in the chair beside her bed and thought of Jess. She wasn't going to have much time to spend with her sister with the way things were going. Time that she'd remember anyway. She sipped her tea, tiredness settling over her as the day caught up with her. Luke would be back tomorrow. She wanted to see him but would be lying if she said she wasn't worried about what she might do next to unconsciously sabotage their relationship.

* * *

Sunlight was streaming through the bedroom window when Reeve woke the next morning. She froze, for a split second unsure where she was. Her head pounded, and she was naked under the covers. Her body ached in the way it might if she and Luke had enjoyed a particularly passionate night of lovemaking. Holding the covers against her, she sat up and glanced around the room. What had happened?

The shrill of the doorbell made her jump. It was a little before eight. It wouldn't be Luke as she was picking him up at the airport at lunchtime, and anyway, he'd let himself in. The doorbell rang again. She got out of bed, slipped on her robe, and hurried down the stairs, wincing as her body reminded her of its soreness. She stopped at the foot of the staircase, squinting at the jacket that was slung across the bottom of the banister. Luke must have come home late last night, and she'd blacked out or had whatever these memory losses were. That explained why her body felt the way it did. She wasn't sure she'd admit that she didn't remember their lovemaking. Not to him anyway.

Relieved that she'd worked out what must have happened, she pulled open the front door. A man stood in front of her, a lopsided grin on his face. He held up two takeaway coffee cups. 'Thought I'd treat us.'

Reeve stared at him. He was familiar, but she couldn't place where she'd seen him before.

He frowned. 'Aren't you letting me back in?'

'Sorry, do I know you?'

He laughed. 'That's the best denial I've ever heard.' He winked and pushed past her into the house. 'Reeve, after last night, I'd say you know me better than my wife does.'

Alarm rushed through Reeve. *His wife.* It was the guy from the restaurant. The one who'd been flirting with her. George something. What was he doing here? He'd given her his card, but she hadn't done anything with it. Had she? She followed him to the kitchen, where he sank onto one of the stools at the counter, his grin wide. 'Last night was amazing. I know you're happily married, but I think we owe it to ourselves to go another round. You said your husband wouldn't be back until lunchtime, didn't you?'

He might as well have punched her. *I cheated on Luke. Oh my God, what have I done?* She hurried from the kitchen to the half bathroom that sat off the hallway and retched into the toilet bowl. *Oh my God. Oh my God.* This couldn't be real. It was a nightmare, and she'd wake up. She steadied herself and took a deep breath.

'Reeve?'

He was still here. She flushed the toilet, her whole body trembling as she ran the taps and splashed cold water on her face.

'Reeve? You're freaking me out.'

She took another deep breath, opened the bathroom door, and came face to face with him. His concern was genuine. On the surface, he looked like a decent guy. How could she have no recollection of having sex with him?

'I'm sorry,' George said. 'Have I done something to offend you? The way you took the lead last night suggested you enjoyed every second of it.'

'I have a medical condition,' Reeve said, 'and sometimes I do things I have no recollection of.'

His eyes widened. 'You don't remember last night?'

She shook her head. 'I don't remember inviting you over. I do remember meeting you at the restaurant.'

His face reddened. 'You invited me. I didn't force myself on you.' He shook his head. 'I feel like such a prick. If I'd had any idea...'

Reeve pulled her robe tight around her and moved back into the kitchen. She couldn't believe she was in this position. She'd cheated with a guy she had no recollection of being with. If he wasn't here now and her body wasn't sore, she wouldn't even know she'd done it. Her phone was on the kitchen counter. She picked it up and looked through the call history and messages. Sure enough, there it was – a text message from her to George inviting him to the house.

She shook her head and forced herself to look at him. 'It's not your fault, and I'm the one who should be apologising. I can see from my phone that I invited you here, and my body tells me we had an active night. But it's not something I'd do when I was in control of my actions.'

'I'll go,' George said. 'I don't know what to say. I feel like I've done something wrong, but I can guarantee you, you wanted it. You practically ripped my clothes off when I walked through the front door.'

Reeve hung her head.

George didn't wait for a reply. He picked up his coffee cup from the counter and walked towards the front door.

Reeve followed him, glad when he took the jacket from the banister. He turned when he reached the door. 'Last night was the best sex I've ever had.' He blushed. 'You said the same. Said I was *more man* than you'd ever experienced before. I'm sorry you don't remember it. I hope you can sort out whatever this medical thing is.' He turned and let himself out.

Reeve waited until she heard his car pull away from the house before locking the front door and sinking onto the bottom stair of the staircase. She'd cheated on her husband. *Cheated.* She had no recollection of it happening, but she'd still done it. Was there any way Luke would understand? Would he be able to forgive her? She wasn't sure she'd be able to forgive herself. Yes, she might be sick, but this was a whole other level of betrayal. The one thing she knew for sure was she couldn't be trusted on her own. She needed help, and she needed it now.

* * *

By the time she needed to leave to pick up Luke from the airport, Reeve was a mess. She'd managed to strip the bed and change the sheets, finding four condom wrappers and the used condoms in the bin in the bathroom. What was left in her stomach had quickly emptied at this discovery. She'd cleaned the bedroom and bathroom and lit cleansing candles to remove the energy from the previous night. It was unfathomable that she could have had sex with someone multiple times and have no memory of it.

She wasn't sure how she'd even begin to speak to Luke about this. But she would have to. After being away for three nights, she knew what he'd want to do the moment they got home, and right now, the idea of having sex with anyone, including her husband, repulsed her. While she didn't doubt that the sex the previous night had been consensual, she felt violated.

A text arrived as she was collecting her bag, ready to leave.

> I got an earlier flight and am in an Uber. I'm rereading your email of yesterday. I think it's the nicest message I've ever received. I love you. Meet you upstairs in about 30. x

Reeve sank onto the couch. She still hadn't moved when she heard the Uber pull into the driveway and doors slam as Luke got out and took his suitcase from the boot. She knew she needed to get up and greet him, but she couldn't. She couldn't face him.

'Ree?' He called out the moment he opened the front door. 'You upstairs?'

She listened as he moved through the house, searching for her. They rarely used the formal lounge room, and it was no surprise that it was the last room he checked.

'Hey,' he said from the doorway, 'didn't you hear me?'

She looked up. Her eyes blurred with tears.

'What's the matter?' He was by her side in an instant, taking her hand in his. 'What's happened? Is it Bella? News about your dad?'

She shook her head. A lump formed in the back of her throat, making speech difficult.

'Is it your new sister? You had dinner last night, didn't you? Has she done something?'

'It's nothing like that,' Reeve managed to say. 'I've done something. Something that you'll never forgive me for.'

He dropped her hands and sat back, the lines in his forehead and around his eyes deepening. 'Something you did consciously or unconsciously?'

'Does it matter?'

'Yes, it does.'

'Well, I can only hope you still feel that way after I explain.' Reeve took a deep breath, and told him what had happened.

Luke was on his feet within seconds of the words coming out of Reeve's mouth. 'You did what?'

Reeve buried her face in her hands. She couldn't look at him. If this situation was reversed, she couldn't imagine how she'd feel.

'You invited a total stranger back to our house, to our bed, and you had sex with him?'

Reeve wished Luke would lower his voice. At this rate, all the neighbours would know what she did.

When Luke spoke again she could hardly hear him. 'First, you tell me you want to have sex with other men, then there's the situation at school with the Oscar kid, and now you do this, the whole time saying you don't remember doing any of it.'

Reeve forced herself to look at him. 'I don't. I have no recollection of doing any of that, plus other things.' Tears were rolling down her cheeks. 'I need help, Luke. I don't think I can be trusted to be on my own.'

Luke shook his head. 'I'm sorry, Ree. I know it's not you doing these things consciously, but right now, it doesn't make this any easier. I'm going out for a few hours to try to get my head around what's happened.' He started to walk out of the room but stopped and turned. 'Try not to have sex with anyone while I'm gone.' Guilt registered in his eyes as the words left his lips. 'Ignore me. This is just really hard, but Ree...'

She managed to lift her eyes to his.

'I'm sorry, okay. Really sorry. I didn't mean that, but I do need to get away for a few hours.'

Reeve hugged one of the couch cushions to her as the front door clicked shut after Luke. What if he didn't return?

Her phone rang, and she picked it up off the coffee table, hoping it was Luke ringing to tell her everything would be fine. It wasn't. It was Nick.

'Everything okay?' Nick asked.

'Why?' Her question was tentative. Surely he didn't know what she'd done.

Nick sighed. 'You've done it again with Bella, that's all. The gift you sent arrived this morning.'

'Gift? I didn't send her anything.'

'Are you sure?'

She couldn't be sure of anything right now. 'What did I send? Please tell me it was something half decent.'

'You don't remember?'

'No, and to be honest, Nick, it couldn't be any worse than what I've done to Luke this morning.'

'You served him divorce papers? Disowned him?'

'What? No, of course not. Although he'd be in his every right to do that to me.'

'Reeve, you sent her a very detailed letter explaining why you wished you could divorce her, but as that's not something a parent can legally do, that when she's eighteen and comes of age, you'll be disowning her. You said you're planning to have her written out of your will so that none of Martin's estate will go to her. You went on to call her a bunch of very unflattering names.'

Reeve's eyes were shut, and she let out a sound that was somewhere between a moan and a wail.

'I take it you have no recollection of sending it?' Nick's voice was calm and without a hint of accusation, which Reeve was grateful for.

'None at all,' Reeve managed to say. 'Are you sure it's from me? Anyone could put my name to a letter.'

'It's your handwriting. I'd recognise it anywhere.'

Reeve fell silent. She'd taken the time to hand-write a horrible letter and couldn't remember doing it. She knew that it was part of dementia, but that didn't make it any easier to digest. 'What do I do? She'll never forgive me.'

'Look, I'll do my best to explain the situation to her, but she's angry and upset.'

'I need help, Nick. I don't know what to do.'

'Have you got another appointment with that psychiatrist? I know you won't want to be medicated, but at least if you can find out what's going on, there might be some drugs that stop some of this be-haviour. It's worth finding out.'

'I'm seeing her on Monday. Please tell Bella I'm beyond sorry, and I honestly have no recollection of doing any of the things she thinks I've done. Nick, it's as if I'm Alice but ten times worse. It's terrifying.'

Nick was silent for a moment. 'I'll be here for you, Reeve, anything you need. You know that. I'll go and talk to Bella now. I haven't wanted to scare her too much that there could be something wrong with you, but I think it's time we had a proper chat.'

'No,' Reeve said. 'Don't say too much. We should find out what we're dealing with, and then we can tell her. Would it be okay with you if I came over on

Monday night, once we know what it is? Luke might come too if he's talking to me by then.'

'You're both welcome to come to dinner.'

Reeve swallowed the lump in her throat. 'I doubt I'll be able to eat, but Nick, thank you.'

21

Jess organised with Meg to arrive at the Smiths' residence at three o'clock on Sunday afternoon. It gave her plenty of time to pick up Felicity at twelve and take her out for lunch. She wasn't sure how this was going to play out, but she had to do her best to minimise the damage she was responsible for.

'How's it going with the Smiths?' Jess asked as she sat across from Flick at Café Latte.

Flick shrugged. 'It's okay, not as bad as I imagined.'

Jess smiled. 'Hearing that from you is like a normal person saying they love something.'

Flick raised an eyebrow. 'A normal person? Are you trying to give me a complex?'

Jess laughed and handed Flick a menu. 'That came out wrong. Order anything you want. It's my treat.'

Flick stared at her for a moment before consulting the menu.

Does she know something's up? Jess waited until they'd placed their orders and their drinks arrived. 'So,' she said. 'I wanted to talk to you about something I discovered a couple of weeks ago.'

Flick waited expectantly.

'Before I tell you this, I do need to make it clear that this isn't a foster opportunity. Your place is with the Smiths for now and the person I'm going to tell you about is only in Australia for a few days. She'd like to meet you, but she's not able to consider staying or taking you with her to foster.'

Flick frowned. 'Take me with her? A stranger? Why would I want her to?'

Jess took a deep breath. 'When I picked you up from the Novaks' house, you mentioned an aunt who disappeared. I've done some digging and discovered she left Australia twenty years ago and lost contact with your mum and all her friends here.'

Flick's eyes widened. 'You found her?'

Jess nodded. 'She happened to be coming to Australia for a few days and wanted to meet you. Unfortunately, she's returning to Chicago this week, so it is a chance to meet her and possibly stay in touch if the two of you decide to.'

Flick looked around the restaurant. 'Is she meeting us here?'

'No, back at the Smiths' at three. There's heaps of time to get ready, and if you don't want to meet her, I can call her and let her know.'

Felicity sat in silence for a moment. 'What's she like?'

'Mid-forties,' Jess said. She couldn't say much more. Telling a fifteen-year-old that her aunt was a money-grubbing leech wasn't ideal.

'And?'

'And I only met her briefly. She still has her Aussie accent, although she sounds a bit American. She was shocked by everything I told her, which meant it was hard to get a feel for what she was like. She didn't know your mum had died.'

Felicity nodded, accepting this as an explanation. 'Can we go? I don't think I'll be able to eat anything, and I want to change and get ready.'

'Sure,' Jess said. 'I don't want you getting your hopes up, okay? She can't foster, and she's going back to America.'

Flick nodded, but Jess could imagine the cogs

turning in her head. She would have been the same, expecting her aunt would take one look at her and change her mind. That there was no way she'd leave her behind knowing they were related. Jess left money on the table for their drinks, picked up her bag, and followed Flick out of the restaurant, dread filling the pit of her stomach.

* * *

Later that afternoon, Jess was deep in thought as she came through the front entrance of the apartments and smashed straight into Trent.

She jumped back. 'Sorry, I wasn't looking where I was going.'

Trent took her arm and pulled her to one side as the couple from 7B passed them. 'Are you okay?'

Jess shook her head. 'Difficult afternoon. Flick met her aunt, who destroyed every bit of faith I've ever had in humanity. She pretty much told Flick that she'd disowned her sister twenty-five years ago and didn't think much of family or blood ties. She shattered any piece of hope Flick had that there was a family out there for her.'

'Come with me,' Trent said, putting an arm around her. He guided her to the stairwell, up the three flights to his apartment. 'I'll make us some tea.'

Jess nodded and flopped gratefully onto his soft blue couch. 'Thank you.' She closed her eyes, doing her best to push away the memory of Flick's distraught face.

'You know, it's not your fault,' Trent said a few minutes later, placing a tray with a teapot, two cups, and a packet of chocolate biscuits on the coffee table. 'You tried to do something nice, and it didn't work out.'

'You can say that again.' Jess sighed. 'Still, she has the foster family she's with currently. They're nice people, so hopefully it will work out for her. The only thing is – and I haven't told her this yet – they've decided they'll only do a year of fostering. They like her but want younger kids. I'll leave that for a few more weeks before I tell her. She doesn't need that blow right now.'

'Poor kid,' Trent said, pouring the tea. He looked up at her. 'Have you ever considered fostering?'

She nodded. 'A few years ago, I seriously considered it. I event went through the approval process, which takes a few months. The day I was approved to foster was the day I changed my mind. I've such a big workload it wouldn't be fair on the kid. They'd be home by themselves half the time. Also, I can't imagine I'd be any good at parenting as I had such bad role models as a kid. I'm sure Mum was good, but I was young and hardly remember her parenting style.'

Trent sipped his tea. 'I could do it, I guess. I work from home and am quite flexible.'

Jess set her teacup on the table. 'Is it something you've ever considered?'

'No. I always assumed I'd have my own kids.' He smiled. 'Guess I'm getting a bit old for that now.'

'We're always looking for good foster carers,' Jess said. 'If you're ever serious, let me know.'

Trent nodded. 'I'll think about it. And it'd have to be a boy. I can imagine what people would say if I fostered a teenage girl.' He shuddered. 'I guess that's a problem with single guys wanting to foster.'

'It can be,' Jess said.

Trent smiled. 'You'd be a great mum. You'd be such a great cheerleader for any kid you raised.'

Jess blushed. 'That I doubt very much. I grew up with such a dysfunctional childhood. I had no good role models to model parenting on.'

'Yes, but that's a positive. You know what doesn't work. If you're not going to have your own kids, you should seriously consider it, Jess. Sure, little kids would need you home more, but a teenager is more self-sufficient. Most of us grew up letting ourselves in after school. You're usually home by six, and you're available on the weekend.' He laughed. 'They'd probably find that too much. You know kids today; they spend their entire lives on their phones and wouldn't want you interrupting.'

When Jess thanked Trent for the tea and left an hour later, his words continued to play over in her head. Could she really become a foster parent? Felicity's tear-stained face appeared in her mind. She wasn't sure she could take the risk of letting down a child in the way she'd been let down. Not feeling loved or cared for. Being an inconvenience and, at times, a slave. Not that she'd do any of that, but what if she didn't fulfil their emotional needs and made things worse? Looking at how she'd handled the situation with Felicity and her aunt confirmed that was a very real possibility and an excellent reason to stay working in foster care rather than becoming a carer herself.

* * *

Jess's head was heavy the next morning as she dragged herself out of bed. Her sleep had been fitful, with dreams of being a mother – a very bad mother – jolting her from her sleep.

Her phone rang as she walked into the kitchen and switched on the coffee machine. She glanced at the screen and frowned. It wasn't even seven, and Devon was ringing her.

'Hello.'

'Jess, sorry to call this early. It's Devon.'

'Everything okay?'

Devon cleared his throat. 'Yes and no. I've had news overnight that our investigations have tracked down your uncle.'

Jess froze. 'You found Joey?'

'Found information about him. I'm sorry to tell you, but he died in the late nineties.'

'Oh.' Whatever she'd been expecting, this wasn't it. She'd pictured confrontations with Joey where she'd be demanding answers.

'It turns out he'd paid a woman, a Ms Maria Lubcheck, to act as a power of attorney and next of kin if something was to happen to him. He left strict instructions that in the unlikely event of his death, he was to be buried in the Cayman Islands, and no one in Australia was to be contacted. She carried through with his wishes once he died. It was a boating accident – a fire on a yacht. Nothing suspicious, but Mr

Williams and another man died. She said she kept his belongings, which included a motorbike, a small amount of cash, a Rolex, and a few personal items.'

'What about the money? Martin's money.'

'Other than the small amount of cash she kept, she didn't know of any other money. Said Joey had lived frugally from what she'd seen.'

'Really?'

'Further investigations,' Devon continued, 'have uncovered a bank account in Joseph's name in the Caymans with over two million dollars in it. The account was last used a few days before his death and then sat dormant for many years. As per Cayman law, the monies reverted to the government.'

Jess was finding it hard to digest all of this. Joey was dead. He had stolen the money, and now it belonged to a government?

'We can start proceedings to try to retrieve the money,' Devon said. 'The government will return the money, less fees, if the correct legal channels are engaged.'

'Wouldn't they consider it Joey's money?'

'It's quite complicated,' Devon agreed. 'We'd need to start legal proceedings at this end to show that Mr Williams stole the money and then go from there.'

'I'm happy for you to do whatever you think Martin would want,' Jess said.

'Okay, leave it with me,' Devon said. 'There will be a lot of hoops to jump through, but I know Martin would want me to jump through them. To say he was upset about Joseph Williams's actions towards you and your mother would be an understatement.'

Jess ended the call, poured her coffee, and sat down at the kitchen counter. *Joey stole the money.* While she'd known this outcome was a strong possibility, deep down she'd hoped he would be proven innocent. She closed her eyes, an image of her mother appearing in her mind. While this process might prove Joey to be a thief, it also confirmed he was a murderer. Her mother would still be alive if it wasn't for his greed. A tear escaped the corner of her eye. One person's actions had singlehandedly shaped and ruined her childhood, and there was nothing now that she could do about it.

22

'I think I'm going to be sick,' Reeve said as Luke manoeuvred the car along the busy Nepean Highway towards East Brighton. In less than twenty minutes, she'd be sitting across from Patricia, learning her fate.

Luke took a hand off the steering wheel and placed it on her knee. 'There's nothing we can't handle together. Hopefully this appointment will give us some answers to what's going on and a treatment plan. Don't automatically assume it's dementia. It might be something else.'

Reeve fell silent, her mind instantly imagining the worst version of 'it might be something else'.

Good news, it's not dementia. It's a brain tumour. Terminal.

They arrived at Patricia's a few minutes before their scheduled appointment, allowing Reeve to gulp in the sea air to help calm her nerves.

Luke took her hand and led her into the waiting area of Patricia's studio. The psychiatrist was quick to greet them and show them into her consulting room.

'Okay,' Patricia said once they were all seated. 'I know it's been a distressing time for you, Reeve. Luke's filled me in via a phone conversation on the happenings since I last saw you, and it's obvious that we need to get on top of the issue.'

'Do you have the results?' Luke asked.

Patricia nodded. 'Unfortunately, the scan does show considerable widespread cortical atrophy.'

Reeve's heart sank. She remembered this being part of her mother's issues and that it was monitored with reasonable regularity to check for further decline.

'There was no sign of tumours, strokes, or fluid build ups; however, high levels of beta-amyloid were present.'

Luke took his head in his hands, shaking it to and fro. 'All signs of Alzheimer's.'

'Unfortunately, yes,' Patricia agreed. 'And with the

genetic link, plus the results of the cognitive testing, I'm afraid to say that it looks like we are dealing with a rather aggressive form of early onset dementia.'

'Like my mother?'

Patricia nodded. 'It's very unfortunate, Reeve, but we can start with medication. As you know, it won't cure anything, but it may relax you and reduce aggressive behaviour.'

'It didn't do much for Mum.'

'There's no guarantee you're experiencing what your mother did. Research has moved along, and different treatments are being offered.'

'Mum died a year ago,' Reeve said. 'How different are things now?' If it had been ten years ago, there would be some comfort in believing research had advanced, but one year didn't give her much hope.

'There are a few different drugs to experiment with,' Patricia said. 'I've written you a script for Memantine. It blocks glutamate and prevents too much calcium from moving into the brain cells and causing damage. In addition, I'll write you a script for Risperidone. It's a tranquilliser that helps with aggression. I'll give you some information to read up about it as it does have its risks attached.'

'I'm going to have to go into care, aren't I?'

'Eventually, it's likely,' Patricia said. 'Right now, it's

a matter of working out the best medication to keep you in your own home. I would recommend putting your affairs in order.'

She smiled as Reeve's mouth dropped open. How had Patricia guessed that she might not choose to stay around?

'I'm not suggesting you're about to die. It's best to have everything in order while you're of sound mind. If you were to deteriorate quickly, I'm sure you'd like the peace of mind that you'd put someone in charge of your wellbeing. An enduring power of attorney, for starters, is a good idea. I'd suggest you decide who you'd like to nominate in this role and then have a lawyer organise the documents. Also, if you choose a care facility while you are still capable of doing so, it will be much easier for your family if and when the time comes, knowing they are carrying through with your wishes.'

Luke reached for her hand, but Reeve ignored him and kept her hands firmly clasped in her lap. She remembered the day her mother signed the forms to make her father her enduring power of attorney. It had made sense to Reeve at the time. It was a practical step in looking after her mother. Now, however, she realised how her mother must have felt going through that process – signing away her right to make her own decisions. Reeve knew it was necessary, but it was terrifying to acknowledge there would be a time when she'd need someone else to make decisions for her.

An hour after walking in, she allowed Luke to guide her back to the car, the two scripts held tightly in his hands. Reeve thought of her mother as tears rolled down her cheeks. Medicating Alice had been the start of the end. Once it had started, she'd never been the same.

* * *

CLIENT MEETING SUMMARY

DATE: September 9
Client: Reeve Elliot & Dr Luke Sheffield
Duration: 90 Min
MRI Summary: High levels of beta-amyloid. Considerable widespread cortical atrophy.

Reeve Elliot accompanied by husband, Dr Luke Sheffield. Delivery of MRI results indicating Reeve is suffering from early onset dementia. I have prescribed Memantine and Risperidone.

The recommendation has been made for Reeve to nominate an enduring power of attorney and consider care facilities.

Distress mounted in frustration at the end of the session, and an angry outburst from Reeve ensued. Dr Sheffield was able to calm his wife by holding her and stroking her hair. Her aggression was aimed at me. The glazed look in Reeve's eyes is, according to Dr Sheffield, a signal that her actions are unconscious, and she may have no recollection.

Appointment regularity to be increased. Next appointment scheduled for Friday of this week.

* * *

Having someone else to think about other than herself helped Reeve process what Patricia had told her and work out how she was going to tell Bella and Nick what had been revealed. She'd sent him a text earlier saying they'd come over at seven-thirty, after dinner. He'd immediately replied, insisting they come for dinner as he'd originally offered.

Now, as she placed the white chocolate brownies, Nick's favourite, in a plastic container, she felt stronger than she had all day. She owed him. He was there for her in the background, she knew that, and she knew she could trust he was doing everything possible to make this easier for Bella.

'You sure you want to do this?' Luke asked, jangling his car keys as he came into the kitchen. 'I'm sure Nick could talk to her.'

Reeve shook her head. 'No, I need her to understand what's happening. We sheltered her from Mum, and to be fair, Mum usually attacked me and certainly not Bell.'

'You look a lot stronger than you did earlier.'

'I feel it. As much as I didn't want the diagnosis, I feel like I can move through the next stage. Telling people, hoping the medication works, and taking things from there. At least I can stop wondering if I'm doing all the things you and others are telling me I'm doing. I need to accept that it's not the real me and need others to understand this. I've asked Sloane to meet us at Nick's too.'

Reeve's phone pinged with a text message. She picked it up, frowning. 'And Jess apparently.'

'Jess?'

Reeve nodded. 'I thought I knew what I was doing today, but I have no recollection of asking her. Looking at this, I sent it after the session at Patricia's.'

Luke raised an eyebrow. 'You did get a bit aggressive at the end of the session, Ree. Not sure if you remember? You were mad at Patricia. You calmed down quickly, but maybe you were still in that frame of mind when you sent Jess the text.'

Reeve stared at him. She didn't even want to know what she'd said to Patricia. 'What frame of mind? The crazy one?'

Luke's cheeks coloured. 'The forgetful one.'

Reeve shook her head. It wasn't his fault that she was doing all these crazy things, but sometimes she wished he wasn't there to witness any of it and report back to her. She scrolled up to find the message she'd sent earlier.

> Hi, this may sound weird but wondering if you'd like to meet the family this afternoon? I have some news to break concerning my health and would love to include you. If you'd prefer to meet them another time, that's fine.

She looked up at Luke. 'At least I didn't say anything horrible to her. She's asked for Nick's address and said she'd love to be included.'

She sent back a quick text. 'I've told her to come

thirty minutes after everyone else. I'd better explain who she is before she gets there.'

Reeve's strength began to fail as she walked up Nick's driveway clutching the brownies in one hand and Luke's hand in the other.

Luke gave her hand a gentle squeeze. 'This takes amazing courage, Ree. However Bella reacts, the rest of us will be here for you.'

Nick hugged her when she arrived, the concern in his eyes speaking volumes.

'Where's Bella?'

'In her room, refusing to come down,' Nick said. 'I'll go and have a chat.'

'Want a hand, mate?' Luke asked.

'That'd be great, thanks. I expect it might take both of us to talk some sense into her.'

He was right, and five minutes later, all three of them returned to the living room where Reeve had done her best to make herself comfortable.

She moved to the edge of the couch when Bella came into the room and flopped into the chair farthest away from her.

'Okay,' Luke started. 'We're here to listen to what your mother has to say. This isn't about apologies for past behaviour because there is absolutely no reason she should be apologising.'

'You think?' Bella practically hissed the words.

'I do,' Luke said. 'Hear her out, Bell. Okay?'

Bella shrugged, and Reeve took a deep breath and began.

As she spoke, she desperately wanted to pull her daughter into a hug. With each word she spoke about the diagnosis, treatment, and likely long-term effects the illness could have, Bella's anger was replaced with sadness. Reeve's heart ached for her daughter.

'You honestly had no idea you did any of those things?' Bella finally said.

Reeve shook her head. 'No, and I have no idea where it even comes from. I understand how painful it is, Bell. My mum did and said such awful things that at times I vowed I'd never visit her again. I do understand how you feel. Granddad was much more understanding and tolerant than I ever was. I don't know how, as some of the things she said to him were unforgivable, but I think he'd done enough research to realise that the person saying and doing the horrible things wasn't Mum. It was like an alien or monster had taken over her thoughts and actions. If you can separate us into two people, it might be easier. Hopefully you won't see as much of the alien version of me now that I've been given some medication.'

Reeve found herself unable to control the tears

when Bella moved onto her couch and hugged her. 'I've been so horrible. Dad said you were sick, but I didn't want to believe him.'

'I didn't want to believe it either.' Reeve noticed Luke checking his watch. 'Need to be somewhere?'

His cheeks reddened. 'No, but I'm aware that Jess could arrive at any minute.'

Reeve was immediately contrite. 'Sorry, yes, I'd better explain who she is.' She turned to Bella. 'Remember the woman you were speaking to at the funeral? Jessica?'

Bella nodded. 'Yeah, I was sure I knew her from somewhere. Who is she?'

'And why is she coming here?' Nick added.

'It turns out she's my half-sister,' Reeve said. 'Your aunt,' she added for Bella's benefit. 'Granddad had a few secrets that we're only now finding out about.'

Bella's mouth dropped open. 'You're kidding. He cheated on Nana?'

Reeve nodded. 'Around the same time she would have found out she was pregnant with me. I had dinner with Jess last week. She's lovely. She had a very difficult childhood thanks to Dad. She was in and out of foster homes, as her mother died when she was five. She's open to getting to know us. I know it's a huge shock, and hopefully you won't feel too badly about your grandfather.'

She turned to Nick, who looked surprisingly guilty, and frowned.

'What?' Nick said.

'Why do you look like you've got something to hide?'

'Yeah, mate,' Luke added, 'you're very red.'

'You knew, didn't you?' Reeve couldn't believe it. Her ex-husband knew, and she didn't.

'Not exactly. When things didn't work out with us, Martin had a chat with me. Said he was disappointed that I'd messed up, but he wasn't one to judge. That he'd done something a lot worse many years ago. Something that he regretted every day, and he had a lot of respect for the fact that I'd admitted what I'd done. He didn't tell me about Jess, but I assumed he'd had an affair.' He turned to Reeve. 'It wasn't my place to tell you.'

A knock on the front door silenced all of them.

'I'll get it,' Reeve said. 'Be nice, okay?'

She opened the front door to find Sloane and Jess standing there. Both had concern written all over their faces.

'You okay?' Sloane asked.

Reeve took a deep breath, refusing to dissolve

into the puddle of tears that threatened. 'I will be. Come in. There's some news to share, but first, I need to introduce Jess.' She smiled at her half-sister. 'You met Sloane briefly at the funeral. Sloane, this is my sister, Jess.'

Sloane's mouth dropped open. 'What?'

'Yep, my sister. The one that my daughter, husband, and ex are dying to meet properly.'

23

Jess hadn't been sure what to expect when she'd received Reeve's text message. Her thoughts had been consumed with the phone call from Devon earlier that morning and the news of Joey. At first, she'd wondered if the request to join the family for a meal was to discuss this, but realised quickly, as the conversation turned to Reeve's health, that it wasn't. She'd been introduced to Luke, Nick, and Bella properly. She'd met them all briefly at the funeral, but this was in a very different context.

As Reeve asked them to gather around, she couldn't help but appreciate Reeve's taste in men. Both her ex-husband and current husband were lovely and gorgeous, as was fifteen-year-old Bella.

'I've never had an aunt,' the teenager had said with a shy smile.

Now, as Reeve described the issues she'd been having, the results of the MRI, and the uncertain future ahead, Jess's heart contracted as raw pain flashed in Bella's eyes. She could only imagine what that must be like for a fifteen-year-old to hear. The fierceness of her protectiveness came as a shock. One that must have registered on her face.

'You okay?' Reeve asked. She'd finished talking about her diagnosis and answering questions, and Sloane had offered to help Nick dish up the lasagne he'd cooked. Luke and Bella had joined them, leaving Reeve and Jess to talk.

Jess nodded. 'A little overwhelmed. I haven't been part of a family that cared about each other since Mum died.'

'Oh Jess,' Reeve said. 'Here's me thinking I've got problems, and then look at what you've been through.'

'The two aren't comparable,' Jess said. 'My stuff's in the past. This is your present and future. I'd like to be part of it, Reeve. Help you in any way I can. Whatever you need. For you and for Bella.'

Reeve nodded, her eyes filling with tears. 'I've known you for, what, two weeks, and you feel like family. You're a total stranger, but there's something there. I can't describe it.'

'I know. I felt the same way when I first met you. I guess it's the bond of family.' Jess wiped her eyes. She couldn't believe how emotional she was feeling. It was more than having met her sister. It was the thought that she could lose her as quickly as she'd found her.

'You're thinking about the future, aren't you? That I might become someone different. Someone you wished you'd never met.'

Jess shook her head. 'Half true. I'm worried about the future, but I'll never wish I'd never met you. This is honestly one of the happiest moments of my life. Bella's so gorgeous too. I can't believe I have a niece.'

'What about you? When we had dinner, you said you'd been through a breakup, but you never elaborated. I assume there aren't kids.'

Jess laughed. 'Correct. I'm never having kids. I'm getting too old, but after my experience in foster care, I promised myself I'd never put a child through that.'

'But why would you think your child would end up in foster care? It would be unlikely.'

'I'm sure my mother would have thought that too,' Jess said, 'before she was killed.'

Reeve nodded. 'It's a shame. Kids are amazing.

Although mine hasn't been talking to me for the past few weeks so I'm probably not the best person to rave about parenting.'

'Lasagne is served,' Nick announced, interrupting them. 'Bell's tossing together a salad.' He grinned and ushered them all into the kitchen.

Jess had to wonder as she watched the ease with which he and Reeve spoke to each other why they'd split. They appeared to be the perfect couple with the perfect teenager, except for the fact that Reeve had remarried.

She asked Sloane about them after they'd all finished eating and the two of them insisted on clearing the table while the others took the brownies into the living room.

'I think Nick would do anything to get Reeve back, but he cheated on her, which was a deal-breaker,' Sloane said. 'We were all devastated when they broke up.'

'Why did he cheat?'

'It was a few years before her mum died,' Sloane said. 'She was getting hard to handle, and Reeve and Martin weren't sure what to do. Reeve needed Nick's support, but she was stressed and wasn't much fun to be around. We all copped it, and I guess Nick found comfort somewhere else. He felt so guilty that he told her.' She lowered her voice. 'I know he asked Martin for advice on what to do.'

'And Martin told him to fess up? That's a bit of a double standard.'

'No, he told him to never utter a word to anyone.'

Jess's mouth dropped open. 'Okay, maybe that's worse. But certainly more in keeping with his own track record. But Nick still told her?'

Sloane nodded. 'He assumed she'd forgive him. But I think for Reeve it was more than just the cheating. Money was an issue in their relationship. Nick could never understand why Reeve wouldn't accept her father's help. He was a multi-millionaire and both Reeve and Nick were working their butts off in order to get by. Martin wanted to give them money, Nick wanted to accept the money, but Reeve stood in the way.'

'She wanted to be independent,' Jess said.

Sloane nodded. 'Which I understand, but I'm not sure that she's completely independent now. I think you'll find Luke pays for a lot of their lifestyle, which Nick must find frustrating.'

'It's not her dad though,' Jess said. 'Luke works hard and so does Reeve, so perhaps she views it differently. Have they been married long?'

'No, they met when Reeve's mother was in her

final stages of life and married a few months later. I guess it hasn't even been a year yet. He's a good guy and adores Reeve. I just hope he can handle what's coming.'

Jess nodded. 'He's going to be tested over the coming months and years, that's for sure.'

Sloane sighed. 'Having lived through Alice's diagnosis and the years that followed, I can say that unfortunately, we all are.'

* * *

Jess was still smiling when she arrived at work the next morning. She'd left Nick's the previous night with the realisation that she was part of a family. A loving, caring, close-knit family. It was the strangest thing that had ever happened to her. There was an underlying connection between her and Reeve, and Bella too.

She had two weeks before officially taking over as CEO. She pushed open the door to her office with a feeling of anticipation. She had a meeting at three to announce her replacement, and she was having lunch with Reeve. The previous night had been lovely, but it had been about the bigger picture, the family and those who loved Reeve. She was looking forward to it being the two of them.

'Jess.' Marlee broke into her thoughts as Jess stored her bag in the large drawer in her desk.

'Sorry, but there's been a mix-up. I've got a guy in reception saying he has a meeting with you. Something to do with next quarter's funding. It's not in your calendar, and I wasn't sure whether you knew about it? It's possible it was one of Stuart's meetings, and he's palmed it off on you now that you'll be filling the CEO position.'

Jess frowned. 'That's strange. Stuart didn't mention it. Can you offer him coffee and put him in one of the meeting rooms? I've got a couple of things to do, and then I'll meet with him.'

Five minutes later, Jess pushed open the meeting room door and froze. Dean Blackwell sat at the head of the table, his arms folded across his chest.

'Hello, Little J.'

Her breathing quickened, and she found herself holding the table to steady herself. 'What? How?' The effort to get the two words out was more than she could handle.

He held up a newspaper and threw it across the table to her. 'Saw this. It made me think it was about time we caught up. Been a long time.'

Jess glanced at the paper. It was an article about Martin's death with photos from the funeral. There was a photo of her and Reeve sitting together with the caption, *Who Will Inherit the Elliot Fortune?* She quickly scanned the article. It said nothing about her being Martin's daughter, so why was Dean here?

'You need to leave,' Jess said, looking up at Dean and doing her best to steady her breathing. 'Right now, before I call the police.'

He laughed. '*You* call the police? That's my threat, not yours. After what *you* did.'

A wobble started in Jess's legs. She'd put all of this behind her. She'd moved on.

'That's right. Thought you'd get away without me ever knowing, didn't you?'

'What do you want?'

He pointed at the paper. 'That photo suggests you might be due an inheritance.'

'No, it doesn't. It shows me at a funeral, talking to a friend who happens to be his daughter.'

'Well, that's good news for me. That you're friends with the daughter, because even if you're not in line to inherit, she is.'

'And?'

'And you owe me, and your *friend* can help settle that debt.'

Jess stared at him. She owed him a knife to the chest. That's what she owed him. 'Are you crazy? You should be in jail.'

He laughed again. 'Once more, you seem to have our roles reversed. *You* should be in jail. You've got death on your hands, which I'm sure the authorities would be very interested in hearing about.'

'And you want money?' How did he know what had happened? He'd disappeared and hadn't been around to witness the fallout.

He grinned, his eyes narrow and dark. 'Now you're cottoning on. I would like a very large sum of money to help me with the trauma your actions have caused.'

'I can't do this,' Jess said. 'I need you to go. Whatever you've been told isn't true. Just leave me alone.'

Dean stood, pushing an envelope towards her. 'I'm sure Sandy had no reason to lie to me about what she witnessed after I left. She was only nine or ten, but she still remembers what happened. Now, the envelope contains my request and my terms. You'll find bank details in there too. I've gone out of my way to make this easy for you. Call me if you've got any questions, and if I don't hear from you or receive the required funds on the dates provided, I'll be speaking with the police.'

'You could never prove anything.'

He shrugged. 'Willing to risk finding that out, Little J? Sandy is happy to talk and say what she saw and what she was told to cover up.'

Jess sank into a chair once he'd left the room. Her breathing was erratic, and it was likely she'd pass out any minute. She lowered her head between her knees, willing her insides to settle. She never expected to see him again. What if he did report her? She'd covered up the worst things a person could do. She'd lose everything. Her job, her friends, her reputation, and Reeve.

* * *

Jess did her best to plant a smile on her face and pretend that everything was alright when she met up with Reeve for lunch. But the moment her sister looked at her, she knew she hadn't fooled her.

She'd waited until they'd placed their orders and were seated in a discreet table at the back of the cafe before asking the inevitable. 'Are you okay?'

Jess nodded, doing her best to keep the smile on her face, but even she knew it was wobbly. 'Why wouldn't I be?'

Reeve frowned. 'You look like you might be sick

any minute, and your hands are shaking.' She reached across and placed her hand over Jess's trembling fingers. 'What can I do to help?'

The concern and compassion in Reeve's voice caused Jess's eyes to fill with tears. 'Sorry – difficult morning.'

'Is it something to do with Dad?'

Jess considered her questions. 'Inadvertently, I guess.' She didn't want to risk losing Reeve, but she couldn't keep this to herself either. 'Someone from my past turned up at the office this morning. There was a photo in the paper of you and me sitting together at Martin's funeral with a headline questioning who is going to inherit the Elliot fortune.'

'What? No one except for us even knows about your connection to Martin.' Reeve's eyes narrowed. 'Do they?'

'No, and the article doesn't say anything about my relationship with him,' Jess said. 'It was a sensational headline to stir things up. But the guy who turned up saw that photo and assumes I'm in a position to get money, either through inheritance or via my connection to you. He wants a cut.'

Reeve sucked in a breath. She waited as a waitress set their coffee orders down on the table. 'Why would he think you'd give him money?'

Jess didn't meet her eyes, her gaze fixed on the napkin dispenser. 'He believes he has information which could cause problems for me if it was released. He's using it to blackmail me.'

'And would the information cause problems?'

A tear ran down Jess's cheek as she nodded.

As Reeve stared at her, Jess knew she was wondering what could be so bad that someone would be willing to blackmail her.

'You can't give him money, no matter how bad the information is. He'll continue to ask for more.'

'I know,' Jess said. 'But I can't risk the information being released either. It would cost me everything. My job, my relationship with you, my friends. I might even go to prison.'

'Prison? We should speak with Devon,' Reeve said. 'He'll know what to do. Are you free tonight? I'm sure he will make himself available if we contact him.'

'I'm not sure he'll be any help,' Jess said. 'I can't tell him what happened.' She stifled a sob. 'I thought I'd left it all behind me.'

'How long ago did this happen?'

'Twenty-five years.'

Reeve's eyes widened. 'What? You would only have been fifteen – Bella's age. There's nothing you could have done at that age that you would need to worry about now. You were still just a kid.' She smiled. 'Honestly, Jess, think about it. If Bella did something awful, she'd get a slap on the wrist, even if it was bad enough to end up with the police. It might be twenty-five years on, but they'd take into account that you were fifteen at the time. I'd tell this guy he's not getting anything. Even if he reveals the big secret, your age will play a huge part in how anyone will react.'

Jess locked eyes with her. 'Even when they find out I killed my son?'

Even as the words left her lips, Jess regretted them. The colour drained from Reeve's face, and her mouth dropped open.

'What?'

Jess looked around the coffee shop, making sure no one was listening. 'I killed my son, Reeve. He was only hours old, and I suffocated him.'

Horror flashed in Reeve's eyes. Jess could only imagine what she was thinking.

'Not deliberately,' she added. 'He was born at three a.m., and I was exhausted from the birth. They put him next to me to feed him, but I fell asleep, and when they came in to check on me, I'd rolled over on him, and he'd suffocated. I was so out of it they couldn't even wake me.' Tears ran down her cheeks. 'I woke up to find my baby gone. They decided it would be too traumatic for me to see him. The decision was made before I even got to say goodbye. He was so small, so helpless.'

'But you can't be blamed for that,' Reeve said.

'Yes, I can. It was karma. Through the whole pregnancy, I'd wished I'd miscarry. I couldn't raise a baby, and I was terrified of giving birth. But within minutes after he arrived, that all disappeared. I fell in love with him instantly. This little human had been living inside of me for nine months. All I wanted to do was protect him.' Her voice cracked. 'And instead, I killed him.'

'Oh hon, I'm so sorry,' Reeve said, 'but you can't blame yourself. What happened to you was an accident. A terrible, terrible accident. Surely the nurses made you realise that. And the police too. You weren't charged, were you?'

Jess gave a brief shake of her head, avoiding Reeve's eyes. She picked up her coffee and sipped it.

'As traumatic as what you went through was, it's not something this guy can hold over you. People would feel tremendous sorrow for you, not animosity.'

Jess didn't respond. She couldn't tell Reeve the whole truth.

'Did someone lead you to believe it was your fault at the time?'

Jess nodded.

'I'm so sorry that happened. You should have been given counselling, not made to feel like that. I'm also surprised they took your baby without giving you the chance to say goodbye. Did you see anyone?'

'No. There's more to it, Reeve. I'm not sure I can tell you. If what I've already told you hasn't changed your opinion of me, the rest will.'

Reeve managed a small smile. 'Hey, don't forget I'm currently suspended from school for sexually harassing a student, I've abused most of my friends and my daughter, and I invited a stranger into my bed.'

'What? A stranger?'

Reeve shuddered at the memory. 'Don't ask. To be honest, I think you're the only one I haven't offended. And even then, I imagine you're too kind to tell me what I have said or done that I have no recollection of. And as an added benefit, with my memory issues, unfortunately, or possibly fortunately, if I'm shocked by your revelation, I may not remember anything you tell me.'

Jess couldn't help but smile. Reeve had a self-deprecating way of speaking about herself that you couldn't help but love her for. She was going through such a rough time, yet Jess could see she was genuinely concerned for her. She took a deep breath. 'I've never told anyone about this, and I'd appreciate it if it was kept between us.'

'I may be going nuts, but you can trust me.' Reeve frowned. 'I think you can, anyway. This version of me can be trusted. The other one I have no control over.'

Jess took another deep breath. 'I guess I'll take the risk. In response to your question of did I see anyone, no, I didn't. No one even knew about Leo's birth or his death, other than those of us present.'

'What? Hold on, someone must have, or this guy wouldn't be threatening you.'

'No one outside of my foster family knew. They were ashamed that I was pregnant at fifteen and kept me hidden once I started showing. They'd organised a private adoption, and my baby would have gone to its new home later the day he was born. My foster mother, Carly, worked as a midwife, so there was no need to have anyone but her to attend to me. My foster parents were angry with me for what I'd done. I think that's why they took Leo, and I didn't get to say goodbye. It was one of the punishments they handed down. Carly knew I'd changed my mind about keeping him and had made it very clear it wasn't an option. She and Mike would have found themselves in a lot of trouble if people knew of my pregnancy.'

'I know you were only fifteen, but that's not completely unheard of. There are a lot of teen pregnancies.'

Jess closed her eyes, her stomach swirling.

Reeve laid her hands on Jess's. 'Really, Jess, you shouldn't have blamed yourself, and the family should have looked after you from day one. What sort of people hide a pregnancy for the sake of appearances? It wasn't the 1950s.'

Jess opened her eyes and withdrew her hand. 'The type of people who hide the fact that a boy in their care was a rapist. A rapist who came to me every night for weeks. A rapist who I told my foster parents about, and they didn't believe me but threatened to tell everyone I encouraged him and that I had made a move on Mike, the foster father, too. They got lots of government benefits for being foster carers, and if anyone had learned of the rape and the fact that I'd told them but they hadn't believed me, they would have been deemed unfit to continue as foster carers and possibly charged.'

'They allowed him to stay in the house after you told them?'

Jess nodded. 'Until I found out I was pregnant. Then they threw him out and told him he was never to tell anyone about my pregnancy. The day he disappeared was one of my happier days in foster care.'

Reeve shook her head. 'You poor thing. You should never have been put in that position.'

Jess could see the anger flash in Reeve's eyes and guessed what she was thinking. 'It's not Martin's fault.'

'It was his fault you were in foster care to start with,' Reeve said. She let out a long breath. 'Anyway, there's not much point going down the road of what-ifs and what could have been. So, the boy disappeared, but someone must have told him your baby died.'

'From what I gather, he's recently spoken with Sandy, the other foster girl who was in the house at the time. She was younger, only nine. A few days after Leo was born, my caseworker appeared at the house. She said to pack our bags, as we were being placed elsewhere. Carly didn't bother to say goodbye to either of us. She just disappeared. But Mike did. He said that I'd damaged their faith in mankind, and they couldn't stay under the same roof. He said I was a flirt and a whore, and it wasn't Dean's fault. It was mine, and if I ever spoke of my pregnancy or Leo's birth and death to anyone that they would make sure people knew I'd killed him. That I'd placed a pillow over his face and suffocated him. That I was a murderer.'

Tears streamed down Jess's cheeks as she spoke. 'I was too scared to tell anyone. Sandy knew I'd been pregnant, but I never saw her again. Until Dean spoke to me this morning, I assumed Sandy didn't know what had happened that day, but it appears she did.'

'And your new family didn't ask about you? You must have been traumatised by what happened. Surely they wanted to know if you were okay?'

'They thought I was another moody teenager. And they'd only agreed to be foster carers so they could use me to help them. They expected me to *pay* for their kindness. They provided me with accommodation and food, and I cooked, cleaned, and looked after their four-year-old when I was home from school and most weekends.'

'Oh Jess, you should have spoken up. Imagine if you had a case like that at Safe Houses. You'd never allow that to happen.'

'I only had two years to get through before I was

eighteen and would no longer be in the system, and I figured it was part of my punishment for what happened to Leo. I went through the motions. School during the day, cooking, cleaning, and looking after their kid when I got home. The busier I kept, the less time I had to think about what had happened. And now, twenty-five years later, thanks to Dean, one of the things I've fought so hard to reconcile in my life is all fresh again. He wants to traumatise and blackmail me.'

'No.' Reeve shook her head. 'We won't let that happen. We'll speak to Devon and find out where you stand legally, and then we'll get rid of this guy. I won't allow you to be hurt again. You've been through enough already.'

Jess smiled at the determination in Reeve's voice. 'Thank you, and thank you for not judging me.'

'You did nothing wrong, Jess. They did. You've been let down so badly in life I don't even know where to start. And you certainly don't need to thank me; this is what family is about. We're there for each other.'

A lump rose in Jess's throat. *Family.*

Reeve smiled. 'We're family now, whether you like it or not. And family looks after each other. Those people shouldn't be allowed to get away with what they did. Have you ever considered tracking them down?'

* * *

Reeve's words played over in Jess's mind as she lay in bed later that night. *Have you ever considered tracking them down?* For the first time since Sam left, the king-size bed seemed big and empty. She'd give anything right now to be wrapped in strong, comforting arms. But it was Trent's face that filled her mind, not Sam's. She shook herself. Where had that come from?

She'd wanted to track down Carly and Mike Grenfell since she'd turned thirty. Something changed when she hit her thirties. She'd matured and realised that hiding from her past wasn't healthy. She'd done as much as look through the foster system to see if they were still registered, but they weren't. They also no longer appeared to be in Melbourne or Victoria. She'd decided it was a sign to leave it alone. To stop dredging up the memories. But now, with Dean demanding money, she needed answers. How could they do what they did back then – hide the fact that they'd had a teenage rapist in their home and then threaten to say she'd murdered her baby? Her poor little boy. There was no record of his birth or his death. She didn't even know what they'd done with his body.

Huge tears ran down her cheeks and soaked her pillow. She'd only been fifteen. She was scared and alone. She could be excused back then. But now? She was forty, about to become the CEO of a large organisation, and Leo deserved better.

She picked up her phone from the nightstand and pulled up Reeve's number.

> Thanks for today. Sorry I was such a mess. In answer to your question, yes, I would like to find them. Do you think Devon would help?

Within minutes the reply came back.

> Definitely. I'll contact him tomorrow and set up a meeting. And Jess, remember, you did nothing wrong. You are a victim in this, and they should be held accountable.

Jess smiled as she looked at Reeve's response.

> Thanks, sis!

A smiley emoticon with a huge love heart came back.

Jess put the phone back on the bedside table, feeling marginally better. It still blew her away that she could feel so close to Reeve and that Reeve was willing to accept that they were related and that she wasn't after Martin's fortune. She'd made it clear that she wasn't, but it didn't mean that Reeve would necessarily believe her.

She closed her eyes, not expecting sleep to come, but two hours later woke to her phone pinging with a text message. She glanced at the clock; it was after midnight. She grabbed her phone. Every now and then, an overnight caseworker needed her help.

> Money grubbing bitch. We all know you're after Dad's fortune and you don't give a shit about any of us.
> Stay away.

The message was from Reeve.

Jess stared at it, her lips curling up at the edges. She knew it wasn't funny. That it was a sign that Reeve was suffering, but it was hard not to laugh. This was not Reeve. It was other Reeve. It's what she would have expected, but the fact that this was coming from the sick Reeve was enough for her to know to ignore it.

Her smile faded quickly and was replaced with sadness. In her dealings with Reeve, this was the first *other* Reeve exchange. It didn't faze her. But what about when this would be all she'd get from her? When *her* Reeve would disappear completely? She'd only just met her, and yet that day would be one of the hardest she'd ever have to deal with. She only hoped it was still a long way away, or there would be advances in medicine that would stop it from ever happening. She found herself crossing her fingers as she returned her phone to the bedside table and turned over in an attempt to go back to sleep.

24

Reeve contacted Devon first thing the next morning. She was still in shock with the story Jess had told her. The poor woman. It was one of the few times since his death that she knew if Martin was alive right now, she would probably kill him. All of this had been avoidable. If Martin had owned his responsibilities from day one, rather than assuming he could throw money at the situation, it would never have happened. She organised a meeting for five thirty that afternoon.

She picked up her phone to send Jess a message with the details, her heart almost stopping as she saw a text she'd sent at midnight the night before. She dropped her phone on the counter.

She'd ruined it. Just when she and Jess were getting to know each other, she'd gone and sent that. Her lower lip quivered. She couldn't catch a break.

Her phone rang, and Jess's name popped up on the display. Her heart sank. This was it. The end of a relationship before it even started.

'I'm sorry,' she said before Jess had a chance to speak. 'I was about to text you with a meeting time to see Devon later today, and I saw the text from last night. I—'

'Hey,' Jess cut her off. 'I wasn't ringing about that. That was *other* Reeve, not you. I know the difference. Don't stress.'

'It didn't upset you?'

'I laughed. But then I was sad, if I'm honest. Not because of what you said, but because I know you're sick, and I hope you never get to a point where you don't know who I am.'

Tears filled Reeve's eyes. 'That's probably the nicest thing anyone's ever said to me.'

'Well, I'm the nice sister,' Jess said with a laugh. 'And you, based on your texts, are not!'

Reeve managed a small laugh; she was grateful Jess was able to make light of it.

'I rang to say thanks for yesterday. You've given

me the strength to do something about this. Dean's getting nothing, other than a lawsuit, I hope.'

'Good. Devon's agreed to see us at five thirty. Will you be able to make that?'

'Definitely. And Reeve, don't stress about the message. How about this. Anytime I get one from you, I'll send one back that's as nasty. That way, you'll know I saw it and that I knew it came from other Reeve.'

'Really?'

'We might as well have fun with it while we can. Obviously, if it becomes distressing, we chat about it and come up with another solution, but for now, it will defuse any concerns.'

Reeve ended the call with a smile on her face. If only she could get everyone to react like that if she sent them horrible messages.

'You look happy.' Luke entered the kitchen and took an apple from the fruit bowl.

'I am. This situation with Jess, although weird, is probably the best thing that's ever happened to me.'

Luke raised an eyebrow. 'Best thing?'

Reeve smiled, knowing he was fishing for a compliment. 'The best thing since you. Is that better?'

'Much better, and I'm glad to see you looking cheerful. Bella seemed to be coming around the other night too.'

'Are you?'

'What do you mean?'

'I don't expect you to forgive me for what I did. It's terrible, and if the situation was reversed, I don't know how I'd feel.'

'Gutted.' Luke took a bite from his apple.

'I don't know what to do or say,' Reeve said. 'It's honestly the worst thing I've ever done.'

Luke sighed. 'It'll all work out, Ree. We both know you didn't consciously invite him over. This one's just harder to swallow than the rest. I'll deal with it, don't worry. Just give me a bit of time.'

Reeve pulled him to her. 'Thank you. I don't know how I'd cope through all of this without you.'

'Which is a problem,' Luke said. 'As you know, I have to go away tomorrow afternoon for a few days. It's that lecture at Adelaide University followed by a tour of the new facilities at the hospital.'

Reeve nodded, not willing to admit she had no recollection of him telling her about it.

'It's only for two nights, but I wondered how you'd feel about asking Sloane to stay here with you, or even go and stay at Nick's? I'd feel better knowing you had someone keeping an eye on you.'

Reeve wasn't sure how to respond. The rational part of her knew it made sense. He couldn't trust her, and realistically she couldn't trust herself, but it was awful as a grown adult to think this was necessary.

He leant forward and kissed her forehead again. 'Think about it. Now, I have to go. I'll be home by eight, okay?'

Reeve nodded. 'I'm meeting with Jess and Devon at five thirty. I'm sure I'll be home by eight, but if I'm not, ring me. We might grab a bite to eat and you can join us.'

Luke smiled. 'You and your new family. What's the meeting for? The DNA test?'

Reeve shook her head. 'No, a problem Jess needs help with. I'd completely forgotten about the test.'

'Well, don't,' Luke said. 'Make sure she is family before you get too invested. I'll look into which is the best one and organise it. I'm pretty sure you can order them online, or I might be able to get one from work.'

Reeve nodded. If she was honest, she'd be devastated to find out Jess wasn't family. She had to be. Why would Martin track her down if she wasn't?

* * *

'Okay,' Devon said, 'I think I've got everything I need.' Reeve and Jess had met at DS Legal a little before five thirty, and the three of them now sat around a small meeting table in Devon's office.

'What do you think?' Reeve asked, glancing at Jess. She could only imagine how hard it had been for Jess to go through the whole story again.

Devon slammed his fist on the desk, causing the two women to jump. 'Sorry, I think I'm channelling Martin.'

'I told you,' Reeve said to Jess, 'he would be smashing things at this point.'

'Which is what I feel like doing.' Devon took a deep breath. 'Leave it with me. I'll get some guys working on this for me. Dean Blackwell should be charged, but being a crime from so long ago, I'm not sure we'll get anything to stick.'

'I just want him gone,' Jess said.

'That we'll have no problem achieving. As for the Grenfell family, I'll track them down and see what I can find out.'

Jess nodded, and she and Reeve stood. 'Thanks, Devon. You too, Reeve. I can't believe after all these years I'm doing this.'

Reeve smiled. 'It's a lot easier with your family on your side.'

'Speaking of family,' Devon said. 'This came for

you.' He shuffled some documents on his desk and picked up a box. 'It's a DNA test kit.'

Reeve took the kit from him and stared at it. She looked at Jess. 'What do you think? Personally, I don't think there's any need. I only want to know the result if it's a positive match.'

Jess gave a small laugh. 'I think we should make sure. For Martin's sake too. If I'm not his child, then he's lived a life feeling guilty and spending a lot of money thinking he was doing the right thing. I have no idea if Mum was seeing more men than Martin when I was conceived, but if she was, then it might explain why she didn't want anything to do with him.'

'But where would that leave us?' Reeve couldn't bear to lose anything else right now. She'd lost her father, Bella to a degree, and her mind was rapidly going. She'd gained a sister, and she certainly didn't want to lose her.

'It leaves us as very close friends,' Jess said. 'As close as sisters, but without actually being sisters.'

'It's a simple cheek swab,' Devon said. 'Do it now if you like, and I'll send it off. You'll have the results in a few days.'

Jess shrugged. 'Let's get it over with. It honestly

won't change anything I've said to you, Reeve. I'll be there for you, regardless.'

Reeve did her best to smile. As lovely as Jess's words were, she was pretty sure if the test came back as a negative match, she would be thinking differently. Why would you want to get caught up with someone with dementia if you didn't have to?

As Devon sealed the box to return the cheek swabs for testing, Reeve thought back to the conversation in Patricia's office about the enduring power of attorney. She closed her eyes, wishing she didn't have to address this.

'Everything okay?' Jess asked.

Reeve's eyes flicked open. 'Yes, sorry. It's my way of avoiding asking Devon something.'

'Oh?' Devon looked up, concern flashing in his eyes. 'What is it?'

Reeve sighed. 'Enduring power of attorney. I need to organise it in case my health deteriorates.'

Devon was silent for a moment before nodding. 'Okay. You'll want to appoint a medical treatment decision maker too. The enduring power of attorney role is more for financial decision making and other personal decisions that don't include health.'

Reeve nodded. 'I'll appoint Luke as both.'

'Okay, I'll organise the forms now. Ask Luke to get

in touch to make an appointment to come in and sign them when he's available.'

It was close to seven by the time they left Devon's office. Reeve had signed the forms, and they would be finalised once Luke made an appointment and signed them.

'Want to get a bite to eat?' Reeve asked. She was glad to have the distraction of Jess and to not have to think about the fact that she'd signed away her independence. 'There's a lovely little Thai restaurant around the corner.'

Jess nodded. 'Sounds great, although after all that discussion about the Grenfells and Leo, I'm not sure I could eat anything.'

Reeve linked her arm through Jess's. 'Then you'll have to watch me.'

25

Jess followed Reeve through the front door of the Thai restaurant, inhaling the aroma of sizzling garlic. Her stomach groaned, reminding her that she'd lived off coffee for most of the day. They were shown to a booth at the back of the restaurant.

'This is nice,' Jess said, relaxing into the squishy seat. 'Now, are you okay? Signing those forms couldn't have been easy.'

Reeve forced a smile. 'No, it wasn't. Still, it makes sense I do it now while I can. Hopefully, I'll be fine for ages and having Luke make the decisions for me is many years away.'

'Many, many years,' Jess said. 'Now, I think after a day like today, I need a drink to help me relax.'

'You don't deserve to relax.'

The male voice brought Jess to attention. Reeve's eyes widened as she looked around to see who was talking.

Before she had a chance to object, Dean slid into the seat beside her. He held his hand out to Reeve. 'Evening, I'm Dean Blackwell. Jess's ex-boyfriend from many years ago.'

Reeve didn't take his hand. Instead, she stood. 'Get out.'

Dean looked surprised by the venom in her voice, but he didn't move. 'I'm not going anywhere. I believe you're a close friend of Jess's. A friend who grew up with the rich old man. The one who recently checked out.'

Jess wasn't surprised to see Reeve flinch at Dean's casual disregard of Martin's life.

'Dean,' Jess said. 'Go. I mean it. You'll hear from my lawyer in the next few days.'

'Really?'

She nodded. 'It's the meeting we've come from. He knows the whole story and will be in touch.' She didn't add that he'd be in touch to run him out of town.

'You've come to your senses then. Finally realised that compensation is due and is the only way forward?'

Reeve sat back down, anger flashing in her eyes. Jess didn't need a DNA test to know that the woman sitting across from her had her back. They were sisters regardless of what blood said.

Jess stared at Dean. 'I still don't understand what you think happened and who told you.'

'Sandy knew part of it, that you'd had my baby. The Grenfells threw me out because of our relationship and never mentioned you were pregnant.'

Our relationship. Bile rose in Jess's throat that he had the audacity to refer to it as that. 'You raped me repeatedly. That's not a relationship. It's a criminal act.'

He laughed. 'Interesting how you've changed the story about what happened. You wanted me. You're a liar if you say otherwise.'

'And you're a complete prick,' Reeve said. She held up her hands in the way of apology when both Jess and Dean turned to look at her. 'Sorry, I shouldn't be getting involved in this conversation, but it's hard not to.'

'You're not the one who needs to apologise,' Jess said. 'This *prick* does. But we can all see that's not going to happen.'

'Me? I'm not the one who killed our baby.

Nothing I did to you, or you choose to make up that I did to you, is worse than that. Now, why don't we get to the point? I expect to be compensated or I'm going to the police.'

'Hold on,' Jess said. 'If Sandy didn't tell you, then who did?'

'Mike Grenfell. I tracked him and Carly down. They're living in Perth.'

'You went and saw them?'

'Didn't need to. A phone conversation was enough. Mike was pretty upset. Said he'd told me to leave because he didn't want a baby wrecking my life. I was only sixteen, and it wouldn't have been an ideal situation. Then when you killed him, he knew he'd made the right decision and that there was no need for me ever to find out. My perspective's a lot different now. I'm in my early forties, and I should have a son in his mid-twenties.'

'Even if he was alive, he would have been adopted out,' Jess said.

Dean shrugged. 'Doesn't mean he wouldn't have come looking, and I would have welcomed him with open arms. My own flesh and blood.' His eyes narrowed. 'I certainly wouldn't have killed him because he was an inconvenience.'

'I didn't kill my baby.' Jess forced the words

through gritted teeth. 'Not like you've been led to believe. Yes, he died, but not through deliberate actions.'

'I don't believe you, and neither does Mike Grenfell. They were witnesses, don't forget. People who chose to protect you. Just organise the compensation, Jess, and you'll never see me again.' He stood.

'I don't have the kind of money you're demanding.'

'How about you make a down payment now and sort out the rest later.' He nodded towards Reeve. 'We both know your friend's loaded, and I'm sure she'll help you out.'

'Please leave,' Jess said. 'I'll be in touch.'

He turned, and relief settled over Jess as he left the restaurant.

'Prick's an understatement.'

The two women sat in silence, both shocked by the encounter, and Jess was grateful Reeve wasn't hounding her, wanting to know how she felt.

'I guess the Grenfells meant it when they said they'd protect themselves at all costs. Lying to Dean even.'

'Maybe they worried he'd say something to the authorities, and then they'd be investigated like you said and lose the ability to foster. Did it ever worry you that they were allowed to take other girls in after you left?'

'Definitely. Once I started working in foster care I looked them up, but they were no longer in our system. I'd hoped that that meant they'd stopped fostering. I did my best to block them out of my mind, but when I turned thirty, it started to really nag at me. I checked again for them but couldn't find them. If I had, I would have reported them.'

'Dean said he found them in Perth. Would your searches have shown the results for Perth?'

Jess shook her head. 'No. I feel awful. I should have searched until I found them. I think part of me still wanted to do my best to forget them and everything that had happened. It was easy to assume they'd moved on to do something else rather than go through the trauma of facing them again.'

'I'd be by your side if you did decide it was time.'

'Would you go and see them if you were in my position?'

Reeve considered her answer. 'Possibly. I think I'd want to confront them. See why they thought it was okay to do what they did. They don't sound like the sort of people who are going to be remorseful, but who knows, twenty-five years have passed.'

Jess sighed. 'The fact that they told Dean I killed

the baby suggests I'm not going to get an apology. Let's wait and see what Devon comes up with. If they're still fostering, then yes, I'll feel the need to do something.' She stopped and smiled at Reeve. 'Thank you, by the way.'

'Me, for what?'

'For being here. Your moral support means heaps.' She smiled. 'And calling Dean a prick to his face was satisfying.'

'I should have punched him in the face,' Reeve said. 'He deserves a lot worse than that.'

Jess nodded. 'Yes, he does.' If she'd been even a little hungry earlier, she certainly wasn't now. 'I don't know if I can eat anything at all any more.'

'Let's order anyway,' Reeve suggested. 'By the time it arrives, you might feel like something.'

Jess nodded and ordered a Penang curry when the waiter came to take their order.

'Order a drink if you want,' Reeve said. 'You could probably use one by now.'

Jess shook her head. 'No, I'm good. A soft drink will be fine.'

'A glass of Pinot Gris,' Reeve told the waiter.

'Honestly,' Jess said when the waiter left, 'I can live without wine, and I want to support you.'

Reeve stared at her for a moment.

'What?'

'I was wondering.' Reeve blushed. 'Luke has to go away tomorrow for a couple of nights for work, and he's worried that if I'm by myself, I might do something stupid like I did last time.'

'The guy?'

Reeve nodded. 'He's suggested I ask Sloane to come and stay or for me to go and stay with Nick and Bella.'

Jess smiled. 'And you think it would be better if we had some sister bonding time.'

'It crossed my mind, yes. I'm sure Sloane or Nick would happily support me, but they're all a bit sad about the situation and keep checking on me. It's much easier being around you. You treat me like I'm normal and laugh when I do something stupid. Like the text the other night. Anyway, if you were happy to hang out tomorrow and Friday night, that would be great.'

'I'd love to. But will you be okay during the day? I'll have to go to work.'

Reeve shrugged. 'Who knows, but that's no different than any normal day when Luke's at work. It's interesting, but I seem to get up to the bad things in the evening. Maybe it's part of my routine.'

'Let's break the routine. I've got a spare room. I'm

within walking distance to St Kilda. You can explore the shops and have a change of scenery.'

'Really?'

'I'd love you to. My place is probably a lot smaller than yours, but it's cute and relaxing.'

'Thank you. Who knows, a change of scenery and I might be a new person.'

26

Nausea churned in the pit of Reeve's stomach as she held the phone to her ear and listened to Sergeant Butler. That someone had murdered her father was too much to bear.

'We've been able to exclude those of you who were close to your father: yourself, your husband, your ex-husband, Jessica Williams, Devon Saunders, and many others. We are, however, investigating business contacts your father was involved with.'

Reeve had thanked her for the update and called out to Luke.

He appeared in the kitchen with his overnight bag in hand, ready for his Adelaide trip.

'They've confirmed Dad was murdered.'

Luke dropped his bag. 'What? Are you sure?'

Reeve nodded. 'They believe the security cameras were disabled, and someone waited until Dad was having a drink in his study before starting the fire. A drug was found in his system that would have put him to sleep, possibly before the fire was started. Their attempt to make it look like an accident didn't fool the police.'

'I'm so sorry.' He moved towards her and took her in his arms.

Tears ran down Reeve's cheeks. 'They've ruled out quite a lot of us already and seem to be focusing on Dad's work contacts.'

'Oh God, Reeve, I really am sorry.' He squeezed her tight. 'I know you don't want to believe that Nick would have anything to do with it, but did they rule out Jess?'

Reeve pulled back from Luke and stared at him. 'Nick definitely didn't do it. But Jess? You think she was involved?'

'I hope not. It's just that she's appeared so close to his death and is inheriting such a lot of money. I know this will sound crazy, but I'm almost wondering if this is some elaborate plan that Devon set up and employed Jess to be part of.'

Reeve shook her head. 'That's impossible. Dad

went in search of Jess before he died. Devon didn't do that.'

'I know, but hear me out. The only person, other than your father, who knew he'd had an affair and another child was Devon. Devon is the trustee of the Elliot Family Trust and also knew Jessica was going to inherit sixteen million dollars. He helped track down Jessica Williams, and everything's unfolded from there. What if she's just someone who looks like Bella? Someone he'll instruct not only to contest the way the will has been left but also the family trust?'

Reeve shook her head. 'Nope. Absolutely no way.'

'You hardly know her, Ree. We don't even know for sure she's related.'

'You met her,' Reeve said. 'She's not even interested in the money.'

'That's what she says to your face,' Luke said. 'Sixteen million dollars is a big payday.'

'We did a DNA test with Devon. The results will be back in the next few days.'

'With Devon? I said I'd organise it.'

'Well, he already did, and we sent it off to get the results.'

'You should get another one done.'

'What? Why?'

'Really? You need to ask why? Reeve, if I'm right

and Devon has set this up, he'll falsify the DNA results.'

Reeve's head was swimming. 'Where's all this coming from?'

'Look, hopefully it's just crazy thoughts, but it's my gut feeling. There's something not right, I know it.' He checked his watch. 'I'll see if I can work it out when I see him this morning.'

'This morning?'

Luke's brow furrowed. 'The appointment to sign the forms to become your enduring power of attorney and medical decision maker. You asked me to go and see Devon, remember?'

'I remember, but I didn't realise you'd already organised an appointment.'

'I said I'd stop by this morning on my way to the airport. It will only take a few minutes. I might ask him a few questions about Jess too.'

'Don't cause any trouble, please.'

Luke leant forward and kissed her on the forehead. 'Of course I won't. I want to make sure you're looked after. Now, I'd better go, but promise me one thing.'

'What?'

'Get another DNA test done to be sure. I can almost guarantee the one you did with Devon will come back quicker than you thought and will be a positive match. I didn't get a chance to get one from work, but I had a look online, and Paternity Testing Australia is probably the best one. I'll see if I can get one couriered here before the weekend, and then you can organise with Jess to do another one. Tell her about the second test before you get the results back from the first one. That way, you can make it sound like you were going to do it regardless of whether it is a positive or negative match. Okay? That way if I'm wrong about all of this it hopefully won't cause any issues with Jess.'

Reeve nodded, although she wasn't sure it was something she'd do. He leant forward and kissed her lightly on the lips. 'I'm not trying to ruin what you've got with Jess; I'm just worried you're being taken advantage of. If Devon's test is a positive match, I can almost guarantee he'll talk Jess into contesting the will and possibly the family trust.'

'Realistically, she'd be entitled to do that.'

'Yes, but as you said, she's shown no interest in the money. If she suddenly changes her mind on all of that, then you'll know you're being conned. Promise me you'll be careful and look out for signs. Invite her over for dinner on the weekend, and we'll do the second test. And please make a different arrangement for the next two nights. Stay here and get someone to be here with you. Actually, leave it with me. I'll organise something on my way to the airport.'

'You?'

Luke smiled. 'Yes, I know the perfect person. I'll see if she's available and surprise you.'

Reeve shook her head. 'No, I don't need any new surprises right now. Let me sort it out.'

Luke picked up his bag and took his keys from the bowl on the counter without responding. He kissed her on the forehead before moving through the internal access into the garage.

* * *

Relief settled over Reeve as she heard the garage door close behind Luke. Regardless of his feelings on the matter, she had no intention of changing her plans with Jess.

An hour later, after cleaning the kitchen and making herself a light lunch, nervous energy fluttered in her stomach as she packed an overnight bag. For the first time in their relationship, she'd lied to Luke. She'd sent him a text saying she'd asked Sloane to come and stay. As she zipped her toiletry bag into the larger bag, her phone pinged with a text from Jess.

> I'm going to leave work early. Devon wants to meet with me at three. Could we meet at his office and go back to my place from there?

Reeve was quick to type her reply.

> Perfect. See you at three!

Reeve could feel nothing but annoyance for her husband when she arrived at Devon's office at three. While the rational part of her knew he was only looking out for her best interests, his suspicions were making her question everything. She'd been looking forward to spending time with Jess, and now she was second-guessing her own intuition around whether Jess was genuine or not. She did her best to push those thoughts from her mind as Jess waved to her as she approached the St Kilda Road office.

'Sorry,' Jess said, panting as she reached Reeve. 'My meeting went later than I expected, and I've had to rush.'

Reeve smiled. 'It's still a minute before three.

You're perfectly on time. Why did Devon want to meet with you?'

The two women made their way through the front entrance of the modern office building and sought out the lifts.

'I think he's tracked down the Grenfells. My foster family,' Jess said.

Reeve instinctively grabbed her hand. 'You okay?'

Jess gave a wobbly smile. 'Not really, but thanks for coming with me. It means a lot.'

They travelled to the twelfth floor in silence and found Devon already in the reception area when they stepped out of the lift. He smiled. 'Come straight down to my office. Coffee?'

They both shook their heads.

'Too nervous,' Jess said.

'Nothing to be nervous about, and I have good news too.' Devon smiled, which surprised Reeve. Surely if this was about the foster parents, then it would be of a serious nature.

They sat at the small meeting table in Devon's office.

'Firstly, I do have news on the Grenfells.'

Jess tensed.

He handed a piece of paper across the table to Jess. 'As you already know from what Dean Blackwell revealed, they moved to Perth twenty-five years ago. Based on the information we were able to collect, it appears they left Melbourne days after you gave birth, and their house went on the market. They arrived in Perth and stayed with Michael Grenfell's sister, Elizabeth, for a period of twelve days before renting a house of their own. A couple of years later they went on to buy a house and that's where they've remained. Mike Grenfell started work with Walcon, a mining company, and has done fly-in-fly-out work ever since.'

Jess's face paled as she listened to Devon. 'What about fostering?'

He shook his head. 'They didn't continue with it.'

'That has to bring a little bit of peace of mind,' Reeve said.

Jess nodded, blinking back tears. 'Sorry, this is all a bit raw still.'

'It's up to you now, Jess, as to what we do with this information. They broke the law, and I believe they deserve to pay. However, for that to happen, you'd be put through a lot of questioning, which I imagine might be traumatic.'

'I need to think about it,' Jess said. She fell silent, and Reeve could only imagine what she must be thinking. She wasn't sure what she'd do in Jess's shoes. They deserved to be punished, but it was twenty-five years later. Were they different people? She sighed, causing both Jess and Devon to turn to her.

'Reeve?' Jess said. 'Are you okay?'

'Gosh, sorry, yes, this isn't about me. I was thinking about the Grenfells and wondering whether they'd used their life in Perth to start again and become better people. Try to make up for what they'd done. Or whether they continued being despicable humans. I guess we'll never know.'

'Not necessarily,' Devon said. 'As I said, Jess needs to decide what she'd like to do. We can do a lot more digging and find out more about them, and we can bring charges against them. Think about it,' he said to Jess. 'There's no rush. It's been twenty-five years already. Take as long as you need.'

He rubbed his hands together. 'Now for the good news.' He took two documents from his desk and passed one to each of them. 'I thought you'd like a copy each. There are two reports here.' He turned to Jess. 'When Martin died, the coroner collected a biological specimen. This meant that a paternity test was able to be done.'

Jess's mouth dropped open. 'You organised that too?'

Devon nodded. 'It's the top document.'

'Oh!' Jess's exclamation had Reeve turn to look at her. Jess reached over and took Reeve's hand. 'I'm too scared to look. What if it's negative?'

Then you won't be entitled to any money. Luke's voice in her head shocked Reeve. She glanced from Jess to Devon. She hadn't said that out loud, had she? Thankfully, it appeared not. Reeve did her best to push Luke's negativity from her mind. Jess wanted this as much as she did.

'The result is on the second page,' Devon said, and the two women turned the page.

Reeve's eyes scanned down to the interpretation section of the document. 'Based on testing results obtained from analyses of the DNA loci listed, the probability of paternities is 99.9998%. This probability...' Reeve didn't read on but looked at Jess. She was Martin's child, which meant she was Reeve's sister.

'The second report is the sibling one,' Devon said. 'The reason I sent off for the paternity one was because I discovered that there could be inaccuracies with sibling DNA tests. Half siblings only share around twenty-five per cent of DNA, and all sorts of factors can come into play.' He grinned. 'Although, as you can see, the report is fairly conclusive.'

'We're definitely sisters,' Jess said. The colour had completely drained from her face now.

'Are you okay?' Reeve asked.

Jess nodded. 'It's what I wanted. I guess the fact it's real is a shock.' She managed a small smile. 'A happy shock. Honestly, I don't know why I'm feeling like this.'

If Luke wanted any proof at all that Jess was genuine, this was it. There was no way someone could fake this kind of reaction to the news.

'Sisters,' Reeve said. 'We're actually real sisters.'

Jess met her gaze, tears glistening in her eyes. 'I can't believe it.'

* * *

Reeve followed Jess back to her apartment, glad that on this occasion, they weren't sharing the same car. Like Jess, she was finding the situation hard to process. It was such a strange feeling. They'd both known it was most likely they were related, yet the actual confirmation left her feeling odd. She wasn't sure if it was Luke's words playing in the background that had thrown her. While part of her wished he'd seen Jess's reaction to the news, what Devon went on to say played right into Luke's theory.

'Now that you have confirmation of your parentage,' Devon had said to Jess, 'what I mentioned when we first discussed Martin's will still stands.' He'd looked apologetically at Reeve. 'If the situation was reversed, I'd be giving you this advice too.'

Reeve had nodded, silently waiting to find out what he was referring to.

Devon cleared his throat. 'Jess is entitled to contest the will, as is anybody for that matter. But being a biological child of Martin's does give her more scope for a successful contest. I would also like to think that if Jess did decide to do this, that it's something that could be settled between the two of you.'

Reeve almost jumped in, saying she was happy to have an equal share of the estate as she'd voiced previously, but Luke had planted the seed of doubt. He'd said the DNA tests would come back quicker than expected, and he said that Devon would push for a larger percentage of the estate to go to Jess. And he'd done exactly that.

'How did you get the test results returned this quickly?' she'd asked.

'A friend who works at Paternity Testing Australia rushed them through for me,' Devon had said. 'I knew you'd want to know as soon as possible.'

Reeve had nodded. 'Yes, we did want to know,

thank you.'

Jess had looked at her strangely. 'This is all a bit overwhelming, isn't it?'

Reeve had nodded.

'Why don't the two of you go off and think about what you'd like to do next. The simplest solution is that Martin's will stands as is. That there is no need to contest it, and probate goes ahead and the monies are distributed. It's part of my job to make sure everyone knows their rights.'

Reeve had raised an eyebrow. 'That depends on who the client is, doesn't it?'

'Of course, why?'

'Well, in theory, Martin is the client, isn't he?'

Devon had nodded.

'And you're suggesting a beneficiary contests the will that he entrusted you with. Is that in his best interest?'

Devon had flushed a deep shade of red. 'I'm sorry, Reeve.' He shook his head. 'You're right. I think I've been a bit caught up in the excitement of Martin finding Jess and then you two discovering you're sisters. I'm a sucker for a happy family and was forgetting that Jess isn't my client. Please forgive me.'

Jess had stared at Reeve, a strange expression on her face.

'Jess,' Devon had continued, 'if you would like to explore any changes to the will, it would be best if you seek your own representation. It would be a conflict of interest for me to advise you any further. I think of you as Martin's daughter, and I know he'd want me to look out for both of you, but on this occasion, I've overstepped the line.'

'That's fine,' Jess had said. 'I can't imagine anything I've already said changing. I'm not sure I want the money he's left me, and I certainly can't see myself fighting for more.'

'I'll leave that decision with you then.'

They'd said their goodbyes, Devon once again apologising to Reeve.

Reeve's phone trilled, breaking into her thoughts. The caller display showed it to be Sloane.

'Hey you, I've been meaning to call you.'

'Me too, hon. Look, I can't chat now. I've got a staff meeting in a few minutes, but I wanted to check something with you.'

'Sure, what?'

'Were you expecting me at your place tonight?'

Reeve frowned. She'd lied to Luke that Sloane was staying with her, but she hadn't mentioned it to Sloane, or had she? 'No. Sorry if I asked you and forgot to cancel.'

'That's okay. Some wires crossed somewhere. I've got to run. Call you soon, okay?'

Reeve ended the call, unable to push the feeling of unease that had settled over her away. The concern in Sloane's voice had been evident. She sighed. She'd apologise to Sloane later. Right now, she had Jess to deal with. She knew how out of character her behaviour would have seemed to Jess compared to the excitement she'd previously exhibited at the thought of them being sisters. She owed her an explanation.

Jess wore a slightly guarded smile as she showed Reeve where to park and helped her with her bag.

She followed Jess into the cosy apartment. The soft colours, a mix of vintage and new decor, was the shabby-chic style Reeve adored. 'Look, I'm sorry,' she said once she'd deposited her bag in the spare room. 'Luke said something yesterday that made me think we should probably do our own sibling DNA test and not rely on Devon.'

Jess raised an eyebrow. 'Really? Why?'

'He's worried that Devon might have orchestrated the whole thing. Finding you, hurrying the DNA tests through, and then suggesting you contest the will. He didn't mention the family trust at least and suggest that was contested.'

Jess's eyes were wide. 'But how would that benefit him? He'd need to contest the will for himself, wouldn't he?'

'Luke's worried he's working with you.' Reeve dropped her head into her hands. 'I'm sorry, it's not something I ever considered, but then he said it, and I'd be devastated if that's what was happening.' She forced herself to look at Jess. 'I was so happy to think I might have a sister.'

Jess's face relaxed, and she smiled at Reeve. 'Me too, and guess what? You do. I can promise you right now, Reeve, the first time I met Devon was at Martin's funeral. To be fair, I can see why Luke would have a problem with Devon's advice. Martin's lawyer shouldn't be encouraging anyone to contest his client's will. But I'm not working with him, and like I've said from day one, I don't want Martin's money.' She frowned. 'Although, something he said to me has me maybe changing my mind on that.'

'He? As in Devon?'

'No, Martin. Let me show you the letter he sent me when he wanted to prove that he'd been sending money each month when I was a kid.' She left Reeve sitting on the couch and went in search of the letter, reappearing moments later. 'Here.' She handed it to Reeve.

'See the bit where he suggests that I might not want the money, but Safe Houses might.'

Reeve quickly read the letter, pressure building in her chest. This was possibly the last letter he'd ever written. She nodded.

'The money could make a huge difference to foster care, and the more I've thought about it, the more fitting it would be. I was only in the system because of him. The system failed me, and now I'm doing my best to make it better. With Martin's money, we could make it a lot better.'

Reeve nodded again. 'It could make a huge difference.'

'But only what he left me in the will,' Jess clarified. 'I don't want any more. He had his wishes, and they should be respected.'

'Really?'

'Definitely. And I'm happy to do another test. If it puts Luke's mind at rest, and yours too.'

'It was really Luke, not me, but it will make life at home a lot easier if he feels comfortable with everything.'

Jess smiled. 'Great, then it's all sorted. Now, let's make cocktails. Don't worry, a virgin one for you, but if you don't mind, I need a drink. After a day like today, I probably need a few.'

27

Jess's mind was racing by the time she got ready for work on Friday morning. She and Reeve had ended up having a lovely night. She'd ordered in pizza, and they'd made a few cocktails. Reeve's reaction in Devon's office had surprised her. She'd initially been offended at the implication that she'd go after more money than Martin had left her, but once she realised it was Luke's concern, not Reeve's, she felt a little better about it. Luke didn't know her, so on paper, yes, it certainly could be a set-up.

She let her mind wander. While she'd like to believe Devon's explanation, that his relationship with Martin left him protective of both Reeve and her, she couldn't help but think that the recommendations he'd made regarding the will and contesting it were entirely unprofessional. She hadn't mentioned to Reeve that Devon was the one who'd encouraged Martin to make contact with her, but was now wondering if she should.

She let herself out of the apartment, her thoughts shifting immediately as she bumped into Trent.

'Hey, stranger. You're up early. I haven't seen you in ages.'

Jess smiled. It had been a few days. 'It's been hectic, which is why I'm going in early this morning. I've got lots to tell you.'

'How about drinks tonight? You're welcome to come to me, or we could go out.'

Jess shook her head. 'No, I've got my...'

He grinned. 'My what?'

'My sister staying.'

'Do we know if she really is the sister yet?'

Jess nodded. 'Test results came back yesterday. Not that I ever doubted it. You saw Bella at the funeral. We're definitely related.'

'Cool,' Trent said. 'Happy to include the sister in the catch-up.'

'You know what, that sounds good. I'd like you to meet her properly. Yesterday was full-on with discussions around paternity and money. A lighter night sounds good. Why don't you come over to my place? I'll text you when I get home. I'm planning to leave early this afternoon.'

'What's Reeve doing today?' Trent asked.

'Sleeping in and then going to explore St Kilda, I think. She doesn't come over this way very often.'

'Too toffee-nosed?'

Jess laughed. 'She's anything but. She's a school-teacher, don't forget. She's very down to earth.' She hesitated. 'Although, she is going through some health issues. Hopefully she'll be okay tonight, but if she does anything weird or says anything strange, ignore her, and I'll explain later.'

Trent raised an eyebrow. 'Intriguing. I can't wait to get to know this sister of yours.'

* * *

Jess finished replying to an email from one of Safe Houses' caseworkers and opened a report on her computer. She had a lot to get through and was still hoping to leave early to spend time with Reeve. She smiled. Her *sister*. She wasn't sure she'd ever get used to the knowledge that she had family.

Her phone rang, and she hesitated when she saw it was Devon Saunders. Reeve's concerns about him concerned her too. He'd certainly never suggested to her that he was hoping to cash in on Martin's estate, and she hoped that it wasn't the case, but from what Martin had told her at their initial meeting, it was Devon who'd encouraged him to find her.

She accepted the call. 'Hi, Devon.'

'Jess, I'm glad you're available. I wanted to apologise for yesterday. I pride myself on my professional ethics and conduct, and Reeve was right. I let Martin down on this occasion. All of you, in fact.'

'Don't worry about it,' Jess said. 'It was probably a conversation we needed to have without Reeve present. Luke's concerned that I might be an imposter after Reeve's money.' She gave a small laugh. 'I guess I should be grateful that my sister has someone looking out for her. I think he's going to organise another DNA test.'

'Why? You've already got the results. Another test isn't going to change them. Maybe I should get my friend at Paternity Testing Australia to give him a call. Talk him through the reports?'

'I'd just leave it alone, Devon. A second test won't hurt, and as you say, if the first one was done properly then the second one will have the same results.'

Devon was silent.

'I appreciate the apology,' Jess said, breaking the silence. 'Did you call for anything else?'

Devon cleared his throat. 'Yes, for a couple of reasons. The first is that Reeve is right. I can't advise you any further on the will other than to suggest you find another lawyer if you choose to contest it or the family trust. I have a great contact at Walter Hennessey I can put you in touch with.'

Unease settled on Jess. Devon was incredibly helpful. Too helpful perhaps? 'Thank you, but I have a lawyer I'll contact if I decide to move forward on that.'

'Okay. Well, the other area I can help you with is the situation with the Grenfell family. I know Martin would want action taken. After all, your son was his grandson, and I'd like to make sure justice is served.'

'Thank you,' Jess said. 'I haven't decided at this stage what I want to do, but I'll be in touch when I do. For now, what information can you tell me about them?'

'I can email you the file. It doesn't tell you much more than what I shared yesterday with you and Reeve, but you might find it of interest.'

Jess thanked him and ended the call. Moments later, the email arrived from Devon with a file from his private investigator. She opened it, her stomach churning as she read the details. A recent photo was included of Mike and Carly. It looked like it had been snapped at the supermarket.

She glanced at the clock. It was already after nine, and she had a meeting at ten. She needed to push all thoughts of the Grenfells and everything they represented from her mind and get on with her morning.

28
─────

Dread filled the pit of Reeve's stomach the moment she switched on her phone. She'd deliberately turned it off the previous night, not wanting to discuss anything that was going on with Luke. Her phone showed eleven missed calls and six text messages from him.

Where are you?

She sent him a quick text.

A last-minute change of plans. Staying at Jess's in Elwood. How's Adelaide?

Her phone rang seconds later.

'I told you I didn't want you staying with her. I told you I'd organise someone to stay with you.'

Reeve held the phone away from her ear, surprised by the anger in his voice.

'Morning, honey,' she said, her tone dripping with sarcasm.

'Jesus, Reeve. You're sick. You should be at home, not with a stranger. I told you I was going to organise something. I cancelled Sloane yesterday and organised Carol James to stay with you.'

'What? You cancelled Sloane...' That explained the phone call she'd received from Sloane the previous day.

'Yes, I sent her a text saying we'd doubled up with our arrangements and wouldn't need her help. She seemed fine with the change of plans.'

Reeve swallowed, grateful that Sloane hadn't told Luke she knew nothing about the arrangement.

'Carol arrived at the house last night and waited for over two hours for you.'

'Carol? Why would you ask her? We don't need to pay someone to look after me at this stage.'

'She's perfect to look after you, and you could consider using her on a regular basis. She did such a good job with your mum. I thought you'd be pleased.'

'Well, I'm not. You need to call her and apologise and explain that *you* messed up. I don't need a nurse, Luke. I told you I'd sort out something for while you were away – and by the way, that *stranger* is my half-sister,' Reeve said. 'Devon had paternity and sibling DNA tests done. We're related.'

Silence greeted her.

'And,' Reeve continued, 'Jess has agreed to do a second test. She doesn't want anyone thinking that she's orchestrating something she's not.'

'You told her what I said?'

'I told her you had concerns and were looking out for my best interests. She understands that and is happy to do another test.'

'Good. We'll do it tomorrow night. Is she coming for dinner?'

'I haven't asked her yet, but I'm sure she will.'

'And you're in Elwood now?'

'Yes.'

'You should be on your way to East Brighton, to Patricia's.'

'What? No, I shouldn't.'

'You have an appointment at ten, which gives you

forty minutes to get there. If you'd stayed at home, Carol would have reminded you.'

'Hold on,' Reeve said, ignoring his reference to Carol. 'Let me check my messages from Patricia.'

She held the phone away from her ear and found her messages with the psychiatrist. The last one was on Wednesday, confirming her 10 a.m. appointment for today. She'd sent a confirmation YES back as instructed. She had no recollection of receiving the text message or replying to it. She frowned.

'Didn't we discuss letting the medication work for two weeks before we went back again?' Reeve asked Luke.

'No, she said she wanted to see you within a week of when you started taking them. I think you need to start writing things down. This stuff's important.'

'Okay. I'd better get dressed and get going.'

'Call me after your session,' Luke said. 'Let me know what she says. And Ree, sorry if I sounded angry. I'm not. I love you, and I'm worried, that's all.'

Reeve hung up, the uneasy feeling that crept over her any time she discovered she'd done something she didn't remember returning. It was only a forgotten appointment. It wasn't a big deal, but that wasn't the point. Was there going to be a day that passed where she didn't do anything out of character or without any recollection?

* * *

Reeve threw a twenty dollar note at the taxi driver, thanked him, and hurried to the entrance of Patricia's house. She was two minutes early, which was a miracle. She followed the winding path around the side of the house to the cobbled pavers that led to Patricia's studio.

'I have to admit,' Reeve said, minutes later as she sat across from Patricia and accepted the ginger tea the psychiatrist offered her, 'this appointment completely slipped my mind. Luckily Luke reminded me this morning.'

'He's worried about you,' Patricia said. 'He called me yesterday and again this morning after he discovered you were staying in Elwood. He wanted to share with me some of the things you've been doing and saying.'

Reeve put down her cup of tea and moved to the edge of her chair. She was pretty sure she didn't want to hear any of this.

Patricia picked up her notebook. 'There have

been several angry verbal assaults this week, according to Luke.'

'Verbal assaults?'

Patricia nodded. 'Apparently, you got very angry with Luke on Tuesday night when he suggested a' – she consulted her notes – 'Jessica Williams was after your father's inheritance.'

'We discussed it,' Reeve said. 'Before he went to work, which was in the morning, not in the evening. I wouldn't say I got very angry. I was a little upset that he was making me doubt her. That was all.'

'Can I read you something?'

Reeve nodded.

'This is a rough transcript of the conversation Luke says you had with him around nine p.m., after he'd returned from work. Luke says you started the conversation along these lines.

'"Would you stop being such a prick."

'"I'm not a prick, I care about you, and I'm worried."

'"You're a jealous piece of shit who hates to see me happy."

'"All I want is to see you happy."

'"Yeah right. You're glad I'm sick, and you probably can't wait for me to die. I know if the situation was reversed, I'd want you dead too."'

Reeve's hand covered her mouth.

'There's another similar conversation the next evening in relation to you deciding Luke was bad for you.'

'Bad for me?'

Patricia nodded and began to read.

"'I wish I'd never left Nick. He was all man, not like you, you weak pussy. No backbone, no guts. No wonder I slept with that guy from the pub. He was ALL man, and I mean ALL. It was the best sex I've ever had. I hate, you Luke. I want a divorce.'"

Reeve stared at the psychiatrist. She'd said all of this to Luke, and he hadn't brought it up? 'Why didn't he say something? Give me a chance to apologise and reassure him I don't feel like that?'

'He knows it wasn't *you* saying these things, Reeve. That's why he didn't ask for an apology. He's very aware that you knowing about these conversations will upset you. He's trying to shield you as best he can.'

'Okay, so why are you telling me?'

Patricia smiled. 'Because while you're still capable of understanding what's happening to you, you need to know. It will help make the eventual transition into care easier if you're aware that things are happening that are outside of your control.'

'Transition into care?'

'It's not something that needs to happen at this stage, but eventually, I'm afraid it is a very real possibility. Your outbursts are happening with more and more regularity, as is your passive-aggressive behaviour. Notes, messages, emails. You've sent your ex-husband a few notes this week, and then I've received some myself.'

'Notes?'

'Emails, to be more precise. You sent me one the night before last.'

Patricia took a selection of pages from her desk and handed them to Reeve. 'The top three are messages to your ex-husband, Nick, suggesting Luke is holding you prisoner and messing with your brain. I hope you don't mind, but I had a brief conversation with him yesterday. Then you'll find two that have been for me.'

Reeve was overcome with nausea as she read her garbled messages to Nick and then her less garbled messages to Patricia. Her face heated as she noted the language she'd used. She looked up at the psychiatrist. 'Is this normal?'

'In what respect?'

'The messages to you are incredibly rude. I feel like I should apologise for that, but I have no recollection of writing them or sending them. What seems strange is the language I've used in them. I called you' – she cleared her throat, embarrassed – 'let's say the *C-word*, rather than make me say it five times. It's not a word I ever use. I can't stand it. I can't even say it now.'

'It's not unusual for dementia patients to take on a whole other personality,' Patricia said. 'Often not a very pleasant one. Each person reacts differently and is triggered by different things. You've been under an enormous amount of stress lately, which could be a contributing factor. Now, I do need to ask, have you been taking the medication I prescribed at the last appointment?'

Reeve nodded.

'Good. It takes a few weeks to work. You might not have seen the benefits yet. Once it does kick in, you should find your aggression is reduced considerably. I'd also be recommending at this stage that you always have someone in the house with you. Your mother did up until she went into care.'

'In the last couple of years, she did, but not at this early stage.'

'Unfortunately, your situation is quite advanced. Either that or it's moving at a rapid speed. I am concerned with the behaviours I'm seeing.'

'Really?'

Patricia nodded. 'Luke told me that he'd organised for the nurse' – she checked her notepad – 'a Carol James, to stay in the house with you while he was in Adelaide. I believe she looked after your mother?'

'Yes, Carol was Mum's carer, but I'm not at a stage where I need permanent care. Mum was a total mess by the time she got to that stage. I'm nowhere near that. Please don't think I'm ignoring your advice. I don't think I'm as bad as Luke has led you to believe.'

Patricia's lack of direct response sent a shiver down Reeve's spine as she watched the psychiatrist write a note on her pad. Was she in complete denial? Did everyone around her believe she was a danger to herself and others? That was the turning point for putting her mother in care.

'This has all been quite a heavy start to our session,' Patricia said. 'Now, let's talk more about your day-to-day circumstances. How is your daughter coping with all of this?'

* * *

CLIENT MEETING SUMMARY

DATE: September 13
Client: Reeve Elliot
Duration: 90 Min

Reeve attended the appointment on her own. She had forgotten about it, and her husband reminded her.

She has been taking medication, but so far, her aggressive behaviour has not changed. This is expected at this early stage. Improvement should be seen over the coming weeks.

Reeve is distressed by her behaviour towards her husband and others. The stress currently surrounding her – father's death, daughter's distancing, new sister – is taking its toll.

I have recommended she consider home help. Her situation is deteriorating rapidly and going into care needs proper consideration. She confirmed she has appointed an enduring power of attorney and medical treatment decision maker.

Next appointment scheduled for Wednesday.

* * *

Tears swam in Reeve's eyes as she followed Patricia's directions to join the Bay Trail and walk the beach route back to Elwood. She needed time to clear her head and hoped the walk would achieve this. She'd done her best to hold it together until she left the psychiatrist's office, but she wasn't sure how convincing she'd been.

The question about Bella had unravelled her. She and Bella had been so close. It was hard to believe that her fifteen-year-old wanted nothing to do with her. She'd rung her numerous times since the dinner where she'd introduced Jess to the family but had received no response. Nick had done his best to get Bella to communicate with her, but she refused, saying it hurt too much to watch Reeve's decline. Reeve understood her daughter's position, but it hurt like hell. She was also worried. Nick had mentioned how much time Bella was spending with Mason Walker. He'd said that he'd spent a bit of time with Mason, and he wasn't as bad as he'd been led to think. Reeve found that hard to believe. Mason was trouble. But what power did she have right now to stop Bella from doing anything?

What she didn't understand was how most of the time, she felt normal. There were the occasions when she'd woken to discover she'd drunk too much or done something awful the night before, but during her waking hours, she seemed to know what was going on. She wasn't losing large chunks of time where she was doing things she couldn't account for... or was she? She felt betrayed by Luke. That he was speaking to the psychiatrist behind her back was more than frustrating; it was upsetting. Why didn't he talk to her about what was going on?

Her phone rang as she was halfway back to Jess's. It was Luke. She stopped and sat on one of the park benches that overlooked Port Phillip Bay and accepted the call.

'Hey, hon, how did you go with Patricia?'

'Why don't you ring her and ask her?'

Luke was silent for a moment. 'Are you okay?'

Reeve sighed. 'Why are you telling me everything's okay and then reporting back to her that it's not? I need to know if I'm doing terrible things so I can stop.'

'We both know it doesn't work like that,' Luke said. 'I can tell you, but you'll have no memory of what you've said or done and it will be upsetting when I tell you. You've been there with your mum. You know what it's like. And I'm sorry, I don't look at it as going behind your back. I'm trying to help you.'

And he was. That was the truth in it. 'Sorry, I guess I'm scared of what's going to happen.'

'Oh, Ree, I'm sorry you're having to deal with any of this. We'll get through it the best we can. If it comes to it, we can afford the best care you could ever want. We should probably start having a look at some options for living. Hopefully, you'll be at home for a long time still, but when the time comes, at least you'll have chosen the place you want to be in.'

'I want to avoid a home until the last possible minute.' She sighed, thinking of the discussion with Patricia. 'Maybe you're right and I should consider having Carol if she's available, or someone else, in the house with me. I still think it's far too premature, but it might be worth looking into her availability at least.'

'Okay. Now, I'll be back tomorrow morning. Are you going to be home or still at Jess's?'

'I'll be home by ten.'

'Great. I love you. Look after yourself tonight, won't you? Try not to do any crazy lady stuff.'

'I didn't last night,' Reeve said, conveniently choosing not to mention the email she'd sent Patricia.

Luke hesitated.

'What?' Had Patricia told him?

'Nothing, I just suspect Jess would be too nice to tell you if you did do something to offend her. See you tomorrow.'

Reeve stared out at the ocean after he ended the call. Was she already at a stage where Jess was being *too nice* to tell her of the terrible things she was doing? She remembered clearly with her mother the day the decision was made not to tell her about her awful behaviour. Her distress and constant apologising after being told was worse in many ways than the aggressive outburst the dementia was causing.

An overwhelming sense of grief settled over Reeve. Right at this moment, she felt an empathy for her mother she'd prayed she would never be in a position to experience.

29

It was early afternoon when Jess realised she'd missed a call from Felicity. She picked up her phone and pressed the call button.

'Hey, Flick, what's up? Are you at school?'

She was greeted with silence.

'Flick.'

'I'm here, and no, I didn't make it to school.'

'How come?'

'I hate everyone knowing I'm a foster kid. It's humiliating. You should hear what the kids say. Please don't tell me I'm silly. You've got no idea what it's like.'

She was all too familiar with what it was like.

'Where are you now?'

'At the Smiths'. I waited until they went to work

and then came home again. I left my window open so I could get into the house.'

'Okay, give me an hour and I'll come over for a chat, okay?'

'I'm not going back to school.'

'I'm not asking you to. I'm suggesting a chat, and as you rang me today, I'm assuming, whether it be conscious or subconsciously, that's what you were hoping for. See you in an hour.'

Jess ended the call and called Shay Smith to let her know that Flick was home and she was going to go and talk to her.

'She's getting difficult,' Shay said. 'We're doing our best, but it's beginning to affect our relationship with the younger girls. I want to help Flick, I do, but she gives us nothing. I don't think she's smiled the entire time she's been here. Not even when Maddie, our ten-year-old, dressed the dog up in a wig and tied a chocolate bar to his collar with Flick's name on it. She took the chocolate and closed her door. No smile. No thank you. No effort.'

'Leave her with me, Shay,' Jess said. 'She's had a rough time and is very guarded as a result. I'd hoped the counselling would be helping, but it seems that it's not.'

An hour later, Jess pulled into the Smiths' driveway. Felicity appeared at the front door before Jess had a chance to knock.

'Can we get out of here? Go for a drive or something?'

'Milkshake?'

Felicity shook her head. 'Nah, being healthy. A juice, maybe. There's a place not too far from here that sells them. We could take them down to the beach?'

'Done.' Jess got back in the car and followed Flick's directions. It wasn't long before they were sipping their juices with the wind whipping across the water into their faces as they walked along St Kilda beach.

'You're wrong, you know,' Jess said. 'When you said you didn't want me to say anything because I didn't get it. I do get how hard it is to be in foster care. To be different and to be teased. It's horrible, and there's not a lot I can say to you to make that better.'

'Great. I assumed you'd bring your magic wand and fix everything,' Flick said. 'So how did you survive the system?'

Jess took a deep breath. 'I barely survived. When I was your age, I had something happen to me that took its toll. After it happened, I was moved from that family to another foster family who used me as their slave.'

'Slave?'

'Pretty much. I was expected to cook and clean and look after their four-year-old after school and on the weekend. I did it for nearly three years and left the day I turned eighteen.'

Felicity stared at her. 'And I was upset at being teased. Why didn't you say something to someone? If I told you the Smiths were treating me like that, you'd remove me from the house.'

'I would,' Jess agreed. 'I didn't say anything as I considered it my punishment.'

'Punishment? For what?'

Jess took another deep breath. 'When I was fifteen, I was fostered by a couple who were awful. There were two other foster kids in the house, one of them being a sixteen-year-old boy.' Jess did her best to keep her voice from wobbling. 'He raped me repeatedly, and the family did nothing about it.'

Flick stopped walking and turned and stared at Jess, her eyes wide.

Jess continued. 'I couldn't tell anyone outside of the family because I was too ashamed, and the foster parents threatened me not to. Then I found out I was pregnant.'

She went on to tell Flick the rest of the story. About Leo's birth and death and the threat she'd received from the Grenfells if she was ever to tell anyone.

'Why are you telling me all of this?' Flick asked. 'Is it to make me feel sorry for you and put my own problems in perspective?'

Jess smiled. 'No. I guess I wanted you to know that I do understand where you're coming from. I had an awful experience in the foster system. I can relate to you.'

'They're hardly the same scenarios,' Flick said. 'I'm being teased, not raped.'

'Yes, and how you choose to deal with that is what will shape the outcome. I'm not proud of how I dealt with my situation. That I walked away from that family and allowed them to threaten me and then believed I needed to be punished. I should have spoken up straight away. I should have told the truth, and I should have asked someone for help. That's why I'm proud of you. You're having a hard time, and you rang me for help.'

'And you've told me a horrible story to guilt me into thinking I don't have it too bad.'

'That's not the point of me telling you,' Jess said. 'I want you to think about how you're reacting to the teasing. Are you getting angry? Are you walking away? Are you showing that it upsets you?'

'All three,' Flick said. 'Angry first, then walking away, then upset.'

'Okay. That's what we need to work on. How about you change the narrative. When a kid teases you, don't get angry; start a conversation.'

Flick looked at her as if she was mad.

'I'm serious. Give me an example of what someone says to you.'

'Hey, Flick, the unwanted chick. Any family members killed themselves today?'

Jess flinched. Why were kids so cruel? 'Okay. You respond with a smile and say something like, "No suicides today, how about you? The family all breathing?" Then laugh as if they've made a great joke. As silly as it might seem, it'll confuse them, and you'll find they move on to someone else.'

Flick looked sceptical.

'Try it, okay?'

'And if it doesn't work?'

'We'll regroup and come up with something else.'

Flick nodded and continued walking along the beach. She stopped again after a few hundred metres. 'You know you've told me that you never stood up to anyone when you went through the experience you did? So, is this a case of do what I say, not what I do? You run away from your problems, but I'm expected to deal with mine.'

Jess shook her head. 'No, you've inspired me to do something about my situation. It might be twenty-five years later, but it's not too late. I've found out quite a bit this week about both the boy who raped me and the family I was placed with.' She went on to tell Felicity what had happened with Dean reappearing and finding out the family were now in Perth.

'I need to confront them, find out why they did what they did and whether they feel any remorse.'

'And if they don't?'

'I'm not sure. I guess I'll find out what my legal position is and go from there.'

'You're really going to do that?'

Jess nodded. 'Yep. I'm going to stand up to the people who hurt me. Are you?'

'I'm not sure.'

'You can. You're strong, you're brave, and you're an inspiration. How about this. I'll go and deal with my past, and next week, once I return, you agree to deal with your present.'

Felicity nodded slowly. 'Okay, but I want to know what happens. Whether you get the apology you're after and whether you decide to press charges.'

Jess held out her hand. 'Deal.'

* * *

Jess hurried home after her last meeting, hoping Reeve had found enough to entertain herself for the day. She wasn't sure why she was worried. She was a grown woman and lived less than fifteen minutes away. If she'd become bored, she could easily have gone home.

She unlocked the front door, surprised to hear laughter coming from inside. Trent poked his head out from the living room as she pushed open the door.

He grinned. 'Arrived a bit early. I hope you don't mind.'

'As long as you haven't been harassing Reeve.'

Trent pretended to look offended. 'Harassing? We've been getting to know one another and I've been entertaining her with lots of stories about you.'

'Oh great, that's all I need. She'll probably run a mile now.'

'No, I won't,' Reeve said, joining them. 'Trent's only told me good things.'

'Shouldn't you be working?' Jess asked. 'He's an author,' she added for Reeve's benefit. 'Which he's probably already told you.'

Reeve punched Trent playfully on the arm. 'You said you were a freelance journalist. That's hardly the same.'

'I'm both. I do less of the journalist work these days.' He turned to Jess. 'Anyway, let's get you a glass of wine, and you can tell us about your day.'

'Tea will be fine,' Jess said.

Reeve shook her head. 'I bought you two delicious bottles of Pinot Gris this afternoon as a little thank you for having me to stay. Ignore me and open one. I might even have half a glass.'

'Atta girl,' Trent said.

'You haven't been forcing Reeve to drink, have you?' She knew what Trent was like. He loved wine, and she usually drank far too much when she was with him due to his encouragement. 'She isn't supposed to be drinking.'

Trent laughed. 'I haven't forced Reeve to do anything. We've had a long chat about our experiences with dementia, and I understand to an extent what she's dealing with. My grandmother was a victim to it too.'

Jess winced as pain flashed in his eyes. 'I'm sorry.'

He shrugged. 'One of those things. Now, Reeve's told me everything about her and why she shouldn't be drinking, but she's also keen to do an experiment. So, it might as well be with a delicious wine.'

Jess raised her eyebrows. 'Is that a good idea?'

'Come and sit down,' Reeve said. 'I want to ask you something, and then I'll explain.'

Jess followed them into the living room, curiosity getting the better of her.

'You promised you'd tell me if I was doing anything nasty, didn't you? That we'd make light of it until it was happening regularly or becoming distressing.'

Jess nodded. 'Yes, I said I'd send you back a nasty message if I got one from you.'

'So nothing's changed? I haven't sent you so many horrible messages that you've decided to keep it from me?'

'Of course not.'

'Good. So, just to clarify. Did I get angry last night or do anything that you know I have no memory of?'

'No. You had your suspicions about Devon and what he might be up to, but that was all. You didn't get angry. We discussed all of that before dinner and then had a nice, relaxed evening.'

'I remember all of that, and then we went to bed around eleven. Is that right?'

Jess nodded. 'Yes, it was a few minutes before. And that was it. You went to sleep, I assume, and so did I. I would have been gone this morning when you woke up.'

Reeve smiled. 'Good, that means I didn't do anything crazy.' She went on to explain her appointment with Patricia and that she'd become angry with Luke and had also sent Patricia offensive messages.

'Tonight, I want to do an experiment if you're happy for me to? Just one glass of wine to see if I start abusing you or Trent. If I do, can you record me with the video on your phone?'

Jess nodded. 'If you're sure you want to see it?'

'I still find it hard to believe I'm doing all of these things,' Reeve said. 'It'll give me some proof.'

'You think Luke's making it up?'

Reeve shook her head. 'No, I wish he was. But to believe it I need to see it for myself.'

Trent poured them each a glass of wine and held his up. 'Let the experiment begin.'

Jess held her breath as Reeve sipped her wine. She was conscious of Trent watching her, and her cheeks heated up as he burst out laughing.

'Sorry,' he said, turning to Reeve. 'I'm not trying

to make light of what you're going through, but I think Jess thought you'd take a sip, and your head would explode or something.'

'She's right to be worried,' Reeve said with a smile. 'You should hear what I called the psychiatrist in my messages to her. Words I've never used in a sentence before were used multiple times to reinforce the inappropriate message.'

Trent's eyes widened in delight. 'Tell me. I might use it in my book.'

Reeve blushed. 'I can't repeat it. Let's say, the word that rhymes with punt.'

'You called your psychiatrist that?'

Reeve nodded. 'Add a few other expletives to it to get the full impact. I'll apologise to both of you in advance if I do anything like that tonight.' She took another sip of her wine and looked at Jess. 'How was your day? Did you give any more thought to the Grenfell situation?'

Jess nodded. 'I'm going to book flights and confront them.'

'I'm coming too,' Trent said immediately.

'And me,' Reeve added. 'You can't do this on your own.'

'No, I think I do need to do this alone,' Jess said.

'Absolutely no way,' Trent said. 'This is huge, Jess.

Whether you like it or not, we're coming with you. I'm happy to stay in the background, but these people covered up the death of a baby and accused you of murder. They're not rational people. It's too dangerous for you to go by yourself.'

'I agree,' Reeve said. 'You don't know what you're going to be confronted with when you get there. It's likely to bring up a lot of repressed emotion and sadness. Like Trent, I'm happy to be there in the background, but if you need me, I don't want to be four thousand kilometres away. I want to be by your side.'

By the time the Thai food they'd ordered arrived, they had flights to Perth booked for Sunday, returning on Tuesday.

'I can't believe I'm going to do this,' Jess said. 'If it wasn't for Felicity, I'm not sure that I would be. She's right. I'd be a much better role model if I had dealt with my own problems rather than run away from them.'

'She said that?' Trent asked.

Jess nodded. 'Yep, full of fifteen-year-old wisdom. Although, she's right. I do need to deal with it. It hangs over me like a black cloud throughout the year, getting worse at certain times.' She didn't elaborate on how the anniversary of Leo's birth and death affected her. She took a week off and generally stayed in bed.

A little after eleven, Trent said his goodbyes, assuring Reeve she'd been perfectly behaved all evening. He said he'd meet them on Sunday morning and would drive them to the airport.

30

The next morning Jess insisted on taking Reeve out for breakfast before she went home.

'You know, Trent likes you,' Reeve said as they sipped their coffee. 'He's a lovely guy.'

'He likes me as a friend.'

Reeve raised an eyebrow. 'More than that.'

Jess shook her head. 'Did he say something?'

'No, but I'd say he'd do anything for you.'

'As I would for him. As a friend,' she added.

Reeve smiled as Jess blushed. Maybe something would happen between Jess and her neighbour. With everything Jess had on, she doubted it was a priority, but it was nice to think it was a possibility.

'Now, about tonight,' Jess said, changing the subject. 'Why don't I come over at about five. Unless Luke changes his mind about the dinner invite after he hears our plans for Perth.'

'He'll want to do the DNA test, so I doubt he'll cancel. He might refuse to feed you,' Reeve said with a wry smile. She knew he'd be angry at her for deciding to go to Perth without consulting him. Well, maybe not angry, but certainly concerned. 'He needs to get to know you. He'll relax once he sees the results from the second test. He's overly cautious. His father took his life a few years before I met him. He'd been cheated out of money by someone, which left him bankrupt. Luke, therefore, has huge trust issues around money.'

Jess's mouth dropped open. 'I wish you'd told me that earlier. That explains why he'd be cautious. Tell him I'll be happy to do whatever test he needs if it will make him feel safer around me. I should probably make it clear to him that I don't plan to contest the will or the family trust. There's no way I'd want to undermine Martin's wishes on any of it.'

While Jess's words were comforting, Reeve was left wondering about Devon. She imagined Jess only knew that contesting the family trust was an option from something Devon had told her, and it didn't sit right that her father's lawyer would bring this up. She did her best to push away her concerns about Devon, but it was getting more and more difficult.

Concern was only one of the emotions Luke expressed later that morning when Reeve told him her plans for the weekend. He'd arrived home before lunch, and she'd be lying if she didn't admit that his reluctance to take her to bed didn't sting.

He'd placed his coffee cup on the kitchen counter and sighed when she suggested it. 'I'll get there, Ree. I need more time. I know you didn't know what you were doing with that guy, but it still hurts knowing you had the "best sex of your life" with someone else.'

Reeve decided to leave it alone. There were bigger issues to discuss this weekend.

'Jess is coming over at five,' she told him. 'To do the second DNA test and to stay for dinner if you'd like her to?'

'Is there any reason I wouldn't?'

'I'm going to Perth with her tomorrow.'

'What?'

She went on to explain the situation with Jess's foster family and her need for some answers and, hopefully, closure.

'Why does she need you to go?'

'She doesn't. I insisted. So did her neighbour, Trent.'

'Hold on. There's a guy going too?'

She nodded. 'He didn't want us going alone in case something happens.'

Luke shook his head. 'This is ridiculous. What if, in the middle of all of this, you have an episode? They're happening all the time now.'

'We'll deal with it if it happens. They know what to expect.'

'Really?'

'Yes, I've filled them in. Trent's dealt with dementia before, so we'll be fine.'

'I don't even know what to say. You're going to traipse to the other side of the country with a woman you hardly know and could be after your money, for what? So she can put closure on something that happened twenty-five years ago?'

'Yes, except for the bit about my hardly knowing her and her being after my money. Listen to her tonight, okay? She wants to clear the air with you.'

Luke rolled his eyes. 'I'm going to unpack. Let me know when she's here, and I can dust off my scam detector.'

'Dust off my nice husband while you're there, would you? The one I love and married who, up until recently, was always there to support me. I seem to have lost him.'

'Lost him?' He stared at her. 'I'm bending over backwards to be supportive, and this is the thanks I get. At least when you are with it, which I assume you are now, I'd expect you to make more of an effort to appreciate me. Thanks for the email, by the way. It was a pleasure to wake up to.' He turned and left the kitchen.

Reeve's stomach clenched. She'd checked with Jess as soon as she'd woken up that she hadn't done anything she'd regret the night before, and Jess had assured her they'd had another lovely night, and there'd been no signs of her dementia. She'd quickly checked her text messages but hadn't taken it to the next step and checked her email.

She took her phone from her bag and opened her Gmail client and looked in the sent items box. Her heart sank as she opened a message sent at midnight to Luke.

Conniving, Untrustworthy, Narcissistic, Tainted = CUNT = U.

She shook her head. What was it with the other Reeve and the C-word? Did that Reeve have any other words in her vocabulary? If she was honest, she was gutted. She'd believed she'd gone two days without doing anything out of character. Being with Jess had relaxed her, and she hoped that was what she needed. It appeared it was not the case.

She sighed and moved into the kitchen, determined to get a start on dinner. She'd make her porcini risotto, Luke's favourite, which would hopefully put him in a better mood.

A little before five, Luke opened a bottle of Sauvignon Blanc, poured himself a glass and joined her in the kitchen. The DNA test kit sat on the kitchen bench.

'I'm sorry about the email,' Reeve said.

He sighed. 'I'm sorry for how I reacted. It's been a stressful few days, and I guess that kind of topped off an awful week. I lost a patient yesterday.'

Reeve put down the mushroom she was slicing and moved over to wrap her arms around him. 'Oh hon, why didn't you say something earlier?'

'I figured you have enough on your plate right now. He was only forty-six. Telling his wife was difficult, to say the least.'

Reeve hugged him to her. 'I'm so sorry.'

A knock on the front door signalled Jess had arrived. Reeve pulled away from him. 'Can we discuss this later?'

Luke nodded and sipped his wine while Reeve went to let Jess in.

'Hey.' She embraced her. 'Thanks again for the last couple of days.'

'No need to thank me, that's what being sisters is all about, isn't it?'

They both laughed, and Reeve led Jess into the kitchen. She smiled at Luke, who was now sitting at the counter, his glass of wine in front of him.

'Nice to see you again,' Jess said.

Luke nodded and picked up the DNA test kit.

'Luke!' Reeve admonished, but Jess laughed.

'It's okay. Guilty until proven innocent.' She turned to Luke. 'Why don't we get this over with, and I'll go home. Once you have the results, perhaps we could consider all having dinner together and getting to know each other.'

Luke shifted uncomfortably on the stool. He obviously hadn't expected Jess to be this direct.

'It's not a big deal,' Jess reassured Reeve. 'I'll be devastated if the first DNA tests prove to be wrong, but honestly, I can't see how it could be.'

'It could be if someone tampered with them,'

Luke said. 'Someone who was looking to get a share of Martin's estate that they're not entitled to.'

'I've made it very clear to Reeve and Devon that I have no intention of contesting the will,' Jess said. 'The one thing I will agree with you is that Devon's behaviour seems unprofessional, but I can assure you I'm not working with him. Anyway, I feel like a broken record about all of this. Let's do the test, and I'll go. I need to pack for Perth. I assume Reeve's told you our plans, and I assume you're stopping her from coming?'

The corners of Luke's lips curled up, and Reeve could tell he was trying to suppress a smile. Jess was full-on when she chose to be.

He picked up the kit and took out the swabs, handing one to each of them. 'We can ask for the results to be sent via text. I'll use your phone number,' he said, looking at Reeve as he filled in the paperwork. '*Sisters?* can be the password.'

The two women completed the cheek swabs and signed the relevant forms. Jess turned to Reeve once the process was complete. 'Did you want to meet at my place tomorrow? Or we can pick you up on the way.'

'I'll take Reeve to the airport,' Luke said. 'What time do you need to be there?'

'Two.'

'Fine, we'll see you there then.'

Jess hesitated.

'What? I'm not going to stop her, Jess. I hope you know what you're getting yourself into. If Reeve has a meltdown on the plane, you'll wish you'd never suggested this.'

'It's not what I was going to say. I was going to suggest that we all go to the post office right now and post the DNA kit off. That way, we'll all be confident that no one has tampered with it.'

'I don't really think that's necessary,' Reeve said. 'But there's an express post box on the corner on Toorak Road and Osborne Street. We could walk there. It's only about five minutes away.'

Luke picked up the package. 'Okay, let's do it.'

* * *

As they wound their way along the Tullamarine Freeway towards Melbourne Airport the next afternoon, Luke turned and glanced briefly at Reeve before returning his focus to the road.

'I'm sorry.'

Reeve stared at him. 'Isn't that my favourite phrase?'

He smiled. 'I think you've worn it out. The difference is I know what I'm apologising for, whereas you're apologising for a million things you didn't know you did.'

'Okay. What are you sorry for?'

'For going off the deep end about Jess and about the DNA tests. Honestly, I'm not sure what's come over me. I hope for your sake that the second test confirms you are sisters. You deserve to have someone else in your life who loves you as much as I do.'

Tears welled in Reeve's eyes. 'It'd go a long way if you apologised to her.'

He nodded. 'I will before you go today.'

Reeve smiled, her heart swelling with love for her husband. 'This is one of the many reasons I love you,' she said. 'You admit when you might be wrong, and you do something about it.'

'What if I'm right, Ree? About Jess. And I hope I'm not. But what if I am? What if she does have an ulterior motive? To be fair, she's a very good actress if she is conning us, but she could be.'

'We deal with it when we know for sure. Innocent until proven otherwise. Right now, she needs me to be with her for something that has nothing to do with Dad or money, except she wouldn't be dealing with this if it wasn't for my father abandoning her when she was a baby.'

They pulled into an empty space in the short-term parking area. Luke got out and took Reeve's bag from the boot. 'I won't stay. I'll take you through to the gate lounge to meet them, apologise to Jess, and then go. Is that okay?'

'Of course it is. I'll ring you when we arrive.'

Luke nodded. 'Look after yourself. It worries me, you going off like this. If I didn't have a full schedule tomorrow, I'd come with you.'

'There's no need. I'll have people with me the entire time. If I do anything crazy, they'll be there to look after me.'

Luke nodded, took her hand, and together they walked into the airport.

31

Jess had expected Reeve to cancel on the trip to Perth, which in all honestly would have been fine. She would have preferred to do this alone, but now, as they waited in line to check their bags in, she had no choice but to accept that Trent at least was going with her.

'Still nothing from Reeve?'

She shook her head, checking her phone one more time. 'Based on Luke's mood last night, she probably won't be allowed to see me ever again. He wasn't very impressed with me turning up.'

'And he is here to apologise for that.'

Jess turned at the sound of Luke's deep voice. He stood on the other side of the rope from the check-in line. 'I'm sorry, Jess. I'm protective of Reeve, and I couldn't bear to see her hurt. She's had so much to contend with in the last few weeks, I don't want her having to process something else.'

'Neither do I,' Jess said.

'Good. Then we're on the same page. I hope everything goes okay in Perth,' he added. 'Reeve's told me what you're going to do, and I'm shocked that you've had to deal with anything like that. Call if you need anything while you're there.'

Jess nodded, surprised and touched by Luke's genuine concern.

'Now, I promised Reeve I'd drop her and go and not make a huge scene before I did.' His smile slipped, and he lowered his voice. 'Look after her, Jess. Her behaviour's been strange. Her outbursts can be random. She can go days at a time without any-thing, and then suddenly, something triggers it. She's not violent, which is the main thing.'

'Don't worry,' Jess assured him. 'I'll look after her.'

He smiled before turning to Reeve, who had been observing their exchange. He took her in his arms. 'Call me when you get there.' He kissed her lightly on the lips. 'Remember, I love you, and I'm sorry about all the extra stress. I'll make sure I'm on top of that by the time you get back.' He lowered his voice and whispered something in her ear.

Reeve smiled and kissed him. 'I'd like that, very much.' She blushed. 'Ignore any random messages you receive from me while I'm away.'

Luke kissed her lightly on the forehead. 'Will do. Now, I'll leave you to it. Have a good trip.'

Jess watched as he walked back towards the entrance doors. He'd certainly mellowed since the previous day.

'Random messages?' Trent asked.

As they moved slowly forward in the queue, Reeve explained the email message Luke had received from her.

'Do you usually email him?'

'No. Normally I text, but from time to time, I seem to revert to email. It's what got me in trouble at the school to start with. The school and I assumed I'd been hacked, but I was suspended before they could check whether my email had been accessed. But then more and more things were happening, and the Oscar situation...' She blushed as she filled Trent in. 'It's become pretty clear that it is me and probably was me emailing as well.'

Trent nodded. 'Do you have all the emails?'

'In my sent box, yes. Why?'

'Can I have a look at them when we're on the plane? It's giving me all sorts of ideas for a story, and I'd love to see what you're saying in them.'

'Always researching,' Jess said and laughed. 'Be careful what you let him read, Reeve. You'll end up in his next book.'

'You should be more worried,' Trent said. 'Look at this situation that you're letting me tag along to.'

'Letting you? Like either of you gave me a choice.'

He shrugged and nudged her forward towards the bag drop.

* * *

Jess had planned to watch a movie and tune out everything on the four-hour flight to Perth, but the conversation between Trent and Reeve became more and more intriguing as he read through the emails in her sent box.

'It's easy enough to check if your Gmail has been accessed by an unauthorised device or person,' Trent said, clicking on her account. 'See here.' He pointed to a table showing the recent activity on her account. 'It shows us that your account has been accessed from a mobile device and a browser, and the IP addresses are different.'

'So someone has been accessing my email?'

Trent shook his head. 'I'm assuming you use email when you're away from home.'

'Occasionally.'

'Then this will be your phone.'

'And there's no other devices using it?'

Trent scrolled through the list. 'No, it doesn't look like it.'

Reeve squirmed in her seat. 'Confirming it's me sending the messages.' It was not a big surprise, but all along Reeve had hoped there might be another explanation.

'Possibly,' Trent said, opening one of her messages. 'Although, it's interesting how many times you use the C-word in these messages.'

Reeve blushed. 'It makes me cringe. It's literally the only word in the English language I have a real problem with.'

'You're an English teacher, right?'

Reeve nodded. 'High school. Both general English and literature.'

'And yet your alter ego – we'll call that version of you that for now, if that's okay – has poor English.'

'What do you mean?'

'Look at the messages you've sent. The grammar and punctuation are consistently poor in them. Your alter ego seems to love the comma splice, uses the incorrect version of there, their, and they're, and seems to prefer US spelling. Although some of that might be your email program correcting the words.'

Reeve looked through some of the messages. He was right. The English was appalling. 'It's probably why all along I've said I didn't send them, and they don't sound like me.'

'Can I make a suggestion?'

Reeve nodded.

'Let's suspend this email account, and I'll set you up a new one with new passwords that I won't even tell you. I'll write them down in case you ever need them, but it will mean that I'm the only person who could possibly hack into your account and send a message from it. If the messages from you continue, then we'll know you're sending them, but if they don't, it could be that someone else is accessing your account and has a way to hide the fact that they're accessing it from a different IP address.'

Reeve's pulse raced. 'You think that's possible?'

He shrugged. 'In the world of hacking, I imagine anything is possible. You've had tests and everything, but you don't exhibit any of the signs I saw with my gran, who had dementia. We're spending a few days together, so who knows, I might see them, but it would be good to rule everything out.'

'Unfortunately, you probably will see them,' Reeve said. 'Jess has.'

'No, I haven't.'

Reeve frowned. 'I sent you that message, remember?'

'Okay, I've seen a message, but I haven't seen any of the behaviour that you, Luke, or Nick have described.'

'Nick?'

'When I came for dinner that night, he mentioned a few of the things you'd said to Bella, that's all. He was worried about you and wanted to reassure me that you were a lovely person.'

'That's your ex-husband?' Trent asked.

Reeve nodded. 'That was nice of him.'

'It was,' Jess said. 'Now, we should all relax. It's going to be a big day tomorrow.' She put her headphones on, sank back in her seat and closed her eyes. She still needed to formulate what she was going to say to the Grenfells.

* * *

The following morning, Jess took a deep breath and, with Reeve on one side of her and Trent on the other, walked with her head held high up the front path of Mike and Carly Grenfell's home in the Perth suburb of Fremantle. She'd hardly slept and hadn't been able to keep anything other than a weak cup of tea down that morning. But with Reeve and Trent flanking her, she had added strength that she was grateful for.

She took another deep breath before rapping on the front door.

A voice on the inside called out. 'Mike, love, can you get the door?'

If that was Carly, she'd certainly softened in the last twenty-five years. Back in her time, she would have screamed at him to 'open the bloody door!'

She heard footsteps on the other side, and the door opened. An older grey-haired version of the Mike Grenfell she knew smiled at them. 'Can I help you?' His eyes searched her face as if she was familiar, but he couldn't seem to quite place her.

'Is Carly home?' Her voice was a nervous squeak.

'Sure, I'll get her for you. Can I ask who wants her?'

'Jessica,' she said.

Mike stared at her again before nodding. 'Love,'

he called as he walked back into the house, 'there's a Jessica at the door for you.'

'Jessica?'

'Sorry, love, I didn't ask. She's familiar. From church perhaps.'

Church! They'd changed their tune if they were going to church.

Reeve moved beside her. 'Okay?'

She nodded as footsteps returned to the front door. Carly Grenfell stood in front of her. The woman who twenty-five years ago had treated her like a dog.

Carly frowned, like Mike, trying to place her. She forced her lips into a smile. 'Can I help you?'

Jess nodded. 'I'd like to speak to both you and Mike. My friends and I arrived from Melbourne last night.'

'Melbourne?' Carly's face paled.

'Yes. I'm sure you remember me, don't you, Carly?'

'Jess? Jess Williams?'

Jess nodded.

Fear filled Carly's eyes. 'Oh sweet Jesus. Mike!'

Her husband returned to the door, hearing the panic in Carly's voice. 'Everything okay?'

Carly shook her head. 'It's Jess. Jess Williams from Melbourne.'

Mike turned and stared at Jess. 'Get out of here. I mean it. Get out of here, or I'll call the police.'

Trent stepped in front of Jess. 'Why don't you do that, Mr Grenfell. I think they'd be interested in hearing what Jess has to say.'

Mike looked around. 'Keep your voice down. We don't want the neighbours knowing our business.'

'Perhaps you should invite us in then,' Trent said. 'Jess would like, and deserves, an explanation from you.'

Mike hesitated before opening the door. The three of them were led down a long hallway to an open and airy living room which opened out onto a large back garden. A cubby house sat in the middle of the lawn with a small blue swing hanging off it. Jess froze. *Are they still fostering? Devon's investigation assured me they weren't.*

'What do you want?' Carly asked.

Jess turned to face her. 'Are you still fostering?'

Carly's eyes travelled to the cubby house. 'No, we stopped after we left Melbourne. Mike's sister, Elizabeth, has a son and a grandson. Mike built the cubby house for him.' She placed her hands on her hips. 'Is that what you came to find out?'

Jess shook her head. 'No, I want an explanation for why you did what you did to me.'

'We didn't do anything,' Mike said. 'You did. As you know, and as I'm happy to tell the police if you want to get them here.'

Carly shook her head and sighed. 'No, Mike. This day has been coming for a long time. Jess deserves the truth.'

Mike's face paled. 'What?'

Carly held up her hand. 'Let me say what needs to be said.' She motioned for them all to sit. Once they had, she began to talk. 'We did an awful thing to you, and we've tried to live a better life ever since.'

Jess wasn't sure what she'd expected to hear, but it wasn't this. She'd assumed an apology would be the last thing she'd get from these people.

'We were scared,' Carly continued. 'You became pregnant under our roof, which was unforgivable. We threw the boy out, but we would have lost our right to foster if anyone knew. We'd fostered for years. It was our way of coping with the fact that we couldn't have children. We would have done any-thing for that not to be taken away from us, and un-fortunately, you became the victim in it all. When your baby was born, we panicked.' She lowered her eyes. 'He died due to complications with the birth.

Complications that if we'd taken you to the hospital might not have happened.'

'Hold on. I fell asleep and smothered him by accident.'

Carly shook her head. 'You passed out due to a postpartum haemorrhage, and the baby died while you were unconscious. Your blood loss was extensive, but you recovered.'

'But you made me think I'd killed him. Not only that, but then you threatened me and said you'd tell the authorities I killed him if they found out about my pregnancy.'

'We panicked,' Carly said. 'It was a horrifying situation. We'd already covered up your pregnancy, and this was taking it a step further.'

'What happened to Leo?'

Carly looked at Mike.

He cleared his throat. 'I drove out to the Macedon Ranges that day to the state forest. We'd placed him in a small wooden crate, and I buried him.'

'Would you know where that spot is now?'

'Possibly,' Mike said. 'It was twenty-five years ago, but I'd probably remember. When I got back to the house, Carly was a mess. Said we needed to call the police and tell them what had happened. But I said no, that we needed to make sure you were okay and then we would leave the state and start again, which is what we did. We made sure you were okay first.'

'Was that for my health, or so no one knew I'd given birth?'

'Honestly, the latter. We wanted to put it all behind us and never think about it again. My sister lived here in Perth and was having some difficulties herself. We hoped coming and helping her would help make amends for what we'd done.'

'What about the family who was going to adopt the baby?' Jess asked. 'Weren't they suspicious?'

'There was never a signed agreement,' Mike said. 'I contacted them and told them that you'd had the baby and had decided to keep him. They were upset, but there wasn't anything they could do. The adoption was never through legal channels.'

Jess took a deep breath. So that was it. After all the years of wondering, in a matter of fifteen minutes, she had all her answers.

'And you've lived here ever since?' Reeve asked.

'Yes. And we've changed, become much better people. We were affected by what happened with Dean and Jess's baby. We couldn't have that happen in our house again, which was one of the reasons we chose to stop fostering.'

'If you were so affected,' Trent said, 'why did you

tell Dean about Jess and the baby and that she killed him? He's come after her for money recently, trying to blackmail her.'

Carly's mouth dropped open. 'I never told him anything of the sort.' She turned to Mike. 'Did you?'

Heat rose in his cheeks. 'He called me recently, completely out of the blue. I thought that story would get rid of him. I did say to him that he'd be in trouble with the police if the circumstances of the pregnancy were ever revealed. I'm sorry, I should never have said anything. We'd moved on, and I just wanted to get rid of him, not relive that awful time.'

Jess looked to Reeve, who had tears in her eyes. These people were not the monsters she remembered. It appeared the situation with Leo had affected them greatly too.

'We found God when we got to Perth,' Carly said. 'We've done our best to make up for past sins, Jess. I'm devastated that you went through what you did. I imagine it was very difficult for you after your baby's death.'

Jess nodded. Understatement of the century.

'What do you need from us, Jess?'

Jess cleared her throat. 'I came here for closure. To find out what happened to you. Whether you ruined anyone else's lives and what you did with Leo.

Probably the one thing I would like to be shown is where he was buried.'

Carly looked at Mike. 'You should do that for her, love. It's the least we can do.'

'But what if this is a set-up? What if she's going to say I murdered him and buried him there?'

Carly looked Jess in the eye. 'Is that what this is?'

Jess shook her head. 'I just want to know what happened to my baby.'

'Mike's working until Thursday. We could both fly to Melbourne next weekend and show you.'

'Really?' Jess looked at Trent, who'd uttered the word at the same time as she had.

'Yes,' Carly said, standing. 'Now, I'm sorry, but I need to lie down. I hope you can understand that this has been a shock.'

Jess, Reeve, and Trent all stood. 'Of course,' Jess said. The older woman in front of her, full of remorse and compassion, was hard to equate with the woman she'd hated for twenty-five years.

'Leave your details with Mike, and we'll make arrangements for the weekend.' Tears filled Carly's eyes. She took Jess's hands in hers. 'I've never forgiven myself for what we did to you. I'm not asking for your forgiveness, but I do want you to know that. There's not a day that's passed that I haven't prayed for your baby.' She dropped Jess's hands and turned and disappeared into a room off the living area.

Jess swallowed the lump in her throat and followed Reeve and Mike down the hall to a small table that stood by the front door. Mike handed Reeve a pad and pen and asked for Jess's details. She wrote them down, then looked around, realising Trent wasn't with them. 'Trent?'

'Coming.' His voice travelled down the hallway from the living room they'd been in. 'Sorry, think I was too shocked to move. This hasn't turned out how I was expecting.'

'Me either,' Jess said, doing her best to blink back tears.

Trent didn't acknowledge Mike. Instead, he took Jess's hand in his and led her out to the rental car.

Tears ran down Jess's face as Trent pulled out of the driveway and drove in the direction of their hotel.

'I expected anger and denial, not a reasonable explanation,' Jess said. 'They look like they suffered too.'

Reeve squeezed her hand. 'I'm glad they did, Jess, I really am. It shows that they were human, after all. The situation appears to have shaped who they became. It made them better people. As much as I hate

that that was at your expense, it is at least one positive. Isn't it, Trent?'

Trent glanced in the rear-view mirror at them
and nodded before returning his gaze to the road and
maintaining his silence.

32

The mood was subdued as Jess, Reeve, and Trent boarded the flight back to Melbourne the next morning. Jess settled back in her seat with her headphones, leaving Trent and Reeve to talk.

'How are you doing?' Trent asked Reeve. 'This has been a pretty big couple of days, and you have all your own problems to think about.'

'This has been liberating, not thinking about any of that. And anyway, I have no idea when I do something crazy. It's only if someone tells me. For all I know, I went back and abused those arseholes. Told them what' – she blushed – 'what C-words they are.'

Trent laughed. 'You can't say it, can you?'

Reeve shook her head.

'Well, I can tell you that you haven't done any-thing on the dementia scale since we left Melbourne. I checked your new email account this morning, and there was nothing to worry about there.'

'So it's possible that it is someone else sending the emails and they can't now that they don't have access?'

Trent nodded. 'It's a possibility. The messages sent from your account in the past were random as far as how often they were sent. There were times that a week, even two, passed without a new message. We need to give it a bit more time to be certain.'

'Thanks for setting that up,' Reeve said. 'At least if I do start sending nasty messages, we'll know that it's me. I keep thinking about you noticing how bad the English is of dementia Reeve. You wouldn't think you'd forget something like that, even if you are on another planet. If I can put sentences together, then surely I can punctuate them.'

'Actually, I googled that last night,' Trent said. 'It's been bugging me as it is such an obvious way to con-firm these messages aren't from you.' He lowered his eyes, not meeting her gaze. 'Apparently, dementia can cause language problems that extend to writing. Spelling, grammar, and punctuation may decline.'

'Oh.' Reeve lapsed into silence, not willing to

admit that Trent's suggestion that maybe she wasn't writing the messages had given her the slightest glimmer of hope.

The flight attendant appeared at the end of their aisle, offering drinks. Trent ordered sparkling wine for all of them.

Reeve shook her head, but he insisted. 'You're seat-locked between Jess and me, thirty thousand feet up. You can throw a fit, I guess, and we'll have to restrain you, but other than that, what do you think might happen?'

Reeve accepted the wine, nudging Jess and pointing to her small bottle and cup.

Jess smiled, poured the wine into the cup, and downed it in one large gulp, not removing her headphones.

Trent laughed. 'She deserved that. Okay, let's enjoy ours and then my guess is the effect it's going to have is we'll both pass out. I don't know about you, but I'm exhausted. I'm surprised they even serve alcohol this early.'

'It's a connecting flight from South Africa,' Reeve said. 'That's probably why. It's probably still yesterday or the middle of the night for some of the passengers.'

Trent was right. The champagne, as delicious as it

was, went straight to Reeve's head, and she was out like a light, only waking when the plane suddenly shuddered forward. She opened her eyes, her hands gripping the armrests.

'We've landed,' Trent said. 'You've been asleep for three hours.'

Reeve smiled. 'Good, so I didn't do anything I need to worry about.'

'You had a dream where you were calling my name out *very* loud,' Trent said. 'Like this, *oh Trent, oh Trent, oh my God, Trent.*'

'Ignore him,' Jess said as Reeve's cheeks heated. 'He's teasing. You did nothing of the sort.'

Reeve elbowed him in the ribs. 'No teasing the dementia chick, okay? I'll believe anything you tell me. You do realise that, don't you?'

'We shouldn't tell you about the chicken impersonation and how you tried to lay an egg, then?'

Reeve looked to Jess, who rolled her eyes and shook her head. 'No chicken, no egg.'

'You're no fun at all.' Trent pouted. 'What's the point of having our own crazy chick if we can't tease her?'

Reeve laughed.

'I'm glad you find him funny,' Jess said. 'I think

most people in your situation would find him highly offensive.'

'I like that he's not giving me any special treatment,' Reeve said. 'I hope I know him well enough that when I do something crazy, he probably won't tease me.' She turned to Trent. 'Am I right?'

He shrugged. 'You can read me like a book.'

Reeve returned her focus to Jess. 'How are you doing?'

'I need some time to get my head around everything that's happened and then plan for the weekend.' She locked eyes with Reeve. 'Do you think you could come with me? I don't think I could visit Leo's gravesite on my own.'

'Of course.' Reeve's eyes filled with tears. 'Sorry, I just can't imagine what you're going through right now.'

Jess managed a small smile. 'A huge range of emotions, to be honest. Finding out I didn't kill Leo is massive, but it doesn't bring him back.' She reached over and took Reeve's hand in hers. 'But I do have a new sister and a niece, and I'm not sure I could ask for much more than that.' They remained holding hands as the plane taxied to the gate.

Jess nudged Reeve as they disembarked the plane and entered the gate lounge. 'Luke's waiting for you.'

Reeve's eyes locked with her husband's. He looked every part the handsome doctor, deep in thought with his hands in the pockets of his black jacket. When they reached him, he took her into his arms and kissed her with a ferocity she hadn't experienced in a long time.

She laughed as she pulled back from him. 'Did you miss me?'

'You could say that.'

'Ms Elliot?'

Reeve turned, freezing instantly as her eyes met Oscar Ryan's.

'Oscar?'

'My family are at the next gate lounge waiting for my aunt to arrive,' he said. 'I was just getting a drink from the vending machine' – he held up a bottle of water – 'and saw you. I wanted to say I'm sorry. I didn't want to get you into trouble or fired. You did so much for me.'

Reeve's eyes filled with tears. 'No, I'm sorry. I've found out that I'm sick, and I have no recollection of what I did, but I'm incredibly regretful. I hope one day you can find it in your heart to forgive me.'

Oscar looked from Reeve to Luke. 'She's sick?'

Luke nodded. 'Afraid so, and as Reeve said, we are very sorry for what happened. Once Reeve's diagnosis is official, we'll be finalising a compensation package with the school to go towards your pain and suffering.'

'I'm not sure about that any more,' Oscar said.

'Any more?' Reeve said.

Oscar blushed. 'If you were sick, then you shouldn't be punished, that's all.'

'You shouldn't be talking to us, Oscar,' Luke said. 'Your parents and your lawyer could cause further problems for us if they think we initiated this conversation.'

Oscar stared at Luke, hesitating for a brief second before turning back to Reeve. 'Really, I am sorry. I never intended for any of this to happen. I'd better go. My aunt's plane will be here any minute.'

Reeve nodded, touched by his words. 'He's a good kid,' she said. 'I'm sorry that he was involved in all of this.'

They walked as a group towards the baggage claim. 'I'll be pleased to go home, go to bed, and not think for a few days,' Jess said.

'Me too,' Reeve said, sliding her phone from her bag as it pinged with a text message. She glanced at her phone and then at Jess. 'It's our DNA test results. They're back, and we can log in online to view the results.'

'Log in? They don't email or post them to us?' Jess asked.

Luke nodded. 'It's standard, which is why I find it interesting that Devon had hard copies. Hard copies he may have printed off, or he could easily have produced himself.'

'Let's hope he printed them off and they were correct,' Reeve said.

'The login we set up is your phone number,' Luke said. 'The password's sisters with a capital S and a question mark at the end.'

Reeve glanced at Jess. 'You ready to do this?'

Jess nodded.

Reeve keyed in the password details and waited as the pages on Melbourne's DNA Diagnostic Centre loaded. The first page gave an explanation of how the tests were done and what to expect. Reeve scrolled through to the page titled *Results*.

The DNA data does not support the biological relationship.

The pain that hit her was so intense it caused her to gasp. She looked at Jess, whose eyes were wide, like a deer caught in the headlights.

Reeve's legs crumpled beneath her, and she had to sit down.

They were not sisters.

* * *

Reeve was in a state of shock as she sat in the passenger seat of Luke's Mercedes. She hadn't spoken another word to Jess. She'd collected her bag and allowed Luke to lead her out of the airport. What she and Jess had shared since they met was more than what most family would ever share, and it was only a few weeks. She felt an inexplicable link to the other woman, which a family tie explained. Grief was overwhelming her. It was as if her sister had died, which, in a way, she had.

Luke squeezed her knee, the familiarity of the gesture bringing her some peace. 'I'm sorry it's turned out like this,' he said. 'I know your dad was close to Devon and respected him, but it seems he and Jess have worked together on this. It's such an elaborate scheme to steal your father's money. If you decide to prosecute, he should go to jail.'

Reeve didn't respond. *Prosecute* Devon? And Jess? With everything Jess was going through, would that be something she could even consider bringing herself to do? Was Trent part of it too? She wasn't sure she'd ever trust anyone again. She was so gullible. Although it was possible Jess was innocent in all of this. That Devon had set her up. Reeve dismissed the thought as soon as she had it. Why would Jess share an inheritance with a lawyer if she wasn't in on it? But what did that mean about Devon? He and Martin had been friends for years. It wasn't as if he'd set up the friendship or their client–lawyer relationship to steal his money from the start. Devon was wealthy in his own right. Not Martin Elliot wealthy, but still beyond comfortable. Had he seen Martin's death as an opportunity? A shiver ran down Reeve's spine.

'You don't think Devon had anything to do with the fire, do you?'

Luke glanced at her before returning his eyes to the road. 'I hope not, Ree, I really do, but I think we should make the police aware of this latest development.'

Reeve nodded and rested her head against the car window, mental exhaustion taking over. Not that long ago, she was happily teaching at school, loving being a mum to Bella and wife to her handsome surgeon husband. How had things changed this dramatically and this quickly?

33

Jess didn't know what to do or say. She'd tried to talk to Reeve, but Luke had protected her, telling Trent to get Jess away from his wife.

In the end, she'd done what he said, grabbed her luggage and followed Trent out to the short-term parking terminal.

'I don't understand,' she kept repeating. 'Why would Devon's result say one thing and Luke's another?'

'Luke's convinced this is a setup,' Trent said as they drove back towards Melbourne. He turned to Jess. 'I'm going to ask you this once only, and please know, I'll believe without question what you tell me. Okay?'

Jess nodded.

'Does Luke have any reason at all to believe you and Devon are working together?'

Jess almost laughed at the absurdity of it, but Trent's question was serious. 'No, he doesn't. Weeks ago, I was contacted by Devon out of the blue, saying his client, Martin Elliot, wanted to meet with me. He explained who Martin was, and it went from there. Although Martin did tell me that Devon was the one who encouraged him to find me in the first place. Martin was dealing with cancer and Devon made him realise that if he wanted to meet me, his time was running out. I guess he could have had an ulterior motive. He's also suggested to me that I'd be entitled to contest the will if I chose to, and the family trust, but that's all. He's never suggested he'd take a percentage as payment.' She thought back to her dealings with Devon. 'He acted unprofessional at times and when Reeve and I called him on it, he apologised and agreed that he should have Martin's best interests looked after and no one else's. I don't know him well enough to know whether he's telling the truth or not.'

'Maybe you need to organise another DNA test. Luke might have tampered with this new one.'

'But I saw Luke post the DNA test. I saw our

swabs go into the box before it was posted. We literally did the test in the kitchen, packaged it up, and went to the post-box together. There was no opportunity to switch out the swabs or do anything else.'

'Then it could be a case of the test being wrong.'

'Possibly. Devon did a paternity test from Martin's DNA the first time because he said that sibling DNA tests can be inaccurate. Maybe it's as simple as having a third test done?' Jess said. 'There must be somewhere Reeve and I can go together to get one done that no one can tamper with?'

Trent nodded. 'I'm sure there would be. Let's look into it as soon as we get home. Do you think Reeve will agree to another one? She looked devastated.'

Jess blinked back tears as she pictured Reeve's face when they saw the results. The pain in her eyes had mirrored Jess's. It was heartbreaking to think that Reeve now believed she was a fraud. 'What if it comes back negative too?'

'Then at least you'll know for sure,' he said. 'Leave it with me. When we get home, I'll see if I can find a lab that does them on-site.'

Jess sunk back into her seat in silence, her mind frazzled with everything that was going on. When they reached the apartment block, she thanked Trent and said she needed to be on her own.

'I'll come and check on you tonight, okay? I'll bring some dinner.' He hugged her and continued up to his third-floor apartment.

* * *

Jess had to drag herself out of bed when she heard knocking on the door a little after six. She assumed it would be Trent and knew he wouldn't go away until he knew she was alright.

'Soup and fresh bread,' he said, holding out a small tray to her. 'I thought you might need comfort food.'

Jess was tempted to take the food and ask him to leave, but she was touched by his thoughtfulness and knew she owed him a big thank you for everything he'd done in the last few days. She invited him in to eat with her. There was enough food for two, especially as she had no appetite.

'I found a DNA testing lab that does legal paternity tests,' he said as they sat across from each other at the small dining table. 'They're more accurate than the home ones you've used so far, and you have to go into the lab to have them done so there's no question of anyone tampering with them. Do you want me to talk to Reeve for you? It's more expensive than the ones you order online but not too bad.'

'Honestly, I doubt there's any point. She's unlikely to take your call, let alone go along for another test.'

She was right. Trent called Reeve and then sent a text message but got no response. He got to his feet. 'What's her address? I'm going to go around and see her.'

An hour later, he was back, jaw clenched. 'She wouldn't talk to me.'

'Did Luke say that and send you away?'

'No, she came to the door. She told me that she couldn't believe she'd put her trust in me and that I should be ashamed of myself. I tried to explain and mentioned a third test, but she just laughed, said I must be dreaming, and slammed the door. I can try again tomorrow if you like?'

Jess shook her head. 'Let's just leave it for now.'

Trent hesitated.

'What?' Jess asked, knowing that look. The look that suggested he had more to say. But he kept his mouth closed, hugged her again, and left the apartment.

34

Luke glanced at Reeve as he manoeuvred the Mercedes in the stop-start traffic along Nepean Highway. 'I'm sorry you have to deal with all of this, I really am. It's bad enough having to cope with illness, but to have everything with Jess to contend with too, it's too much for anyone.'

Reeve gave a small nod. She agreed with him on all of this. The utter betrayal was devastating. Her stomach had been in knots since slamming the door in Trent's face the previous evening. She'd ignored a call and a text from him, and then, just before eight, he'd appeared at the house wanting her to do a third DNA test.

'You've got to be kidding,' she'd said. 'What the

hell is wrong with you? Are you getting a cut of what-ever Jess manages to rob from me?'

'It's an independent test, Reeve, done on-site at a lab. You have one test that says you aren't related and one that says you are. Don't you want to find out the truth? What if you are related to Jess, and you've just walked away?'

A strangled laugh had left Reeve's lips. 'The truth. That's a joke. She'll need a legal test done if she ex-pects to inherit from my father's will, so I guess if you really aren't involved in her and Devon's scheme, then you'll find out the truth at that point too. I will be seeking new legal representation, and that will be something we will insist upon.' She'd slammed the door, not willing to pursue the conversation any further.

'Reeve?' Luke's voice broke into her thoughts.

She turned and managed to smile at him. 'I'm sorry.'

He met her gaze. 'What for?'

She nodded. 'I should have listened to you about Jess and about Devon. Your gut instinct is a lot better than mine.'

Luke smiled. 'You don't have to be sorry. You're a victim in all of this. I'm only glad that we worked that out before they cheated you out of your inheritance.'

He rested his hand on her knee, and they travelled in silence the remainder of the drive to Patricia's.

* * *

CLIENT MEETING SUMMARY

DATE: September 18
Client: Reeve Elliot & Dr Luke Sheffield
Duration: 90 Min

Reeve presented with disorientation at times today during our ninety-minute session. She started the session quite articulate, relaying the events of the past few days. As she spoke more about Jessica Williams, the woman she had been led to believe was her half-sister, she became upset and confused. The impact of the relationship being based on lies has affected Reeve greatly.

Reeve turned on her husband during the session, lashing him with an aggressive outburst which was hard to follow. Her rambling words turned to screaming at him as she became more agitated. Luke confirmed these outbursts had happened on numerous occasions in the past twenty-four hours since the situation with Jessica Williams had unfolded. Stress is a contributing factor to Reeve's condition.

I am alarmed at the rapid decline in Reeve and have recommended to Luke that she not be left alone. He is hoping to have a full-time carer in the home as soon as possible and will take time off work until this happens. During her outburst, she mentioned ending it all. This is not the first time that suicide has been suggested. She will require twenty-four-hour supervision, and I have recommended that a care facility be determined quickly.

Follow-up session scheduled for next week.

* * *

'I feel like I'm living in a dream,' Reeve said as Luke drove away from Patricia's East Brighton home. 'A nightmare, to be more accurate. I don't feel right in myself. If I was out partying every night, I'd expect to feel this depleted. It's hard to explain.'

'It's mental exhaustion,' Luke said. 'That combined with the medication. You need to give yourself a break. Let's get you home and put you to bed.' He hesitated.

'What?'

'On top of mental exhaustion, I've noticed that after you've had an episode, you appear exhausted, like it's taken it all out of you, that's all.'

Reeve closed her eyes. 'An episode? I wouldn't call a session with Patricia an episode. If anything, she's given me a few coping skills to deal with everything that's happened.'

Luke gave her a sideways glance. 'You went off at me in there.'

Reeve's eyes widened. 'No, I didn't. I filled Patricia in on everything that's happened. I know I got a bit heated talking about Jess and Devon, but I think she'd understand that it's affected me.'

'Ree, you went nuts at me in there. I mentioned that I was suspicious of Jess from the start, and you turned on me. You were screaming to the point that the only word I could make out was the constant use of the C-word.'

'What? No, I didn't.'

'Why do you think Patricia moved next to you on the couch and put an arm around you?'

Reeve stared at Luke. Patricia stood up at one stage to open the window as the room was a little stuffy, but she'd never sat down next to her. Had she? The session seemed to have disappeared very quickly, and Reeve had been surprised when the ninety minutes were up. Was that because she'd blacked out most of it? 'I don't... I don't remember any of that.'

Luke nodded. 'I know you don't. And for that very reason, I'm going to call Carol and see if she's available. I think you need someone with you throughout the day. I'm supposed to be working the next five days straight, but you shouldn't be left alone. I'll take time off until we have Carol or someone else in the house full-time. I'd be too scared to leave you while you're like this.'

'Scared?'

He nodded again. 'In amongst your ramblings with Patricia, you mentioned you'd end it all before going into care. I couldn't live with myself if you did that, Ree. I love you so much. If you're that upset about going into care in the future, then we won't let that happen. We'll get someone full-time for now to look after you, and if you get to the point that you do need further care, I'll stop working. I'm a doctor and can easily handle it.'

Reeve knew she should show gratitude towards Luke, but she couldn't. Even this scenario, which was a lot better than going into care, was awful. She couldn't put him through watching her deteriorate the way her mother had. At least she'd had a reprieve when she'd left the hospital each day. Living with Alice twenty-four hours a day would have been another thing altogether.

She closed her eyes. Her head was heavy, and she wanted to curl up in a ball. She'd seriously considered the idea of ending her life the previous night but hadn't expected to voice it to Luke or Patricia. But then again, she hadn't expected to abuse them either.

Since returning from Perth on Tuesday, Jess had
done her best to push all thoughts of the Reeve situation from her mind and concentrate on her work.
However, it was harder to push thoughts of Leo away.
Now, as she sat at her desk late on Friday afternoon,
she was overwhelmed by a blanket of anxiety that
settled on her shoulders. Carly Grenfell had contacted her the day before, confirming that she and
Mike would be arriving mid-morning on Saturday
and would meet her at the main entrance of the
Wombat State Forest near Daylesford at one o'clock.
They would then walk into the forest together so that
Mike could show her where Leo was buried. She'd
asked Trent to accompany her for emotional support

and for protection. As much as she would like to believe that the situation had changed Carly and Mike for the better, she didn't want to put herself at risk. For all she knew, they might be planning to bury her in the forest too.

Her mobile phone rang as she debated between finishing another report or packing up and taking her work home with her. She glanced at the screen, her heart rate rapidly increasing. It was Carly Grenfell.

'Carly?' The phone line was noisy, as if she was out somewhere busy.

'Yes, Jess. Look, I'm sorry, but Mike's had an accident. I'm at the emergency department with him now. He's crushed his hand.'

'Oh no, that's awful.' Jess's heart sank. 'You're cancelling on tomorrow, I imagine?'

'Postponing. Can I contact you in a few days once we know how bad it is and when he'll be up for travelling? He's in a lot of pain.'

'Of course.' Jess ended the call after telling Carly she hoped Mike would be okay. She leant back in her chair. It had been twenty-five years. Another week or two wasn't going to make any difference. There was nothing to stop her from going out to the forest tomorrow anyway. Of course, she'd have no idea where

Leo was buried, but she'd still be able to be within proximity of him. She'd have to let Trent know. As the Grenfells weren't coming, it was a trip she'd rather do on her own. Almost at the exact second she thought of Trent, her phone rang again. She smiled when she saw the caller display.

'I was just thinking of you.'

'Are you at the office?' The urgency in Trent's voice had Jess sit up straight.

'What's the matter?'

'I need to come and see you. It's important.'

'It's not about Reeve, is it? I'm not sure—'

Trent cut her off. 'No, it's about the Grenfells.'

Jess was silent for a moment. 'I just spoke with Carly. Mike's had an accident, and they aren't coming this weekend. I was about to ring you.'

'Jesus,' Trent said. 'They're unbelievable. Stay put. I won't be long.' He ended the call, leaving Jess staring at the handset.

Ten minutes later, a message flashed on Jess's computer screen from Marlee at reception.

Jess, your friend Trent is here. Can I send him to your office?

She sent a quick response.

Yes, please.

She stood and walked over to her office door. She poked her head out and beckoned to Trent, who was already on his way down. 'In here.'

Trent's face was red, and he was breathing hard. He had a folder under one arm and seemed completely out of sorts.

'Did you run here?'

'Yes.' He checked his watch. 'We've only got two hours, so this needs to be quick.' He moved inside her office and sat down across from Jess.

'When we were in Perth earlier in the week, something didn't sit right with me,' he began. 'The way in which the Grenfells told you what happened to Leo. It was all too easy. They didn't seem to hide anything, just laid it all out as if they'd been expecting you to turn up.'

'Maybe they did expect I would turn up one day,' Jess said. 'They'd changed. Finding God and being much nicer people. I'd still never want anything to do with them, but they weren't the monsters that fostered me.'

'I disagree,' Trent said. 'Do you remember when we were walking out how I stayed in the living room for a few minutes by myself?'

Jess nodded. 'You said you were in shock.'

'I wasn't. I was snooping. There were photos all over the far wall from where we were sitting. I went and looked at them. They were mainly of the boy, the nephew they mentioned. From when he was younger through to his current age. There were also a few of him with his wife and son.'

'Okay, so what?'

'Jess.' Trent had calmed himself, and his voice was gentle. 'Both the nephew and his son looked like you.'

Jess stared at Trent. 'Like me?'

Trent nodded. 'I didn't say anything because I didn't want to get your hopes up if I was wrong.'

'You think the photos were of Leo?' *Leo? Alive?*

Trent nodded again. 'I spoke with Hamish, who referred me to a private investigator in Perth. He's spent the last two days digging up information.' Trent took a deep breath. 'Mike Grenfell's sister died three years after Mike and Carly moved to Perth. She didn't have any children. The boy they referred to as their nephew is registered officially as their son, Ashley Michael Grenfell, born on May 16, 1994.'

Jess's mouth dropped open. 'Oh my God. They kept Leo? Although that date's wrong. He was born on May 2.'

Trent nodded. 'That's how it appears. His birth was registered as a home birth witnessed by a Susan Grey—a registered midwife who I believe is also Carly's sister. As you have sixty days to register a birth, I guess they could have picked any date as long as they hadn't had to take Leo anywhere for medical attention.'

'I met Susan,' Jess said. 'They were both midwives.' Bile rose in her throat as the enormity of what the Grenfells had done hit her with full force. 'Sorry. I think I'm going to be sick.'

Jess hurried out of her office to the shared bathrooms, only just making it into a stall before the contents of her stomach emptied. She flushed and washed her hands and her face before walking slowly back to her office. They'd stolen her baby. But he was alive. *Leo was alive.*

Trent was pacing to and fro and stopped as she entered the office.

'What do I do now? Call the police?'

'If that's what you want to do. You'd be entirely within your right. Keep in mind he's a twenty-five-year-old man, so there might be another way to do this.'

Jess sat down and motioned for Trent to do the same. 'What are you suggesting?'

'I've booked two tickets on a Qantas flight to Perth.' He checked his watch again. 'It leaves at five-thirty. We've got about half an hour to get home and pack an overnight bag and then race to the airport. If it was me, I'd want to confront them and go from there. I thought you might feel the same way.'

Jess grabbed her bag and her phone. 'I do. I definitely do.'

* * *

It seemed like a surreal dream as Jess packed a bag, drove with Trent to the airport, boarded the plane, and a few hours later landed in Perth. Trent had booked a two-bedroom apartment in Fremantle, not far from the Grenfells, and after a night of tossing and turning, Jess showered, dressed, and by six that morning, was sitting waiting for Trent to wake up.

She startled when a little after six, the front door to the apartment opened, and Trent appeared with a small takeaway tray housing two large coffees and two brown paper bags. 'I thought you were still asleep.'

'It's eight o'clock Melbourne time, don't forget,' Trent said. 'Which means this is likely to be a very long day.' He handed her the coffee and one of the paper bags. 'I know you won't be hungry, but you should eat something for the energy. We have no idea how today will turn out, so best to be as well prepared as possible. Have you thought what you're going to say to them?'

Jess nodded. It was all she'd thought about all night. 'It's probably going to turn nasty. They put on a great act for us on Monday, but that's exactly what it was, an act.' She drank the coffee and nibbled on the blueberry muffin Trent had purchased. 'Thank you, by the way,' she suddenly said. 'I can't believe you've done all this for me. Private investigators, booking flights. It's beyond anything I could ever imagine. I'll reimburse you for everything, of course.'

Trent blushed. 'I'm not worried about the money, Jess. It's you I'm worried for. I just hope that today turns out how you want it to.'

Those words repeated in Jess's head as they drove the rental car to the Grenfells' house. She knew exactly how she wanted today to turn out. She wanted the Grenfells arrested and Leo to come back to Melbourne with her. She couldn't help but smile as the thought popped into her mind. She wasn't silly enough to think either would happen. Although the first was possible if she did choose to call the police.

She and Trent had talked late into the night, and

he'd reminded her that as far as Leo was concerned, Carly and Mike were his parents. The private investigator's research had suggested he'd had a happy childhood and had gone on to marry and have a son of his own. What he was going to learn would be a huge shock, and having the police involved and threatening the people he considered his parents could turn him against Jess. She would need to be careful.

Trent pulled up outside the Grenfells' house and switched off the ignition. 'Ready?'

'No, but I don't think I ever will be.' Jess pushed open the car door with trembling fingers. Trent came around to her side and offered her his hand, which she took gratefully.

She drew in a breath, doing her best to calm her breathing as Trent rapped on the front door. They stood and waited as footsteps hurried to open it.

The door swung open, and Carly took a step backwards. 'Jess? What on earth are you doing here?'

'We need to talk,' Jess said. 'Is Mike home?'

'He sure is.' Mike's booming voice floated down the hallway. 'Who's asking?'

'Love, it's Jess. She's dropped in.'

Silence greeted the announcement.

'Don't worry,' Jess said, 'I know you lied about

Mike's accident. He doesn't need to hide his hand from me.'

The colour drained from Carly's face. 'What do you want?'

'An explanation.'

'Mike.' Carly's voice rose an octave. 'You need to come here, now. Mike!'

Mike entered the hallway. 'What's going on?'

'Ashley Michael Grenfell,' Jess said. 'That's what's going on. You know, the man you said was your nephew but is, in fact, registered as your son. I'd like a DNA test.'

Mike looked to Carly and back to Jess. 'Leave my house, now.'

Trent stepped towards Mike, in an intimidating stance. 'We can come back with the police, or we can talk this through as adults. Jess wants to meet Ashley, and she wants him to know who she is. We can either do this through legal channels or try to do it in a way that doesn't destroy your relationship with Jess's son.'

'He's our son,' Carly said. 'His birth certificate proves that.'

Trent gave a wry laugh. 'It proves that you stole a baby and broke the law. Your sister, who I believe was your attending midwife, has also broken the law. A DNA test will be very quick to sort this out.' He let out an exaggerated sigh and turned to Jess. 'Come on. We might as well go straight to the police station. I thought this would be a waste of time.'

'Hold on,' Mike said. 'Let's all calm down and talk about this. Come in, and we'll make some coffee. You've given us a shock, that's all.'

I'll bet we have, Jess thought as she made her way through the house to the living area.

Carly organised coffee and brought it over, her hands visibly shaking as she placed it on the table between the two couches. She sat down, fidgeting with her skirt. When she finally looked up at Jess, her eyes were full of tears. 'We gave him a good life, Jess. You knew we couldn't have one of our own, and your baby was our chance. You weren't planning to keep him, and we knew we would love him as if he was ours.'

'You planned it all along?'

Mike nodded. 'We didn't want you coming to find him at any stage, which is why we led you to think he'd died.'

'You led me to think I killed him. There's a big difference, Mike.' She practically spat his name, her anger escalating. 'And then you lied your arses off on Monday. God, I believed your act. Thank goodness Trent didn't.'

'We loved him with everything we had.' Carly's voice was barely a whisper. 'If you tell him now, you'll ruin everything we built with him.'

'I'm not going to tell him anything,' Jess said, a sliver of guilt edging its way into her consciousness as relief filled Carly's face.

Tears ran down Carly's cheeks. 'Thank you. I don't even know what to say.'

'I'm not going to tell him anything,' Jess repeated, 'because you are. You're going to call him now and ask him to come over, and you're going to tell him that you are not his biological parents. That you're only just learning now that the adoption agency you used was an illegal operation that took babies from young mothers and placed them with families. You had no idea that I'd been told he died during childbirth and have only recently found out from the midwife who attended the birth that he didn't die and was adopted out.'

'You've thought this through,' Mike said.

'Of course I have. Now, we'll be waiting in the car across the road. We have his address, so if you choose to ignore what I've asked you to do, we'll go around and visit Le— I mean Ashley, and tell him exactly what happened. And I mean the real version of events, not what I've just offered you as a way out.' She didn't wait for their response. She turned and walked back along the hallway with Trent following.

* * *

Jess was grateful for Trent's company as they sat across from the house.

'You were amazing,' Trent said. 'Scared me, so I can only imagine how they're feeling.'

'They're devastated,' Jess said. 'Ridiculously, I feel bad for them. They've had Leo for twenty-five years and would feel like he belongs to them. Regardless of the circumstances, I imagine they'll feel a great loss.'

'Leo,' Trent said. 'You'll have to get used to calling him Ashley.'

'If he'll see me,' Jess said. 'There's part of me that's worried he won't want anything to do with me.'

'You did nothing wrong, Jess. You're the victim in all of this.' Trent's head turned as a car approached, indicated, and turned into the Grenfells' driveway.

'It's him,' Jess said as a tall, lean man stepped out of the blue Toyota. She drew in a breath. His blonde hair was ruffled, and as he turned briefly and glanced in their direction, she could see his narrow jawline and striking cheekbones. He locked eyes with her for a split second before turning and walking towards the house.

Trent reached across and took her hand as Ashley disappeared inside the house. He squeezed it, not needing to say anything. They both seemed to be holding their breath.

It was close to an hour later when the front door opened again, and Ashley appeared with Carly and Mike by his side. He stopped in the driveway and stared across at the rental car.

'We should get out,' Jess said.

They opened their doors, stepped out of the car, and crossed the road. Nerves and nausea churned in Jess's stomach. She was about to meet her son. Her real-life, grown son.

Ashley stepped towards them, his eyes wide and brow furrowed. 'I'm sorry,' he said to Jess. 'I know you've come a long way, and I know you want to spend time with me, but this is far too overwhelming. My life's changed in the last hour, and I don't think I can do this now.'

Jess nodded. 'I'd love to talk with you anytime you're ready. But keep in mind, Ashley. Your life hasn't really changed.'

'My life is a complete lie,' he said. 'It has definitely changed.'

'Not a complete lie. You've had two people love you and bring you up as their son. You're part of a family who cares for you very much. That hasn't changed and never will. I'm not looking to split up your family. I'm just hoping to get to know you. Carly and Mike will always be your parents. The people who raised you. I can never take that place.' If she was honest, it almost killed Jess making this little speech, but it was in the wee hours of the morning, as she tossed and turned and thought about what she wanted from today, she'd realised that what she wanted and what was in Ashley's best interest were two completely different things. She grew up knowing that nobody, other than her mother, wanted her, whereas Ashley had grown up feeling wanted and loved. She wasn't going to take that from him.

Ashley nodded, her words seeming to sink in. He ran a hand through his short hair and managed a smile for Jess. 'You look like me.'

Tears filled her eyes. 'I was just thinking the same.'

'Can I get your number?' Ashley asked. 'I need some time for all of this to sink in, and then I'll probably have a million questions. Maybe we could have a Zoom call in a week or two once I've worked out some questions to ask you.'

'Of course,' Jess said, partly disappointed that he didn't want to spend time with her now but also relieved that he thought he would want to down the track. She took a business card from her wallet and handed it to him. 'Please call as soon as you're ready.'

He nodded, taking her card and putting it in his pocket. He stared at her for a long moment before opening his car door and slipping inside.

36

Reeve had been tempted many times over the weekend to contact Jess. As much as she felt betrayed and hurt by what had happened, she was also aware that Jess would have met with the Grenfells and visited Leo's gravesite. She just hoped Trent had been there for moral support.

Now, she sat on the window seat in her bedroom overlooking the back garden. It was late afternoon, yet she was still in her pyjamas, as she had been since returning from the appointment with Patricia on Wednesday.

'Reeve?' Carol's voice was soft as she entered the bedroom with a tray in her hands. 'I've brought you some tea and your afternoon medication.'

'More medication? It feels like I'm taking far too much.'

'Well, it seems to be helping,' Carol said with a smile. 'You've only had one episode in the five days I've been working here, which is very good news.'

Reeve could only imagine how red her cheeks were.

'There's no need to be embarrassed.' Carol gave a low chuckle. 'I've been called a lot worse.'

'I doubt that,' Reeve said. She'd been horrified to learn that on Carol's first morning, she'd thrown her breakfast dishes at her and was apparently very imaginative in her use of the C-word when telling Carol exactly what she thought about having a day-time carer.

'I've worked with dementia patients for many years,' Carol said. 'If I took any of it to heart, I'd have quite a complex. Now, did you want to shower and get dressed after you've had your tea? I must leave on the dot of five today as I have another engagement. Luke's organised for your friend Sloane to come and visit until he returns from work.'

'I remember. But no to the shower. I just don't have the energy.' It was true. Even though she'd done nothing for days, she was exhausted.

Carol patted her arm gently. 'You've had a big upset, Reeve. While I know Jess didn't die, it's still the type of loss that requires grieving. Give yourself permission to do that.'

Reeve nodded. Carol was probably right. She'd stayed in bed for days after her father died and was doing the same again now. It was different, though. Her father hadn't manipulated or betrayed her. He hadn't led her to believe that they were close when he was really just after money.

A tear ran down Reeve's cheek as the pain of what Jess had done washed over her again. She picked up the medication and quickly swallowed it. As much as she disliked taking pills, the benefit of these was they numbed her, and right now, she doubted she'd get through this without them.

37

Jess agonised for over a week once she and Trent arrived back in Melbourne about Ashley contacting her. She'd heard nothing from him when shortly after the Monday morning staff meeting, she unexpectedly received an invitation to a Zoom meeting. She shut her office door, accepted the call, and found herself staring at her son.

He'd smiled at her, instantly causing her heart to contract. His features were similar to hers but also to her mother's. They'd spoken for close to two hours, learning all about each other. The first thing was that he preferred to be called Ash, not Ashley.

'I'm sorry I didn't spend time with you while you were in Perth,' he said. 'It was all such a shock.'

'I completely understand,' Jess said. 'I'd be happy to come back over for a weekend or at any point when you've got some time to catch up. I'd love to meet Jed and Kristin.' It was hard to believe she had a grandson as well as a son. A ready-made family to get to know.

They'd ended the call agreeing to Zoom again the following week, which would give Ash some time to think about dates for a visit.

Jess had sat in stillness at her desk for a long time after the call. After some initial awkwardness, it had been easy to talk to him. It was strange calling him Ash after thinking of him as Leo for years, but other than that, she felt completely at ease with him.

Jess picked up her phone, about to call Trent and fill him in on the Zoom call, when it rang. It was Dina Murphy, Felicity's new caseworker.

'Everything okay, Dina?'

'No, it's Felicity. There's been an accident.'

Jess stood. 'What kind of accident?'

'Car. She had a fight with the foster father. She stole his car and wrapped it around a post about half a kilometre down the road.'

'Is she okay?'

'I think so. A broken leg possibly, but nothing too serious.'

'She's fifteen. Does she even know how to drive?'

'I'd say no based on what she's done. They've taken her to St Vincent's, and she's been asking for you.'

'Me?'

'Yes. I was about to go to her but thought I'd see what you want to do. There's no point two of us going.'

Jess grabbed her bag and started heading out of the office. 'I'll go to her. Thanks for letting me know, Dina. I'll keep you updated.'

Jess reached the hospital in record time. She parked before hurrying into the large reception and waiting area. She went straight up to the nurses' station. 'I'm looking for Felicity Chandler. Fifteen-year-old. Car accident.'

The nurse checked the computer. 'She's waiting to go into surgery. Are you a relative?'

'Caseworker,' Jess said, showing her identification. 'She's in the foster system. I'd like to see her.'

'Sure. Hold on, and I'll get someone to take you down.'

A nurse appeared and guided Jess down the sterile corridor. Felicity was lying on a stretcher, her face contorted in pain. Relief flashed in her eyes when she saw Jess, and Jess reached for her hand.

'You okay, chickie?'

A tear escaped the corner of Felicity's eye, and she shook her head, wincing.

'Relax,' Jess said. 'You can tell me everything later, once they fix you up.'

'I can't go back there. Chris will kill me. I trashed his car.'

Jess placed a hand on her shoulder. 'Don't talk. It's only a car. We'll sort it out, okay?'

Felicity's face relaxed.

'Now, we need to concentrate on getting you better. Dina called me. She's worried about you too.'

Felicity's face tensed. 'She doesn't understand me. Can't you be my caseworker?'

In her role as CEO, Jess wasn't supposed to take on individual cases, but there was something about Felicity that nagged at her. She was a girl that no one seemed able to help. The exact reason Jess had become involved in foster care: to make sure all kids had a voice and didn't slide through the cracks in the system.

'I'll do you a deal,' Jess said. 'You pull through all of this with flying colours and without too much complaining, and I'll be your caseworker. Okay?'

Felicity's eyes shone with tears of relief before she closed her eyes.

'Are you Felicity's mother?' A doctor in scrubs appeared next to the bed, pushing a clipboard at her. 'I need a signature.'

'I'm her caseworker. She's in the foster system.'

'Okay, great.' He handed her the clipboard and took a deep breath. 'Sorry, it's been frantic in here today. Too many accidents.'

'Is she going to be okay?'

'Definitely. She's made a mess of her leg. It might need some screws and pins to get into place. Her shoulder's dislocated, and we'll fix that up under general anaesthetic too. We'll be a couple of hours. The nurse will be out to collect that clipboard and to prep her shortly. You can wait with her if you like.'

'Okay, thank you, Doctor...' She looked for his name badge, but he wasn't wearing one.

'Sheffield,' he supplied for her. 'Now, I'd better go.' He tapped Felicity's hand. 'I want to hear all about your joy ride once we fix you up. Someone told me you robbed a bank. That means a big tip for me after I've operated.' He winked, managing to get a smile out of Flick.

'He seems nice,' she said as he disappeared down the corridor.

'He does,' Jess said. 'Dr Sheffield.' The name sounded familiar. Wasn't that Reeve's husband's surname? Reeve had opted to revert to her maiden name after her divorce from Nick, but she was pretty sure that was his name. He was a Dr Sheffield too, and she had a sneaking suspicion he worked at this hospital. What were the odds of two Dr Sheffields? Slim, she imagined. But at least she was dealing with this one and not Reeve's husband.

* * *

Two hours after she'd been wheeled off for surgery, Felicity was returned to the ward, groggy but semiconscious.

'The surgery went well,' the nurse confirmed. 'Dr Sheffield will be able to tell you more when he returns a little later.'

'Is there more than one Dr Sheffield at the hospital?' Jess asked.

The nurse shook her head. 'Not that I'm aware of.'

'I know a Luke Sheffield who I was led to believe is a doctor here,' Jess said. 'He had his scrubs on and might not have recognised me in this context. It was probably him. How embarrassing.'

The nurse laughed. 'Probably. It is Luke Sheffield who you spoke with. Is he an ex-boyfriend?'

Jess shook her head. 'Nothing like that, but he's someone I'd prefer never to see again.'

'Well, I'm sorry to break it to you, but he'll be here within the next twenty minutes to talk to you.'

Ten minutes after the nurse left, a tall man with crinkly blue eyes and a black clipboard entered the room.

'Ms Williams?'

Jess nodded.

'Sorry about earlier,' he said. 'It was busy, and I had to rush off. Everything went well with Felicity's operation. Good news, too. We've been able to set the fracture back in place without any plates or screws. She'll be in a cast for six to eight weeks.'

Jess stared at the doctor. 'You're Dr Luke Sheffield.'

He grinned. 'I am.'

'Okay, this is strange. Is there another Luke Sheffield who's a surgeon here or at the Alfred maybe?'

He shook his head. 'There's a Jacob Sheffield who works in maternity, but he's a midwife, not a surgeon. I don't know all of the staff at the Alfred, so he might work there. Now, we'll keep Felicity in with us for a few days and monitor her. Unfortunately, I think the police will need to come in for a little chat based on the nature of the accident and the stolen vehicle. Luckily the only person she injured was herself. Hopefully the court will consider a couple of months out of action punishment enough.'

Jess nodded, still trying to get her head around the situation. It was obviously a coincidence, but something still didn't sit right.

Once he left, she picked up her phone and rang Trent. 'Can you do me a favour?'

'Sure, anything.'

'Find out where Reeve's husband works. His name's Luke Sheffield. He's a doctor.'

'Leave it with me.'

Five minutes later, Trent rang her back.

'He's a surgeon at St Vincent's. Supposedly working in the A&E tonight.'

'Are you sure?'

'One hundred per cent. I rang Reeve.'

Jess sucked in a breath. 'You did what?'

'I said a friend had had an accident, and I wanted to know which hospital to take him to. Apparently, he's working tonight, so he should be there. Not that I'll be taking anyone. Why did you need to know?'

Jess fell silent for a moment. 'Something weird is going on. I'm at St Vincent's. Felicity's been involved in a car accident. She's okay, but she's being treated by Dr Luke Sheffield.'

Trent groaned. 'Just your luck.'

'No, you don't understand. I've met him, and the Luke Sheffield who works at St Vincent's is not Reeve's husband.'

38

A knock on her bedroom door brought Reeve out of a fitful sleep. She glanced at the clock. Five thirty. Carol would be gone by now. 'Come in,' she called, her voice croaky.

Sloane poked her head in, her face creased with concern. 'Hey, hon. Luke told me what's been going on.'

Reeve pulled the cover over her head. 'I'd run a mile if I were you. I'll probably call you something awful in a minute.'

Sloane forced a laugh.

'My phone hasn't rung, has it?'

Sloane shook her head. 'Not that I heard. Why, are you expecting a call?'

'No, but I had a strange call from Trent, Jess's friend, a little while ago. He wanted to know where Luke worked as a friend had had an accident.' She frowned. 'I hope it wasn't Jess he was talking about.'

'You didn't ask?'

'Honestly, I didn't want to know.'

'I don't blame you after everything she's done. Now, I'm going to go and make us something to eat. I'll be about forty-five minutes, and then we can have a picnic on your bed, okay?'

The last thing Reeve wanted was food, but she was grateful for Sloane's care. She did her best to smile and nod before slipping back under the covers. She closed her eyes, trying to rid her mind of all thoughts. It was one of the coping exercises Patricia had shown her. She took deep breaths in, exhaling in a long, slow fashion and repeating.

Sloane reappeared a short time later with the promised tray of food.

'Thanks,' Reeve said, sitting up and inhaling the delicious aroma of Sloane's chicken, pesto, and mushroom fettuccine. 'And thanks for being here. This is such a nightmare.'

Reeve's phone rang, interrupting them. It was Trent again.

'Reeve, I arrived at the hospital with my friend a

little while ago, and it appears there's a problem with Luke. The hospital was going to ring you, but I said I could come and pick you up. I'm on my way to you now.'

A pounding started at the front of Reeve's head. 'Luke? What's happened?'

'I'm not sure. It appears he's having memory issues.'

'Did he hit his head?'

'Possibly. Look, I'll be there in about five minutes. Can you wait out front?'

Reeve ended the call and explained the situation to Sloane.

'I'll come with you.'

Reeve hurried from the bed, the pesto dish quickly forgotten, and threw on jeans and an old sweatshirt. She followed Sloane downstairs and out of the front door. As good as his word, Trent arrived a few minutes later.

'I don't know anything much,' Trent said, 'but I knew you'd be concerned.'

They arrived at the hospital twenty minutes later, and Reeve, grateful that adrenaline had kicked in and she was operating as if she had energy, leapt out of the car, ready to rush inside.

'Hold on,' Trent said. 'Hear me out for a second,

okay? Things are a little bit crazy and unexpected in there tonight. I need you to promise that no matter what you hear about Luke or anything else, you'll listen with an open mind.'

'I thought you didn't know what was wrong with him.'

'I don't know for sure, but if I told you what I believe to be true, you'd deck me.'

Reeve turned to Sloane. 'Have I had an episode on the way here? Because I honestly have no idea what he's talking about.'

'No, you've been completely normal,' Sloane said. 'We travelled in silence.'

Reeve turned back to Trent. 'Is Luke hurt?'

'He absolutely will be,' Trent assured her as he put a hand on her back and guided her into the hospital.

* * *

Jess looked up as Trent ushered Reeve into Felicity's hospital room with Sloane trailing behind them. Reeve stopped. 'What's going on? Why's she here?'

Jess stood. 'I need you to hear me out, Reeve. Something strange is happening.'

'You're telling me. Where's Luke? Trent said there was something wrong with him. I'm worried sick.'

'Sit down.' Jess indicated the chair she'd vacated. 'I want to tell you what I know.'

Reeve glanced at Sloane, who looked as confused as she did, before sitting.

'One of our foster kids, Felicity' – Jess nodded towards the occupied bed – 'was brought in and treated by Dr Luke Sheffield tonight. She had a car accident.'

'Is she okay?' Reeve asked, looking at the sleeping teen.

'She's going to be fine, thanks to Luke,' Jess said.

'Okay. This was obviously awkward for you, but I'm glad he treated Felicity regardless of your connection. But why am I here, and why did Trent tell me Luke was having difficulty remembering who he was?'

'Luke's coming back in a few minutes,' Jess said. 'You can ask him yourself.'

'Okay.' It was anything but okay, but Reeve refused to engage in further conversation. Luke could explain what was going on.

'Reeve, this is Dr Sheffield,' Jess said as a tall blonde-haired doctor entered the room. He flashed her a brief smile before picking up the clipboard from the end of the bed and checking it over.

Reeve looked to Sloane. 'Is this a sick joke? I know you all think I'm going crazy, but I'm pretty sure I'd recognise my husband.'

'I have no idea,' Sloane said, looking genuinely confused.

'This Dr Luke Sheffield,' Jess said, 'is a trauma surgeon who works at St Vincent's.'

'There are two of them?' Sloane asked.

'One,' Dr Sheffield said, looking from Sloane to Reeve. 'Although it seems to be causing some confusion tonight.'

'Hold on,' Reeve said. 'My husband, Dr Luke Sheffield, has worked here for eleven years. He previously worked at the Alfred. He's a trauma surgeon.'

Dr Sheffield frowned. 'That's my rap sheet. Look, why don't I send someone from admin down to see you. There's probably some rational explanation for all of this. If your husband is a surgeon who works for St Vincent's, I'm sure they'll be able to locate him.'

'They should. He's working tonight.'

'Great. I'll send someone down, and I'll check on Felicity again before the end of my shift. Everything's looking good.'

He returned the clipboard to the end of the bed and left the room.

Reeve turned to Jess. 'Please explain what's going on?'

'Okay.' Jess looked to Trent and took a deep breath. 'We have reason to suspect that Luke is not who you think he is.'

Reeve's mouth dropped open. 'What are you talking about?'

'We think he's taken on someone else's identity.'

Reeve gave a dry laugh. 'I think you're both going crazy. His licence, passport, everything has his name on it. He's Luke Sheffield.'

'That might be his name,' Trent said, 'but he's not a doctor, that much we're certain of. It's not hard to change your name if you want to impersonate someone.'

Reeve shook her head. 'You're crazy. I met him at this hospital. He's a doctor.'

'Or someone looking for an opportunity,' Jess said. 'You met him when your mother was dying, and Martin had terminal cancer, right?'

'He outlived his diagnosis, but yes, when I met Luke, Dad's life expectancy was about three months.'

'And you had a whirlwind romance and got married within that timeframe.'

Reeve nodded. 'Luke wanted Dad to be at the

wedding, so we rushed ahead faster than we might have otherwise. What are you suggesting, Jess?'

'That Luke possibly targeted you as someone about to inherit a large estate. Developed a relationship with you and put himself in a position to access the funds once they came to you.'

Reeve snorted with disbelief and turned to Trent. 'Is this for real or for the plot of an upcoming book?'

'Reeve,' Trent said, his expression more serious than she'd ever seen him, 'I don't think there's anything wrong with you. I think you're the victim of an elaborate plan of Luke's. Whether it started out this big or whether it's grown as it's needed to, I don't know.'

'Hold on. You say there's nothing wrong with me? The MRI and my psychiatrist would argue with that.'

'Okay, let's tackle one thing at a time. Firstly, your husband is not a doctor.'

An administration staff member arrived as Reeve digested this information. She confirmed what Jess and Trent had already told her. Luke was not a doctor at this hospital.

Reeve's head was swimming. None of this made sense. Maybe this was another episode, but at this moment, she was lucid through it. Maybe once it ended, she'd forget it all, and she'd find out later about how she embarrassed Luke coming into the hospital and saying he wasn't a doctor. She could only imagine how that was going to play out. She wasn't listening to them any more. She stood. 'You're both crazy, and I'm going home.'

'No,' Jess said. 'I can't let you go home to a lying psychopath.'

'Luke's not that. He loves me. He's my husband.'

'Your husband who has pretended to be a doctor to access your inheritance?' Trent said.

'Why would he pretend to be a doctor? I fell in love with Luke for who he is, not because he's a doctor. Why would he lie?'

'To convince you he had his own money and didn't need yours.'

'He does have his own money,' Reeve said. 'He's loaded.' Her words petered out. Was there any truth to what they were saying? That her husband wasn't a doctor? That their relationship had been manufactured?

Reeve's phone rang. She glanced at the screen and froze. 'It's him.'

'Answer it,' Sloane said. 'Ask him where he is and what he's doing.'

'Hey, hon,' Reeve said, covering her phone with

her hand, hoping to block out the hospital noises and praying she sounded as normal as possible.

'Thought I'd give you a quick call before you go to bed to tell you how much I love you. And I wanted to check Sloane was with you.'

Reeve looked at Sloane. 'Yes, she is. But where are you?'

Luke laughed. 'What do you mean? At work?'

'Where do you work again?'

'Are you serious?'

'Sorry, I feel a bit funny, that's all.'

'Oh no, you're probably having one of your episodes. I'm at the hospital. St Vincent's, remember? I'm a surgeon here. Have been for eleven years.'

'And you're the only Dr Luke Sheffield on staff.'

Luke laughed again. 'Yes, and okay, time for you to go to sleep. Finish up your tea and have a good sleep.'

'My tea? How do you know I'm drinking tea?'

She caught Trent raising his eyebrows towards Jess as they listened to Reeve's side of the conversation.

Luke laughed again. 'Because you have it every night. Look, finish it off and lie down. I doubt you'll even remember this conversation in the morning. Night.'

Reeve stared at her phone as he ended the call. 'Supposedly, he's here working, and he said something about finishing my tea.'

'He's probably been drugging your tea,' Trent said. 'This whole thing is a crazy set-up.'

'Why would he drug me?'

'I'd say to either kill you or get control of your money. He doesn't have control, does he?'

'As of about a week ago, he does. Dad's estate hasn't been distributed yet, but I have investments worth a few million that Dad insisted I have when Mum died. I've never touched them, but they are in my name.'

'Okay. We need to call the police and ensure all of your accounts are frozen,' Trent said.

'And we need to get some tests organised,' Jess said. 'DNA for Reeve and me, and a drug test for her. See what's in her system.'

Reeve's head was spinning with what was being suggested. Could Luke really have done this?

'No,' Reeve said. 'I need to speak to Luke. Find out exactly what's going on.' She stood, her legs shaking, and turned to Sloane. 'Can you take me home, please?'

Sloane's eyes widened in alarm. 'I don't think that's a good idea, Reeve. Luke might be dangerous.'

'If Luke wanted to hurt me, he would have done it already,' Reeve said. 'I need answers, and I'm going to get them. You can give me a lift, or I'll get a taxi.'

She turned to Jess. 'If this all turns out to be more of your lies, I'll be pressing charges. I just want to make that clear.'

Jess opened her mouth to speak but closed it again. She shook her head. 'I wish it was, Reeve. For your sake, I really do.'

* * *

Reeve glanced at the clock behind the breakfast bar. It was past midnight, and still no sign of Luke. Had someone tipped him off? Reeve had ignored all of Sloane's protests when they arrived back at Reeve's.

'You can't do this alone, Reeve. What if he's violent?'

'Luke's not a violent person. Whatever's been happening, I'm sure there will be a reasonable explanation. After everything Jess and Trent have done, this could be another set-up.'

'And if it's not?'

'Then I'll sort it out.' She'd shut the car door firmly and walked up the path without looking back.

Now, two hours since Sloane left, she rubbed her

temple, willing the headache that was forming to disappear. She tensed as the garage door rolled open. He was home. She did her best to breathe normally and remained seated at the kitchen counter.

The internal door to the garage opened, and Reeve heard Luke slip his shoes off and put them on the shoe rack. He then appeared in the kitchen doorway.

'Ree? What are you doing up? It's after midnight.' He smiled and ran a hand through his hair. 'I'm exhausted. Busy night at the hospital.'

Reeve stared at him. She loved him so much. But was it possible he'd lied to her, manipulated her, and tried to steal from her?

'Ree? You okay?'

Reeve shook her head.

Luke put his briefcase down on the kitchen counter and moved towards her. He reached for her hands, but she shook her head and moved them away.

'I was at the hospital tonight.'

Luke's eyes widened. 'What? Why? Are you okay?'

'I met trauma surgeon Dr Luke Sheffield. At St Vincent's.'

The colour drained from Luke's face. 'What?'

'Jess and Trent were at the hospital and were introduced to Dr Luke Sheffield. The only surgeon by that name who works at St Vincent's. They called me in to meet him.'

Luke stared at Reeve, fear flashing in his eyes. It was in that instant she knew it was true. He'd lied to her. She sucked in a breath, trying to push the bile that was rising in her throat down.

'I think you're having one of your episodes, Ree. How about I make you a nice cup of tea, and then we'll go to bed?'

Reeve shook her head. 'The drug-laced tea.'

'Okay, I'm confused,' Luke said. 'What are you suggesting?'

'I'm suggesting that you're not who you've said you are, our marriage is a sham, and you're after my money. Or more precisely, my father's money.'

Luke managed a pitying smile. 'Ree, hon. You're sick. Of course I'm Luke Sheffield.' He reached in his back pocket for his wallet. 'I can show you my licence if you want proof.'

'Proof of what? That you changed your name and then lied about who you are?'

Luke hesitated. He stared at her for a moment before kicking at the kitchen counter. When he faced her again, the fear in his eyes was gone. It was replaced with anger. 'I did what I needed to.' He turned as if he was about to leave the kitchen.

Reeve slammed her fists against the counter. 'Don't you dare leave! You owe me an explanation.'

Luke stopped and slowly turned to face her. His cheeks were red, his face full of hatred. 'I don't owe you anything.'

Reeve stood. 'What did I do to deserve what you've been putting me through? Making me believe I have dementia. Setting me up, I assume to steal my money. I thought you loved me.'

Luke stared at her for a moment. Gradually the anger in his face was replaced with a sneer. 'Well, I don't. This was about your father's money. It was never about you.'

Reeve's legs wobbled, and she grabbed the kitchen counter for support. Even with all of the evidence stacked against him, part of her had hoped he would be as shocked as her, and there would be another explanation. That he really was the man she'd fallen in love with.

'And you'll be pleased to know that the debt your father owes my family is already being paid off.'

'You've transferred money?'

He nodded. 'From your mother's investments. It's

not the fortune of your father's I was hoping for, but it's a start.'

Reeve shook her head. 'You don't think the police will be able to track down where the monies have gone?'

He took a step towards her. 'There will be no police involved. You're sick, Reeve. Your psychiatrist can vouch for that. You have tests that show your dementia is progressing quickly. No one will believe anything you have to say.'

'It's not just what I have to say. Jess and Trent were at the hospital, and they met the man you're pretending to be.'

'No, they met a Dr Luke Sheffield. I never said I was a doctor. You did. Think back to when we met. I was visiting my aunt who was sharing a room with your mother. We were introduced and started dating. You wanted to impress your family, so you told them I was a doctor. I played along with it. But in the last few months, you've acted as if you really believe I'm a doctor.' He shook his head. 'I know it's dementia, but it doesn't make it any easier.'

Reeve stared at him, unease creeping over her. 'I don't have dementia, and that story you just told me is exactly that, a story. I don't exactly know how you've done it, but you've set me up.'

Luke shook his head. 'The police won't believe it's a set-up. I've not been able to stop you from drinking or taking drugs. Patricia's reports corroborate all of this.'

Reeve faltered. *Patricia.* How would Luke have convinced a professional to work with him? She swallowed. He must have intercepted the test results before Patricia saw them or paid someone to falsify the results. She couldn't think of any other explanation. 'She didn't say anything about drugs.'

'That you'd remember. You're sick, Reeve. I might not be able to convince you of that, but with Patricia by my side, I'll be able to convince the police. They'll think you're batshit crazy by the time I'm finished.'

'No, they'll arrest you. You do realise that tests will be done, don't you? They'll work out quickly if you've been drugging me.' Confused was an understatement as to how Reeve felt. On the one hand, Luke was saying it was a set-up to steal her father's money, and on the other, he was talking as if he really believed he could convince the police she was ill. She shook her head. 'I don't understand what you're doing. You set me up. You convinced me you loved me. You married me, and for what? So you could take everything from me?'

Anger flashed in his eyes. 'Yes.'

Reeve sucked in a breath. 'And now what? Do you honestly think you'll get away with it? I still don't understand why you chose me. Yes, Dad had money, but why do you think he owed you anything?'

'He murdered my father.'

Reeve continued clinging to the kitchen bench, surprised her legs hadn't given way. 'Murdered? What? That's ridiculous.'

'If it weren't for your father, mine would be alive today. In my eyes, that's murder. You might think Martin was a great guy, but I can tell you now, he wasn't. His business dealings were a disgrace. The day my father died, I made the decision that I would get even one day. That day's arrived.'

Nausea churned in the pit of Reeve's stomach. Her father had admitted himself that he wasn't proud of everything he'd done in his business life. 'I'm sorry for whatever he did. But he's dead. He's not aware of anything you've done or are doing.'

Luke laughed. 'Yes, I'm aware he's dead. An eye for an eye and all that.'

Bile rose in Reeve's throat. 'You killed him?'

Luke shrugged. 'Not that anyone has proven. Now, I need to get organised. I'd hoped I'd have you institutionalised before you worked anything out. Guess I underestimated you.' He turned and hurried from the kitchen. Reeve heard his footsteps on the stairs. She imagined he planned to fill a suitcase and disappear. She walked slowly from the kitchen and followed him. She needed more answers.

'You followed me up here?' He laughed as he moved towards the walk-in wardrobe. 'You're dumber than I thought.'

'You killed my father?'

'I assisted in his premature death, yes.'

'And you're not a surgeon?'

'Nope. I was a plumber before I met you.'

'Where did you go every day when you were supposed to be working?'

'My mother's. She lives in East Brighton.'

'And she knew what you were up to?'

He nodded as he pulled open a drawer and rummaged through it. 'Knows and helped.' He took a container from a drawer and turned to face Reeve. 'Can you grab me a glass of water?'

'What?'

'Water. You're going to need it.' He opened the container and pulled out a bag of pills. 'To wash these down. I'm your power of attorney, so if you kill yourself, guess who has control of your estate?'

Reeve's legs trembled. He was crazy, really crazy. She should have listened to Jess and Trent and left the authorities to confront him. She turned and ran from the room, her heart pounding. She raced to the top of the stairs, taking them two at a time as Luke crashed down behind her. She reached the front door and wrenched it open at the same time as his hand slammed down on her shoulder.

'I don't think so.'

She screamed as he kicked the door shut and spun her around to face him.

'Shut up, you crazy bitch. Do you hear me?' He grabbed her hair before she could respond and pulled her towards the kitchen.

Reeve's hands flew to her head, trying to get him off her, but his grip was too strong. They reached the kitchen, and he pinned her body against the benchtop while he grabbed for a large glass. She struggled while he filled it with water, but it was no use.

'You can do this the hard way or the easy way,' he said, her hands still pinned.

She spat in his face, earning herself a slap so powerful her teeth ached.

He grabbed a handful of the pills, forcing her mouth open as he shoved them in and forced the glass of water to her lips. She spat the pills back in his face, earning herself another slap. She screamed, and at the same moment, the kitchen door flung open.

Nick stood in the doorway. 'What the hell?'

Luke lunged for him, but Nick deftly sidestepped him, picked up a wine bottle from the kitchen bench, and smashed it over his head. Luke crumpled to the floor in a puddle of red wine.

Nick turned to Reeve as Sloane, Jess, and Trent appeared in the kitchen, their faces reflecting Reeve's shock. Nick put his arms out and brought her to him. 'Are you okay?'

She buried her face in his chest, shaking her head. No, she was not okay.

39

With Luke in custody, it took over a week to unravel what was going on. It was confirmed that Rohypnol was present in Reeve's system, which was the same drug found in Martin's system. Luke, once he regained consciousness, was arrested for the suspected murder of Martin Elliot and was facing numerous charges for his manipulation of Reeve.

'I can't believe any of this,' Bella said as Reeve and Jess attempted to explain the situation to her and Nick.

'Me neither,' Nick said. 'Let me get this straight. Luke's been working towards this since he met you?'

Reeve nodded. 'His real name is Thomas Parsons.'

'Why did he target you?'

'A few years ago, his father committed suicide after my dad withdrew an investment from his company. According to Devon, Wesley Parsons's company was involved in illegal dealings, and Dad withdrew a very large investment when he found out. The company went bankrupt, and Wesley killed himself.'

'But didn't Carol introduce you?'

Reeve nodded. 'She did. From what we've learned, Carol's brother had invested in Wesley Parsons's business and lost close to a million dollars when the company went bankrupt. When Carol was offered the position to look after Alice, she took it, wanting revenge. From what she's told the police, she couldn't go through with her original plan, which was to make Alice's life unbearable. She was a nurse foremost and couldn't do anything to hurt another person. She was, however, good friends with Wesley Parsons's widow. She got her involved with Mum's care, and between the two of them, they came up with the plan to introduce Thomas to me so that he could get the revenge on Martin that they felt the Parsons family and Carol's brother were entitled to.'

'Your marriage and the stepdad stuff was all fake?' Bella asked.

Reeve nodded, a lump rising in her throat. She'd

fallen for a conman. Completely and utterly head over heels with a man who'd killed her father and was either going to kill her or have her locked up. Worse, she'd brought him into her daughter's life.

'And he tried to make you look like you had dementia?'

She shivered. 'And did a convincing job of it. I could have been medicated and locked up for the rest of my life.'

'But wouldn't tests or scans have shown there was nothing wrong with you? The psychiatrist could hardly have made all of that up,' Nick said.

Reeve gave a wry laugh. 'Patricia, my psychiatrist, also happens to be Thomas Parsons's mother. Wesley's widow.'

Bella sucked in a breath. 'No way. You mean she wasn't a real psychiatrist?'

'No, she was a psychiatrist. One who was presented with an opportunity for revenge and took it.'

Nick's mouth dropped open. 'They were all in on it?'

Reeve nodded. 'A very elaborate set-up that started when Mum was ill. From what I've been told, it was Carol James who recommended Patricia as Mum's psychiatrist. Carol was aware of Dad's cancer diagnosis and initial prognosis that he only had a few months to live. She, Patricia, and Luke schemed together to devise a plan to take as much of Dad's fortune as possible. Only none of them counted on Dad living for as long as he did, so Luke took matters into his own hands.'

Reeve closed her eyes, a wave of nausea flooding over her. That she'd been the target of such a scheme was unthinkable. She'd thought after her marriage to Nick ended that she'd have difficulty trusting anyone again. After this, she knew for sure she wouldn't be able to.

'Are you okay?' Bella asked.

Reeve opened her eyes and forced a smile. 'Yes, sorry. It's still hard to believe. I played right into Luke's hands when I suggested I see Patricia. I had no reason to distrust Luke or Patricia. She tried to cover all her bases. Even wrote up reports after each of our sessions that read as if I have dementia, and she had numerous concerns about me and made recommendations for care.' She shook her head. 'They planned every detail. You know, a couple of times, I was sure someone was watching me as I went to my appointments. As Luke spent his days and nights at her house when he was supposed to be working, it was probably him.'

'This is crazy,' Nick said. 'So, what, he drugged you, and that made you do and say horrible things?'

'It's beginning to look like the majority of what I did or said was in written format,' Reeve said. 'All done by Luke when I was passed out in the evenings. He was drugging my tea. The chamomile tea leaves were laced with Rohypnol. I was out cold most nights.' She shuddered at the memory of the night that she'd been tricked into thinking she'd slept with George. George, who, according to the police, was a man by the name of Austin Yves. He was a friend of Luke's and was being questioned for his involvement. She wasn't sure whether to be relieved that she hadn't slept with a stranger or disgusted that it was Luke who'd violated her while she was unconscious. He'd never even gone to Sydney. Instead, he'd stayed close by to orchestrate all the awful things she'd been led to believe she'd done – the emails and text messages, the wine, the one-night stand. Even the call to Sloane had been Luke using a voice changer app to sound like a very drunk female.

'But what about you and Jess and the DNA results?' Nick asked. 'You said you all did that together.'

'We did,' Reeve said. 'But neither Jess nor I checked the form he filled out. He wrote down my phone number incorrectly and put the password as "sisters question mark" with a lowercase s. He then sent in another kit with DNA he got from somewhere else and put in the phone number and password details he'd told Jess and me he'd used. It was such a simple way to trick us. I'll never sign anything again that I haven't read every word of.'

She turned to Bella. 'I didn't write the letter you received. It's been examined by the police and they've been able to confirm that someone has forged my handwriting. Luke must have paid a handwriting specialist to do it. But it doesn't explain what I said to you, about Granddad saying you were a "little slut". I can't explain that other than to say the drugs must have affected me.'

Bella frowned. 'You never said it to my face. I came home, and you and Luke were talking in the lounge room. He came out, angry, saw me, and apologised. Said he couldn't believe that Granddad would ever call me a little slut and to assume it wasn't true.'

'Hold on. I never said any of those things to your face? What about when I called you a spoilt little bitch?'

Bella shook her head. 'Luke apologised to me. He was upset on my behalf – blamed dementia. He was so convincing. There were a couple of other occasions too when he dropped in to see me and Dad, said how worried he was and repeated some of the things you were doing and saying. He even cried one night when he dropped in.'

Nick's face contorted in anger. 'He sat in my lounge room crying one night he was so upset about everything. I consoled the prick. Often his visits to us were followed up with horrible emails or text messages supposedly from you.'

'That bastard,' Reeve said. 'I honestly can't believe he manipulated the situation to the extent he did. And I can't believe I'm so gullible.'

'We all are,' Nick said. 'I hated that you were with someone else but thought he was a decent guy. I wonder how he afforded the fancy car and everything else?'

'Thomas Parsons last worked as a plumber,' Reeve said. 'The last twelve months he's run up over two hundred thousand dollars in credit card debt. I expect he was planning to use Dad's money to pay that off.'

'What does this mean?' Bella asked. 'There's nothing wrong with you?'

'Other than my poor taste in men,' Reeve said, before smiling apologetically at Nick. 'Sorry. No, there's nothing physically or mentally wrong with me. The MRI was of someone else's brain, and Patricia Fields is currently in custody for using it falsely, amongst her other misdeeds. Carol's being questioned, although I'm not sure they'll get her on anything. Other than introducing me to Luke under false pretences, I'm not sure she's done anything wrong.

'The only situation that hasn't been resolved is the one at school. Unfortunately, that looks like it's separate from all of this. The Oscar situation, that is. Dale Cross and the nasty email was Luke, but Oscar's situation is different.' She thought back to how they met him at the airport and how he'd seemed worried and concerned that he'd got her in trouble. 'That one I'll have to live with. The positive in all of this was the DNA test Jess and I had done earlier in the week.'

'It's pretty cool to have an aunt,' Bella said. 'Especially one like Jess.'

Reeve nodded. In amongst the shock of everything that had happened, having confirmation that she and Jess were sisters was a huge relief. The thought of Jess, Trent, and Devon all working together to steal her father's fortune was almost as devastating as what Luke had done.

'Now, Jess and her friend Trent are meeting me at Fredricco's for dinner. Are you guys up for it? There's something important she wants to ask our opinion about. She's hoping you'll both come.'

'Is it about her son?' Bella asked.

Reeve had been astonished when during the week, Jess had filled her in on Trent's discovery and their hurried trip to Perth. She shook her head. 'I don't think so. She's done a few Zoom calls with him and is slowly getting to know him. I think they're talking about meeting in person soon. But no, I think it's about something else. She hoped you'd come, Bell. She mentioned something about wanting a teenager's opinion.'

Bella smiled. 'I really like her, Mum. I'm so glad it turned out she is your sister.'

'Me too,' Reeve said.

'I'd like to come,' Nick said. 'I'd like to get to know Jess better. And protect you from any more crazies,' he added with a wink.

'You've been amazing through all of this. Really, you have. Luke might have killed me. It was certainly his intention.'

'No one could have predicted what he was up to. I'm just glad that Jess called me that night to let me know what was going on. But remember one thing: I'll always be there for you. Always. I wish...' He sighed. 'Well, you know what I wish.'

She nodded. She did, but right now, she couldn't give any thought to men or relationships. 'We should get going.'

'Can I meet you there?' Bella asked. 'I promised I'd drop some homework off to Grace.' She hugged Reeve. 'I'm sorry that I've been such a bitch since Granddad died. I thought you were doing all those terrible things and that you hated me. And once I knew it was dementia, I couldn't deal with that either.'

Reeve hugged her daughter. 'I completely understand, and hopefully you'll never have to deal with me and dementia again. Now, Dad and I will meet you at Fredricco's. Ring if you need us to come and get you from Grace's.'

Bella nodded.

'I'm still trying to get my head around everything,' Nick said with a laugh as they got organised to leave. 'I wish Martin was alive to hear how this all played out.' He stopped laughing as Reeve's face fell. 'Sorry, that was insensitive, especially as his life was ended early.'

'He would have died from cancer at some stage,' Reeve said, 'but Luke robbed him of the chance of getting to know Jess and saying his goodbyes. I'll never forgive Luke for what he did to me, but of everything, I think that's the worst of all.'

* * *

Reeve and Nick were seated at Fredricco's in time to relax with a drink before Jess and Trent arrived.

'You're handling this all well,' Nick said. 'I thought you'd be a mess.'

Reeve plastered on a smile. 'Don't worry. I am most nights. I can't stop replaying our relationship in my head. There were no red flags for me at all with Luke. You hear stories about people losing all their money to conmen. I thought I'd be smart enough to see through one.'

Nick nodded, then smiled and waved at someone behind Reeve. 'Just Bella,' he said as Reeve swivelled in her seat.

'Oh no.' She turned back to face Nick.

'What's the matter?'

'Bella's with Oscar Ryan. You know, the kid who's accused me of sexual harassment.'

Nick frowned, his face reflecting Reeve's own thoughts. What on earth was she doing?

Bella reached the table, with Oscar Ryan and his parents next to her. They all looked remarkably uncomfortable, except for Bella, whose eyes were dancing. She nudged Oscar. 'Go on, tell her.'

Reeve looked at Oscar's parents. 'I have no idea

what Bella's doing, but I'm pretty sure our lawyers wouldn't be pleased with this situation.'

'It's okay,' Ted Ryan, Oscar's father, said. 'Oscar needs to clear something up.'

'I'm sorry, Ms Elliot.'

Reeve frowned. 'For what, Oscar?'

'You never said any of those things I accused you of. I was paid to say you did.'

Nausea churned in Reeve's stomach. 'Paid?'

He nodded. 'I was offered twenty grand. I assumed it was a joke at first, but then the money appeared in my bank account.'

'Who offered you the money?'

'I don't know. A guy came and spoke to me after practice one afternoon. Said he was working for someone else. He said there would be more if I needed it if I went along with his scheme. He told me what to say and do. It was so much money, and it meant we could afford for Dad to get his cataract operation done now rather than wait nine months with the public system. His vision was getting worse, and his job was on the line. You can't drive a truck if you can't see. My parents were struggling enough, even with me on the scholarship. I knew it was wrong, but I also knew that you were loaded and probably didn't need the job. You would survive financially. Also, the guy told me you were sick, and that I'd be doing you a favour as you'd ultimately do something that would get you fired anyway.'

'We're incredibly sorry,' Oscar's mother said. 'We had absolutely no idea that Oscar had acquired the money this way. We were led to believe that one of the football sponsors had provided a cash sponsorship. We'll repay the money as soon as we can.' She blushed. 'We understand from Bella that your husband may have stolen the money from you.'

'Possibly,' Reeve said. 'I can check the files, and if he did, we can work something out. Were you able to get the cataract operation?'

Oscar's mother nodded. 'Yes, it meant we were bumped up the list rather than having to wait for the public system. Other than taking some holiday time while he recovered, Ted didn't lose his job or too many hours as a result.'

Reeve smiled. 'That's one good thing at least.' She turned to Oscar. 'You know, if you'd asked, I would have helped you. Maybe not given you the money outright but certainly worked out some way to do a fundraiser or something like that.'

Oscar hung his head.

'All I need you to do is tell the truth to your

lawyer and to the school,' Reeve said. 'It'll be humiliating, I'm sure, but it's what will make this right.'

'He'll be in there first thing tomorrow,' his dad said. 'Once again, we're incredibly sorry and very grateful that you're not threatening to sue us. We'd understand if you did.'

Reeve waved her hand, dismissing the notion. 'Oscar's a good kid who made a questionable decision. Let's move on from this and not repeat it.'

She smiled as they apologised one last time and left the restaurant. She turned to Bella. 'How did you know?'

'He's said a few weird things to Mason lately. Keeps asking about me and if I'm alright. It was Mason who said to me the other day that he suspected Oscar was involved in some way. He offered to beat the truth out of him, but I said that'd make you hate him even more than you already do.'

Reeve's cheeks coloured. 'I don't hate him. It's his reputation that's concerning.'

'As is yours to anyone who believes that you've been doing the things everyone's saying you've been doing. Mason's reputation is mostly made up. Sure, he's had a rough upbringing, but he's got a good heart.'

Reeve nodded. She could hardly dispute this

when he'd gone out of his way to help her. She wasn't one to judge anyone else right now. Luke proved her own judgement was terrible.

'There's Jess and Trent,' Bella said, waving as the couple entered the restaurant.

They all stood as Jess and Trent reached the table, exchanging hugs and laughter as they did.

'How great is this?' Jess said once drinks had been ordered. 'We can finally enjoy each other without worrying about the next crazy thing that's going to happen.' Her face clouded over the moment the words left her lips. 'Sorry, hon. I know you've lost a husband in all of this.'

Reeve smiled and reached across and squeezed Jess's hand. 'I'm beginning to think I've gained a lot more than I've lost. Now, before I forget, I spoke to Devon today, and he said he was having trouble trying to get hold of you. I think he was worried that you might still be wary of him.'

Jess laughed. 'God no. I think between the two of us, we've apologised so many times for doubting him that he's sick of hearing about it. I spoke to him an hour ago. It was about my uncle. He wanted to let me know that he'd started the process of retrieving the money he stole. Joey's bank account sat dormant for years when he died, and the money reverted to the government. But according to Devon, there's a process to apply directly to the Treasury Department to recoup the money. If he's successful in retrieving anything, it will go back into Martin's estate for distribution.'

'But it was your money. Dad thought he was giving it to you. It shouldn't go into the estate.'

'Let's talk about that later,' Jess said. She looked around at the group. 'Right now, there's something bigger I need to discuss. Something I need all your advice on that's much more important than money or anything from the past.'

40

Trent took Jess's hand as they made their way along the hospital corridor to Felicity's room. They'd enjoyed dinner with Reeve, Nick, and Bella the previous night, and Jess felt a new level of confidence after confiding in her sister, niece, and Reeve's ex-husband.

Flick was scheduled to be discharged in an hour, and Jess was hoping she'd be happy with what had been organised.

'Thanks,' Jess said to Trent.

'What, for holding your hand?'

Jess smiled. 'No, for supporting me in what I'm doing now and with the whole Ash situation.' She smiled. 'I'm getting used to calling him that at least.'

Trent stopped outside Flick's room and pulled Jess close to him. 'You're truly amazing. Do you know that? I can't begin to imagine what you've been through, and yet here you are smiling, happy, and about to do something incredibly selfless.'

Jess smiled. 'You're amazing yourself, and I wouldn't call this selfless. It's going to give me an enormous amount of pleasure.'

Trent searched her eyes with his before leaning forward and kissing her lightly on the lips. She returned the kiss before pulling away. 'Took your time, Mr Finlayson.'

Trent laughed. 'I've wanted to do that since I first met you. But you had a boyfriend, and I didn't want to ruin our friendship either. You say you can't confide in boyfriends. I'd choose our friendship over a half-arsed relationship.'

Jess leant towards him and kissed him, this time more firmly. 'I think you're one of a kind. A best friend and potential boyfriend all in one.'

'Potential?'

Jess pulled away and laughed. 'You've proven yourself as the best friend I've ever had, but I haven't had much proof on the boyfriend side of things, other than that kiss, which I will say held a lot of promise.'

Trent pulled her to him again, this time kissing her with a passion that took her breath away.

'Okay, "potential" might be the wrong word,' Jess said, coming up for air. 'That was pretty special.'

'As are you. Now, go and make Flick understand how special she is. I'll meet you back at the apartment later. I think you should do this alone.'

Jess gave a nervous smile. If someone had told her a few months ago she'd be doing this today, she would have laughed at them. She just hoped that wasn't Flick's reaction too.

* * *

Jess lost her nerve the moment she walked into Felicity's room and saw the look of defiance on the girl's face. She wasn't sure her announcement was going to be received the way she'd imagined, so she decided to tackle it a different way.

'How come you're collecting me and not the Smiths?'

'You're not going back to them,' Jess said. 'They weren't too impressed with the stolen car and the poor role model you've ended up being for the younger girls.'

Flick had the good grace to blush with embarrassment. 'Fair enough. I don't blame them. I'd prob-ably give up on me too.'

'To be fair to the Smiths, they did offer to have you back, but they were only available to foster you for another nine months, and we had someone else come forward who was keen to have you, hopefully long-term. Now, come on, let's get you discharged and get you out of here. I went by the Smiths' yes-terday and picked up your belongings. You don't have to see them again unless you choose to.'

Felicity considered this for a moment. 'I'd like to. I owe them an apology, and the little girls too. I was a shitty big sister.'

Jess smiled. 'The fact that you can see that is a huge step forward. Let's get you settled in your new home, and we'll call them and set up a time to visit.'

Flick nodded and allowed Jess to push her out of the hospital in a wheelchair, her crutches in hand.

'The home I'm taking you to belongs to a single woman,' Jess said as they drove away from the hospi-tal. 'She's in her forties, has a good job, and lives in a two-bedroom apartment. She's agreed to have you on a trial basis to see how it works out. She went through the approval process many years ago to be-come a foster carer but then got cold feet. You'll be her first experience at fostering, and she's open to making it a permanent arrangement if you both get along.'

'How many cats does she have?' Felicity asked, rolling her eyes.

'None that I'm aware of. No live-in boyfriends either, although I believe she's dating a nice guy who we've had police checked in case he's at the house at any time.'

Felicity nodded.

'It's a second-floor apartment,' Jess said, 'but there's a supply lift she's got permission for you to use while you need the crutches.'

'I think I'm going to be sick,' Felicity said as they neared the front gate of the apartment block. 'I can't do this again, Jess.' Tears welled in her eyes as the tough guy facade melted away.

Jess's heart went out to her. She knew this feeling. Turning up with a bag housing all your worldly possessions and having no idea what type of person was going to be on the other side of that door. Praying it would be someone who would love you and provide you with a home. And in her job, Jess had come to realise that this was the reality for many foster kids. They got that loving family. For some, they got their dream. For others, they got a situation that they were okay with; but for a kid like

Flick, she'd gotten the bad draw more often than not.

Jess took her hand. 'You'll be okay. I've met this woman, and I already know she's going to like you a lot.'

'You can't know that.'

'I can, actually. Now come on, let's go and check out your new home.'

* * *

'What do you think?' she asked Felicity a few minutes later as they stood in the living area of Jess's two-bedroom apartment.

Felicity looked around as if she expected the woman to jump out of a cupboard at any minute. Finally, she'd lowered her voice to a whisper. 'Where is she?'

The vulnerability in Felicity's face brought tears to Jess's eyes. She stepped forward and hugged her. 'Welcome to my home, Flick. I hope you'll want it to be yours too.'

Felicity pulled away, disbelief written all over her face. 'Really? You're going to let me live here?'

'*Let* is not the right word. I would love to invite you into my life. To live with me, and hopefully, if you enjoy being here and feel safe, you'll choose to stay.'

'For the next three years?'

'Longer, hopefully. If we do this, it's to become a family. We go into it seriously, wanting it to work. I'll never be your mum. I know that, but I'd like to be someone you can rely on and know cares about you and loves you.'

Felicity continued to stare at Jess, tears running down her cheeks.

ONE MONTH LATER

As they waited in the gate lounge to board the flight back to Melbourne, Reeve watched as Jess said her goodbyes. Ash, Kristin, and Jed had insisted they come and wave them off.

Reeve had been surprised and touched when Jess had invited her and Bella to join Trent, Flick and herself on their first trip to Perth to visit Ash and his family.

'You're so much a part of this, Reeve, I'd really like you to come,' Jess had said. 'He's your nephew, don't forget. There's a lot he's asked about Martin that I haven't been able to answer. He'd love to talk to you.'

A feeling of warmth had enveloped Reeve as she realised that, of course, Jess's son was also related to her and Bella. Her family was continuing to grow in the most unexpected of ways.

They'd had a wonderful five days getting to know Ash. Reeve had ensured that they gave Jess plenty of time alone with him, but they'd also shared meals together as an extended family and had even taken a trip across to Rottenest Island to see the quokkas. Reeve was pretty sure that Jess had taken at least two hundred photos of Jed doing his best to get close to the little marsupials. She didn't blame her; he was an adorable little boy, and the quokkas were incredibly cute.

Reeve waved to Ash, Kristin and Jed as the flight was called, and she, Felicity and Bella presented their boarding passes and, with Felicity still on crutches, slowly made their way down the air bridge and onto the plane. She'd leave Jess and Trent to say their goodbyes in private. They'd all had dinner the previous night on the decked terrace at Cha Cha on Fremantle Wharf, and Ash and Kristin had been excited at the prospect of coming to Melbourne at Christmas. Ash had never been to Melbourne, and now discovering it was where he was born, he was keen to visit the city and learn more about Jess's life.

'You'll be able to show Ash Martin's legacy,' Reeve had said with a smile. It had been a discussion with

Felicity that had given Reeve the idea of what to do with the land Martin's burnt down house stood on. The Toorak location was worth a fortune. Rather than sell it, Reeve had suggested to Jess that they use the insurance money and some money from Martin's estate to build a large house that could be used for emergency accommodation for children in the foster care system. Jess had been overwhelmed at Reeve's generosity with the suggestion, although she had questioned how Martin's neighbours would react to the suggestion.

'That's irrelevant,' Reeve said. 'I think Dad would like us doing it. He told me before he died that he had some things to put right in his past, and while his will did that for some people, a project for Safe Houses would be helping a lot of people over many years. I'd like to remember him and have him re-membered for his generosity rather than anything else.'

Now, as they took their seats on the aircraft, Reeve marvelled at how much her life had changed in such a short space of time. She wouldn't lie. Grief hit her at times she least expected it. She was grieving her father and her marriage. She'd started seeing a psychiatrist recommended by Devon who was helping her understand that nothing that had happened was her fault. Reeve knew she had a lot to come to terms with and also knew she wouldn't be able to move on until Luke and Patricia had been sentenced. It was, however, a relief to know that they'd both been remanded in custody while awaiting their trial dates.

Reeve pulled herself from her thoughts and smiled as Bella laughed at something Felicity said. The two girls had become firm friends, and while Martin's contact at St Margot's had offered Bella a place starting next term, she'd declined it. Felicity was attending the local high school, and Bella decided that would suit her too. Mason had also moved to the high school and had promised Reeve he would act as Bella's bodyguard. Reeve had to admit, her feelings towards Mason had changed considerably. He and Bella had become great friends, but Reeve would be lying if she said she wasn't relieved that friends was all they were.

Jess and Trent appeared and sat down across the aisle from them. 'Swap with Reeve for a minute, would you?' Jess asked Trent.

Reeve stood and took Trent's seat as the passengers continued to file onto the plane. 'How are you feeling?'

'Strange. I have a son and a grandson. I've gone

from thinking my only family was a long-lost uncle to having this huge family. It's amazing.'

'It is,' Reeve said. 'What about his father? Did he ask about him?'

Jess nodded. 'He was devastated when I told him how he was conceived, but I had to draw the line somewhere as far as fictionalising what happened. It's bad enough to have lied about what the Grenfells did, but that was to protect Ash. Dean Blackwell, however, is not someone I'm going to offer the same opportunity to. I had Devon file a restraining order against Dean on my behalf and I can guarantee he'll regret contacting Ash if he ever decides to.' She smiled. 'My son is very protective of me, and Blackwell will learn that the hard and painful way if he makes contact.'

'Good,' Reeve said. 'He deserves nothing less.'

'I'm still blown away,' Jess said, 'by how much I've gained since Martin made contact with me. And I don't mean financially.'

'It's the same for me,' Reeve said. 'I've lost Dad and my marriage, but now I have you, Ash, and Flick. I hope Ash does come for Christmas like he said they might last night.'

'Me too,' Jess said. 'It's a strange feeling, but it really is as if he's part of me. Jed too. It's this deep sense

I feel. We can sit in silence, and it feels right.' She squeezed Reeve's arm. 'Like I do with you. You know, when Luke's DNA test came back negative, I knew it had to be wrong. There's no way you could feel this kind of connection without having some deeper sense of belonging to each other.'

Reeve nodded, her lips curling into a smile. 'How do you explain the deep sense of connection you and Trent seem to have formed?'

Jess smiled. 'He thrives on drama, so it appears I'm his soulmate.'

Reeve laughed. 'What if things settle down now and life becomes ordinary?'

'Then the wedding's off, according to Trent.'

Reeve raised an eyebrow. 'Wedding? Are you for real?'

'Shh,' Jess said, glancing across the aisle. 'Maybe in the future. It's all happened far too quickly. With all that's been going on, we've hardly had a chance to go on a date. I've gained a family and become the guardian of a fifteen-year-old in the last month. The romance has hardly had a chance to develop. But I think it will.'

She glanced at Trent, who was sitting with his eyes closed, his lips curling up at the edges as he eavesdropped on their conversation.

He opened one eye and looked straight at Jess. 'Not maybe. Definitely, regarding that wedding, Jess. But I agree, a date first would be good. Any chance you could have Flick for a sleepover one night, Reeve?'

She grinned, and he closed his eyes, a satisfied smirk on his lips.

'And I thought you and men were a bad combination,' Reeve said.

'We generally are. But Trent's different,' Jess said. 'Really different. I've never felt like this about anyone.' She lowered her voice and turned to Reeve. 'And I've had Devon check him out. Police check and the whole lot. And guess what?'

'What?'

'It's the strangest thing.' Jess's eyes danced with delight. 'He's actually the person he says he is.'

ACKNOWLEDGEMENTS

Having a book published is always a team effort, and I would like to thank several people who helped take this seed of an idea through to publication.

Firstly, a big thank you to Janine, Judy, Maggie, Ray, Robyn and Tracy for providing feedback on early versions of the story, and to Judy and Robyn for reading later drafts to provide further feedback.

To the lovely Christie Stratos of Proof Positive. Thank you for applying your meticulous editing skills to the first, self-published version of this manuscript. It is always a pleasure to work with you.

To the team at Boldwood Books. Thank you for the opportunity of re-publishing this story and the efforts of the entire team to not only offer it to a wider market, but to ensure it is a success.

To my assistant, I wouldn't enjoy this process without you by my side each day. You are simply gorgeous, and your purrs of encouragement are never taken for granted!

Lastly, to my lovely readers who continue to purchase, download, listen to, and borrow my books – thank you!

ABOUT THE AUTHOR

Louise Guy bestselling author of six novels, blends family and friendship themes with unique twists and intrigue. Her characters captivate readers, drawing them deeply into their compelling stories and struggles. Originally from Melbourne, a trip around Australia led Louise and her husband to Queensland's stunning Sunshine Coast, where they now live with their two sons, gorgeous fluff ball of a cat and an abundance of visiting wildlife.

Sign up to Louise Guy's mailing list for news, competitions and update on future books.

Follow Louise on social media:

f facebook.com/LouiseGuy

BB bookbub.com/authors/louise-guy

ALSO BY LOUISE GUY

My Sister's Baby

A Family's Trust

Boldwood

Boldwood Books is an award-winning fiction publishing company seeking out the best stories from around the world.

Find out more at www.boldwoodbooks.com

Join our reader community for brilliant books, competitions and offers!

Follow us
@BoldwoodBooks
@TheBoldBookClub

Sign up to our weekly deals newsletter

https://bit.ly/BoldwoodBNewsletter